MERCY'S SONG

SARAH HANKS

Praise for Mercy's Song

Mercy's Song could not be a more timely book. At a time in our history when the treatment of people of color in the church, in the justice system and in society period has stood up in the face of the Body of CHRIST and asked, "What are you going to do about this," in comes Sarah Hanks with Mercy's Song. This book is a bridge between Believers in CHRIST who have not had to suffer the ravages of an upbringing that was plagued by broken homes, drugs, violence, gangs, police brutality and sub-par schools and those Believers who have been afflicted by this and so much more at the hands of their country.

Mercy's Song is a well-written story that draws you in quickly. You immediately feel a kinship to the characters. GOD's love, care, comfort and compassion is displayed in the relationships of this book. Your heart will be touched by the confusion and despair of jail as DeAndre struggles to hold on to his faith, his sanity, and his love throughout this ordeal. Sarah captures the capricious grit of jails in America. To my surprise, she even shed light upon the understanding, passion and loyalty that so many CHRISTians in prison have for each other while making hard decisions and facing the challenges of jail in a way that properly represents JESUS. Through the unfortunate circumstances and bad decision made by DeAndre, she shows how GOD moves both subtly and explosively in our lives. All while clearly presenting the full gospel of JESUS CHRIST.

As someone who has literally spent half of my life in prison (23 out 46 years)—being a committed CHRISTian 17 of those years—I have not read a book that so clearly expresses GOD's heart for HIS incarcerated children. Mercy's Song is a necessary read for Believers who want to see the entire Body of CHRIST healed, healthy and active in the Kingdom of GOD.

> ~ Demeyon Watie, Author of *The G.A.M.E. You Reap What You Sow*

Mercy's Song opened my little world to the agonizing choices of a slave. Dragged me across the borders of customs and culture to show me pleasures and pains of a real person.

> ~ David Warner Parks, PhD, Author of *The Boy Who Closed the Sky*, First Impressions Award Winner

Sarah Hanks takes readers on a powerful journey of mercy, forgiveness, and love in action through the thought-provoking and heart-breaking stories of her characters. I could not read it fast enough and found myself thinking about it long after I'd finished.

> ~ Jamie Ogle, ACFW First Impressions Winner

Sarah Hanks seamlessly weaves the past and the present together in this timely—and timeless—novel of grace, love, consequences, and mercy. A well-written, heart-wrenching, uplifting, and memorable read. You'll devour it.

~ Chris Posti, Author of *The Shortest Distance Between You and Your New Job* and *Marriage On and Off the Rocks.*

MERCY'S SONG continues the beautifully crafted story of the tragic intersection of Natassa and DeAndre's life. Sarah Hanks has crafted the second book in a series that compassionately weaves together a story of the roots of racial inequity with the hard work of reaching toward each other—in spite of our differences, excuses, and justifications. MERCY'S SONG highlights the struggle we all face, the balance of forgiveness with justice. Can the unforgivable be forgiven? Can justice prevail where mercy is needed? Or does mercy render justice impotent? A beautiful addition to the continuing story of *Mercy Will Follow Me*, MERCY'S SONG gives us a glimpse of what can happen when flawed people choose to move toward each other even when needless tragedy takes us places we never wanted to go. Sarah is a gifted storyteller and in MERCY'S SONG, she shares her gift with us.

~ Angie Stumbo, Author

Sarah Hanks has produced an incredible account that takes you from past, to present, and back again through the eyes of her characters in an indelible way. I found myself deeply immersed in each character and couldn't wait for the next chapters to be reviewed! Her careful research into the history of the characters—into their lives, their perspectives, and into their loves—shows clearly in the story, and it's impossible to read the books without finding yourself in their pages. Although these books tackle generations' worth of difficult situations and struggles, Mercy (as it will) wins over all.

These books were a wonderful read, and I eagerly anticipate their conclusions.

~ Cassidy Cooley

Sarah has masterfully done it again! Mercy's Song not only continues with the powerful story began in *Mercy Will Follow Me*, but Sarah seamlessly intertwines a multitude of scenarios that will have every reader asking God to search their own heart. Whether it's identity, parenting, marriage, social issues, grief, unforgiveness, etc., Sarah doesn't leave one stone unturned, challenging every reader to go deeper into their own stories as they travel deeper with the characters into their journey. Mercy's Song doesn't just tell a good story, it is a gateway to freedom as readers connect their own story lines with those of the characters and receive the hope found in reading their testimonies. Every turn of the page is a new opportunity to be undone! This series has forever transformed my idea about fiction novels!

~ Brandie West

Mercy's Song hooked me from the beginning with its authentic Christian characters. Their struggles with their faith through difficult circumstances resonates. The historical elements put contemporary race issues into perspective. An unforgettable read, that you won't want to end.

~ Pamela Baker, Writer, Goodreads

reviewer

Sarah has done it again! Mercy's Song thrills with its twists and turns. This book has some of the characters from the first book in this series, *Mercy Will Follow Me*, and adds in a few new ones. I loved reading this story and seeing some of my old favorites again. Sarah has expertly woven the story line together and has gone to great lengths to help the reader connect with the characters. I found myself cheering for them as the story progressed and feeling their sadness when they dealt with loss and regret. The close of every chapter left me hungry for more, I didn't want to stop reading.

~ Melissa Jacobs, Author of *Livin' the Dream*

I couldn't wait for the continuing saga of Natassa, DeAndre and Mercy! Sarah doesn't disappoint. Another story that zigs and zags, keeping you on your toes. Just when you think you know what will happen next, Sarah takes you another way. This book was well worth the wait!

~ Janell Harris

There are always at least two sides to every story. And Sarah Hanks pulls back the curtain on the complexity of it all. Mercy's Song will break your heart for what breaks God's heart—in the best way. Through these fascinating characters, the author shines light on stories that have long been hidden in darkness and shame. Open the pages to gain new understanding and compassion for the complexity of the human heart, including your own.

~ Brittany Roach

A second installment of a series that is quickly becoming a favorite of mine. A book of love, REDEMPTION, and forgiveness, woven through two different life stories, providing for a magnificent tale of God's Mercy.

~ Tara Geller

In Mercy's Song, Sarah Hanks moves seamlessly between past and present from a modern-day prison cell to the shackles of slavery in pre-Civil War America. She takes you into the hearts of her characters as they struggle with love, loss, and forgiveness. We ache alongside DeAndre, Mercy, and Natassa as they choose to do what is right at great personal cost, and we see God at work in their lives, carrying them through the storms.

~ Sherry Shindelar, Author, ACFW
First Impressions Winner

Mercy's Song continues the stories of modern day and historical Mercy characters. Sarah has weaved stories with unexpected twists turns but by the end of the tales, be ready to participate in surprise forgiveness. As a researcher myself I also appreciate the amount of accuracy and detail that Sarah has put into both story lines.

~ Dr. René Burress

SonFlower Books

Dedication

This book is dedicated to my brothers and sisters in Christ behind bars here in the United States and across the world, as well as to those who have chosen to engage in prison ministry. Your stories of endurance through heart-wrenching circumstances have inspired me. I pray that your light may shine brightly, piercing the darkness surrounding you and bringing many into freedom.

Remember the prisoners, as though in prison with them, and those who are badly treated, since you yourselves also are in the body. (Hebrews 13:3 NASB)

Acknowledgements

No labor of love is accomplished alone. Mercy's Song has been a labor of love indeed, and I am so thankful for the amazing network of people I've had supporting me along the way.

Thank you to my dream team of readers—Melissa, Janell, Rene, Shannon, and Cassidy. Your feedback has been invaluable in this process.

Thank you also to the Scribes tribe of AFCW for critiquing my work and spurring me to become a better writer. You've all taught me so much and this novel is immeasurably better from all those red lines and comments.

Thank you to Michele Pyatt and Dance Again Ministries for allowing me to peek through the window of your prison ministry and meet the amazing men you work with. I learned so much from you and from them.

To my husband Kevin and all eight of my beautiful children, thank you. You've been so patient with me as I've transitioned into a full-time writing career. I love you most.

And to my Lord who has blessed me abundantly and loves me unconditionally, thank You.

Prologue

December 11th, 2010, Crawford County, Nebraska

A newborn wail permeated the hospital room, eliciting the response of everyone within earshot.

Well, nearly everyone.

Brandon stood, but Bethany beat him to the bassinet and scooped the baby up, shushing her sweetly.

Next to Bethany hovered Natassa's sister Olivia. She stroked silky newborn wisps of hair.

Even Laura inched to the edge of her chair as if she, too, wanted to cuddle the new life before her. Though she hadn't come to the baby shower, Brandon's sister-in-law showed up at the hospital with a balloon in hand two hours after Natassa gave birth.

Only Natassa's mother sat ramrod straight in the corner of the room, unmoved by the commotion surrounding her granddaughter. She looked as if she wished to bolt but invisible chains bound her to the chair. Hours before, at the baby shower, a twinge of hope sprung up inside Natassa as her mother laid a hand on her and at least assented to Bethany's prayer for her and her child.

Natassa shook her head, still trying to take it all in. Once her water broke at the gathering, they had to rush to get to the hospital on time.

When Mercy came, she came swiftly.

"You're sure they said everything's okay?" Natassa put a hand on Brandon's arm, his flannel shirt soft beneath her touch.

"Sweetheart, relax. She's fine. Perfect Apgar score. Perfect birth. Perfect baby." He kissed her forehead. "Perfect wife."

"It's just … none of our others came early."

"Three weeks isn't that early, babe."

Natassa was about to seek further reassurance when the sound of Bethany singing stole her attention.

> Mercy. Sweet mercy.
> Good Lord, we need Your mercy.
> Every morning. Every morning.
> Your mercies are new.

Bethany swayed back and forth holding Mercy, serenading her.

"Hey." Natassa couldn't stop herself from interrupting. "That's the song from the journal. From Mercy's Journal. Is that how it goes?"

"Shoot, sugar. I don't have a clue how the tune's supposed to go. I just done made one up to go along with the words and that suits me fine. Looks like it suits your Mercy girl fine too." Bethany continued to rock the newborn.

A soft knock sounded at the door and Maureen and Charles dragged themselves into the room, their faces somber as if they came to a funeral instead of a birth.

"Hi, little sister." Maureen strode over to Natassa and stooped over her hospital bed. "Sorry I couldn't make the shower. Work stuff. But here." She thrust a small pink gift bag in Natassa's general direction.

Brandon took it and put it with the others.

"Thanks for coming, Maureen." Natassa gripped her sister's hand.

Natassa's mom popped up and enveloped Maureen in a hug, nearly clinging to her. "I'm so glad you're here."

"Misery loves company," Brandon whispered in Natassa's ear.

She snickered.

"Here, Grandma." Bethany slipped Mercy into Natassa's mother's arms. "Why don't you hold your grandbaby for a while?" She stepped back.

Mercy whimpered.

"It's okay. It's okay, baby." Natassa's mother's voice sounded soft yet laced with discomfort. "Look, Maureen. It's not that bad. The baby doesn't even hardly look black at all, thank God."

Natassa catapulted up, her wide eyes searching Bethany's expression. "Mom!"

"What?"

"Why would you say something like that?"

"Like what? Do you want a black baby, Natassa? Sweetheart, come on. Use common sense. I know you like hanging around all those … people down there in the city, but you're not black. You're white as they come. Stop trying to be something you're not."

"Brandon …" Natassa whispered through clenched teeth, her eyes pleading.

"What's that, babe? You're hungry? I'm sure you're sick of this hospital food. How about your mom and Maureen go and find you something better to eat, and I'll go ahead and hold Mercy for a while. Sound good?"

Natassa mouthed "Thank you," and Brandon stood and took Mercy into his arms.

Natassa's mom jammed her hands on her hips. "I don't think there's any decent food in this building. We might have to drive for miles."

"If that's what it takes, I'm sure it will be worth the wait. Right, babe?"

Natassa nodded, but the women looked unconvinced.

"Hey, Chicka, sorry it took me so long to make it back here." Breanna breezed into the room, out of breath and with a bag dangling on her arm.

"Breanna," Natassa brightened. "I'm so glad you're back."

"Do you realize how difficult it is to find a huge blue bow? For a baby, I mean. Pink ones, I could have bought her a dozen pink ones. Or purple. But blue? I'm surprised she's not walking yet with as long as that took me."

Breanna dug into the gift bag, plucked out a bag of M&Ms, and tossed it on Natassa's lap. "That's for Mama."

Natassa snorted. "Thanks."

"She needs something more nutritious than that," Natassa's mom interjected from across the room.

"Now you, little missy." Breanna knelt beside Brandon. "Or should I say little Mercy. You had better like bows 'cause your mommy has a thing for them. And I hope you like blue because it's your mommy's favorite color." Breanna plucked the bow out of the bag, ripped off the tag, and gently placed it on Mercy's head. It slumped over one eye.

"It's too big." Natassa's mother huffed.

Bethany chuckled. "She'll grow into it." She turned and smiled at Natassa, then gestured around the hospital room. "This whole thing done feel like it's too big for the lot of you, but you'se gonna grow into it. Trust me. Wait and see."

1

February 3rd, 2014 , Crawford County, Nebraska

Everything DeAndre Scott owned fit in the back of his Corsica. He'd stuffed a dozen canvases, three boxes, and two suitcases into his trunk and back seat, along with some old busted up dreams and perhaps new ones that just needed some TLC to take flight.

Lord, is there still such a thing as new beginnings?

As he rolled into Crawford County, he slowed his vehicle to a crawl. Subtle changes had taken place over the past three years. A new gas station on his left. An office building ahead on the right. But mostly everything else looked the same.

There was nowhere else to go. *Who else in this whole wide world will give me a chance?*

Cruising into the parking lot of Java Joe's, he idled for a minute and stared at the mural. The rich shades of teal, blue, and orange spelling out the name in bold lettering, the smattering of people fellowshipping, coffee cups in hand. He'd painted himself in the left corner, the only person of color in the mural. Not unlike the town itself.

"It looks ... Wow! Just wow! Amazing work, Dre!" Rob's voice echoed in DeAndre's memories.

Man, he could use a pat on the back right now.

God, please don't let this be another dead end.

He got out of the car and entered the building almost reverently. This place that had granted him a new start in life. If not for Java Joes … He shuddered.

The bell jingled, unearthing memories.

He scanned the shop for familiar faces and disappointment crested as he found none. No Rob or James, Patrick or Eddie. No one he knew— unless … Why did the girl behind the counter look familiar? Her blonde hair made her skin seem as pale as a model he'd seen on a billboard for alabaster makeup. He stepped into her line, the only line.

"Welcome to Java Joe's. How can I help you?"

She tilted her head slightly, then her eyes lit up. "DeAndre, right? Is that you?"

He nodded, his mind scrambling to place her face with a name.

"It's me, Janell. I trained you here, remember? Oh, I let my hair grow out. And lightened it."

"Janell. Yeah. I took your job." Why hadn't he remembered her? But she looked so … different. More mature than she had then. But then again they had both grown a lot since he first walked through those doors.

"Then I took it right back." Her laugh sounded like a song.

His smile broadened.

"So—what can I get you?"

He ordered and paid.

"So, James? Rob? Patrick? Any of them still around?" DeAndre propped his elbows on the counter. The line stretched behind him, but he wasn't eager to leave the conversation.

"Yes, but the flu. This winter's been brutal. I'm the last man … uh, woman standing. I had to call some guys who haven't worked here since the summer to help out, but they can't get here until the afternoon."

DeAndre stepped aside as Janell assisted the next customer. Only one other person worked in the back, and he scrambled about, helping her out front as well as working drive-thru. The bell over the door jingled again. He should leave her to do her job, but her smile snagged him, kept him close.

"I can help." After all, he didn't have anything better to do. Other than sit in a corner booth and sip his coffee, watching Janell. He could do that all day.

"Seriously?"

"Sure. I mean, if it isn't against protocol."

She blew a stray hair from her face. "I don't know or care about protocol at this point. I'm swamped. Grab an apron."

DeAndre slid back into the routine. He and Janell worked well together. They anticipated one another's needs, talked without talking, danced without dancing. Hours flew by like mere minutes.

"Whew." Janell wiped her brow with the back of her hand. "We've slowed down. You can take a break now."

He reclined against the counter next to her and caught a whiff of vanilla that didn't come from the lattes. "That's okay. None needed." *I'd rather stay with you.*

Could he extend their time together further? Would she laugh him off? Shoot him down?

When business finally slowed, he gathered up his courage. Time to ask her the question he'd put off for the past three hours.

"So, I planned on connecting with Rob tonight. I don't know anyone else in town besides the guys here. Seeing as how they're all sick, would you want to grab a bite to eat after work? You could fill me in?"

He couldn't discern her expression. Did she think him corny for asking? Did she feel sorry for him?

"Sure."

It didn't matter. He'd take it.

Sitting across from her in La Mexicana made him forget about everything else, everything but that moment. Everything but her as she stuffed her face with chips and salsa.

"Aren't you going to eat anything?"

"Oh. Yeah." He picked up a chip. He wanted to smack himself across the head.

"Why do you keep staring at my hair?"

"The king is held captive by your tresses." *Did I just say that? OMG, I said that out loud.*

She paused with a chip midway to her mouth. "Don't tell me you're throwing down some Song of Solomon pick-up line." Then she laughed with her eyes and he forgot his name.

"Wait, you know it? Song of Solomon. The Bible?"

She shrugged. "College and Career group at church does a Bible study on Tuesday nights. We did Song of Solomon last summer."

"Ah. I did a piece on that … pick up line, as you call it."

"A piece? A piece of what?"

"Art."

"Art? Okay, wait. Start at the beginning. You're an artist?"

So he did. He started at the beginning. How he had been scribbling in notebooks all his life and doing graffiti art on buildings in the hood but how he'd never thought he was good enough to do anything worth anything until the guys from Java Joe's told him differently.

And how he would never have met those guys if she hadn't gone away to college. When her position as a barista opened up, the manager Jim gave him a chance to break free of the cycle of his neighborhood. Rob and Patrick had helped him get his GED and apply for art school and he had gotten a scholarship.

The waiter brought their food and he tried to focus on telling his story instead of the way she loaded her fajitas so full they overflowed from the sides, dripping onto her plate as she ate.

"The scholarship kept getting renewed. Got me through three years. Then it ran out. I tried to get a job out there, pay my own way. But paying rent and bills stretched me, let alone tuition. I could only scrape by. I thought maybe it was a sign that I needed to move on. Come home. Only I'm not sure where home is anymore."

Janell twisted her lips together and nodded slowly. She sat forward and … Were her eyes glistening? But then she shook her head as if to banish whatever she was about to say, to do. She sat back and crunched a chip.

"So, the piece you were talking about, when did you do that?"

"Interpretive Art. One of my teachers was a believer. He challenged us to interpret Biblical symbols and allegory in our artwork. He got me searching through the whole book of Song of Solomon looking for material. Some of those guys had a real good time with that one, but in the end, I landed on 'The king is held captive by your tresses.' All of those strong symbols and that's the line I couldn't get away from."

"I wish I could have seen it."

"You can. I have it in my car."

"Really?"

He nodded. "I've got most everything I've done in the trunk of my car."

Her eyes glistened with tears. "Life doesn't always end up the way you planned it, does it?" Regret dripped from her voice, thick like honey.

"No." A world of pain seemed to hide behind her question.

"What about you? What's your story?"

She closed her eyes and shook her head. "Another time?" It sounded like a plea.

"Does that mean you're giving me another shot? I didn't completely blow this?"

Her eyes opened wide as she slid her hand across the table in an invitation. His hand met hers. Their fingers intertwined. He stared at the dark and light, cradled together. In another time, another place, it would be unthinkable. But here and now, perfectly acceptable. Even in Crawford County. Maybe the entire reason he came back was for the woman in front of him. Only God knew. And this? This equaled perfection.

He paid the check and held her hand as they walked to his car. He had to drive her to Java Joe's where she'd left her car. If only he could take her home, see where she lived. Get more of an idea of what made her tick.

On the drive back to Java Joe's, she filled him in on how Rob made assistant manager and Patrick worked at Java Joe's some on the weekends but hustled at a start-up IT company during the week. The two of them still lived at the same house, though Patrick was pretty serious with a girl. Janell assumed he wouldn't be there for too much longer before marrying her. James remained the manager of the coffee shop and still as kindhearted as ever.

DeAndre careened into the parking lot and angled his Corsica next to her Beetle. The lights from the other stores in the strip mall still shone, though Java Joe's on the corner stood dark, his mural only faintly illuminated by the nearby streetlamps.

"So, how far of a drive do you have?" DeAndre's mouth quirked. Years ago, on his first day on the job, she'd asked him a similar question.

"My parents live about ten minutes north of here."

"And you live with your parents?" He fished for information. Hopefully he didn't seem creepy, like a stalker.

"Yep."

"Cool." Having two loving parents who were willing to support and encourage you in life sure seemed like a gift to him.

"Cool? Trust me. It's anything but cool."

"Oh."

"Sorry. I don't mean to take it out on you. Show me your painting, DeAndre. The Song of Solomon one."

She smiled up at him. Her hair glinted in the light streaming from the streetlamp.

They got out, and he popped the trunk. "You gotta promise not to make fun of it."

"Make fun of it?"

"Promise."

"Okay."

He shuffled through dozens of canvases and then pulled it out, angling it toward the stream of light. A king stood clothed in scarlet and purple, holding a scepter. Before him bowed a woman with her hair flowing all around him, covering the canvas. Her hair wove around the king's ankles, around his wrists, and around his waist.

Janell stared. Silent.

"Sooo, what do you think?"

"DeAndre,"—she was so quiet that he could hear her breath—"I'm trying to take it all in."

"It's a 16 × 20 inch canvas. There's not much to it."

"There's so much detail."

He looked at it again. Okay, she had a point. He did spend quite a bit of time on this one.

"Can I ask you something? I don't know how to ask it."

"Go ahead."

"The king is black. Why?"

He shrugged. "Why not? Do you think everyone in the Bible looked like you?"

A pause. "I guess not. I never really thought about it before."

"You go to the art museum, and you'll see pasty white Jesuses everywhere. That's because pasty white men painted them. Jesus was a Jewish man, Janell."

"Yeah. I guess so."

Her eyes traversed the painting inch by inch.

"The girl. What color is she? The dress covers up her skin. All you can see is her hair. It's not black, but dark brown?"

"Like yours," he whispered. Could he? Would she mind? He reached out and took a strand of her hair, rubbing it between his fingers. So soft. She never took her eyes off the painting, didn't pull away. Did that mean she was okay with it?

"So, you like it?" he asked.

"Like it? Are you kidding me? It's the most beautiful thing I've ever seen."

He chuckled. She needed to get out more. "You can have it."

"What? DeAndre, no. This is a masterpiece. You don't give it away to some girl you just met."

Tentative, he reached out and touched her cheek. When she closed her eyes and gave a soft smile, he gently pried her face away from the painting until she faced him.

"Janell, you aren't just some girl I met. I painted this for you. I just didn't know it at the time." He ran his hand through her hair. "The king is held captive by your tresses."

Her lip trembled, and he kissed his fingers and touched them to her lips. He didn't dare do more, or he might scare her away.

She turned into his arms and clung to his shirt. "Thank you."

"You're welcome." He wrapped his arms around her. Her small body pressed against his. She was so fragile, so soft.

"I have to go." She swallowed hard. "You coming by the coffee shop tomorrow?"

"Will you be there?"

"Of course."

"Then I'll be there."

He placed the painting in her trunk, then watched until her taillights completely disappeared.

2

The sun's warmth kissed Natassa's face as she lounged on the park bench. A fragment of spring had sneaked in amid perpetually bleak winter days. Friday morning, the playground teemed with children and parents, eager to release pent-up energy. Natassa had dressed the girls in hot pink to help keep better track of them in the crowd, but she wasn't worried. Their older brothers were keeping an eye on them, and David especially was turning out to be a fierce protector of his sisters. She could take a deep breath, relax, de-stress from everything that had been—

"Beautiful day, isn't it?" A slender woman with a bob of curly red hair plopped down on the bench next to her.

"Yes, it is." Natassa angled her body into the direct path of the sun to soak up its warmth. "Perfect."

"Brody, my four-year-old right there, is playing in the sandbox, and Jamison, my six-year-old, is over there waiting to go down the green slide. Which ones are yours?"

"I have those two older boys and those three girls in the hot pink shirts." Natassa pointed.

"Oh."

David ran over to the bench for a drink from his water bottle. "Mercy does not want to stop swinging, Mom. I keep trying to get her to do something else, but she says, 'Again. Again.'" Grinning, he shook his head and plopped down on the bench on the other side of Natassa. "I asked Daniel to take over for a minute."

"So, are they all yours? Because my sister fosters, and I think it's the best thing in the world." The redhead put her hand on her heart as if pledging her sincerity.

"They're all mine." Natassa's smile tightened.

"You adopted her, then. That's so amazing. Where did you get her from? A lady from my church adopted from Ethiopia, and I think it's so precious. I mean to take a child who had nothing and to give them a home is admirable, for sure."

"It looks like my son is getting tired of pushing her on the swing, so I'm going to take a turn. Enjoy your day." Natassa jumped up from the bench and jetted to the swing.

"You too. It's a beautiful day." The redhead called from the bench.

Natassa looked back, but David was no longer sitting down.

"Why did you do that?" He spoke in her left ear.

Natassa yelped. "Oh my gosh, David. You scared me. I didn't see you follow me."

"Why, Mom?" His face bloomed red, his teeth clenched.

"Why what?"

"That lady. You told her you adopted Mercy. Ethiopia? What was that?"

"I didn't say anything of the sort. She assumed."

"You didn't correct her."

"Why should I?"

He threw his hands in the air. "Because it isn't true. How could you let her say stupid stuff like that and not even say anything?"

"What would you have me do, David? Tell a stranger my entire story? Explain to her why Mercy is a different color than the rest of us? I don't owe her anything."

"So, you're going to lie?"

"I didn't lie."

"You didn't tell the truth either."

"Maybe I just wanted to enjoy a day at the park." *Without having to justify my decisions to my thirteen-year-old.*

Natassa stopped at the swings, but David stormed off in self-righteous anger. She always said or did the wrong thing in his eyes. *But what is the right thing? Shouldn't I be old enough to figure that out?* But somehow, she couldn't. So, she did the only thing she could do: fix her eyes on Mercy. She smiled at her little girl, gave the swing a big push, and then lost herself in the giggle that ensued.

Later that afternoon, after she'd washed away all the sand from the park, Natassa sat alone on the couch, browsing listings of farmhouses on her computer.

David came downstairs and sat next to her. "Sorry I blew up at you." He scooted on the couch beside her. Her heart made space.

"It's okay. I get it."

"It's just … I get those questions, like all the time. I'm so sick of it. I'm ready to deck someone."

"Want to move out to the middle of nowhere with me? Be a farm boy? We'd never have to answer to anybody except some cows and corn." She angled the computer toward him.

"Are you serious?"

"I dream sometimes."

"Do you just want to get away from Grandma?" David smirked.

She covered her mouth. "What? No." *Perceptive child.*

"I can't imagine Dad in overalls." David waggled his eyebrows.

She chuckled.

"Actually, Mom, sometimes I don't get questions. A lot of times, people don't say anything, but then it's like I know they are thinking it, and that's almost worse. Like this big awkward bubble waiting to pop. I keep thinking I should pop it first and get it over with, but I don't know how. The longer I wait, the bigger it gets. The worse it gets."

His words were all too familiar. For the same reason, she constantly avoided the conversation. "I'm sorry this is hard for you."

He glanced up at her from under his long lashes. "I know it's hard for you too."

Was this kid thirteen or thirty? "Don't worry about me."

Concern etched lines into his furrowed brow. He struggled right along with her. She needed to be a better example, to find a better way to deal with things.

* * *

Before sunrise on Saturday morning, Natassa kissed Brandon goodbye and headed out the door toward the city of Renada. The kind of kiss that made her toes curl and lingered in her thoughts far past Crawford County lines. The kind of kiss she once assumed she would never receive from her husband if he knew she went to the city, and yet here they were. Years after her double life of sneaking around with her St. Anthony's Baptist Church "family" ended, she had his full approval.

Okay, so not his full participation, but he did come with her to St. Anthony's once a month, and that was a blessing. And it wasn't like they could both work in the food kitchen on Saturday mornings anyway. Someone had to stay home with the children.

No matter how early she left in the morning, Bethany always beat her there, gloves and food service hat donned and ready to go.

"Good morning, sugar. You ready to serve up some Saturday morning breakfast?"

"Sure am."

Within minutes, a half-dozen others filled the basement kitchen of St. Anthony's Baptist Church. The scent of bacon, eggs, and pancakes permeated the air. A half-hour later, Bethany opened the doors, and the long line of hungry people filed through.

"Georgia. So good to see you." Natassa greeted an elderly woman who shuffled in, bent over a cane. She wore the same dress—navy blue with faded red roses—every Saturday morning with a matching navy sun hat, rain or shine.

"Nice to see you too, Tasha." Georgia nodded. "You got my eggs done up how I like 'em?"

"You bet I do. Two fried eggs right here, set aside for you."

"I don't like them scrambled eggs, no ma'am."

"I know you don't, Georgia. I'll carry your plate to your table for you." Natassa took Georgia's plate of fried eggs and biscuits and gravy to her usual spot next to Gary, Sam, and Francie. Bethany called it the Old Folks Table, and they were some of Natassa's favorite people to serve. Sam's wry humor made everyone laugh, though he could be cantankerous. And Francie was ninety-two years old, but didn't look a day over sixty. One day, Natassa had asked her about her youthful appearance.

"What's your secret, Francie?"

"Lean in close, and I'll tell you something good." Francie summoned Natassa close with her finger.

Natassa leaned in, her ear inches from Francie's mouth.

But Francie didn't whisper. "Black don't crack, baby."

The whole table erupted into laughter, Natassa included.

Natassa enjoyed the children too. Most of them scarfed down their breakfast. Were they getting enough to eat at home? Probably not. She couldn't save the world, but she could help fill some bellies on Saturday morning. The children taught her a few handclaps, and she played along with them. She wasn't very good, but that made them laugh. Their laughter and their faces lighting up with happiness soothed her weary soul. In some small way, she was making a difference in the world.

When the doors to the fellowship hall closed and the volunteers began the arduous task of cleaning up, Bethany and Natassa stood side by side washing dishes.

"You thank that husband of yours now, you hear?" Bethany stood elbow-deep in suds.

"I will. I always do."

"Before he started writing checks, all we could give these people was some oatmeal and toast with jam. Look at how much happier they are with a full meal like the one we give them now. They bust'n at the seams." Bethany handed Natassa a plate to rinse.

"Yeah. I just wish Brandon were here to see it." He missed out on meeting the people affected by his money.

"He's seeing it in you, sugar."

Natassa nodded. Sure, but …

"Don't you go being down on that hubby of yours. He's a fine man. One of the best I've ever known. He's probably playing Barbies with Mercy right now. Don't you think for a minute he don't want to get his hands dirty." Bethany gave her a solid stare before handing her another plate. "We mighty thankful for the money he's giving."

How did Bethany always seem to do that? Lay her insides bare and exposed? She shuddered. Okay, so Bethany was right. Brandon was an amazing father to all of their children, Mercy included. She hadn't been sure if Brandon would ever be able to bond with a child that wasn't his biologically. A child that came to them through such tragic circumstances. And yet, when Brandon adopted Mercy as his own, he did so without reservation. He protected her like a shield. Her hero. And he should be Natassa's hero too. So what if he didn't share her desire to be in the city, helping those in need. He supported it. He funded it.

"You're right." Natassa placed the last plate in the dish drain.

"Mama's always right, baby girl." Bethany patted her cheek, leaving a trail of suds.

It had been nearly four years since Natassa pulled into the parking lot of St. Anthony's Baptist Church, intending to look at the stained glass windows. Instead, she'd been drawn inside by this woman who became a second mama to her. It had been exactly what she needed then. And needed still.

"Thank you," Natassa whispered, her throat clenched with emotion.

"Aw, my sweet sugar." Bethany wrapped her in a hug. She smelled like cigarette smoke and Diet Coke. Like belonging. "Natassa with a *T*. I done love you like my own, you know that."

Natassa squeezed back, unable to form the words to convey all this woman meant to her.

"Now you run on home to the rest of your family. I bet they've been missing you."

"Okay. See you tomorrow."

"This ain't your Sunday to be down here, is it?"

Natassa ran through the schedule in her mind. "I guess not." Disappointed ballooned in her. She would have to wait until next Sunday to go to St. Anthony's Baptist Church. This Sunday, her family would be attending their church in Crawford County. "Next Saturday, then."

"It's a date."

"I'm going to beat you down here."

"You can try."

* * *

That night, a flush of peace came with the usual nighttime routine. After Brandon read to the children, she followed up by singing to each one, just as she had done since David was a baby. Stepping into Mercy's room, she smiled at the way her daughter remained transfixed by the glow-in-the-dark stars they had placed on her ceiling months ago. Wouldn't the wonder have faded by now? But no. Mercy's fascination persisted.

Sitting on the side of Mercy's bed, Natassa smoothed the covers over her daughter and began to sing her personalized version of "You Are My Sunshine."

Then, Natassa sang the song that she reserved for this child, the song that Bethany first sang to her within hours of her birth. The song that "Good Ole Mercy"—as Natassa and

Bethany now called her in order to distinguish between the two—sang back in the 1800s.

> Mercy. Sweet mercy.
> Good Lord, we need Your mercy.
> Every morning. Every morning.
> Your mercies are new.

She sang it to the tune Bethany used that day, though neither of them knew the original tune. Mercy's journal had changed Natassa's life forever. When would Bethany give her the rest of it? She'd said Natassa wasn't ready. What did that mean? When would she be ready? How could she get there? Three years had gone by since she'd read the first part. Why did Bethany have to be so stubborn?

Natassa prayed with Mercy, kissed her goodnight, and then moved on to Hope's room. After singing and praying with Hope, Faith, and Daniel, she stepped into David's room. He stood, putting a CD away on his shelf. Natassa's breath caught, and tears stung the corners of her eyes.

"What, Mom? What's wrong?" David's eyebrows squished together.

"Nothing. Nothing's wrong. It's just … We had a deal. I told you when you were taller than me that I would quit singing to you and look at you now." She pressed her lips into a thin line to keep from falling apart.

David walked up to her, only proving her point. He was growing up. Too soon. Too fast. "No, Mom. It's the shoes." He kicked off his tennis shoes. Sure enough, now she stood a half-inch taller at most. But she'd take it. "I think we still have a few more nights of you singing that stupid baby song to me." He winked, then plopped down on his bed. In a voice choked with emotion, she sang David's version of "You Are My Sunshine," then prayed with him and tousled his hair.

She turned to walk out the door.

David's voice snagged her attention. "I won't take it away, Mom. Your sunshine. I'm here for you. I've got your back."

His eyes brimmed with sincerity. He had so much of his father in him.

"Thank you. I appreciate that. I appreciate you. But you are also allowed to just be thirteen, okay?"

"Yeah. Okay. Good night."

Natassa rolled her eyes. "We both know you aren't going to bed. You'll be listening to music for the next two hours. But good night anyway."

Downstairs, Brandon waited to wrap her in his arms.

"You are an amazing mother." He kissed her.

"And you are a fabulous father, my dear." She ran her hands through his hair as he drew her closer.

"What do you think about trying for another baby?"

Stunned, she drew back and searched his eyes. Was he joking? No. He was serious.

She deepened the kiss.

* * *

Natassa woke up to pounding on their bedroom door. Yawning, she stretched and smiled as she brushed against Brandon sprawled out next to her. Then, she checked her watch.

"Brandon, wake up. It's nine thirty." Natassa shook her husband, but he buried his face in his pillow.

"Huh? What?" he asked, voice muffled.

"We're going to be late for church. Like really late."

"Hmm? What's going on?" Brandon rubbed his eyes.

"Babe, get dressed. It's nine thirty. Nine thirty," she repeated.

"It's Sunday?"

"Uh-huh."

"We'll never make it."

The pounding intensified.

"One minute, girls." Natassa hopped out of bed and rushed to get dressed.

Brandon sat up. "What if we went to St. Anthony's instead? It would buy us an extra half hour at least."

Natassa paused in the middle of zipping up her dress. "Are you serious?"

"Sure. It's the only way we'll make it to church today."

"You're right. Let's do it." Since St. Anthony's Baptist Church started later than Cornerstone Church in Crawford County, they had just enough time to get dressed, eat a quick breakfast, and dash out the door. They could make it before the second bell.

In the kitchen, Natassa found puddles of milk on the table and Cheerios scattered across the floor. The girls must have already helped themselves to breakfast.

She grabbed a rag. "Well, at least I don't have to feed you this morning. Mommy and Daddy slept really late, so we are going to St. Anthony's Church this morning instead."

"Sure, whatever." Daniel poured himself a glass of orange juice.

"I get to see Grandma today." Hope jumped and clapped.

"Yes, baby. You get to see Grandma Bethany. Only please don't say that around … Grandma." Natassa would never hear the end of it if her mother heard the girls call another woman grandma.

"No!" Faith stood in the middle of the kitchen, fists clenched at her sides, eyes wide.

"What? What's wrong?" Natassa squatted down beside her daughter.

"We're supposed to go to Cornerstone this morning. It's on the calendar. See." Faith pointed to the family calendar where Natassa had clearly marked their Sunday schedules. "St. Anthony's is next Sunday."

"I know, Faithcakes. That's how it was supposed to go. We were supposed to go to Cornerstone today and St. Anthony's next Sunday. But sometimes plans change. Sometimes we have to be flexible."

"I don't want to go to black church." Faith stomped her foot, her face reddening.

"What? Why?" Natassa reached out to hug her, but Faith broke free and ran out of the kitchen and toward the backyard. Natassa started after her.

"Let her go." Brandon put a hand on her shoulder.

"What does she mean she doesn't want to go?"

"She doesn't like when people spring things on her. Give her a minute to process." He stood behind her and rubbed her shoulders, but that didn't ease her tension. St. Anthony's was her first choice, but not her daughter's. Just when her husband got on board, her daughter jumped ship. Would they ever be fully unified as a family?

She watched Faith out the window, her heart churning. Faith paced back and forth, clearly in turmoil. Finally, she plopped down on the porch swing, and Natassa went out to her.

"Can you tell me what's on your mind?" Natassa sat next to her.

"I'm different there, Mommy. I don't like being different."

"You're the only white child in your class, you mean?"

"Yeah."

"Does anyone say anything to you about it? Is anyone mean to you?"

"No. Not really. But I feel it. Like I'm not one of them. Like I'll never be one of them. There's nothing I can do to fit in. I'll be different forever."

"Hmm. That probably doesn't feel too good, does it?"

"No." Faith sniffled.

Natassa drew her close. "So, do you think the best thing we could do as a family is to always go to a place where you are with people who are exactly like you and where Mercy is the one who feels different? Who feels like she doesn't belong? Would that be a good solution?"

"No." Faith wiped her nose on her sleeve. "Probably not."

They sat in silence for a couple of minutes. What could she say? How could she cross this bridge?

Finally, Faith looked up. "Could I stay in the big service with you?"

"Absolutely Faithcakes."

During the service, Faith sat right next to Natassa and watched as dozens of members of the congregation passed Mercy back and forth throughout the singing and preaching. At three-years-old, Mercy really should be going to class. She wiggled and wouldn't stay quiet, but no one seemed to mind. Everyone loved her, and all the women adopted the title of "Auntie" to Mercy. Doted on and adored, Mercy soaked up the extra attention.

Service let out, and Mazy came over to hand Mercy back to Natassa. "It's about time for me to do this girl's hair again."

"Yes. Let me look at my calendar and call you this week."

Faith tugged on the hem of Natassa's dress.

She bent over. "What do you need, Faith?"

"Mercy fits here." Such a simple statement. And so true.

"Yes."

"I can do this. For her."

Tears and a smile vied for first place as Natassa whispered, "My brave girl. That's what love is all about."

3

DeAndre pulled up in front of the address Janell had written down on a piece of notebook paper—124 Steward Ave. Her handwriting made it seem as if every letter and number were italicized. Not exactly sloppy, but not quite neat either. It wouldn't fit in a box. Like her. If it took the rest of his life to figure her out, it would at least be an adventurous one. He laughed. Hard to believe that a girl had him thinking in that direction. And tonight? Maybe this was a step—or a leap—down that path.

It wasn't like he planned to meet her parents or anything. This was their first official date after much unofficial time spent together, mostly on the clock. She'd also helped him move into Rob's place, which took all of ten minutes and consisted of unloading his trunk. She had stayed for pizza afterward, but the guys were all there so that hardly counted as a date. They did talk on the phone nearly every night lately, sometimes for hours. Mostly about nothing, really. That girl could talk about everything and never say much that really mattered, never get around to telling her story. Next time, she'd say. This had to be "next time," didn't it? Their first official get-dressed-up-and-pick-you-up date.

"Pull up on the street outside my house. I'll be waiting," she'd said.

Except he didn't see her. How long should he wait before walking up to the door? He checked the time. Only five minutes early.

A flash of a green dress flew into DeAndre's peripheral, but it didn't come from 124 Steward Ave. DeAndre shook his head. What was this about? Janell darted from the front door and down the path of the house next door. She looked back, then made a quick right, dashing a few feet before seeing him. Then, she slowed.

Maybe she wrote the address down wrong. Maybe she was visiting the neighbor. There had to be an explanation other than that she didn't want her parents to see him.

He took a few deep breaths.

She smiled at him shyly, differently than she usually did. Should he say something? Ask her about it? And ruin their evening before it began? She put her hand on the door. No. He wouldn't say anything yet. He'd wait and see.

"Good evening," she said in a singsong voice as she slid into the car. Ugh. He should have opened the door for her. *Way to win her over. We're off to a great start.*

"Hey. How are you?"

"Excited. Will you tell me where we're going now?"

"We're going to go see someone you know." He tried to shake off the negative vibes. If only he could get into that sweet spot he'd been in when he first pulled up.

"Someone I know? What on earth?" There it was again, that laugh that sounded like a song. So, she wasn't going to talk about whatever just happened. He could forget it for now, couldn't he? If she kept laughing like that, he could forget most anything.

He stole glances over at her while he drove. Instead of stewing earlier, he should have complimented how amazing she looked in that dress. She talked about a few funny customers she'd had that day, impersonating their accents and body language. From experience, she'd likely nailed it. She was good at that, noticing people, seeing them, hearing not only what they said but how they said things. He just made coffee. He had nothing to add to the conversation, but he wouldn't change a thing.

Finally, he pulled into a parking spot, and Janell looked around.

She crinkled her nose. "We're meeting someone I know at the art museum?"

He chuckled. "I hear they have some great pictures of The Big Man Himself. You know Him, right?"

"Oh, Big J? Yeah, we go way back."

He fidgeted with his keys. Was this a stupid idea for a date? "Is this okay? Because we could do something else if—"

"No, this is great. I haven't been here since my middle school field trip, and I don't think I paid any attention. I was too busy wondering if Roy Cateroni was going to ask me to the spring dance or not."

"Did he?"

"No."

"Idiot."

"I think the majority of middle school boys would fit into that category."

"I don't disagree."

"What could be better than going to the art museum with a real artist? This is perfect. What are you waiting for? Get out of the car." She slid out and strode toward the entrance. Once again, he'd missed his opportunity to be a gentleman and open her door. Chagrined, he caught up with her and grabbed her hand.

Janell towed him along with a zeal for life that was virtually absent from the streets he grew up in. Whenever it had leapt up within him, Reg had been there to stuff it down. But now with Janell, it sprung up in him again, busting out, reaching high.

Once they stepped inside, Janell slowed, savoring piece after piece. She would step back, as if taking in the big picture, then step closer. Her eyes traced the paintings inch by inch. She tilted her head while examining details most people would gloss over. DeAndre spent more time studying her than the paintings.

"The pictures of Jesus are in the next wing." He pointed to his left.

"Oh, I've already found them."

"What? Where?" He hadn't left her side, and they'd seen nothing but landscapes.

She took his hand again and led him over to a painting. "Right here. This is a picture of Jesus if I've ever seen one."

"It's a sunset and a canyon."

"Yes." she nodded. "And He's all over it. His majesty and beauty."

DeAndre shook his head. What was he to make of this woman?

"He's over here too. This one's my favorite." She led him to a watercolor of marigolds.

She continued to point out what she considered to be pictures of Jesus as they viewed a still life of a mother holding her baby, an elderly woman smiling, and a child sleeping.

"You see Him in everything, don't you?"

She shrugged.

"How are you not an artist?"

She tried to look exasperated but her smiling eyes betrayed her. "Because I can't draw or paint or sculpt."

"Have you tried?" She had an artist's eye. She could probably do wonders with a brush in her hands.

"You should see my old art projects, DeAndre. Hideous. I'll stick to what I'm good at."

"Which is ?"

Her mouth pursed, and her forehead scrunched. "Appreciating the art." She started to walk toward the next wing, but he tugged her back to him.

"I didn't mean you're not good at anything. I … I want to know you, Janell. What makes you tick, what you're passionate about. What your dreams are, you know?"

"No. I don't know. That's the problem. But I'm getting pretty good at figuring out what I'm not good at, so by process of elimination, I'll figure it out eventually."

She pursed her lips, hinting at one thing she'd be good at. He stepped close, running his hand down her arm. She gazed up at him, taking a step closer.

A tour group came into the wing, the shuffle of their feet breaking the quiet magic between them. A few people stared at them, then abruptly looked away.

"Let's go find Jesus," Janell whispered.

"Good idea." Though he consented, DeAndre glared at the tour group, whose backs were turned to him. He'd been so close.

"Found Him," Janell called out, much too loudly for an art museum.

He found her standing before a watercolor of Jesus and the Samaritan woman at the well. A very white Jesus and a very white Samaritan woman.

"So, His hair is light brown with a reddish tint, I guess." DeAndre rubbed his chin. "Good to know."

"He's so pale. You'd think with all the time He spent outside teaching He'd at least have a tan. And He looks old. Much older than thirty-three." Janell pointed toward the woman in the picture. "The artist put so much detail into the Samaritan woman's dress, though. It makes her look like a woman of wealth and good standing, like she had the world at her fingertips. We get how broken she was, but you wouldn't be able to tell it by looking at her. I wonder if the artist intended that. Like how Jesus can look through the person who seems to have everything all together and see right through the facade, straight to the heart."

"That's deep." How deep did the mind inside her pretty little head go? More importantly, how far would she let him in?

Janell moved on, grabbing his hand and tugging him along. They stood before a lithograph entitled *Jesus Christ*.

"Still pasty." DeAndre grimaced.

"Yeah, but at least He doesn't look old and tired. He's got that manly beard going on that looks like it's been curled under with a curling iron."

"What's that in His hand? A diary?"

"A Bible?"

"Wasn't the Scripture on scrolls?"

Janell shrugged.

They looked at a dozen other pictures of Jesus, each time noting the discrepancies between the depiction in front of them and the reality. Janell seemed enchanted with a colorful depiction of the ascension from the 1600s done with egg tempera, wax, and gold paint on parchment. "It's exquisite."

"I guess." DeAndre glossed over the piece, unimpressed.

"You guess?" She turned toward him.

He wrinkled his nose.

"So, this is why you brought me here? To prove your point that no one paints a black Jesus?"

"No."

"Really? Because I thought you were going to talk about the *art*, DeAndre. Instead, all you're talking about is how white the Son of God looks in all the paintings. You're right, okay? Pasty white men painted them, and they aren't accurate depictions. But your depiction of the king in Song of Solomon isn't accurate either." He started to interject, but she held up a finger. "And just because they are not accurate doesn't mean there isn't something to appreciate in them. There is beauty all around us. Art doesn't have to be perfect to be beautiful."

With a breath, DeAndre blew out all the defenses that had risen in him. "Okay." He held up his hands in a truce.

"Now we are going to the last wing of modern art, and you are going to stick your nose up in the air and explain the pieces in there to me like a true artist. Deal?" She rocked back and forth from the balls of her feet onto her tiptoes, eyes twinkling.

"Yes, darling." He tilted his nose up and held his arm out to her. Okay, so she had him. She had him good. His mouth tipped in a smile.

* * *

After the art museum, they sat across from each other at Bristol's. Janell devoured her steak salad, loaded with extra dressing. Cute.

"My mom ate salads, but not like that." Why had he said that? His mother would be horrified. *Don't ever comment on what a woman eats, or how.*

She chuckled, then shoved another huge bite into her mouth. "Tell me about your mom, DeAndre." She spoke with her mouth still full, a dribble of dressing cresting the corner of her lips.

"She loved my dad. The end." He forked a bite of mashed potatoes into his mouth. No sense dredging up the past.

"Come on. You went to school in Chicago, right? Didn't you see her? She lives there, doesn't she?"

"Yeah. I thought when I moved there we'd reconnect, but nothing happened how I planned." He fiddled with his napkin. "She lives in a one-bedroom apartment, works a lot of hours. No room for me at her place or in her life, I guess."

"That can't be true." Janell frowned.

"I think she's seeing someone and doesn't want me to know about it. She kept making excuses, being all secretive. I'm not sure. Something's up, and that's the best that I can figure."

"She's a grown woman. She could remarry if she wanted. Why would she hide that from you?"

"It'd be hard for me to see her with someone other than Pa. She knows that. But it's just that … I wish I could find somewhere where I fit. I was the odd one in my old hood, always wanting to break free. Then I came out here and—

don't get me wrong—the boys have been great to me, but I don't exactly blend in.

"So, I went away to this school that's supposed to be multicultural or whatever, and I hung out with some people of color, some black dudes, some Latinos, and I looked like I fit at least. But they were raised in the suburbs and had all these experiences that I didn't have, and they'd never seen the things I'd seen, so I felt out of place there too."

He sat back and puffed out his cheeks. "And then I thought at least I can feel at home with my Ma, but even that didn't work out. I can't seem to find my place."

Janell put her fork down and took his hands in her own. "What about now?"

"Getting closer," he whispered.

He stared into her eyes. Yes, his place was in there somewhere.

The waitress came and refilled their drinks. Reluctantly, he let go of her hand to finish his meal.

"I have a business proposition for you," Janell said in between bites.

"Go on." He paused with his fork midway to his mouth, curious.

"You told me your dream is to own your own studio. If you sold most of the pieces in your trunk, you could rent the little place on Main that used to be a stationery store. You'd make enough for the first and last month's rent and the deposit, plus supplies. I added in a little extra for a cushion. I went online to get an idea on pricing; I'm not an expert, of course."

"And how do you suppose I sell those pieces?" He cocked an eyebrow. "Through a website like a million other struggling artists? It'd get lost in cyberspace."

"Actually, I've already talked to Jim. He's cool with you hanging your pieces in Java Joe's and having them for sale there. You can put them online as well but displaying them at Java Joe's is a win-win for them and for you."

"You talked to Jim?"

"You're not mad, are you?" She winced.

"No, just surprised." And confused. Why was she going through all this trouble for him?

"I know you can do it, DeAndre. You can sell those pieces, paint more, and get your studio. Live your dream. Find your place."

"You're so … confident."

"I can see it. I see it in you."

"And you think you're not good at anything?"

She sat back in her seat, biting her lip. "Maybe that's what I'm good at. Making other people shine."

"Marketing. You should have majored in marketing."

She threw her hands up. "Now you tell me."

"What did you go to school for anyway?"

"Prelaw." She scrunched her nose.

"What happened?"

"I flunked out." Janell framed her hands as if highlighting a newspaper headline. "Shining star goes away to college on a full-ride academic scholarship and flunks out. Couldn't make the grade. Couldn't cut it. Couldn't handle the pressure. Came home disgraced. Now works in the same coffee shop she worked in as a teenager in high school." Her voice cracked. "Shame of her family."

"But you're so smart."

"I was." She studied her plate and whispered, "I don't know what happened."

"I'm sorry."

She straightened and waved her hand in front of her face. "Hey, no biggie. I can always live with my parents for the rest of my life. Be a barista." She wiped the corners of her eyes with her napkin.

"No deal. You'll find your way. We both will."

"Together?" Her eyes searched his, wide and wanting.

"Yeah. Let's do it together." He reached out and took her hand again and brought it to his lips.

By the time they'd finished dinner, he'd nearly forgotten how their night had begun. Until he pulled onto Steward Ave. She'd given him the wrong address earlier. It might ruin such a wonderful evening, but if they weren't honest with each other, how could they possibly do this thing "together?"

"So," he ventured. "Do you want me to drop you off at 124 or 126?"

She groaned.

"You don't want your parents to know that I'm black." He'd been naïve. Of course, the color of his skin would matter.

"No! DeAndre, why would you say that?" Her hand flew to cover her heart like a pledge of sincerity.

"Umm …"

"You people always think it's about race. It's not." But then she flung that same hand between them, and it hovered there, accentuating the otherness.

"You people?"

"Oh, just stop." She dropped her hands to her sides as if laying down arms.

DeAndre pulled over at 124 and faced Janell, taking a deep breath. He should hear her out. "Continue."

"My parents, they had these big hopes for me. Big dreams for their baby girl. I'm an only child. Only one child to make the parents proud. I had two career choices in their eyes: a doctor or a lawyer. That's not going to happen. When they figured that one out, they set their sights on me at least *marrying* a doctor or a lawyer. Or someone extremely wealthy or successful. Someone to make up for how pitiful I am. They hate that I work at Java Joe's. If I bring home a guy that works there too …"

"So, if I was a wealthy black doctor?"

"Welcome to the family."

Janell blushed. She probably hadn't meant to go down that road on a first date.

"You think so?"

"I really don't think your color is going to be an issue. And I'm going to have to make them love you as much as I do so that they can be okay with waiting until your art takes off."

"Say that again."

"I don't think your color—"

"No, the next part."

She stilled. "I didn't mean to say … Not like that. Not here. It's too soon."

He brushed a strand of hair from her face. She closed her eyes and swayed into his palm. Angling her face toward him, he kissed her like he'd wanted to do all evening. She leaned into the kiss, eager and full of life. They parted breathless, pressing their foreheads against one another.

"I love you too, Janell. I know it's fast and there are barriers, but we'll work it out. Whatever comes, we'll work it out."

She smiled. "Drop me off in front of my house. We can start there."

4

———————

Eight months later

DeAndre clasped Janell's father's hand. The meeting had gone so well that a tide of emotion hit him. Relieved. Pleased. Hopeful.

"We'll be happy to have you in the family, son." Mr. Brodigm placed a firm hand on his shoulder. "We've enjoyed having you around these past months."

The nervous energy DeAndre had been harboring rushed out in a mixture of a sigh and a chuckle. "I'm honored, sir."

Janell had been right. A trend, he was finding out. She insisted on her parents seeing his art before they laid eyes on him and before they had a clue that black hands had painted those pieces. Though he could have taken offense, she knew her parents best, didn't she? And he needed to roll with her agenda.

Turned out it was a brilliant plan. Janell brought them into Java Joe's and told them the guy she was dating painted those amazing landscapes and still lifes. That he was about to have his own studio. That he was a rising star. She believed it, they believed it, and he started to believe it too.

They loved his work before they knew him. So, when Janell casually mentioned, "Oh, by the way, he's black," she said it only took some minor adjusting in their paradigms. By the time they met face to face, they looked at him like a person with dignity, not a poor black boy from the wrong neighborhood.

"How about a toast?" Mr. Brodigm grabbed a bottle of champagne from a cabinet in the corner.

DeAndre fidgeted. "Sorry, sir. I don't drink alcohol." Not anymore. Not ever again.

His future father-in-law considered him for a moment, then retreated back to the cabinet and snagged another bottle. "Sparkling cider?" He held it up in DeAndre's direction.

"Yes. That sounds great." His shoulders dropped in relief.

Mr. Brodigm extracted two wine glasses from the cabinet and filled each to the brim with cider. "To you and my daughter. May you find every happiness together."

They clinked their glasses. Perhaps their wedding picture would end up on the wall in the living room. Currently, three of his paintings were hanging on display.

And now he was about to become part of the family.

Time to shop for a ring. Also, time to tell Mama.

After getting home from the Brodigms', DeAndre called Mama. It took five rings before she picked up.

"Hello, Dre. How are you doing?" Dishes clattered in the background. *She must be cooking.* He could almost taste the gumbo.

"I'm good, Mama. Real good." He paused—about to tell her he had some news—but she jumped into the empty space.

"You been going to church?"

He rolled his eyes. "Yes, Mama." He could finally give her the answer she longed for. Janell's church wasn't in Crawford County, and it wasn't so white. Not exactly an equal mix of races, but the closest he'd seen. He felt mostly at home there, at least not the odd man out.

"That's good to hear." Satisfaction resonated from her voice.

He breathed in her acceptance. Did a man always yearn for his mother's approval?

"Well, I'd best be going."

"Already?" He looked at his phone. They'd been talking for less than four minutes.

"You caught me in the middle of making dinner." Her tone turned defensive.

"I ..." He stumbled over his tongue. "I-I wanted to tell you that I met a girl." Eight months ago, but he'd hardly talked to Mama since. And he needed to tell her he'd met Janell before he mentioned that he was about to propose to her.

"That's nice, dear." More clanging of pans. A cabinet thumped closed. "You take care now."

DeAndre let out a breath and closed his eyes. "You too." He hung up the phone.

* * *

Eight months. DeAndre had spent eight months with the woman next to him, sharing meals and stories, laughing until they couldn't breathe, talking on the phone until one of them fell asleep. He had rolled into Crawford County a defeated man, and Janell had inflated him with life. This kind of happiness wasn't supposed to be possible. Not for someone like him.

He'd fully immersed himself in her world, spending ample amounts of time with her family. He must really love this girl because he even played Scrabble with them—God help him. Good thing they counted brand names of paint, or he would have thoroughly humiliated himself each and every time. The Brodigms were cutthroat. It made sense that Janell would feel the intimidation and pressure to make them proud. Could he come through for her? Be her golden ticket? He was so close to getting his studio and trading his makeshift workspace in Rob's garage for a sweet spot with decent lighting. If he could sell two more of his bigger pieces, he'd be in.

Of course, he'd spent a pretty penny on that ring.

He'd hidden it in the bottom of his bag and brought it with him everywhere he went, though he didn't plan on asking her until Friday night. Sometimes waiting seemed too hard, and if he had an opportunity, he'd ask her right then and there without the candlelight and fanfare. He'd already rehearsed his proposal a hundred times or more. She'd say yes, wouldn't she? Of course, she would. She loved him. They talked about their future together all the time. Yeah, their relationship had moved fast, but not too fast. He couldn't wait to marry Janell Brodigm.

Now, they were fulfilling her request to see his world—or his old one. He'd spent hours at the home where she grew up, but she had yet to see the neighborhood where he used to live. She wanted to get a taste of where he came from. Fine. They could drive by the apartment where he grew up, sneak past the house Reg and he lived in, and view some of his murals. He just wasn't going to take her down St. Anthony Street. This woman and his new life didn't belong there. Even if that was his best mural.

As they got closer to Renada, his heart rate rose. He rolled his head back and forth trying to ease the tension in his neck. Flexed his fingers. It would be okay. This was just a quick tour. He wasn't going back for good.

As they turned onto Ninth Street, the distinctive click of the car door locking sounded through the car.

He cast a gaze at Janell. "Why'd you do that? Because you saw a black person?"

She reared back. "No. Because this is a bad part of town."

"Seems like the same thing to me. Why do people like you want to lock people like me out of your world?" He grimaced at his tone. *Shut up, D. You know that's unfair.*

"People like you?" Her eyebrows arched high. "Dre, this city has the second-highest homicide rate in the country. It's wisdom. I'm not trying to lock anyone out; I'm trying to protect my world. It's not like you're dangerous. It has nothing to do with you, nothing to do with the color of your skin."

DeAndre shook his head, pushing down the familiar brew of emotions inside. *It's not like you're dangerous.* If only she knew. Thank God she didn't. His eyes and throat burned as he struggled to hold the torrent of shame and fear in. She could never, ever know what he had done that night on St. Anthony

Street. Sure, God had forgiven him. But that didn't mean this lovely lady beside him would feel the same way.

"Why are you shaking your head?" Her tone softened.

At the stoplight, he turned and took her in. So innocent. So beautiful. So … nervous in his natural habitat. What was he thinking? Did he have a right to hang onto her, knowing where he came from? What he had done? But how could he let her go?

"How can this work, Janell? You and me? You're right. It's not just the color of our skin. We're from different worlds, and there's this chasm between us."

She clutched his clammy hand, sought his eyes. "Then paint a bridge." Her lips pursed in determination.

He coaxed them open with a kiss that escalated in passion until a car horn interrupted them.

"Green light." Janell drew back, breathless.

"Good thing."

* * *

Nervous energy sped through DeAndre's spine and out through all of his limbs. He couldn't stop shaking his leg. He couldn't keep himself from pacing. He kept talking too fast, no matter how much he tried to slow his roll.

Tonight's the night.

He'd reserved the entire patio of The Rivera and double-checked to make sure they planned to turn the twinkle lights on. He'd hired a violinist. He had the painting ready and the ring nestled in his pocket.

Now, to wait for seven o'clock. He got off work at five o'clock. Janell wasn't on the schedule but planned to meet some woman at Java Joe's at three, something about a babysitting job. He'd pick her up at six thirty at home, talk to her parents for a few minutes, and get to The Rivera by seven o'clock. And then? Then, he would ask her the question that would change their lives forever.

He was a wreck at work all day. Rob knew what was up and kept laughing at him, but James asked if he was okay.

"Yeah, boss. Sorry, I messed up those orders."

"No big deal." But he kept eyeing him with a look of concern.

DeAndre never made mistakes, and he'd tallied five in one day. Good thing the boss didn't keep such close records.

When Janell came in at two thirty, DeAndre's mood lifted. "I like your hair like that." He handed her the latte.

She tossed loose curls over her shoulder and stared up at him through dark lashes, her cheeks red. He almost asked her right then and there, leapt over the counter and dropped to one knee, brandishing the ring in front of a line of waiting customers. But he stood frozen in time, unable to move, unable to do more than breathe in the sight of her.

"I'd better get to my table." She sounded breathless, as if they had sneaked a kiss in the utility closet.

DeAndre watched her sit and continued to steal glances her way.

Right at three o'clock, the bell above the door jingled. Natassa Bloomington walked in. His stomach plummeted. Her hair looked different, shorter, but it was definitely her. He ducked behind the counter and pretended to look for something, anything.

After a few minutes of fiddling with straws, he stood and scanned the area. Natassa was sitting at the table with Janell. *Oh no. That's who Janell is meeting with? That's who she's babysitting for?*

Rob shouted an order to him. He made it with shaking hands. As he slid the cup across the counter, he stared over at the two women again.

They laughed and talked like best friends.

His head swam. He stumbled into the counter.

"DeAndre?" Rob's brow wrinkled. "Take a break, man. You're due."

He nodded, unable to force words past the lump in his throat. He ripped off his apron and started to rush toward the back exit to get some air.

Janell's voice stopped him. "DeAndre, come here. There's someone I want you to meet."

He froze. Could he refuse? She waved him over. He forced a smile. *Get it together, DeAndre. Go over there and say hi. You've done it before. You can do it again.*

He forced one foot in front of the other and stood before the two women. "Natassa, this is my boyfriend, DeAndre. DeAndre, this is Natassa. I used to babysit for her other girls Faith and Hope, and now she's looking for someone to babysit part-time for Mercy."

Janell gestured to a little girl wedged on the other side of the booth next to Natassa. A little girl with light brown skin and puffy black hair. He stared at her, then looked at Natassa, then looked back at the girl. All with the same grin pasted on his face. Was Natassa's husband black? When Natassa started talking, he shook off his stupor. What had Janell said?

"That's so interesting, DeAndre. You know, those paintings look familiar to me. They remind me of this mural on St. Anthony Street. I have friends at a church down there."

"DeAndre has several murals downtown. One of a bird—"

"Flying out of a skull?"

"Yep. That's the one." Janell's eyes brightened.

DeAndre nodded, casting glances at the girl, trying to put together the pieces. Could it be?

"Are you familiar with St. Anthony's Baptist?" Natassa asked DeAndre.

He blinked a few times, trying to clear his mind. "Yes. I went there when I was a little boy. I knew Old Ezra before he was blind."

"Old Ezra. Really? What about Bethany?"

"Everyone knows Bethany."

"Gama Befany!" The little girl clapped.

He opened his mouth to ask. Shut it, then tried again. He had to know. "How old is she?"

"Three. She'll be four in December."

He coughed but recovered his smile despite the ringing in his ears and churning in his stomach. "Excuse me. I need to get back. Nice meeting you."

Then he rushed to the bathroom where he retched and groaned. He had a child. A child who sat across from the woman he loved. But was he about to lose everything?

5

"So, did you like her?" Natassa buckled Mercy into her car seat.

"Yeah. She's funny." Mercy scrunched up her nose and stuck her tongue out to one side, mimicking Janell's earlier action.

Natassa laughed. "She is funny, isn't she? She used to be Faith and Hope's favorite babysitter. They would beg to have her come over."

"When's she coming to play?" Mercy kicked her legs.

"I don't know yet, honey. Mommy has to check and see when they have a class that works with Janell's work schedule."

Mercy cocked her head.

Natassa shrugged. "We'll have to see."

A real estate agent. She could hardly believe it. After all these years of pouring herself into her home, she was about to set off on a grand adventure. Anticipation twirled within her. She could do this, right? She never finished college, but she could take the classes, pass the exam, and make her way in the real estate world.

She popped in a CD of Bible memory songs for Mercy and merged onto the street. What had gotten into her? Too much time surfing Zillow perhaps? But she could help people find their new beginning. Their fresh start. This wasn't about the money. She'd flown through some extremely rough air and then finally landed in a place of healing. Now that she'd come out on the other side, this seemed like a redemptive step in her journey. Moving other people forward.

She'd told Bethany as much, but her adoptive mama only answered with an "Mm-hmm. Is that so?"

"What's that supposed to mean?" Natassa had asked.

"Oh, nothing. Nothing that you won't find out eventually."

A horn blasted behind her, and she startled. When had the light turned green? How long had she been holding up traffic? She waved an apology and drove forward.

Why couldn't Bethany just say whatever she was thinking? And why couldn't she be happy for Natassa's new journey? Bethany's approval meant more than Natassa would admit.

Her actual mother had said, "It's about time you found something to do other than babysitting Mercy."

"It's not called babysitting when it's your own child, Mother." Natassa had gripped the phone so tight her knuckles had been stiff for hours.

At least Brandon supported her. And Breanna. She could count on them to cheer her on.

"Janell likes brown people." Mercy's voice rose over the music.

Natassa shook herself from her internal monologue. "What, baby?"

"Janell likes brown people. She liked that brown boy."

"I think you're right." Natassa said. DeAndre, the young black man, had blatantly stared at Mercy as if he had never seen a biracial child before. Then again, maybe he hadn't ever encountered one in Crawford County. Years ago, DeAndre had worked at Java Joe's. She might have even stared at him when he first came to town, so who was she to judge? Janell thought highly of him, and she trusted Janell's judgment, didn't she? Wait, wasn't he the one who spilled her coffee that one time she went through the drive-through? Maybe he was just awkward. Janell probably had a soft spot for that type.

"I like brown people too." Mercy laid her head back against her car seat.

"Me too." Natassa smiled at her daughter in the rearview mirror, but her smile fell quickly. Something wasn't right. Something that had to do with DeAndre. She gasped when she made the connection. DeAndre had painted the mural on St. Anthony Street. With her picture on it.

* * *

DeAndre paced back and forth between Rob's living room and dining room, the thud of his shoes softening as he stepped onto the carpet and intensifying to a clunk again as they turned onto the hardwood. He paced like a caged animal, desperately looking for a means of escape. A window. A door. A loophole. Something somewhere that would allow him to go back in time to this morning before his world rocketed out of control. Or better yet four years earlier so that there'd be no need for the panic plummeting in his gut.

Oh God, You forgave me, right? You did. You washed my sins away. As far as the east is from the west. Natassa forgave me too. He reached into his back pocket, tugged out his wallet, and extracted the well-worn note she'd written: *I forgive you. God will forgive you too.*

If I'm forgiven, why does it feel like something is not right? Like something's left undone?

His insides churned, and he pushed the palms of his hands onto his eyes. The answer shouted at him. Glaringly obvious. But, Oh God, how could he go through with it? He had so much to lose.

Don't ask this of me. Please. Can't there be another way?

He stared at the ring box sitting on the dining room table. It wasn't supposed to be this way.

A pounding on the door made him jump. *No, I'm not ready. Please, God. Just a little more time.*

"DeAndre? Rob? Is somebody home?" He couldn't quite decipher Janell's tone. Confused? Exasperated? Worried?

He wiped his sweaty palms on his jeans, tried to slow his breath.

"Rob? Where's my boyfriend? Will someone please tell me what's going on?" She sounded near tears, and he trudged toward the door. *God help me.*

As he opened it, Janell fell into his arms.

"Rob's not here. All the boys are out tonight." A lame opening, but at least he managed to say it without hyperventilating.

"Dre, there you are. Oh my gosh, you worried me sick." Janell pulled back and started waving her arms around like she always did when she got riled up. Normally, it amused him, but now it compounded his grief. "What in the world? What was with the cryptic text: *Can't pick you up. Left you something on the patio of The Rivera.* I text you back, but do you answer? No. I call you. Do you answer? No. So, I drive *myself* to the fancy-pants restaurant, and are you there? No!

No, you're not. Your painting is there, but you are not. What's your excuse, huh? Give it to me." She flung her hand in the air.

"Did you like the painting?" DeAndre rubbed the back of his neck, sheepish, and attempting to postpone the inevitable a little while longer.

"The painting. Oh my gosh. I left it on the porch. Hold on." She grabbed it from outside and set it on the dining room table.

"This is the most beautiful painting I've ever seen. I mean that, DeAndre. Nothing has captured my heart more."

They stood side by side, taking in the scene before them. The painting featured DeAndre on one side and Janell on the other with her long hair flowing in the breeze. Their hands stretched out toward each other, and each took a step on the bridge that spanned between them, over turbulent waters below.

"You said to paint a bridge." His voice trembled.

"And you did."

She reached out and took his hand. He ran his thumb along hers. Her soft skin stirred a longing that would never be fulfilled. This was most likely his last evening with her, rendering each moment sweet and yet painful.

"Now will you tell me why you left the painting, but you weren't there?"

He nodded. Then shook his head. A sob escaped, and he pulled her close to his chest.

"DeAndre, what's wrong?"

"I love you. I love you so much."

"I love you too. What's the matter?"

"Sit down. Please, sit down." He motioned toward the couch in the living room and made a vain attempt to dry his eyes with the bottom of his T-shirt. The tears kept flowing.

"You're scaring me." She perched on the edge of the sofa, knees knocking together.

He kneeled in front of her. "You're so beautiful. The kind of beauty that shines out from you is rare. Life shines out from you. You believed in me. From that first day, you believed in me."

"Of course, I do, Dre." Janell held her hand out to him.

He thrust his hand between them and shook his head. "But Janell, you know who I am now. I am a changed man. I didn't grow up like this. I didn't … I'm not … I did things I'm not proud of."

"We all have, DeAndre." She leaned toward him.

His heart cracked. "You don't understand."

"I do."

"Janell, why is Natassa's girl mixed?"

"What? Why are you changing the conversation?" Janell sat back, crossing her arms and rolling her head to one side. "Well, if you're embarrassed about today, that makes two of us. You totally stared at Mercy. Gaped at her. I guess that throws some people, but I didn't expect it to throw you."

"Do you know her story?"

"Yeah. She was raped in the city and they decided to keep the baby. They're a white couple with four white children and one little girl who doesn't look like the rest of them."

"I did it," DeAndre whispered, doubling over, tears coursing down his cheeks.

Silence blanketed the room. Her shocked expression blurred through the haze of his tears.

Finally, she croaked out a question, "What?"

"I raped her."

"DeAndre, no. No!"

Sobs racked through him. "Oh God, Oh God."

Janell stood and walked to the far end of the room, staring at him with tears zigzagging down her cheeks. The distance grew between them like a regret-filled chasm now. His soul reached for her but only grasped at the air as it fell from the charred remains of the bridge he had burned years ago, before he had known such beauty existed in the world. He plummeted into the turbulent waters.

Deep in Natassa's eyes flashed a core of resilience. She had overcome, risen above the atrocity done to her. But DeAndre would drown. And he deserved to drown.

"She doesn't know that it was you." Clarity dawned through her tear-drenched voice.

"No. But she forgave me." He told her the story, his own voice shaking. Then, he told her what he had to do.

She nodded curtly, lips pressed firmly together, arms folded tightly around herself. What was he hoping for? That she would talk him out of it? Tell him it wasn't necessary? Pave another path?

"I'll leave you to it, then." She turned quickly, nearly sprinting toward the door.

"Janell, wait." He reached out.

She spun around and stared at his hand, still holding herself soundly. "What for?" Her whisper begged for hope.

He couldn't give what he didn't have. "Take the ring. On the table. I planned to propose tonight. You can sell it. Fund the beginning of one of your dreams instead of trying to prop up mine."

Her hand flew to her mouth. "You were going …"

"I was going to ask you to marry me."

She bit her lip, tears flowing freely down her cheeks again. "I was going to say yes. Whenever you got around to asking."

"It would have been perfect."

She shifted her weight from one foot to the other, shaking her head. "A lot of good that does us now." But she grabbed the ring box from the table.

"Take the painting." His voice rang desperate in his ears.

"I don't want the painting."

"I painted it for you."

A long moment passed with waves of anguish passing across her face. Then, she swallowed hard and said, "Sell it to someone who can look at it without their heart shattering. Sell it to someone who can still believe that love is enough."

6

———

Natassa finished loading the last plate into the dishwasher.

Mercy bounced into the kitchen, holding out her phone. "Mommy, your phone is singing."

"Thanks, baby."

Unknown number. Natassa sent the call to voicemail. *Ugh. If you're going to be a real estate agent, you're going to have to get used to taking calls from strangers.* But she did not want to hear how she could make four-thousand dollars a week from home, using a simple system.

"Come on, sticky fingers. Time for your bath."

Mercy giggled and dodged her playfully as Natassa chased her around the kitchen, wiggling her fingers and making silly faces.

Scooping her up, Natassa carried Mercy into the bathroom. After she bathed and dressed her daughter, she walked out of the bathroom and straight into Brandon.

She jumped with a yelp. "Oh my gosh, Brandon." She put her hand on her chest. "You scared me to death. What are you doing home?"

"I tried calling first. You didn't answer."

"Sorry. I was bathing Mercy. I must not have heard my phone."

Mercy emerged from behind Natassa and hugged her daddy's leg.

He rubbed Mercy's back, but tension radiated from him.

His jaw clenched, and his shoulders were rigid. "Natassa, we need to talk."

"What's wrong?"

"My brother's in the living room. Laura is here to watch Mercy."

"Brett and Laura are here? Brandon, what's going on?" Her eyes widened, and her pulse rose.

He didn't answer, just nodded toward the living room. She inched forward. Laura sat on the edge of the couch. Brett stood by her, arms crossed, looking out the window.

Mercy bounded to them. "Uncle Brett! Aunt Laura!"

"Hi, sweetie," Laura oozed.

Brett smiled, but it didn't reach his eyes.

Laura reached for Mercy's hand. "I hear you have quite a Barbie collection. Can you show me?"

Mercy nodded, grabbed her hand, and led her to the playroom.

Natassa's eyes roamed back and forth between the two men, who glanced back and forth between each other. In the silent room, her heart pounded in her ears. An adrenaline rush threw her off-balance. The panic was too familiar.

"Natassa, sit down." Brandon took her arm, guided her.

She perched on the corner of the couch, her knees and hands pressed together, her eyes wide and searching. More uncomfortable silence ensued as the two men communicated with each other through their expressions. Every second stretched, leaving her nerves taut.

"Tell me."

Brandon nodded at Brett.

Brett pinched the bridge of his nose. "Your rapist turned himself in today."

"What?" Her hands trembled, and her voice sounded far away in her ears.

"A man came to the station claiming that he was the one who assaulted you in 2010. They're still waiting for the DNA results from the lab, but his story lines up. Exactly."

She clutched her hands to her stomach to settle the shaking. Her palms began to sweat. "Why now? After all these years?"

"He didn't say." Brandon put a hand on her knee. "They need you to come down to the station, honey."

"Me? Why?" She shook her head. "No, no, no."

"The detectives need to talk to you. They need to verify that they have the right guy."

"Why? I already gave my report. Why do I have to do this again?" Panic laced her words. "I've moved on. We've all moved on."

"Breathe, honey." Brandon knelt in front of her and put his hands on her shoulders. His gaze found hers.

She tried to maintain eye contact, to match her breathing with his, but in the back of her mind the wine bottle fell from her hands, the glass shattering.

The raspy voice said, "Have at her D," as foreign hands grasped at her.

They'd shoved her out of the car. Her head smashed against the concrete. Her face scraped against loose gravel.

She felt dirty again in an instant.

Blinking away the images, she shook her head as tears fell. "I don't want to go in."

Brandon took her hands in his. "I know. But you need to."

"Just a quick testimony. I'll make sure they don't badger you." Sympathy pooled in Brett's eyes.

Natassa took a series of deep, shuddering breaths. She had to calm down. As she did, a picture formed in her mind. And a sickening feeling returned to the pit of her stomach.

She whispered, "What's his name?"

"Scott," Brett answered. "DeAndre Scott."

Natassa sucked in a breath and held it until the room hazed over. Then finally, she crumpled into a sob that turned into a mourning wail. It came from a place deep inside. A place she had thought long healed. A place where her raw wounding resurfaced.

She had seen her assailant's face. He had painted hers. He had seen her daughter. Their daughter?

No, her daughter.

And now, after years of only having a voice to haunt her, she would have a face. One with … kind eyes? An awkward smile? From a man who knew Bethany and Old Ezra. The two scenes didn't mesh together. Both versions brought her a piercing internal ache.

*　*　*

Could a man die from shame?

With each roll of the finger on the ink pad, another layer of heaviness settled over DeAndre. When they tested his DNA, what did they find? Did it have the markings of a criminal? When they scanned his retinas, what did they see? Pools of guilt staring back at them? He tried not to notice the peeling paint and rust in the room, tried to ignore the layer of dust that lined the table in the corner. He'd landed himself in jail, not the Ritz, and he swallowed back the bile that rose in his throat. He deserved everything they threw at him.

He declined his one phone call. Who would he call? Mama? He couldn't bear to hear the strain in her voice when she heard what he had done. He'd write her a letter instead.

When the guards stripped him down and hosed him off, he could have melted into the floor. Nothing could have prepared him for this level of degradation. He stood so small at the mercy of this gigantic system.

A lady guard pointed to a table where he grabbed his mat, sheet, towel and washcloth. A finality settled over him.

"Remember, innocent until proven guilty. Just don't tell any of the other prisoners why you're in here." Her eyes were just short of kind with a weariness etched in the lines around them. It was as if she tried to care but couldn't invest another ounce of her emotions. She'd seen too much.

"Thanks." He gave her a final glance before following another guard to his cell.

Was it only his imagination, or did every eye bore into him as he entered his pod?

"Here's your cell." The guard gestured to DeAndre's right.

He took a deep breath and stepped inside.

A man twice the size of DeAndre stood leaning against the wall with his arms crossed around his chest. His muscles bulged beneath his T-shirt. DeAndre's chest tightened. That man could crack his skull with one blow.

"Name's Gray." He sneered at DeAndre. "Whatcha in for?"

"None of your business." DeAndre feigned a confidence and aloofness he didn't possess.

Gray snorted. "This'll be interesting."

7

Natassa pounded the dough, slamming it against the powdered cutting board. She kneaded it with clenched teeth and white knuckles. And tears. The tears had been coming and going for days. She attempted to keep them at bay around the children, but they seemed to have a mind of their own, leaking out on their own accord. Making their presence known whether convenient or not.

A knock sounded at the door, and she ignored it—probably another callous reporter scoping out an interview. She continued to knead the bread. Applying pressure. So much pressure. How much pressure could someone contain before they exploded?

"Nat? C'mon, Chicka. Open up." Breanna's voice called out through the closed door, and something in Natassa leapt toward it. She wiped her hands on a towel and rushed to turn the knob. She fell into her friend's waiting arms.

"I'm sorry. I thought you were a reporter."

"No, but I played one on TV."

Natassa chuckled.

Breanna pulled back, rested her hands on Natassa's shoulders, and looked her friend in the face. "Sorry, probably not the time to joke. You've been through it, eh? I've got two hours and a gallon of mint chocolate chip."

Mercy ran up and hugged Breanna's leg.

"And hello, Mercy Girl. How's my Sweet Pop? I brought you an Elmo movie and a popsicle for a treat afterward. How about that?"

Mercy squealed and jumped up and down.

Breanna set Mercy up with her movie and proceeded to the kitchen with the ice cream.

Natassa placed the bread dough in a bowl to rise.

"What? You're making your own bread now? Like a pioneer woman?" Breanna slid out a barstool at the kitchen island and sat, inspecting her with those piercing eyes that saw too much.

Natassa bit her cheek. Breanna raised an eyebrow.

"You just don't know what's in store-bought bread nowadays. All of the additives. High fructose corn syrup. It's better to make my own. It's better that I know what goes into our bread. It's better if I can …"

Breanna cocked her head.

"If I can control what we eat."

"Okay." Empathy etched lines around Breanna's eyes and mouth.

"If I can control something. Something for goodness' sake." Her voice wobbled. "Everything is spinning, spinning wildly out of my control, and I reach out to grasp something solid, and I'm holding air in my hand. I need something, at least one thing to allow me to feel grounded even for a minute." She wiped her cheeks with the backs of her hands.

Breanna took a tissue from the counter and held it out. "And you chose bread."

She grabbed the tissue. "We had the ingredients."

"I wish you would have called me when you first found out. I tried calling, but your phone was off."

Natassa shook her head. "No phones. No TV. No radio. It's everywhere. Everywhere."

Breanna blew out a breath. "Okay, then. I get it. I'll just have to come check in on you." She sought out Natassa's gaze. "Did you have to go to the station?"

Her eyes welled up with tears again as she nodded. "Oh, Bre. I thought I'd put this all behind me—that I was over it. And now I feel stupid for being so naive because it's obvious that I'm not." Her shoulders shook as she sobbed harder.

Breanna slipped off the barstool and came close, placing an arm around her.

"I feel like … like I've been in a car wreck or something because everything hurts. Every part of me is tender and aches and—"

"Mommy? Are you okay?" Mercy stood next to them, looking up at Natassa with wide, solemn eyes.

Natassa swiped her eyes with her shirt sleeves. "Yes, baby."

Breanna crouched before Mercy. "Your mommy is feeling sad right now. Do you remember the story *We're Going on a Bear Hunt*?"

Mercy nodded.

"It's like this sadness is that long wavy grass. Mommy can't go over it. She can't go under it. She's got to go through it. But she's going to get through it, and she's going to be okay." Breanna turned and looked up at Natassa. "She *will* get to the other side, I promise you."

* * *

After Breanna left, Natassa finally worked up the courage to turn her phone on. She found a flurry of group texts from her mother and sisters and a voicemail from Bethany.

She rolled her eyes at the text chain.

Mom: *I found a beautiful rental house you could stay at until this all blows over—5 stars.*

The attached picture showed a quaint country ranch.

Maureen: *That's gorgeous! And what a steal.*

Olivia: *How are you doing, Natassa?*

Mom: *I saw your house on Channel 5. When's the last time you trimmed your bushes? They're overgrown. Makes you look shabby.*

But she sank into Bethany's voice message.

"Hey, sugar. I wanted to see if you would be up for coming to dinner Wednesday night. I sure do miss you."

Natassa jumped at the opportunity to talk with her spiritual mother and mentor, grasping for some clarity and peace to calm the storm that raged inside of her.

On Wednesday, she climbed the mountain of stairs to Bethany's apartment.

Bethany wrapped Natassa in a bear hug. She didn't mind being nearly smothered, needing her mama's comfort.

"Sit, baby girl. The lasagna's almost done." Bethany settled into the worn armchair catty-corner from the sofa.

Natassa dropped onto the couch, comfortable and safe in Bethany's cozy apartment.

"When I saw the news, I could hardly believe it. DeAndre Scott." Bethany shook her head and tsked.

"You knew him." Natassa's voice came out flat, dazed.

"Why yes, I did."

Natassa told her, with a shaky voice but only a few tears, about her meeting with Janell and speaking with DeAndre about St. Anthony's. About the way he stared at Mercy and stumbled over his words. And how she had later connected him—and her face—to the St. Anthony Street mural.

Bethany sat in silence for a moment, as if deep in thought.

"Is something wrong?" What a dumb question. In a story like this one, what wasn't wrong?

"Janell, you said?"

"Yeah. Janell is his girlfriend."

Bethany's brow furrowed. "I could be wrong, but this Janell might be showing up at Saturday breakfast at the church. A girl named Janell called me yesterday and asked if she could volunteer. Of course, I told her to come on down. She'll be there bright and early."

"Janell? How would she?" Natassa sat back, stung. "Why would she?"

"I don't know. That's something you'd have to ask her."

"Ask her? I don't want to ask her. I don't want to see her." Natassa's voice pinched. "Call her back. Tell her she can't come."

"Oh, sugar. I understand how this must tear at your wounded heart." Bethany sat forward and placed a hand on Natassa's knee. "I'm so sorry you're hurting. But the church has never turned away a decent volunteer. Not ever. If it's too much for you to be around her, why don't you stay at home Saturday? I can talk to her about coming in every other week. You two could alternate for now."

Natassa recoiled. "You mean, you don't want me to come every Saturday?"

"Natassa, baby. You aren't unwanted. You've gotta know that. I've just got to do what's right by everybody. And Janell, well, she's gotta be hurting too."

Natassa crossed her arms around herself. "Not as bad as me."

The timer buzzed. Bethany rose to take the lasagna out of the oven and then returned to sit on the sofa next to Natassa.

"You could be right. Probably are. But playing a comparison game with pain never seems to end well for anybody. You are fully entitled to feel whatever you'se feeling and so is she. Pain is pain. Hurt hurts. It won't hurt you any less by claiming you have more of it."

Bethany rubbed her back and kissed her on the head. "Think about it. I'll understand if you stay home Saturday. No harm done."

She nodded, biting her lip.

"Now let's eat."

As they ate, Bethany asked Natassa questions about how she found out DeAndre had turned himself in and how she was holding up. She talked about the nightmares that had returned and how she once again felt a chasm of distance between herself and the Lord. And she talked about Mercy.

"Now that I know what he looks like, I looked at Mercy and all of a sudden, instead of seeing my precious girl, I saw his cheekbones. I saw his face in hers. I felt as if someone slapped me. I love her. And she hasn't changed, but I can't unsee him. I wish I could unsee him. I wish I could go back …" She'd barely taken two bites of her lasagna, and her napkin was soaked with snot and tears.

Bethany took her hand. Then she bowed her head as if praying silently. Natassa prayed too, although the only prayer she could form was *Jesus, help me.*

"Hold on, sugar. I'll be right back. I gotta give you something." Bethany left and came back a few minutes later with a three-pronged folder that she handed to Natassa.

"What's this?"

"The rest of Mercy's journal."

"What? Seriously?"

Bethany nodded.

"Why are you giving this to me now? I've begged you for it for years."

"I had to wait for the right time, sugar. You're ready for it now. You thought you were all done with the hard work of healing, and when you're above the dust, you're liable to look down on those sitting in it. If you'se gonna walk with Good Ole Mercy, you gotsta walk *with* her, and that means you can't be afraid of getting dirty yourself."

"I don't know what you're talking about."

"Healing ain't something you check off a list, baby girl. Been there. Done that. Move on."

"I never said—"

Bethany held her hand up, cutting her off. "You'll get to understand what I'm saying. Walk with Good Ole Mercy and see what she has to show you this time."

Natassa nodded but stewed inside. *She withheld the journal from me for years because I was doing okay? Because I was healed? And now she's giving it to me, why? Because I'm a mess? As if that's a good thing.*

"You know I love you, right?" Bethany patted Natassa's knee.

"Yes." Natassa found a smile.

"Good." Bethany's eyes twinkled. "You can be mad at me all you want as long as you know I love you."

8

———

August 26, 1842, Georgetown, South Carolina

I guess you don't rightly realize all you'se have to be grateful for until it flies off and you'se left with nothing 'cept the air thick with memories. I've done got a good master and missus at Hopecrest, and I'm here with Mama like I's been wanting to be all my life, but I loathe to admit I sure do miss being a house slave. Harvesting rice drains the life from my body, but I's determined not to let it drain the light from my mind no more. No matter how tired I am at the end of the day, I got to make time to write in here again.

I's only been here two years, and sometimes I do fear I ran the wrong way—God forgive me. If only I could have had Mama and my freedom at the same time. My dreams at night tease me with first-class dining on steamers bound north. Of the river's breeze snatching wisps of hair from my braid as I stand on deck, listening to the water lapping the bottom of the boat. Freedom to me will always sound and smell and taste and feel like a steamboat ride.

It ain't no use to think this way. Mama don't. She's content with her lot. 'Course she never did eat no fancy food. She's never had someone call her Miss and look her straight in the eye, expecting her to hold their gaze instead of lowering her eyes in subjection. She's never been treated like a person and not merely a slave. I think being treated like I did might have done something to me, some irreparable damage to my ability to settle into the blanket of slavery and cozy up into it.

* * *

August 29, 1842

Mama done stumbled in the field today. She lost her footing. Nearly toppled on her face. I dropped my rice hook and ran to her, ignoring the shouts of the overseer. She done said she was fine. Dizzy in the heat is all. She seems feeble to me, but she keeps telling me she's as strong as ever.

It's not the first time she's lied to me.

I try not to let that bother me none.

* * *

September 1, 1842

Just one more day cutting the crop. There's always extra work come both planting and harvesting time. I cut three rows of rice at a time. Mama's only cutting two, but at least she's sure-footed now. You never want to be too good at managing your field or they'll give you two fields next season. You got to walk the line of being just good enough to earn your own time but not so good that you'll warrant extra work for Master. We cut the stalks a foot off the ground and lay them on the stubble. Then tomorrow we gots to go back and bind up the stalks with string and then load them into the flat boat. When the flat boat gets the stalks up out of the fields, we gots to carry them on our heads up to the barn. Then, we get a break before we have to thresh. Maybe a day or two while the rice cures.

Mama could sure use that break.

I hope she can make the trek to the barn.

* * *

September 3, 1842

Mama ain't a field hand no more. She collapsed halfway to the barn, sheaves spilling everywhere, slaves yelling from all directions. I's already made it to the barn, thinking if I could get my load done right quick, I could come back and take hers too, but I was too late. By the time I got to her, Jonah was carrying her to the Big House. Jonah with his taut muscles gleaming with sweat and sun. "I've got her. I've got her, Mercy Girl."

When he called me Mercy Girl, I forgot my worry for a second, and my stomach did a flip. His eyes met mine, and it's like they dug deep down into me and saw things no one else be seeing. I'd admired Jonah from a distance before, but we'd never had occasion to be close enough for our eyes to touch. He works Oak Tree Field, and Mama and I work Little Bird. I guess now I work Little Bird alone.

There's another field in between the two—in between Jonah and me. Two canals that might as well be rivers. I ain't got a right to be shy, seeing all I been through and the courage that took root in me to get me here, but I can't seem to do nothing more than look at him and dream. I don't know what's wrong with me. How I can be thinking about this man when my mama's strength is fading?

The missus said Mama could be a basket weaver instead of a field hand, which is a mercy. Her body can rest now, though her hands may be hurting something fierce.

I still worry. I can't help it.

9

As the sunrise peaked through her bedroom window, Natassa closed the journal and stared at the cover. She trailed her fingers over Mercy's name on the front. Good Ole Mercy had regrets about choosing her mother over freedom? Second thoughts? She couldn't call them regrets, could she? If Mercy had it all to do over again, she'd make the same choice.

Wouldn't she?

The questions followed Natassa as she showed up at the church twenty minutes early on Saturday morning. She couldn't take the chance that Janell would get there before her. Of course, she could have stayed home and avoided all confrontation, but this was *her* refuge. Her church. Her church family. She was here first, and she wouldn't budge. She came prepared to stand her ground.

"Natassa, you're here!" Bethany hugged her extra long and hard. The scent of bacon and sausage wafted through the air. "I'm proud of you. You might be aching, but you're ready to give back, even if it's difficult. Shows how far you've come."

"I don't know if I'm ready, but I'm here." Natassa looked around the kitchen. At least serving breakfast to needy families would give her something to keep her mind off of things. Perhaps Janell wouldn't even show. It could be a different Janell.

Natassa grabbed six dozen eggs from the refrigerator. The others in the kitchen talked to each other as they diced and fried, sizzling sounds echoing through the space. But Natassa didn't say a word. What if Janell acted like what happened was Natassa's fault? What if Janell made excuses for him? She cracked the eggs harder than she needed to and had to pick a half dozen shell pieces out of the bowl. Once, she accidentally missed the bowl entirely and made a gooey mess on the counter and her hands.

As she wiped the mess up, a voice made her head snap in the direction of the entrance.

"Hi, I'm here to help. I talked with a Bethany over the phone."

"Yes, that's me," Bethany said. "You must be Janell. It's so nice to meet you. Welcome."

Natassa took several deep breaths as Bethany wiped her hands on a towel then came around and shook Janell's hand.

Then, their eyes met. Janell's mouth fell open.

"Natassa, I didn't know you were going to be here, I swear." She shifted her weight from one foot to another, her eyes sinking down, then skittering around the room, then shifting down again. "You probably don't want to see me."

"You got that right," Natassa muttered under her breath, but she kept her face neutral.

"I should leave." Janell took a step toward the door.

"Nonsense." Bethany wrapped an arm around Janell, drawing her in. Drawing her close. "You are welcome here. We'se always looking for people to help."

Janell looked to Bethany as if pleading for understanding. "DeAndre said he came here as a child. That he knew you. He grew up in this neighborhood, right? These were his people. I am trying to wrap my brain around things. I'm trying to figure out how the man I was ready to marry could be sitting in jail right now." Her words raced out nervous and quick. "I don't understand. But I remembered what he said about St. Anthony's Baptist, and I searched it and found out about this opportunity to serve. I wanted to come and learn about his world. At least a little. I swear I didn't know Natassa would be here. I don't want to hurt her."

So that was why she came. Natassa's resolve to be civil melted with the mention of her rapist's name from Janell's lips.

"Then leave. Leave me be. Let me have my corner of peace." Heat burned in Natassa's face, and furry laced through her words.

"Natassa." Bethany's voice resounded through the fellowship hall, nearly echoing off the walls. When she spoke again, it still held a firmness that made Natassa tremble. "You are hurting, and I'm so sorry about that, but your hurt doesn't give you the right to wound. This girl didn't know you were going to be here. This caught her off guard." Bethany's glance said more than her words. *You knew, but Janell didn't. You chose this. She didn't.* "We'se gonna have to try to make this work, and if you can't figure out how to be in the same room with this sweet girl—who ain't done nothing to you—then you need to go home."

The tears flowing down Janell's face matched Natassa's own. They stared at each other. Janell's eyes wide and pleading, as if saying, "give me a chance." Natassa's eyes were hard and dry, much like her heart. How could she change that? Could she choose to soften? Bethany was right in that Janell was innocent. She just loved someone who wasn't.

"Fine." Natassa turned back to the eggs, whipping them in a frenzy. The whisk clattered against the sides of the bowl.

"That's a start." Bethany placed the women on opposite sides of the kitchen, tasking Janell with plating the food alongside her. Natassa avoided all eye contact but eavesdropped in on their hushed conversation. Motherhood had honed her ability to snoop.

"So, you knew DeAndre as a child?" Janell asked Bethany.

"I sure did. He came from a good family. A church-going family. His mama sang in the choir. His pa was an usher before he died. When his mama moved away, he stopped coming around."

"What was he like back then?"

Bethany chuckled. "He doodled in that notebook of his throughout service. Never did bother me none, but his mama took it away from him 'cause she figured it was disrespectful and he'd best be paying attention to the preachin'. Then, guess what he did? He grabbed them old hymnals and doodled in the margins. We got dozens of hymnals with his drawings in them. His mama eventually gave him his notebook back. Guess she figured if he was gonna draw anyway, it'd be best if he didn't do it in the hymnals."

Janell's laugh grated on Natassa's nerves. This was her rapist they were talking about.

"He was going to be a famous artist. I know it. He has it in him. You should see some of his art now." Janell sounded full of pride. *Sickening.*

"Oh, I don't doubt it. He was good even at ten."

Janell sniffled. Natassa turned just enough to see her wiping her eyes. Bethany enveloped Janell in a hug.

"It's going to be okay, sugar. You'se gonna get through this. I know it seems your whole world's come crashing down, but this story ain't over, baby girl."

Sugar? Baby girl? I'm her sugar. I'm her baby girl. Tears stung Natassa's eyes again as she started cracking the next batch of eggs.

Why am I here? I should go home. I'm a mess. An envious mess. The petty web of feelings tangled up around her heart. How could she cut through them? They wouldn't pack up neatly or push away easily. She was a grown woman, and yet fear controlled her. Would Janell take her place in Bethany's heart? Supplant her? Leave her as an orphan?

When the doors opened and members of the community arrived, bringing with them a buzz of conversation, Natassa managed to keep it together—barely—and to avoid Janell. But serving the people didn't bring her the joy it normally did.

Every young boy who came in could have been a young DeAndre. Every woman could have been his mother. Every man could have been his father. Somehow the people she had grown to love became a reminder of the man she hated. Hated? She knew better than to embrace that word, yet there it was.

What about the note she'd written to him? *I forgive you. God will forgive you too.* Did she? Now that she had a face and a name, did that change her heart? Where was the freedom that had enveloped her when she'd written those words? Only darkness surrounded her now.

DeAndre wasn't the only one in prison.

Natassa put an empty tray in the dirty pile and marched up to Janell, who stopped scrubbing a pan and stared at her.

"He won't talk." Natassa shoved her hands on her hips. "There were two men who assaulted me. DeAndre had an accomplice. He won't tell who it was. You could get him to talk. He's got to trust you."

Janell's eyes widened, then she pursed her lips. "I could try."

"Please, Janell. It's important to me. And maybe it should be important to you too."

"I'll see if I can talk to him."

"Thank you." Her mouth made a firm line. "And make sure he knows that Mercy is my daughter, not his. Mine and Brandon's."

Janell nodded. "I will pass that along."

Natassa offered a wobbly half-smile, and Janell returned the gesture with a tentative shy one of her own. Natassa didn't so much make a choice to love or forgive as much as to *not* do the opposite. What did Bethany say? *That's a start.*

10

DeAndre glanced at the clock for the third time in seven minutes. Would visiting hours ever arrive or would he lose his mind?

"Hey, D. Chill." Gray's voice boomed from his place on the top bunk, his legs dangling over the side.

DeAndre peered up at him from the lower mattress, as far away from Gray's legs as he could scoot. "I told you, the name's Dre."

"You shake the bunk again, D, and I'll smash this tray upside your head."

"Sorry." DeAndre stilled his jittery knees. He pushed his mush of pinto beans around with his fork. No way could he eat this slop no matter how much his stomach growled after the sorry excuse for a breakfast that morning. At least the chicken patty sandwich had been edible. Not good, but edible. He was a criminal, right? Who was he to complain about the food?

What little he did eat tumbled in his stomach, threatening to exit. Forty more minutes, and he would see her face again. *If* she showed. And he wouldn't blame her if she didn't.

He finished his lunch, but didn't have anything else to do but wait, so he sat there while Gray heckled him. Thankfully, that was all he did, being too stoned most of the time to do more than intimidate with his size. The others called DeAndre green since he was new to their world and completely unfamiliar with how things worked on the inside. Then Gray slapped the nickname D on him, and he'd regressed to his former self.

Only he didn't fit here, didn't belong … and he was determined to keep it that way. They tried to get him to give them sexual favors in exchange for candy, cigs, soap, or drugs. He refused and ignored their taunts. Then they tried to take what he wouldn't freely give. What had he gotten himself into? So far, he'd managed to fend them off with bribes instead of his fists. He only prayed he could continue to do so.

Now he tuned everything else out and brought to mind every detail of Janell's face. The way the lines around her eyes crinkled when she laughed. The way her smile slowly broadened until it opened wide, like the dawning of the sunrise. Her hair falling gently around her face.

DeAndre's mouth turned up in a slight smile, which faded when something hit him in the head. He glanced down at the hard roll that came to rest next to his foot. Obviously, Gray had thrown it at him.

"Hey D. Answer me when I talk to you." Gray hopped down.

DeAndre stared.

"I said, who you got visiting your sorry little—"

"My girlfriend. Ex-girlfriend."

At that, the guys in neighboring cells heckled, shouted obscenities, and made crude jokes. DeAndre stared at the clock. If only time would pass quicker.

"My girlfriend overdosed on heroin a month after I got in here." Gray crossed his arms. "Everyone forgot to tell me until I asked my brother about her a month after she died. Missed her funeral."

"I'm sorry." DeAndre spoke automatically before the fullness of what Gray had revealed sunk in. His stomach turned sour. What it would be like to lose someone he loved? A permanent loss on this earth. And because he didn't know what else to say, he added, "I'll pray for you." He instantly regretted saying it. Not because it wasn't true, but because it sounded shallow.

Gray snorted. "You still believe in God, D?" He mumbled an obscenity. "You ain't been here long enough. Your God may be out there"—he nodded in the general vicinity of the front door—"but He sure ain't in here. Get your head around that right now."

DeAndre opened his mouth, but then shut it. What could he say? The "right" answer was the Sunday School answer that the omnipresent God filled every nook and cranny of every space. Even prison cells. But the Sunday School answer that made sense on the outside didn't fly as well on the inside. Sure, DeAndre still believed. How could he not? What else was there for him to believe in? But he didn't carry enough faith to share it, to pass it around, and parcel it out to the boys in the cells.

He shoved his tray aside. The guard should call his name in thirty-five minutes. Butterflies swarmed his stomach. He moved to the front of the cell as if that would make time pass faster. He plopped down on the cement floor and laid his head back against the wall.

"It ain't true." A hushed voice came from the neighboring cell. "God is just as much in here as He is out there."

DeAndre turned his head as if expecting to see the man beside him. Who said that?

"Yeah, okay." DeAndre drew his knees to his chest. Who was this man? What were his motives?

"I'm Luis." The man spoke with confidence and breathed assurance into DeAndre that something solid and good still existed in the world.

"DeAndre."

"Nice to meet you. There's a Bible Study on Thursday nights from seven until nine in the chapel. I hope to see you there."

"Okay." DeAndre couldn't wait to meet this man. Who could sound so sure when everything seemed to be whipping around him in some chaotic storm? He stayed in that position, head pressed against the wall waiting for Luis to speak again, but he didn't. DeAndre glanced at the clock yet again.

She would come, wouldn't she? Afternoon visiting hours started at one thirty, and she said she'd be there. Her vague email had left room for his insecurities and questions to wrestle.

His email to her had used up the entirety of his 6,000-character allowance. Begging. Pleading. If only he could see her again. Could he make things right between them? Did she know he loved her fiercely? Could she ever forgive him?

She responded to his lengthy diatribe with ten words: *Okay, I'll come for a visit. Be there around 1:30.*

Not a hint of what she felt or thought. But she was coming. That had to say something.

DeAndre stretched his legs on the concrete floor, then pulled his knees back to his chest. His leg continued to bob up and down even as he held it fast. He looked around his cell. How had his life come to be contained in a five-foot-wide by eight-foot-long cell? The metal bunk bed took up half the room; the toilet and the sink on top of it took up most of the rest. He could stand with his left shoulder against the bed, and his right shoulder would touch the wall. The light above them shone so dim, he had trouble reading. *This.* His life had come to this.

DeAndre listened as his cellie began to snore. He waited. And waited. Anxiety tore at him, threatening to rip off his skin and leave him bare.

When the guard called DeAndre's name, he startled. He jumped to his feet and had to concentrate to keep in step with the guard. He couldn't let his heart run ahead.

When Janell walked into the visitor's room, DeAndre's breath caught. Tears welled up and spilled over. He quickly wiped them away. Crying in jail could get him jumped. She looked that much more beautiful contrasted with the ugliness around him, the evil of what he had witnessed within the past week "on the inside." Her purity radiated from her, making him ache. He hurt in places that he had been trying to wall off. One look at her, and those walls came crashing down.

"Hi." Her voice sounded small and soft as she sat on the edge of her chair.

"Hi." He stared at her. Drank in the sight of her. No glass stood between them, and they didn't need to use a phone to communicate. Only a wide metal table separated them.

She sucked in a breath. "DeAndre! You have a black eye!"

His hand fluttered to his right eye. "Oh. Yeah. A guy decked me the other day for bumping into him on the way to the showers."

"What? On accident?"

"Yeah, on accident."

"And he punched you?"

"Yep."

She grimaced.

"Everyone here is on edge. All the time. It's like you can never let your guard down. Always high alert."

"How long, DeAndre? What are they saying?" She bit her lip, confining her tears to the corners of her eyes.

"The sentencing is next month."

"Did they give you any idea of how long you're going to be in this godforsaken place?"

He sighed. "It's a felony, Janell. Probably ten years."

"Ten years! Are you kidding me? You turned yourself in. Doesn't that count for something? Won't they give you some kind of leniency? For not having a criminal record?" She waved her arms around again, and he offered a sad smile.

His mind raced back again to the day he walked into the station to turn himself in. After they read him his rights, he talked with the investigator. They explained to him that he'd committed a felony and how with a felony on his record, he would be on the sex offender registry, which would affect his ability to find employment for the rest of his life. A felon. He was a felon.

Should he tell her about the plea bargain offer?

No. Definitely not.

"Thank you for coming to see me. Seeing your face—"

"I actually came because Natassa had a couple of messages she wanted me to relay."

DeAndre sat back. She might as well have slapped him. *Natassa?* How did she make it into the conversation?

"She needs to know about the other person involved, DeAndre. The accomplice. Supposedly, you aren't talking. I'm not sure why you won't say who it is, but it's important to her. She's got to have that missing piece of information so she can have closure."

"You've talked to her about this?" Nausea rose within him.

Janell took a deep breath and let it out slowly. "Not much, but enough."

"Janell, I can't. I can't rat him out. I came forward out of my own free will. He's got to do the same if that's what he wants to do. I'm the one who committed the main crime. I can't do that to him. Not even if—"

"Not even if what?"

He hesitated.

"Not even if what?" Janell repeated, sitting forward in her chair.

He couldn't bear to look her in the eye. "Not even if they would lower the charges and give me four years instead of ten."

"What?" She catapulted out of her chair, then, at a look of warning from the guard, slammed back down again. "Have you lost your mind? DeAndre, you turned yourself in because it was the right thing to do. Telling the whole truth of what happened and who was involved is the right thing to do as well. And six years." She threw her hands up. "You would throw away six years of your life? For what? Whoever you are protecting needs to own up to what they did."

"I'm sorry." He had nothing else to say. The truth was he'd gone back and forth on the issue, racked with guilt on both sides, praying night and day for the answer of what to do. The solution eluded him. But Reg had written to him and asked if he could visit. He was scheduled to come in next week. Perhaps then DeAndre would gain some clarity.

"Think about it, DeAndre. Think about all you've put Natassa through. If you could do this one thing to make it right with her."

"This one more thing?" He glanced around him.

"Yes." Her voice sounded somber. "This one more thing."

"What's the other message?"

"Hmm?"

"You said Natassa had a couple of messages for me?"

"Oh. She wanted you to know that Mercy is hers. And when you get out, you are not to try and have anything to do with her."

DeAndre winced. What did she think? That he would get out of jail and make a run for her daughter? "Point taken."

Janell moaned. "I hate this."

"Me too."

"What do you need?"

"Deodorant," he answered without hesitation.

Janell lifted an eyebrow.

"I'm not safe in the showers."

"Oh my gosh." She put her head on the table in front of her. "I can't. I just can't."

"It's okay." It wasn't, but that was what he was supposed to say. It was his job to comfort her.

She sat up, her face pale. "I can't bring you anything though, can I?"

"You can give money." The moment the words were out of his mouth, he was blanketed with shame. He'd asked his ex-girlfriend for money for deodorant. A month ago, he had bought her a diamond ring.

She didn't seem fazed. "And then you can buy deodorant in there?"

"Yes, at the commissary. Deodorant and maybe a warmer blanket. There's no heating or air-conditioning in here."

Janell shuddered but nodded. She stood to go.

"You'll come back, won't you?" DeAndre's voice cracked. "Please say you'll come back. I need you, Janell. I need to see you. I need to know that there's still beauty …" He tasted salt on his tongue.

"I'll try." Her chin trembled.

He watched her walk away, committing the sight of her to memory for a future canvas.

11

———————

The muffled sound of the television resounded from the living room. Natassa stilled, ceasing to stir the flax muffin batter, tilting her ear toward the sound. The news. Brandon had turned on the news.

She yanked the hand towel off the rack and scrubbed the specks of batter off her hands. Then, she tossed the towel on the counter before stomping into the living room.

"What do you think you're doing?" Her face pinched in anger even as a voice of reason whispered into her ear. *It's been over a month since DeAndre's arrest, Natassa. The man has every right to turn on the television.* She clenched her teeth, pushing that voice away.

Brandon merely glanced at her from where he sat on the edge of the sofa, hands clenched between his knees, brow knit in concern.

Something was wrong. Natassa's pulse catapulted. "What is it? What's going on?"

Brandon didn't take his eyes off the screen. "They're about to announce the grand jury decision in the Ferguson case."

"Huh?" Natassa shook her head, trying to make his words take shape in her brain.

"Michael Brown. Darren Wilson. The shooting in Ferguson. They're about to announce the verdict. Shh."

Michael Brown? The name did sound familiar. Where had she heard it? In the city, right? At the soup kitchen, some of the people had been talking about Michael Brown. What had they said? *Injustice. Unarmed. Police brutality. Killing our sons.* Natassa shook her head again, staring at her husband. Why did he look so concerned? Where was Ferguson again?

"Why do you care, Brandon?"

"Natassa, quiet." His jaw firmed.

"Why do you care, Brandon?" she repeated slower, deliberate.

He sat forward. Then, the court reporter read, "Not guilty." He threw his hands in the air.

"Not guilty? Is that good? Or bad?"

"I don't know. I just don't know."

"Brandon, I don't have any clue what's going on right now. I don't understand why some grand jury decision in Ferguson matters so much to you." Before she could ask, *Where is Ferguson anyway?* Brandon pushed ahead.

"There are rumors of riots. Mass chaos like what happened in August, only worse. In August, they rioted and burned down a gas station. What are they going to do this time? They've already issued a no-fly zone over Ferguson. The governor of Missouri declared a state of emergency in anticipation of protests."

"Okay, so ..." This was happening in Missouri, a different state, which didn't answer the question of why it was a big deal to him.

"Three days ago, authorities arrested two men for buying explosives they planned to detonate during protests."

Natassa stared, waiting.

"So, protests could break out in other cities too. Like Renada. They might call Brett in to help with crowd control."

"You're concerned about your brother?"

"I'm concerned about all the men in blue, Natassa. They put their lives on the line day in and day out, sacrificing everything for their communities only to have the people they protect villainize them and treat them like crap." He tossed a hand toward the TV. "You see what it does to Brett. He's a good guy. A great guy. He joined the force because he loves to help people, wants to keep people safe. And yet some people would throw bottles and bricks at him because of his uniform? It isn't right."

"No," Natassa conceded, sitting down next to Brandon, taking his hand.

She felt the weight of guilt on a man who couldn't protect his little sister so many years ago when a car slammed into her while she rode her bike. What if Brandon and Brett hadn't gotten distracted when their parents told them to take care of Clarissa? How would their lives be different if they didn't have to pay for their childhood mistake far into adulthood?

Now Brandon struggled against a tide rising upon his only remaining kin. He couldn't protect his brother either, and he knew it. She kneaded her fingers into his tense shoulder muscles.

"Can you tell me about the case?"

Brandon explained how on August 9th, Darren Wilson shot Michael Brown. How Officer Wilson claimed Brown had struggled with him, reaching for his gun, attempting to shoot him with it. How Brown had just come from robbing a convenience store.

"It sounds cut and dry to me. What's the controversy?"

"Brown didn't have a weapon. Wilson fired six shots and killed him. Wilson is white. Brown was black. An unarmed black man."

There had to be more to the story, but Natassa sat quietly, continuing to massage her husband's shoulders.

"I had no idea any of this was happening." She pressed her eyes closed for a moment.

"You've been wrapped up in your own space, Natassa. There's a big wide world out there."

"Yeah." She nodded. "I guess there is."

"See." Brandon waved his hand toward the television where reports began rolling in of rioters starting fires and police releasing smoke bombs and pepper spray. "It's beginning."

She stared at the screen, helpless. "I'm going to finish making those muffins and go to bed."

Brandon didn't reply, and he still sat in front of the TV when she sank into bed.

* * *

Brandon stumbled into the kitchen the next morning with deep bags under his eyes.

"You look like you have a hangover." Natassa ran a hand through his disheveled hair.

"I didn't drink. I promise."

"What happened?" She passed him a travel mug of black coffee.

"Rioters destroyed two police cars. They torched other vehicles too. The police used tear gas, but twenty-five buildings and businesses burned to the ground." His shoulders slumped. "Firefighters couldn't respond to the fires because of gunshots. Chaos, Natassa. Complete and utter chaos."

The girls ran into the kitchen, chattering and clamoring for breakfast. She attended to them. Brandon kissed her goodbye and headed for work. As she rolled through her morning routine, the question of why spiraled through her brain. As soon as the older ones left for school and Mercy asked to play a reading game on the computer, Natassa turned on the television in their bedroom and watched the coverage of the protests from the night before.

Fires burned across the city, anger launched from the eyes of the powerless, desperation shouted through the night—it called to her. The scene should have frightened her, and yet it beckoned her. At least now she knew Ferguson was near St. Louis.

Their chants: "No justice. No peace." Their cries: "It isn't fair. It isn't right."

The hurt churned in their eyes, hurt that life had packed down low and hard until they couldn't contain it any longer. Perhaps they had to let the pain out before it consumed them. Maybe it had to burn. So what if they burned their whole world down around them

Deep inside, her heart burned with them. She closed and locked her door, dropped to her knees and wept, stifling her cries in the soft edge of her comforter.

* * *

Bethany called later that afternoon.

"Hi, sugar. I don't know if you heard what happened with them riots in Ferguson."

"Yes, Bethany. I did."

"Well, today, thousands of people are gathering in hundreds of cities all over the country. Peaceful assemblies, hopefully. They're having a rally in the city tonight, and a group of us at St. Anthony's are having a prayer vigil out in front of the church. We're gonna pray for our city. Do you wanna join us, sugar?"

"Yes." She had to. Something beckoned her, and she needed to be there. "What time?"

After she hung up with Bethany, she bit her lower lip. What if Brandon didn't want her to go? How could she broach the subject when he got home? She spent three hours working the problem, framing it in a positive, nonthreatening light.

When Brandon walked in, she asked him about his day, took his coat, and informed him what was for dinner. He seemed relaxed, so she casually mentioned, "I'm going to a prayer meeting tonight at St. Anthony's, if that's okay."

"Why?"

She kept her expression light. "For the city."

"Wait, Natassa. There might be protests in the city tonight. Let me check the news again."

"Oh, don't worry. We won't be at any protests. We'll be at the church."

"Yes, but you have to *drive* to the church."

She shrugged. "I'm sure it will be fine. It's not Ferguson or anything. Bethany wouldn't even think of putting me in danger."

Brandon had already pulled out his phone and was searching. Natassa waited, attempting to seem nonchalant while, in reality, her pulse raced. "There's a rally at city hall.

That's six miles away from the church on the opposite side of the highway. I guess you'll be okay."

"Great. Thanks, babe." She kissed him on the cheek.

"You have to promise me, though, that if something happens, if things get out of hand, you'll get out of there right away and come straight home. I can't stand the thought of you being anywhere near danger like that."

"Of course." The anticipation coursing through her made its way to the edges of her mouth.

Brandon eyed her.

"What?"

"I haven't seen you look happy about something in a long time." The unspoken question of *What changed?* hung in the air between them.

"As you said, there's a big wide world out there. Maybe it's time I start thinking beyond myself."

"Okay." He nodded, still not looking entirely convinced.

"I love you, Brandon." *And I'm so glad you said yes, because if you said no, I would have gone anyway.*

* * *

The prayer meeting proved quiet, reserved, unformidable. As if they were a million miles away from the heated anger she had seen on television. Why did she still hunger for something that mirrored the turmoil of her own heart? They asked God for peace—a peace that she'd grabbed ahold of once. Now, that peace was so foreign she might as well ask Him for a star to hold. What about justice? A lightning bolt and thunder. The tumult of a whirlwind. Where was her righteous storm?

But she'd said the words and prayers they wanted to hear. Polite prayers for peace, all while frustration brewed inside of her. Everyone was saying, "Can't we all get along?" But instead, she required God to make the wrong things right. They would douse the fire, when it should be allowed to burn up everything that was wrong with the world. She breathed a sigh of relief when the meeting ended, and she left for home.

Only instead of turning left to get on the interstate, she drove straight.

She just wanted to see …

She made it three blocks before she came across protesters blocking the road. She let their shouts penetrate. "What do we want? Justice! When do we want it? Now!"

Their demands rang in her ears, pulsing through her brain. She whispered the chant with them, choking back tears.

She read the signs: Black Lives Matter. Hands Up, Don't Shoot. Justice for Mike Brown. Stop Killing Us. Then, her eyes zeroed in on one handwritten sign on white poster board. It simply read: Why?

She stared at it, tears beginning to flow. If she had one question for God, it would be that one. Why the heartache? Why the evil? *Why?*

Natassa's phone sang Brandon's ringtone on the seat beside her. She reached to answer it, then pulled her hand away. He'd hear the commotion in the background. Instead, she sent a text: *Just leaving.*

She managed to maneuver her car into a U-turn and head back toward the highway, leaving the external chaos behind. The turmoil in her heart, however, remained ever present. Perhaps she needed to pull out Mercy's journal when she got home.

12

September 10th, 1842, Georgetown, South Carolina

There's a lot of things my childhood mind didn't grasp onto that are plain to me now being older. On Old Master's plantation, Cypress Hill, Mama and I lived in a cabin on the street close to the Big House. Them cabins were mostly for the craftsmen—the blacksmiths, tinsmiths, tanners, and tailors. Plus, the seamstresses and weavers. Not for the field hands. When I was little, I done thought that's all there was, this row of cabins in view of Old Master and the spiteful missus. But Mama was an exception, being Old Master's favorite. Them cabins were nicer than the others.

Away from Old Master's eye be a whole world that my young eyes never explored, a slave village tucked away in the thicket. Here, the field hands lived and tended their gardens, prayed, and sang, and congregated. It was a whole other world I never did know until I came to Hopecrest with the Millers.

Mama and I live in this world with nearly three hundred other slaves. The cabins are more rustic, and any furniture we want, we best be building ourselves 'cause we don't get the castoffs from the Big House out here like they do on the street. Still, being in the village is far better in my opinion. I feel a part of something. A tribe. Even if I don't rightly fit in.

There's Africans here, real ones, who tell tales of the home country and their journey to America. Ones with long or round tribal markings on their faces. They remember living free until they be tricked or stolen. They remind me of Ekundoyo, the medicine man from the Yoruba tribe that I met in Kentucky. His name means "tears have become joy."

Many here have two sets of names: one name the white people call them and an African name they call themselves. They tell all kinds of stories 'bout magic and incantations. 'Bout spirits changing shape at night and slipping into homes, riding on people's chests, leaving their victims feeling as if they be smothering. They pray at dawn with their heads bowed to the ground to some other god that ain't the one in the Bible.

Mama won't listen to a lick of what they say. She done give me a Bible and told me it be the only thing that's true. Said those Africans are speaking about voodoo and witchcraft, which is an abomination to the Lord Almighty. I sneaked off to listen to them weave their stories a time or two 'til they said Mama done been hoodwinked by the white preacher. They said it like they was spitting out her name, distasteful like, and I couldn't abide them speaking that way about her.

I stopped giving them my ear and started reading that Bible each night. While some people wear conjure bags 'round their neck for protection full of black cat ashes, bones, and graveyard dirt, I reckon I got to trust in the Good Lord and His angels.

Jonah lives on the other end of the village with his mama and brothers and one of their wives. I'm trying to think of an excuse to walk on down that way to catch a glimpse of him. I wonder if my skin be too light for his liking, or whether he might like some cream in his coffee too.

* * *

September 15th, 1842

I think Jonah does favor me some. Either that or he's just a flirt. I never seen him to be talking sweet to the girls, though, so I am hopeful. It's threshing time, and we're using the winnowing barn still 'cause the threshing mill they be building on the plantation ain't ready yet. Mama's threshing seed rice in a winnowing basket. You gots to be all gentle-like with seed rice to make sure it's good to plant. My job is to sweep up the grain that falls onto the platform. Sure beats wading knee-deep in the mud, hacking down the stalks.

Jonah's job was to carry the rice up the high ladder onto the platform of the winnowing barn and pour it down the hole in the floor. When it falls, the wind blows the chaff away and leaves the good grain in a heap where I sweep it up for the pounding mill in town.

So, there I was underneath, and he kept peeking at me through the hole as he poured. Looking straight at me, snagging me with his smile. His eyes would reel me in, and I'd forget where I was and what I was supposed to be doing. He'd wink at me and throw some rice in my hair, his eyes dancing all the while.

I acted annoyed, dusting the rice out of my hair, meeting his eyes with an ornery gaze, but then a smile betrayed me. When he looks at me that way, I'm not a slave for a moment and I's just a woman, meeting eyes with a man. We're gonna finish threshing tomorrow. I can't sleep for looking forward to it.

*　*　*

September 23rd, 1842

Jonah took my hand today, and I was a log that met a flame. I ain't felt nothing like it, that hungry burning in my body, that wanting.

We finished threshing the rice, and he climbed down that ladder and headed straight to me. "Hey, Mercy Girl."

I sucked in my breath. I couldn't rightly say a thing, all the words tumbling around in my mind, not daring to string into anything that would make a lick of sense.

"Isaac's gonna preach tonight in the woods. You coming?"

I was about to say something about how I heard Isaac was a good preacher and I'd been wanting to hear him, but then Jonah took my hand in his and all those words done got mixed up again. I couldn't get my tongue to say a thing, so I nodded.

The callouses on my hand rubbed up against his, and he chuckled, rubbing his thumb across one.

"You're a tough one, Mercy."

I nodded again, pleased that he didn't think me weak-minded or feeble. His strength called to mine, making it want to show itself, prove itself. I wanted to be strong for him. Strong enough for him.

Just then, Lewis ran up to me, snatching the magic away.

"Mercy. Mercy, the missus wants you." Lewis put his hands on his knees, breathing hard. He was only a boy, not much older than I was when they stripped Mama away from me. Dust caked the right side of his face and the knees of his trousers. When he licked his dry lips, his face scrunched up, and I could nearly taste the dirt with him.

"Do you know what for?" Jonah asked before I could.

Lewis shook his head no. "Just asked me to fetch Mercy right quick."

"You'd better go." Jonah cast a glance toward the Big House. "See you tonight?"

"Yes." My mouth tipped in a small smile. "Tonight."

My mind whirled as I followed Lewis to the front porch of the Big House.

"I got her for ya." Lewis puffed out his chest.

"Very well." Missus nodded his dismissal. He dashed off toward the barn.

"Good afternoon, Missus." I curtsied.

"Mercy, you play the violin, don't you?"

"Yes, ma'am." I kept my head lowered and angled away from the glare of the sun. "At least I did. It's been a while."

"Do you think you could still play?"

"Yes, ma'am. I reckon I could if I had a bit of time to practice."

"Good. We're having a party at our house in town to celebrate the harvest after we take the rice to the mill. Nelly used to play for us and now that she's gone, we will need another fiddler."

They sold off Nelly after last year's harvest. Her children still lived in the cabin next to ours with their grandma.

"Yes, ma'am." My eyes lowered farther. Both Nelly and her sons had shed tears when they dragged her away with a half dozen others who had tried to run off. The Millers are good people and refuse to mutilate their slaves for attempting to escape, but they won't abide it neither.

You best be knowing that if you try to make a run for it, they will send the dogs after you. When you're caught, you'll be sold. Just like that, they'll wash their hands of you while the people that love you cry themselves to sleep.

"Very good. You will come to town with us tomorrow. The party is set for Saturday. That will give you nearly a week to prepare."

"Yes, ma'am."

"That will be all. Meet us at the wagon at sunup." Missus turned and disappeared inside before I could say "Yes, ma'am" another time. In town? The Millers had a house in downtown Georgetown, in addition to their summer homes in Charleston and Pawley's Island. I would live downtown for a week or so without Mama and far from Jonah.

My steps were slow finding their way back to the threshing floor. I wanted to be a house slave, didn't I? Fiddling would bring me out of the field. I should be grateful to taste a bit of the life I had before. Yet my hand still tingled from Jonah's touch. I rubbed that same callous with my other hand, imagining that it was Jonah doing so. Calling me tough. Smiling his approval.

"At least I have tonight," I whispered to the wind.

When I returned, Jonah wasn't on the threshing floor any longer. Everyone had gone back to work on their gardens. Now that we had harvested for the master, we could harvest for ourselves.

"I'm going to hear Isaac preach tonight," I told Mama as I entered our cabin.

Mama's face lit up like the sunrise. "Isaac's preaching tonight?"

"Yes, Mama."

"I'm so glad you want to go hear the word of the Lord."

I smiled back at her, not mentioning the fact that Jonah had a far greater pull on me than the Almighty. "I'm going to go pick beans."

I grabbed a basket and left before she could take notice of the lightness in my step.

Mama and I had a small garden, not nearly as big as the family next door. A large family with grown sons meant they had enough to sell their extra crop to others, even to the master.

Mama and I could only manage a small plot, and it only brought in enough for ourselves. Still, the beans, cabbage, squash, gourds, corn, and melons gave us a good variety of food to go with our cornmeal and pork. From the master, we got a peck of corn every Tuesday that we had to grind ourselves on Saturday after we finished our work, and we got four pounds of bacon most weeks. The rest we had to grow ourselves. I heard that Jonah has chickens and a hog, but I never been close enough to his cabin to see for myself.

As I picked beans, I daydreamed of harvesting in Jonah's garden, side by side as husband and wife. My cheeks flushed at the thought, and I tried to push it out of my mind, being sensible. I was lucky enough to have Mama. But his dark eyes haunted me.

I imagined sitting close to him at the preaching that night, and my toes curled, anticipating his leg brushing against mine. I picked the beans faster. If I finished up quickly enough, I would have some time to paint china berries.

When I finished picking the beans, I gathered up a handful of dried china berries and painted them with plant dye, so they were blue, red, and green. Then, I strung them up around my neck. I stuck some honeysuckle into the front of my dress to make me smell nice and sweet while I waited for the sun to set.

On the path through the woods, the hard ground felt solid under my feet. How could I even feel a thing with all the callouses on my feet? But I could. The dirt had caked and dried from lack of rain, cracking, and stirring up a small cloud of dust with each step.

So different from the fields where mud squished in my toes and made a squelching sound each time I moved. Two things true and real on the same plantation. If someone were to ask me to say in one word what the land was like, how would I answer? Nothing is as simple as it seems.

Jonah fell into step beside me. My supper churned in my belly. Winny had made sweet potatoes and stew, sharing with Mama and me. If only I hadn't filled myself with so much stew. I felt heavy inside, but maybe it wasn't the stew at all. Maybe I was just full of wishes that had weight.

He asked how our garden was coming along, and I mentioned that I needed to mend the fence to try and keep out the rabbits. He said he'd stop by and take care of that, which was mighty kind of him. Then, he asked how Mama fared, and I asked who he be living with. His Mama and Papa are alive and well. He has eight brothers and sisters still living, three dying when they were little. Two of his brothers are younger and live with his parents and him. The rest are older and married with a couple cabins that they share. The large web of his family connections woke up a yearning in me.

"Do you really have chickens?" I asked.

He laughed, and a breath of sweetness rushed through me.

"Yes, I've got chickens. They give us some good eggs and a mighty fine meal once in a while. I got a hog too. Mama wants me to sell it, but I'm thinking of butchering it come Christmas. I go fishing too. Bought myself a boat; made myself a pole. That's some good eat'n, them fish from the PeeDee."

"You eat mighty fine, then, huh?" No wonder he was hearty and full of energy.

"How about you? You eat'n enough?"

"Enough." We made do, thanks in large part to Winny's generosity. But I hadn't tasted a lick of fish or chicken since I set foot on Hopecrest.

"I'll bring you something tomorrow evening. You work hard. You should get to eat good." He kicked a pebble, and it skittered along the path.

I smiled, but didn't say anything.

"I'm going to be a trunk minder next season." His chest puffed out a little.

"A trunk minder? Wow, Jonah. That's grand."

"Grand?" He chuckled. "Sometimes I can't figure you out. You sound so white when you say things like that."

Too white? My smile fell. He thought me too white. I looked down at my arm, comparing the lightness of my skin with the darkness of his. How could I dream I could fit into his world? A rush of tears threatened, knocking at my eyelids, asking to flood out.

But then he said, "You're a mystery, Mercy. I like mysteries."

I warmed and blinked, the wetness in my eyes taking flight. "Really, Jonah. I'm proud of you. A trunk minder is something special."

He'd be operating the rice trunks, a coveted position in the fields. A man had to be trusted to be allowed that position. Dependable. Faithful.

"Sure is a long way from where I started out as a bird minder." The edges of his mouth turned upward.

"You was a bird minder as a boy?"

He nodded.

Bird minding was an important job but mostly reserved for young'ns. Each harvest time, itty-bitty rice birds flocked to the fields by the thousands, eager for some of our hard-earned crops. Them rice birds would eat the whole thing if the chillun didn't bang pots and pans to scare them out of the fields.

"I never made it into the fields as a child. Was sold away when I was a girl. Spent years being a house slave, sleeping on the floor of the girl I served."

Jonah whistled low. The sound bounced through the woods, and a dove took flight in the tree above us.

"No wonder you talk white sometimes."

I didn't mention how I'd pretended to be white to find Mama again.

We heard Isaac's strong preaching before we even set foot in the clearing. We silenced at the sound, quiet. Reverent. We had to squeeze our way through a crowd. Logs were laid out to sit upon, but they were all filled to the brim. Men and women stood behind them, huddling close to hear the word of the Lord even though Isaac's voice carried just fine.

We stopped and stood side by side. Isaac talked about the plagues the Lord sent on Egypt to free His people. Jonah kept stealing glances at me, distracting my eyes from the preacher. Then, he walked up to a man sitting on the log and said something to him. The man got up, and Jonah led me over to his spot.

"Sit. You've had a long day."

We'd all had a long day. I'd done nothing special to deserve that spot, but I took it without protest. Jonah stood behind me, and for a few moments, his closeness overwhelmed me. Before long, though, the preaching drew me in, and I focused solely on Isaac's words.

"The Lord was on the side of the slaves. He fought mightily on their behalf." Sounds of agreement filled the space, and a spark lit in me.

"You might be thinking, if the Lord is on our side, why do we labor for the benefit of another man? Why must we toil day after day, cowering to our white masters? Where is this mighty God, and why is He not fighting our battles?" Isaac propped his right foot on a stump and crouched over, resting his arm on his knee, his Bible clutched in his hand.

The small clearing was still as it seemed that we all held our breath, wondering with him and waiting for an answer.

"I'm here to tell you, at the right time, God raised up Moses. At the right time, He smote the Egyptians. At the right time, He led His people out of bondage. Our time is coming! Prepare for freedom."

Hoots and hollers resounded, seeming to shake the trees around us, beckoning them into our cause. I couldn't yell, couldn't even utter a sound as mesmerized as I was. Prepare for freedom? Could it be true? Would the Lord deliver us? Could I have Mama and liberty too? That spark in me grew as I tried to put a name to what was filling up inside me. Hope. Maybe it was hope.

Isaac led us in a song that was more shouting than singing. Arms out, hands up, they formed a circle and moved as one to the rhythm of the drums.

> See day's a-comin' (ha'k 'e angels)—Oh Lord
>   Ha'k 'e angels
> Call my mother (ha'k 'e angels)—Oh Lord
>   Ha'k 'e angels
> Throw off de covah (ha'k 'e angels)—Oh Lord
>   Ha'k 'e angels
> Start that a-risin' (ha'k 'e angels)—Oh Lord
>   Ha'k 'e angels
> Who that a-comin' (ha'k 'e angels)—Oh Lord
>   Ha'k 'e angels
> Look out de windah (ha'k 'e angels)—Oh Lord

The dancers whirled across the grass. The pounding of the drums that matched the beating of my heart. I breathed in the energy of the shouts uniting all around me. Anticipation rose within me that the Good Lord was coming for us.

I pushed my voice into the open and weaved it through the crowd of voices to find Jonah's deep one. Our singing danced together, twirled 'round, leapt high, bowed low. It sounded like our two voices were made to be together. I sent a prayer up that it might be true.

Hope bubbled up and pushed aside my fears of being too white, too old, too much of a burden for the steady man behind me. He put his hand on my shoulder then, settling me. The outline of his fingers brought warmth and comfort, but most of all, his strength grounded me

After a couple more chant songs, we transitioned to spirituals.

> My God is a rock in a weary land
>   Weary land
>   In a weary land
> My God is a rock in a weary land
> Shelter in a time of storm.

We sang late into the night and prayed. The darkness around us sank deeper, but we kept on singing. We sang until my voice quieted, and my eyes fluttered closed for a second as my body tried to drag me into sleep.

"Come on, Mercy Girl. Let's get you home." I took the hand he offered, and he pulled me to my feet. He didn't let go of my hand, his grasp tender as we walked back to my cabin.

"I'm going away tomorrow," I confessed as the reality crept its way to the surface.

"Away? Where?"

A twig snapped beneath my feet. "To town. The Millers are taking me with them. They want me to fiddle for them for a harvest party."

He fell silent for a few moments. What was he thinkin'?

"I'll miss you."

I couldn't help but giggle. "I'll miss you too."

An owl hooted in the distance.

"You won't be gone long?"

"A week, I think."

"A week of missing you." He let out a long breath, and its heat swirled around me. I stumbled over a tree root, and Jonah steadied me, putting an arm around my waist. We stopped for a moment, staring at each other in a beam of moonlight. If only he would come closer, hold me tighter. My lips tingled with want for his.

He brushed my face with his finger, and I closed my eyes.

"I never met anyone like you, Mercy."

I opened my eyes to see if he was any closer to kissing me, but he stood the same distance away, his gaze caressing my face. He was close but too far away. He couldn't be close enough for my liking.

"Come on." He tugged on my hand. "Let's get you home."

He took a step, but I didn't budge. Something crazy and bold stirred in me, and before I knew it, the thoughts in my head came right on out my mouth.

"Aren't you going to kiss me?" My face heated up after the words jumped out, and I lowered my eyes, embarrassed for my brashness.

But then he tilted my chin up and met my lips with his. One sweet, soft, and silky kiss. It squelched the fire in me and fanned it at the same time. His lips left mine with a smile, and my insides swirled like how some of the men looked when they had a bit of whiskey at Christmas.

Without another word, he led me on through the thicket. Another owl hooted, and twigs snapped under our feet, but I was altogether somewhere else, floating on a breeze. When we got to my front door, I stood there as he kissed my hand, then he walked backward toward his cabin, his eyes holding onto mine until he was a spot in the distance. I crept inside and fell into bed, replaying the whole evening over and over again, finally succumbing to sleep deep into the night and dreaming of the kiss that my lips could still feel.

13

When Natassa told Brandon that St. Anthony's was hosting another prayer meeting for the city, he balked.

"Is this going to be an ongoing thing?" He sounded irritated.

Natassa shrugged.

"I don't like it."

They stood facing each other in the kitchen. Not only the kitchen island stood between them, but the empty spaces of the heart as well.

"It was completely boring. Not one disgruntled person in sight, Brandon. A bunch of old people praying. I was the youngest person there. The streets were quiet." Near the church at least. She grabbed two mugs from the cabinet and turned toward the coffeepot. "Want some?"

"The police had to use tear gas to disperse the protesters." Brandon raised an eyebrow.

"I saw that." Natassa had watched the news religiously since the day they announced the verdict. "But not until two in the morning or something, right? I'll leave long before then.

And again, the church isn't in that area." She poured him a cup and slid it across the island.

Brandon let out an exasperated sigh. "You're stubborn." He took the mug in his hands and sipped.

She crossed her arms. "Yeah, well, this city is important to me."

Brandon set his coffee down, came close, and rubbed his hands up and down her arms. The smell of dark roast mixed with his aftershave. "Yeah, well, my wife is important to me."

She took his hands in hers. "Fair enough."

"So, you'll stay at home?" Hope saturated his voice, and she hated to crush it.

"Brandon, please understand."

"Ugh." He broke free of her grip and stomped toward the living room, coffee abandoned.

"I'll stay safe," she shouted after him.

"You'd better."

* * *

That evening, she left the prayer meeting early with the excuse that Brandon didn't like her staying late—which wasn't a lie. *Not a lie at all*. But as she drove over the interstate again, guilt crept up her spine.

She parked on the side of the street this time and debated, praying that God would protect her car. Why would he answer that prayer? She shouldn't be there. But she prayed anyway. An angry prayer. *God, I know You didn't protect me in this city, but do You think You could protect my car?* There. At least that was a bit more honest than the prayers she had prayed at the church minutes earlier.

God could take it, right? Because He sure could dish it.

She walked in the direction of the cacophony. She didn't have to walk far. The scene unfolded before her. Down the street to her left, two buildings stood engulfed in flames. From the tattered awnings and wrought iron patio furniture not yet consumed by the blaze, it looked like a restaurant and a hardware store. Dark smoke billowed above them. Sulfur tinged the air. She coughed.

To her left, a car sat tipped on its side with its windows busted. A crowd rocked a police car on its side to her right. People swarmed the streets, glass crackling under their feet. Some wore masks, some had handkerchiefs around their faces. An armored vehicle cruised down the street. A voice boomed from the intercom, commanding people to disperse or face arrest. Police in riot gear faced the crowd, firearms pointed at the sea of people.

Natassa stared wide-eyed, then stumbled backward. She turned and started to jog back toward her car, pulse racing, palms sweaty. On her way, she passed a few young men breaking into a convenience store. The glass shattered and made her shudder. She picked up her pace, praying fervently that God had answered her irreverent prayer and no one had touched her car.

Relief flooded her when she saw her Audi in the distance. She raced to it, heart pounding in her ears. As she slid inside and locked the door behind her, her eyes welled up with tears. *God, You protected my car, and You protected me. I've been so stupid. I'm hurting, and instead of running into Your arms, I've pushed You away. Forgive me, Lord. Help me. My heart is broken. Will You put it back together again?*

As she careened onto the highway, a small sliver of the peace she had been missing for weeks sparked inside her. God hadn't dropped her, and she was going to be okay.

* * *

Janell had texted, asking Natassa to meet her at Java Joe's at ten in the morning. Natassa picked Breanna up at nine thirty. She didn't want to do this alone.

"So, do you know what this is about?" Breanna plopped her purse down and buckled her seat belt.

"No. I didn't ask any questions."

"Any guesses?"

"No idea." Natassa fought a wave of nausea, and her hands shook on the steering wheel as she drove to the place where she had seen DeAndre's face.

"I need to sit in a different booth," she mumbled to herself as she jammed the car into park, but Breanna caught on.

"Whatever you need, Chicka. Do you want me to sit with you?"

They both got out. Breanna eyed Natassa over the top of the car.

Natassa had been mulling that over. "No. Just nearby." She hit the button on her key fob, and two beeps ensued.

"Near enough to eavesdrop?" Breanna lifted her eyebrows in a hopeful expression.

Natassa squared her shoulders. "Fine by me." *You've got this.*

"You sure? You're going to be okay?" The click of Breanna's heels echoed next to the thud of Natassa's flats.

"Yeah." But no, the memories might swallow her.

"I'm right behind you." Breanna placed a hand on her friend's shoulder as Natassa opened the door to Java Joe's. The bell sounded, and her stomach plummeted. His paintings still lined the walls.

Cruel.

And a new one hung front and center. One where a black man and a white woman stood on opposite sides of a bridge, reaching toward each other. It would have been stunning if not for the man who'd painted it.

She ordered a chamomile tea, and Breanna ordered hot chocolate. Natassa slid into a booth, and Breanna sat in the booth right behind her.

"I brought a book to pretend to read," Breanna whispered.

She chuckled despite her nerves. "You'd make a good spy."

"Only I forgot sunglasses."

Janell took off her apron and headed to Natassa's table. "Here she comes," she whispered, trying not to move her mouth.

"Hey, Natassa. Thanks for agreeing to meet me here. I can only sneak away for a few minutes today since Natalie is sick, but I needed to talk to you." Janell slid into the booth across from her and handed her the hot tea she ordered.

"Thanks." Natassa wrapped her hands around the warm cup. "What's up?"

Awkwardness fell between them like a thick fog.

Janell took a deep breath. "I talked to DeAndre."

"And?"

"He wouldn't tell me anything. About the accomplice, I mean. I tried. I did. I told him he was crazy. He could get a plea bargain for turning the guy in, get a ton of time off his sentence. I don't understand why he's protecting this person." Janell's mouth twisted.

"So, you begged me to come in here to tell me that you don't have any information for me?" Natassa asked, deflated.

"Not exactly."

"Go on," she prodded.

"Well, after I talked to him, I went to his house. Rob's house, I mean. Rob let me shuffle through DeAndre's stuff. I found all these old pictures of this guy."

Janell showed her a picture of DeAndre and another African American male standing together.

"Brothers?"

"No. Best friends. I showed the pictures to Rob, and he knew the man right away. Reg. DeAndre used to talk about him all the time. As soon as he mentioned that, I remembered DeAndre talking about his 'buddy' Reg when he first came to work at Java Joe's. He said the reason he didn't want to move in with Rob and the guys was that he didn't want to leave Reg. Rob told me Reg came over once and acted like a total jerk."

"So what?"

"So, Natassa, Reg said something that night about DeAndre"— Janell looked down, cheeks red— "doing a white woman. I think it could be Reg."

Natassa sat quiet for a moment, processing. "Wait, you remembered him talking about Reg when he first started working at Java Joe's. Did he talk about him when you were dating?"

Janell shook her head. "No. Not a word."

"That's strange." Natassa shook her head. "It doesn't add up. If they aren't friends anymore, why would DeAndre protect him?"

"I have no idea." Janell's voice came out quiet, contemplative.

After a couple of minutes of silence, she shifted in her seat. "I don't know how it matters anyway. We don't have any evidence or anything. Without DeAndre's testimony, it won't do any good."

"I thought it might help for you to know."

"Yeah, maybe." Janell had put a lot of work into sleuthing for her sake. "Thank you."

"Rob called Reg a real piece of work. Just awful. He knew right away that Reg was a bad influence on DeAndre. That's why DeAndre had to get away from him. Don't you see?"

Natassa's eyes narrowed. "Wait? Are you trying to convince me that my rapist is a good guy? That this is someone else's fault? Because if this is all about shifting the blame to someone else, I don't think that's fair." She kept her voice down, but her face twisted in indignation.

Janell's shoulders drooped. "You're right. I'm sorry. It's just … Never mind."

Natassa nodded. "Did you give him my other message."

"Yes."

"And?"

"He understood."

"Good."

"I have to get back to work." Janell wiped away a stray tear.

"Hey." She reached for Janell's hand as she exited the booth. Janell's mouth parted in surprise, but she didn't resist as Natassa held her hand. "Thank you for doing that for me. It means a lot. I'm sorry. This is hard for me. For both of us."

"Yeah. I have no idea how God is going to make something beautiful out of this mess."

"Me either." After Janell went back to the counter, she pulled out her phone to check the time. Mercy's face appeared as her screen saver. The truth blasted through her heart. *He already has.*

14

———————

September 24th, 1842, Georgetown, South Carolina

Mama made ash cakes before sunrise, baking them on the hot fireplace bricks. I loved it when she made ash cakes rather than mush and milk. That morning I scarfed them down, half-consumed with hunger, half not hungry at all, so full I was of hopes and dreams. I met the wagon in front of the Big House as the golden hue of the sun first touched the horizon, bringing pink and orange streaks, stretching out for a new day.

Flora came with me, as she was Missus Miller's chambermaid. Monday and June came too. Bella came, of course, with her being the cook. Eli drove the Millers' wagon. The wagons that followed us were filled to the brim with heaps of grain, ready for the pounding mill in town. The rest of the house slaves stayed to keep everything in order. If only they'd chosen Jonah to help take the grain to town, but they didn't. I didn't see a lick of him 'cept in my mind.

The ride to town bumped and jostled us, but everyone brimmed with celebration for the harvest. I simmered with excitement, though rejoicing in the Millers' gain seemed silly when it meant no real profit for the ones who worked the land. Still, this season was over, and they had a mighty fine crop. A good harvest meant there'd be no need to sell any of us to pay debts. We were safe for another year. Relief settled deep in me as we jostled along the road.

The Millers' house in downtown Georgetown settled over me like a whisper when I first laid eyes upon it. It was green with pale yellow shutters framing the windows, all welcoming-like. The porch wrapped itself around the house like a hug. As if fresh air could twirl around the whole thing, gently blowing your hair, whisking all worries away. The porch ceiling was blue like the sky. Flora said that was because blue kept the evil spirits away.

Master Miller didn't park in the carriage house. He let the missus and us out in front, eager to head to the mill. She led us inside and directed us to the attic where someone had laid out pallets for us to sleep on. We was supposed to put our belongings in there, only I didn't have any, so I peered around. Many years ago I'd slept on the pallet at the foot of Mary's bed. Years without field labor. Years without Mama. Seemed like another lifetime lived by another girl.

The missus didn't waste no time sending Flora and me on an errand. She gave us a list of items to purchase from the market. I held the list, all nervous-like. Missus Miller knew I could read and didn't fault me for it, but what of people in town? Would I get in trouble?

"Hand the list to the grocer, and he'll give you what you need. They don't have to know." Missus Miller gave a reassuring smile.

I nodded and turned to follow Flora out the front door.

"Check and make sure he gives you everything. If not, say, 'I thought Missus Miller said she needed green beans' or the like."

"Yes, ma'am." I turned again.

"Oh, I almost forgot. Here." The missus placed a bag of coins in my hand, and my palm warmed at the weight of it. Just like my freedom jar. The last time I held real money—the time when I passed it into the hands of the steamboat captain, the innkeeper, and the carriage driver—I was free. I had to blink to open my eyes to where I was. *Who* I was.

I gave a little bow and then hurried out to meet Flora who waited for me in front.

"Don't we need a pass?" I whispered.

"No. They know me." She led the way to the open-air market on Front Street.

Each house we passed on the way had blue bottles on the bushes, which looked pretty but mighty peculiar. I asked Flora about it.

"Those bottles are there to capture evil spirits. You put the bottle on a branch, and the evil spirit gets in there and can't escape."

"Where'd the white people get that idea?"

Flora done looked at me like I had two heads. "From us, of course. From their slaves."

"And they believe it?"

"Girl, they believe whatever we tell them. Why do you think they paint their porch ceilings blue?"

I shrugged. Mama would spout it as nonsense. How did I feel about it all? Blue bottles and ceilings. White people following African traditions. All these things got mixed up in my head.

The air smelled sweet and felt warm, though fall crept closer. I closed my eyes and took a breath so deep I could have lifted off the street. The town sounded different from the plantation, from the rumble of carriages and wagons to the voices of people greeting each other and vendors announcing their wares. I'd gotten caught up in the activity of it all when I saw her and stopped dead in the middle of Front Street.

We were crossing the street, headed straight for the market. She turned, and I got a glimpse of her face, framed by her blue bonnet.

"Susan," I whispered. Panic rose all up inside me, and I rushed to hide behind a parked wagon. I put my hand to my chest. My heart thumped like a wild horse. She couldn't see me. She couldn't!

"What in tarnation are you doing over here?" Flora came upon me suddenly.

I jumped and tugged her next to me. I motioned for her to pipe down. How could I explain this?

"I saw someone I knew," I whispered.

"So? Go say hello."

"No." I shook my head. "I saw someone I knew as a white woman … a free woman. When I rode on a steamer headed here."

Not everyone knew my story, but Flora did. She knew how I pretended to be white to flee south and find Mama. She'd heard as much from Mama.

"She was my friend, but …" My throat got all tight and hot. "She didn't know. She doesn't know."

"Oh, I see." Flora nodded and gazed into the distance as if the answer to my dilemma lay out there somewhere. "I'm going to go talk to her. Where is she?"

I grabbed her arm and hauled her to me. "No! You can't. She'll hate me for lying to her. I can't bear it."

"I'll feel her out. Ask her if she knew a—what was your white name?"

"Mary." I bit my lip, but that didn't keep the tears from brimming in my eyes.

"I'll ask her if she knew a Mary who took a steamer."

"And then what?"

"I'll say that I know you. Know Mary. Then, I'll let her know you were a runaway slave and see how she reacts. If she seems angry, I'll slink away, and you can stay hidden. But she might want to see you again."

"I'm not sure …" A storm brewed in my belly, thunder and lightning and bursts of wind. I started to sway, lightheaded, and breathless.

"Goodness, child." Flora grabbed hold of my arm and led me from behind the wagon to a bench beside a building. "You come around and sit here. What's the worst that could happen? I'm going to talk to her. Which one is she?"

"The one in the blue bonnet." My voice came out as a whisp in the wind. The world still wobbled around me.

Flora peeked around the corner. "Okay, I see her. I'll be right back."

I sat there, my heart hammering within me. I forced some slow breaths and wiped away tears. When I met Susan, she talked and talked, eager for a new life—or rather for the rebirth of her old one. She treated me as an equal because she didn't know any better, didn't know the truth. She spoke of the loyalty of her slave, and all the while she was speaking to a disloyal one. My time with her was tainted with worry that someone would find out the truth.

If only I could have jumped full into the friendship. Did she enjoy my company? She had asked for my information, so we could remain friends, yet I had given her the name of a plantation that didn't exist. Our friendship could never work. The difference in our stations would keep us apart.

Time seemed to stretch on. It took all my willpower not to glance around the corner and see what was happening. I twisted the sleeve of my dress in my hand, hoping. Praying.

Finally, Flora popped around the side of the building with a smile blooming.

"She wants to see you."

I squinted and shook my head. Truly?

"She was surprised, for sure. When I asked her if she knew Mary, she nodded, eager to find her again. She asked me if I knew where you were."

"What did she say when you told her?" I trembled.

"She didn't say much. Stepped back a bit like someone had slapped her 'cross the face. Her eyes got all big, but then she nodded like she could see how it could be true. I told her the Millers done bought you, so she didn't think you still a fugitive. Then, she asked to see you."

I shook something fierce, but I took a deep breath and nodded as I stood. "Okay."

I followed Flora through a sea of people—slave and free—to where Susan stood, holding onto the arm of a handsome young man. Her eyes grew wider and wider as I came closer.

"Mary! It is you."

I didn't know whether I could look her in the eye, me being a slave and she a white woman. Yet we were once friends on equal footing. I lowered my head but brought my eyes up to meet hers.

"Actually, my name is Mercy." My lip quivered.

"Mercy. I can't believe it's you. I looked for you. I inquired about the Thymes Plantation and found that it doesn't exist. I thought you were pretending to like me to get a ride. It hurt."

I shook my head. "No, I wanted your friendship. Truly. I just knew it wasn't possible …"

"It all makes sense."

I frowned. Right then, nothing made much sense to me at all.

"I live here now." Susan gestured to the bustling streets.

My mouth fell open.

"This is my husband, Samuel." She nodded to the man beside her.

I curtsied.

"Sam is a banker. He got a job here. We live a couple of streets down."

Shame began to wash over me then as I thought of how far Susan stood above me. Her house was likely nearly as fine as the Millers while I slept in a cabin with a dirt floor. Her husband was a banker. The man I longed to marry was a trunk minder. My gaze sank down, my eyes fixed on her fancy black shoes. Standing right there in front of my dusty bare feet.

"I would like to talk with you, Mary. Mercy, I mean. Flora said you belong to the Millers?"

I nodded, embarrassment worming its way down into me.

"I shall speak to them. See if they wouldn't mind hiring you out for an afternoon."

"Hiring me out?"

"Yes. I'll tell them I need some tasks done and request your assistance in exchange for compensation."

My throat went all thick and clogged with emotion. I nodded.

"Very well, then." She smiled. "We shall likely see each other soon."

She took a step forward, then hesitated. Her arms were wide as if she desired to hug me like she did when we parted last. Oh, to feel friendship's arms around me, holding me up. Instead of drawing closer, I nodded again and then turned to go into the market.

Inside the open-air market, I found a grocer selling produce and went to hand him the list, but then stopped in my tracks. Next to his table, beside the melons and corn, beans and brussels sprouts, a man was selling slaves. A young girl stood on a wooden box, eyes sunken to the ground and shoulders slumped. A handful of white men and women gawked at her, making comments about her as though she had no ears to hear.

"She looks sturdy enough. Doesn't she?"

"I want to see her teeth. Show me her teeth."

The list trembled in my hand.

"Don't pay it any mind. Let's do what we came here to do." Flora took the list from me and handed it to the grocer.

Not pay it any mind? She could have been me from years ago, only no tears trailed down this girl's cheeks. Had she already hardened? My stomach churned. I might retch right there in front of everyone. I forced myself to look away from the girl and to the grocer, who packed Flora's basket full of produce, oblivious to the merchandise the trader offered next to him.

I looked over my shoulder, searching for Susan, hungry to see her again, to experience that brief wisp of time when I was free. But she had gone. Only the child for sale remained. So much like the child I used to be, but I wasn't that girl. I wasn't even a young blossoming woman who had tasted freedom. *Who am I now?*

All those memories swirled around me as I placed the coins into the grocer's hands, the weight of freedom lifting from me. Money exchanged. Another life. Another station. The breath of liberty, the strength of courage. All of it lost now to the swamps of slavery.

15

"Heads up D." Gray swaggered into the cell after breakfast.

DeAndre peered down from the top bunk where he had settled. "I heard some interesting information a few minutes ago. Seems like some of the guys cracked your case. Your sex case." The glint in Gray's eyes threatened him.

DeAndre began to sweat. "I don't know what you're talking about." He tried to play it cool.

"Sure, you don't. You're a rapist, aren't ya? Forcible rape, that's what I heard."

"Shut up, man. You don't know nothing." DeAndre turned to face the wall, his heart hammering in his chest.

"You know how we feel about sex offenders, don't ya?"

DeAndre didn't respond. He focused on keeping his breathing even.

"Boy, you better answer when I talk to you." Gray's thick hand clenched DeAndre's arm, yanking him off the top bunk. He crashed with a thud on the concrete floor. His body screamed in pain. Gray kicked DeAndre's head. His skull slammed against the metal rail of the bottom bunk. His vision swam for a second. The bed seemed to lift off the floor and fall again, and the ceiling tilted. He covered his head, and another kick pummeled his arms.

"What's going on here?" A guard stood at the door.

Gray backed to the wall, his hands lifted innocently. "This moron fell off his bed."

The guard looked between Gray and DeAndre. "I'll be right back. Don't you dare try anything." He looked pointedly at Gray, who raised his palms, declaring innocence.

DeAndre's head reeled, and bile rose in his throat as he attempted to sit up.

Gray stooped down, whispering in DeAndre's ear, "You'd better kill yourself, or I'll do it for you."

DeAndre lunged to retch into the toilet. Gray laughed.

The guard returned and banged on the bars with his stick. "Scott, grab your things. You're coming with me."

His pulse kicked up another notch, but he complied, swaying slightly as he reached up to snatch the sheet and blanket from his bed. Then, he grabbed his hygiene kit and the Bible they had given him. Was he in trouble? Were they about to throw him in the hole? Did he even care? He just needed to get as far away from Gray as he could.

The guard led the way down the hall and to another wing. "I'm putting you in a six-cell. You'll be better off."

He opened a cell with five other inmates. A couple of them stared. One barely glanced up at him before returning to his magazine. Two others didn't even take their eyes off the TV.

"This cell is for check-ins from other tanks." The guard motioned for DeAndre to step inside. "Put your stuff in here, and then follow me to medical." One of the guys who'd stared at him pointed to the bottom bunk in the corner, and he plopped his stuff on there.

DeAndre blinked, disoriented and woozy. Were these guys sex offenders as well? Men could check-in for several different reasons when they couldn't make it in their own cells without problems. But they could very well be sex offenders like him.

He followed the guard to medical, his head clearing a bit on the way. Medical was stifling, windowless, and much dimmer than a medical clinic should be. Almost like a vacuum had sucked all the air out of the room. Several guys waited in hardbacked chairs, but with one look at his head, the nurse brought DeAndre to the examination table. He waited there for a few minutes before the doctor sauntered over, looking annoyed and ready for his lunch break.

"This needs staples." The doctor spoke with about as much emotion and compassion as he would ask for staples to hold a packet of papers together.

With the same emotionless efficiency, the doctor numbed his skin and snapped the staples in his head. After they stapled and bandaged up his bleeding forehead at, they drilled him about what had happened.

"Did your cellie do this to you?"

DeAndre hesitated, but then shook his head no. He wasn't a rat and the last thing he needed was to put someone else in the hole and gain Gray's wrath.

"I fell."

The medic eyed him. "Yeah, right. He's going to the hole, which is where you should be too." DeAndre's pulse kicked up a notch as he followed the corrections officer out of medical. Would they put him in the hole? He hadn't done anything wrong. *Please, God. Have mercy on me. I don't want to go to the hole.* If only he could lie down and ease the pounding in his head.

A flutter of relief enveloped him when the guard led him back to his new cell.

"Jeff." A stocky man stuck out his hand.

He shook it. "DeAndre."

"Rob." The dim light barely reflected off the man's bald head.

DeAndre's breath caught as he stood suspended between two worlds. He almost said, "I have a friend named Rob," but stopped himself. It would have been a stupid thing to say, and it probably didn't hold true anymore. He hadn't heard a thing from his "friend" since he stepped inside the jail.

A man with some girth nodded at him from his position sitting at the front of the cell like a watchman. His eyes narrowed, taking DeAndre in. He nodded back, straight-faced, attempting to size this man up to see what he was dealing with. The man was a mystery.

"That's Chris." Rob pointed. "Let me show you the best thing about this cell."

Was he about to point out the all-too-obvious TV? Instead, he bent down next to the metal toilet bolted to the floor. "Look here. What do you see?"

DeAndre raised one eyebrow. Could he trust this guy?

"Do it." Rob gestured toward the spot.

DeAndre hunched down and followed Rob's finger to a small hole where it seemed a metal screw used to be. He peered closer, then gasped. "Outside."

"Yeah, man. We got a great view. You can see the sky, trees, clouds, and grass. We take turns looking."

DeAndre's throat tightened as he realized he hadn't seen anything green or fresh since he stepped foot in jail. He hadn't even realized what he missed until he got that glimpse. "Oh my God," he whispered. It was a prayer.

His head began to throb again, and he stumbled back a step. "Take a load off, DeAndre. You look like you've been through it." Rob pointed to DeAndre's forehead.

His hand followed the man's gaze. His hand brushed against the bandage, and he nodded before plopping down on his bed.

Jeff sat down on the floor next to the toilet and peered through the hole. DeAndre watched him for a moment, noticing how his face altered when angled toward beauty. Then, he lay down and succumbed to the snag of sleep.

* * *

Reg walked into the visitor's room, stooped with eyes fluttering around as if taking in the parameters of a cage he might get shoved into. When he slid in the chair across from DeAndre, the table between them seemed to be the least of the barriers.

Reg looked shorter, somehow, though it had to be a trick of the imagination. Reg had always had the power in the relationship between them. Power to sway DeAndre to his side, persuade him to go along with some crazy schemes. Or at least look the other way. But who had the power now? Ironically, it was the man behind bars.

"Hey, Reg." DeAndre nodded a greeting. Dispelling the awkwardness in the room would be impossible. He didn't try.

"When I heard you was in here, I couldn't believe it." Reg looked up as if he wanted to make eye contact, but it fell just short.

"I'll bet."

"I didn't find out right away. Our TV is busted. Jake told me."

"That TV was on its last leg years ago."

"Yeah." Reg rubbed his hands on his jeans. Were his palms sweating as bad as DeAndre's own?

They sat in uncomfortable silence for a few minutes before Reg asked, "You turned yourself in?"

"Yes."

"Why, D?"

"Because it was the right thing to do."

"Really? You still think so? After being in there for all that time?"

"Yes," DeAndre lied. Or not. He didn't know. Things sure weren't as clear as the day he had walked into the station.

"It didn't erase the past. Didn't atone for nothing, D."

"She got pregnant, Reg. That night."

Reg finally looked him in the eye. "You have a baby?"

He shook his head. "No, Natassa has a baby."

Reg lifted his eyebrows. "But it's yours?"

"It can never be mine."

"Boy, you crazy. Going to jail doesn't take none of that back."

"Maybe not."

"But you still think it was 'the right thing to do'?" Reg used air quotes.

"Yes." DeAndre gritted his teeth, strengthening his resolve. It was, wasn't it? It had to be. But then why was it so hard? Why was doing what God wanted like journeying to hell?

"You like it in there?"

"No." He dared not say more. If he did, he might crack with emotion that he did not want Reg to witness.

Reg folded his hands between his knees and lowered his voice. "I hear they are trying to get you to tell them about some accomplice. But you ain't talking."

DeAndre nodded but didn't speak. This was probably the whole reason Reg came, though he had held a faint hope that his old best friend might want to check in on him. Might stop by because he cared.

"I hear there would be benefits for you if you told them about an accomplice. But that you still ain't talking."

Once again he nodded, keeping his face void of emotion. Free of the hurt that washed over him.

"I was thinking that the accomplice—whoever he is—probably is grateful that you are sticking up for him like that. I mean, I don't know, but that's what I would figure, that he'd be glad you're not a rat."

DeAndre didn't move, didn't speak. Didn't acknowledge what Reg had said. But Reg's words of gratitude dove down into him and found the place where they had played together as boys, where they had grown together as young men. They entangled themselves in that space.

"I also came to tell you some news. Do you remember Tia? Me and her dated on and off years ago."

"I remember." Did Reg think he could forget Tia? She was shyer than the others, not mouthy. Tia had been in and out of foster care. Her pain attracted Reg's like a magnet. It wasn't explosive, but buzzed beneath the surface, drawing the two of them together. Every time they broke it off, Tia seemed happier.

"Well, she's my girl now." Reg smiled then, for the first time since he'd walked in. A hopeful smile that burst into his eyes and seemed to rattle the table between them. It was a smile that didn't belong in this place. That couldn't cohabitate with bondage. "She moved in six months ago. And guess what, D? We'se having a baby. I'm gonna be a daddy."

DeAndre's eyes narrowed as he tried to make sense of the glowing man before him and the news that spilled forth. His friend had always taken every precaution to avoid getting a girl pregnant, and now he was thrilled?

"I'm gonna do this right, D. Like your pa did. I'm gonna take good care of Tia, good care of the baby. I'm working hard so I can provide for them. I'm done fooling around. I cleaned up my act, D. It's the straight and narrow for me, all the way. You know I loved your pa."

Reg's eyes stared into DeAndre's now, pleading. "I'm gonna honor him the best way I know how. By being the best pa I can be."

DeAndre heard what he didn't say. That he couldn't do that if he was behind bars. That his girlfriend and baby depended on him, that they depended on DeAndre to keep his mouth shut. And that in some twisted way, Pa's legacy depended on that too.

The walls closed in on him, pressing closer and closer, squeezing out the space, the air. But he managed a tight smile. "Congratulations."

Reg let out a deep breath, slumping over in what appeared to be relief. "Thanks. That means a lot to me." He nodded profusely. Obviously, Reg had taken it as a promise not to tell.

DeAndre forced himself to nod, though he coughed as he did so. His throat burned.

"I have to go. Got to get back to Tia. Thanks for letting me visit." Reg turned and left.

DeAndre sat and stared at the door for a minute. That was it? They had been best friends for most of their lives, and that was the extent of their visit? Did Reg even care how DeAndre was doing? Were the details too much to bear, or did Reg not have an ounce of compassion? He hadn't even commented on DeAndre's busted-up head. At least not directly.

He dragged himself out of his chair and met the guard waiting to usher him back to his cell. He shuffled behind the impatient guard who turned and sneered at him.

"I don't have all day."

What's the rush? There's nothing—nothing—worth moving for.

* * *

A few hours later, DeAndre sat on his bunk, pen and paper in hand, mulling over what to write Mama. He hadn't written her, hadn't called, couldn't think of how to break it to her that her only son was in jail for rape. Surely her heart would shatter at the news. All of her hopes and dreams for him would be smashed with the consequences of his crime.

The sound of ladies hollering interrupted his thoughts. He looked up toward the direction of the voices.

"It's the girls in G wing." Rob pointed toward the noise. "You can hear them through the locked door."

"They're always calling for attention." Jeff's mouth tipped in a lopsided smile.

"Let's cadillac." Chris got out an envelope that had a string tied to it. The boys started jotting down stuff on scrap paper, presumably to send to the ladies.

"You want to write?" Rob asked DeAndre while shoving his paper in the envelope.

"Nah." DeAndre waved him off.

"The girls get a kick out of it. Come on, D. A little something to brighten 'em up." Rob nudged a piece of paper in DeAndre's direction, and he sighed as he took it. What could he possibly say to bring light to their darkness? He fiddled with his pencil and then threw it down. He couldn't think of any words to string together to offer hope.

A picture came to his mind of a woman chiseling a window opening out of stone with light breaking through the space and cascading over the other women in the cell. He picked up his pencil and drew it. Immersed in his project, he kept his head down and focused on the details. Nothing else mattered. When he looked up, the cell had gone quiet. The boys stared from him to his work and back again.

"Whoa, man. I've never known anyone who could do that." Jeff's eyes brightened.

"I didn't know I still could." His voice choked up, and he cleared his throat to hide the emotion rising within him.

"Put it in the Cadillac." Chris handed him the envelope.

DeAndre did so, and Chris hollered to the ladies to yank on the string, sending the envelope over to the G wing.

About an hour rolled by before the ladies whooped and hollered for them to tug the Cadillac back. It got wedged under the door, and Chris gave it a good yank to free it. When he finally tugged it into the cell, he opened it and started passing out letters for each of them.

"This one's for you, D." Chris passed him a folded piece of paper.

DeAndre unfolded it and read: *Thank you for giving me hope.* It was signed Rachel with an elementary drawing of a flower under the name. DeAndre's throat tightened, and he squinted to keep the tears at bay. Hope. How had he given someone something he didn't know he had to give? A fragile concept in such a space. And yet, if one could touch even a wisp of it, they could keep on going another day. He swallowed and picked up his pad of paper and pencil again to begin a letter to his mother.

* * *

"Whatdaya got back in the pod?" Luis brushed a dark strand of hair from his eyes. He and DeAndre sat in the chapel a week later waiting for the Thursday night Bible study.

"A Snickers." With Janell's money, he'd bought deodorant, a bar of soap, a warm blanket, and three Snickers bars. He'd eaten two of them.

"I'll trade you ramen for the Snickers." Luis held his worn Bible with both hands.

DeAndre shook his head. "No deal."

"What about two packages?" Luis wagered.

He hesitated. "No."

"Two packages of ramen and a stick of jerky."

DeAndre paused. His stomach had rumbled fiercely after the pitiful dinner of black bean soup that was mostly broth. And it wasn't like that slice of whole wheat bread did a lot to quell his hunger. "Yeah, okay."

Luis's grin widened. "Cool. We'll make the trade as soon as we get back."

He nodded reluctantly.

Luis stuck out his hand. "Nice doing business with you."

He shook it. Thankfully, this business proposition was much more favorable than offers he received of a sexual nature.

The Bible study began, and the fourteen men in attendance sat forward, flipping to Matthew and following along. They were studying the Beatitudes. DeAndre could recite them by heart, as could most of the men.

DeAndre had memorized them long ago, back when everything made sense. Back when he had a hope and a future. A real one he could grab onto with both hands, not the slip of one he glimpsed every once in a while. The one that flew away with a breath. The Bible said he still had a future, but was it written for him now?

After all, was he pure in heart? Meek? Merciful? A peacemaker? Or was he a rapist? A criminal? Dangerous? A threat to society? Did any of the promises of Scripture apply to him anymore? Nothing made sense inside these walls. Perhaps he was destined to become exactly who they said he was.

Mama had written him back. He could see the tear stains on the paper, smearing words, melting one word into the next. He had broken her.

How could you, DeAndre? I raised you better than this. Your pa raised you better.

Her voice rang in his head, cracking under the weight of his sins. Her words crushed the life out of him whenever he replayed them.

The Bible study lasted until nine, but DeAndre left at eight. The men were allowed to move at the top of the hour, and he scrambled into the hallway, too tired to muster up hope for another hour. It wasn't worth it. The darkness consumed everything in its path, and it crept closer and closer.

16

Natassa stumbled bleary-eye into the kitchen on Monday morning, headed straight for the coffeepot. Brandon intercepted her. "What's this? Explain this to me, Natassa." He waved a newspaper toward her face.

She batted it away and rubbed her eyes. "What are you talking about?" She yawned and took another step toward the coffee.

"Look at it, and you'll see what I'm talking about." She couldn't make sense of the rage simmering in his voice. Why was he asking her to explain current events to him? And why was he mad about it?

She blinked, trying to clear the remnants of sleep from her brain and took the paper from his outstretched hand. Confusion flipped to dread as she stared at her face on the front of the local paper. Panic tingled up her spine. The picture showed her in front of masked protestors and an overturned, burning car. She looked like an angry participant, willing to do anything to have her voice heard. That had been the moment it had dawned on her that she shouldn't be there. The moment before she had turned to go home.

Brandon's eyes burned hot and accusatory.

Her mouth opened to try to defend herself, but nothing came out.

"I thought you said the protests were far from the church." He spat his words out like bullets.

She winced. "They were."

"You lied? You said you were going to the prayer meetings, but you were really going to the protests?" Brandon gripped the counter, his knuckles white and jaw clenched.

"No." She sighed. "Not exactly."

"Come on, Natassa. We went through years of counseling. Years! I didn't think you'd ever lie to me like that again."

"I didn't mean to."

Brandon threw his hands in the air. "Oh, that's rich."

"I attended the prayer meetings. Every one of them. Twice on the way home, I drove by the protests. Just to see what was happening. To satisfy my curiosity." She pointed to the paper. "That time, I parked and walked down the street a little way. When I saw what was going on, it scared me, and I left. I told God I was sorry for doing it. I knew you wouldn't approve, and I shouldn't have gone. I won't do it again. I promise."

"You promise. You promise? What good is your word to me? You told me you would stay safe, and then I see my wife on the front page of the paper."

"I'm sorry." She leaned over the counter, tears coursing down her cheeks. She was sorry. She meant it. How could she make him see her genuineness?

"Yeah, well …" Brandon stepped back and drained the rest of his mug, then slammed it on the counter. "Don't forget Brett and Laura are coming over for dinner tonight. We'd better hide the paper and hope they didn't see it for themselves, or tonight's going to be interesting."

He pounded out of the room, leaving her to dry her tears and stash the paper at the bottom of the junk drawer. When the children came flooding into the kitchen moments later, she plastered on a smile and dished out cereal while quizzing Faith on her spelling words for that day's test.

David came up next to her and whispered in her ear. "Why was Dad yelling at you?"

"What?" She played dumb and poured more milk into Hope's already full bowl to have something to do with her hands.

"I heard him shouting, Mom. Why?" His eyebrows knit with concern.

"Don't worry about it." She shrugged as if she could bounce all the heaviness off her shoulders and into the sky.

"Are you two going to be okay?" he prodded her with wide, searching eyes.

"What's my next word, Mama?" Faith asked.

"Grow. Healthy things grow." Natassa said to Faith. Then, she turned her attention to David again. "Yes, honey. We're going to be okay. We're going to come out of this stronger than ever. We're going to …"

"Grow?" he offered.

"Yes. Grow."

"No, you already said that one." Faith tapped her pencil. "What's the next word?"

Natassa and David chuckled. Her children were amazing. Once again, a small spark of hope built inside her. Perhaps reading Mercy's journal every night before bed was giving her a different perspective.

* * *

Natassa walked through the house, picking up stray toys and tossing them in a bin. She never looked forward to time spent with Brett and Laura. Ugh. Her attitude was horrible. It wasn't that she disliked them. They were both very kind people. They adored the children, played with them, lavished them with gifts every Christmas.

She rolled out the vacuum and flipped the switch, filling the living room with a hum. Laura made polite conversation and never demeaned anyone. A step-up from Natassa's own family for sure. She couldn't put her finger on why things between them were a bit awkward, as if they were all sitting uncomfortably on the edge of a dining room chair instead of relaxing on a sofa.

A bubble of uncertainty sat between them, a fear that perhaps she had said the wrong thing somehow. Laura never complained. It showed more in a flicker of hurt in her eyes that she would mask in a moment. How could she fix it if she didn't know what she was doing wrong? And if she couldn't fix it, there didn't seem to be much hope of moving forward in their relationship.

And Brett … Brandon and Brett were so close they almost had a "brother" language that no one else could understand. They didn't even have to finish sentences. It was endearing in one way and annoying in another. She was left on the outside in her own home. Laura probably felt the same way. And tonight, the topic of conversation would more than likely revolve around the protests. Hopefully, Brett hadn't seen that paper.

Was spaghetti with meatballs an okay dinner to serve? Maybe Laura didn't like her because she wasn't as good of a cook. Maybe she needed to make fancier meals like her mother did. She could look up some recipes. How much time did she have?

"Mommy, come read to me." Mercy tugged at the hem of her shirt, eyes hungry for attention. Natassa knelt and smiled at her.

"Mercy, baby, do you want spaghetti for dinner?"

"Mmm. Psghetti!"

"Okay. Psghetti it is. Let's go cuddle on the couch and read."

* * *

Brett and Laura walked through the door, grinning like teenagers who'd just fallen in love. *Something is up.* Laura couldn't stop smiling and giggled to herself more than once. They both oozed with enthusiasm over … well, everything.

"Your house smells amazing, Natassa. What's your secret?" Laura asked.

"Oh, it must be the essential oils you're smelling."

"Really? Tell me more."

As it turned out, both Laura and Brett praised the spaghetti dinner. They raved about the flavor, and Natassa had only opened a jar. It wasn't until after dinner that she found out why their guests were bursting with enthusiasm. Once the children were excused to play, Brett said they needed to make an announcement.

"We've got something to share with you." Both Brandon and Natassa sat forward attentively as Brett and Laura grinned at each other. "We thought it was about time to make you an aunt and uncle."

Laughter bubbled up around the table. "You're pregnant?" She beamed at Laura.

Laura nodded enthusiastically.

Natassa jumped up and rushed around the table to wrap her sister-in-law in a hug. "Congratulations!"

"Thanks. It only took us twelve years." Her laughter mixed with tears, and soon Natassa was crying too. The two women sat beside each other for the next hour as Laura spilled her heart about her journey with infertility and how much it hurt each month to not get pregnant. She confessed how every trip to Natassa's house stabbed her with pain.

"I love you guys, and I love your children, please don't get me wrong. It's just that having children came so easy for you. Every time I came here, I'd have to face the 'Why God?' question. It pierced me no matter how much I would try to ignore it."

"It's okay." She took Laura's hand. "I understand."

"No." Laura shook her head. "No, I don't think you do. I don't think you can unless you've been through it. But that's okay. We all have our own paths to walk down. None of them are without pain."

"That's the truth." Natassa got up, grabbed a box of tissues, and brought it over to where they were sitting. "I didn't think you liked me."

Laura blinked. "Didn't like you? Who wouldn't like you?"

That made her laugh. "Do you want a list?" Mainly her mother and sisters, but right now, she could add her husband to it. Perhaps that wasn't fair, but that was how it seemed.

"You are supermom, Natassa. I want to learn everything from you."

"I can teach you how to make spaghetti," she joked. The women giggled together.

Laura had already quit her job as a receptionist for a grocery supplier. "We always knew when we had a baby I would stay home, so it's good to learn to live on one income now. And my job currently is to rest and grow this baby. When it takes this long to get pregnant, you don't take chances."

Natassa scoured the house for her old books on pregnancy and parenting and handed them to Laura. "I found these helpful."

They meandered into the living room where Brandon and Brett talked on the couch with the news flashing on the television in the background.

"Are things getting better or worse, you think?" Brandon asked.

Brett shook his head. "These people are completely out of control. They're using this as an excuse to riot and loot. Half of them don't even know why they're doing it. They only want a new TV."

"Not everyone is causing trouble." Natassa took a step toward them.

"Huh?" Brett turned toward her.

"I mean, isn't that right? That a handful of looters are giving the peaceful protestors a bad reputation?" Natassa offered a half smile.

"What news source is indoctrinating you, Natassa?" Brett's eyes darkened.

"She's gone to a few prayer meetings in the city. At St. Anthony's Church."

"What?" Brett flinched, looking like he'd been slapped. "You've been participating in this crap?"

"No." She threw her hands out in defense. "It's not like I'm chanting and holding a sign. St. Anthony's is on the other side of the highway. We met and prayed for the peace of our city. And even for the protection of the police officers. That's all."

"You can pray at home." Brett's voice sounded stiff.

She shifted her weight. "Yes, but it's nice to pray with others too."

"Do those *others* have a negative view of the police in their community?" His eyes pierced her.

Her gaze darted to the floor. "I don't know. Maybe some of them."

"Do they think Darren Wilson callously murdered Michael Brown?"

"They might." She shifted her weight from one foot to the other, stepping back slightly.

"If you hang around those people, you'll start thinking like them, Natassa. Whose side are you on?"

"Do I have to take sides? Can't I love my black friends in the city and also love police officers? Do I have to pit one against another?"

"Was Darren Wilson innocent or guilty?" Brett's eyes narrowed.

"I don't know. I honestly don't know." She flung her hands in the air. "I'm not smart enough to figure all this out. All I know is a bunch of people are hurting. And hurt people hurt people. And then those hurt people hurt people. And the cycle goes on and on forever until someone is brave enough to stop it." Her voice sounded bold in her ears. A rush of adrenaline shot through her. Was what she said true? And if it was, what was she going to do about it?

Brett pressed his lips into a tight line. "You're right. You're not smart enough to figure all this out. The grand jury declared him not guilty, so let's go with that. Always back the men in blue, Natassa. You never know when you're going to need them to back you."

She also pressed her lips together and then turned and strode into the kitchen. She busied herself with doing the dishes, wiping warm tears from her cheeks with soapy fingers.

"Don't mind him." Laura stood beside her, drying the pans she'd put in the dish drain. "He feels like everyone is judging him right now. Like people look at his uniform and automatically assume that he's a racist barbarian who would murder someone because of the color of their skin. He's afraid for his life. I'm afraid for him. I kiss him goodbye every day and pray that I will get to kiss him hello that evening. Imagine laying your life on the line to protect people, then having those same people spit in your face or throw beer bottles at your head."

"Hurt people hurt people," Natassa whispered after handing Laura a pot.

"Yes." She let out a slow exhale as she wiped away the remnants of water.

* * *

"I know it's not a smart idea," Natassa explained to Janell while holding her cell phone in one hand and turning the steering wheel with the other. "I mean, no lawyer would say this is a great plan. But I thought, I'll say it and see the look on his face, and then at least I'll know."

"Wow. Well, that explains why he wouldn't see me this week."

"Huh?" Natassa squinted against a beam of sun.

"He can only have one visit a week. He saw Reg last week, and now he's seeing you this week. That's why he turned me down." Janell's voice dipped.

"Oh. Sorry, I had no idea."

"No, it's fine. I'm glad to understand why. Good luck. Let me know how it goes."

"Will do." She hung up.

"Well?" Breanna asked from the passenger's seat.

"That wasn't as awkward as I imagined it would be." Surprising. She flipped down the visor.

"Hmm. Interesting." Breanna took a swig of her soda. "So, you're sure you just want me to wait in the waiting room? I can go in with you."

"I want to go in myself. He might not talk as much if you're there."

"Whatever you want, Chicka. I feel like I'm not much help to you in these situations."

Natassa glanced at her friend. "Just knowing that you are on the premises helps."

Breanna bowed her head with a smirk. "At your service."

She found the county jail without much trouble and soon stood in a short line of people waiting to visit with prisoners. Breanna settled in an orange plastic chair in the waiting room. The lady in front of her turned, and the smell of fried chicken wafted.

"Is your boy thrilled for his food visit?"

"Huh?" Natassa asked.

"His food visit. Didn't you know? The boys get two visits a year where we can bring them outside food. They can eat whatever they want, as much as they want. Oh, my boy lives for his food visits. They look forward to them like children look forward to Christmas. The food they get in there isn't worth nothing. Those boys are always hungry. I brought my Sam fried chicken and biscuits, corn on the cob, and slaw. Oh, and brownies. He's going to be wild about my brownies."

"Oh, I didn't know. Is this the only day?"

"Afraid so. They won't have another food visit day for six months."

The woman turned around and left Natassa alone. *Janell should have come today. She would have brought him food.*

Natassa rocked on the balls of her feet. DeAndre was a rapist. He had brutally attacked her. He deserved this hellhole and to eat crappy food. He deserved to go hungry.

Love your enemies.

She ignored the small voice in her head and shifted her weight from one foot to another. If only this line would hurry so she could get this visit over with.

Love your enemies.

Seriously? She moaned. She had just gotten here. Gotten out of her car. Gotten in line. What did God expect her to do? And he didn't deserve good food. Especially not from her.

The weight of conviction bore down upon her as the words of his note reverberated in her mind: *I'm sorry.* And her note back to him: *I forgive you. God will forgive you too.*

Fine! She exited the line and stomped over to Breanna. "I've got to get something."

"Huh?" Breanna stashed her novel in her bag.

"Come with me."

The two women scuttled out to the car, Natassa with her hands jammed in her pockets and Breanna a step behind.

"What's up?" Breanna asked.

"I need to go to the nearest fast-food restaurant and get something to bring DeAndre."

"What? Why?"

"It's food visit day."

"So?"

"So, I'm supposed to do this. I know it doesn't make sense, so don't ask me to make sense of it."

Breanna sat silently in the passenger's seat while Natassa ordered a large value meal and a shake. *The woman waiting in front of you in line brought a feast for her son.* Natassa ordered cookies too.

"So," Breanna ventured, "you're wining and dining him so that he'll talk?"

"What?" Natassa sat back in the driver's seat. "No."

"No?"

"Oh my gosh. Is that what it looks like?" She smacked her palm to her forehead.

"Well …"

Natassa careened back into the parking lot of the jail and rested her head on the steering wheel.

"It's not like that at all. I felt like God told me to love my enemies. And love is a verb, right?"

"You're bringing DeAndre a meal out of love?" Breanna sounded unconvinced.

"Not any love I feel, I assure you." *Oh God, I can't do this in my own strength. I need You to love through me.*

"Okay. If you say so."

Natassa stepped back in line, proud of herself. At least she could tell Janell and get on her good side.

Don't say a word.

Ugh! Why couldn't she at least get credit for following God's prompting?

Her anger dissipated as they led her back to see DeAndre. Her heart beat like it would break out of her chest, and the walls loomed over her like armed guards. She'd march up to him and demand answers. She deserved them. But with each step, her feet slowed, and her shoulders hunched. Fear twisted her stomach into painful cramps.

"Food visits are held in here instead of the usual." The officer rummaged through the bag. She sat down at the long plastic table, waiting. There were four chairs on one side, four chairs on the other. No glass. No barriers. She focused on breathing. Maybe this was a mistake.

Then he came in. Sat across from her. The guard stood at the door. All thoughts left her head.

"You brought food?" His eyebrows raised.

"Yes." She pushed the bag and shake toward him.

He stared at her. "You brought food for me?"

She nodded.

He covered his eyes with his hand. His shoulders began to shake.

He was *crying?*

What could she say? She kept her mouth shut, but tears found their paths down her cheeks as she watched this grown man break down under the power of a value meal.

"I-I can't … I don't think I can accept this from you," he sputtered.

"DeAndre, please. I brought this for you. If you don't eat it, it will go to waste. I want you to eat it."

He shook his head, his face wet and bruised.

"It will hurt my feelings if you don't."

He nodded and tentatively took a bite of a fry. Then, it was as if the taste awakened his hunger. He inhaled the rest of his meal. Natassa watched him enjoy the food.

"I thought you came here to yell at me." DeAndre finished off his last fry.

"You invited me for a visit so that I could yell at you?"

His chin trembled. "I deserve it."

"I came because …" She strengthened her resolve. She hated to ruin the moment, but she had to do this. She came to do this. "It was Reg, wasn't it? The accomplice."

She studied his face.

A flicker of surprise.

"Reg? How do you know about Reg?"

"Janell told me."

He cocked his head "How does Janell know about Reg?"

"She found a picture of the two of you. Asked Rob. Something like that."

DeAndre nodded and sat back in his chair. "Reg was my best friend growing up. His mom was a prostitute, and he never knew his daddy, so my pa took him under his wing. We were tight—Reg and me. Close as brothers. Closer. He was there the night my pa died." DeAndre lifted his gaze to the ceiling.

"He held me while I wailed. We went through some stuff together, that's for sure." He angled his chin toward her, making eye contact. "He visited me last week. He and his girl are having a baby. He works at my pa's old shop. He's a good mechanic. Has a solid job. Worked there for years. He's gonna take care of them good. So, you see," DeAndre sat forward, propping his elbows on his knees, "that's what I know about Reg."

Natassa nodded. No need to press any further. DeAndre had likely told all he was willing to tell. A hostile interrogation would only negate the kindness done. Plus, she was pretty sure she had her answer.

"Okay, then."

"Thank you, Natassa. I mean it. I don't know if I could ever thank you enough."

"You're welcome." She got up, mind reeling and heart throbbing. She walked out on wobbly legs.

17

———

September 29th, 1842, Georgetown, South Carolina

Once the missus put a fiddle in my hand, all that learnin' came back to me in a rush. My fingers remembered what seemed foggy to my mind. They started dancin' on that fiddle, and I found myself smiling big, the light of creating something bright and beautiful dawnin' on me again.

I spent hours practicin' for Saturday's party, content and plum happy. Missus Miller stopped in the study where I played away and told me I was making great progress. I wasn't thinking much about getting better, though.

Playin' transported me into distant memories of a different world. In that that former time and space, I was younger and didn't have an inkling that Mama's health was failing or how to cultivate rice at all. But oh my! Playing made me miss Emma something fierce.

Days passed by, and I didn't hear a lick from Susan. What if she had changed her mind? Maybe she'd done some thinking and decided it'd be best to leave me be. Maybe the wrong I did to her swelled up so big she couldn't get around it. Or perhaps she couldn't push past the difference between us—a difference new to her but forever known by me. It was just as well. If I never saw her again, I wouldn't have to decipher how to act around her, how to teeter the line between slave and friend.

The missus told me we'd be going to church Sunday and had me try on an old silk frock of hers. It fit like a dream, except I'd sprouted up since coming to the Millers, so it came up a mite short. I stood taller than the missus now by at least a head, which brought Emma up again, and a sad longing settled in me.

Silk. I had never felt something so soft and fine caressing my skin. The fabric wrapped me up in butter and as pretty as a princess. The missus smiled her approval, but then she got a look at my feet.

"Oh my. You don't have any shoes, do you?"

"No, ma'am."

"Well, we'll see if we can remedy that." She disappeared up the stairs, leaving me alone to twirl and pose in the dress. It didn't have a hoop with it, which was fine by me as I didn't know how to walk and sit in one of them hoopskirts anyways.

The children in the slave village liked to play at making hoopskirts out of branches in the thicket. I'd watch them fumble about, and I'd thank the Good Lord that I didn't have to manage one of them hoops. The silk frock suited me fine without a hoop undergarment.

When I heard the missus's feet trek down the steps, I stopped my primping and posing and lowered my head in anticipation of her arrival.

"Here. See if these will work." She handed me a pair of heeled shoes in a magnificent shade of gold.

Looking at them, they would be too small for my feet, but I was too in awe of them to say as much. They looked like something a queen would wear, so delicate and fancy. I prayed to God that I could fit my feet inside of them. I sat down and pushed and prodded, managing to squeeze enough to get them on. The missus stood and watched me struggle but didn't say a word about it. I tried to stand up in them but stumbled back down.

"It'll likely take you some time to get used to them, but they'll suffice, will they not?"

She seemed confident I'd get the hang of walking in them, so I nodded. Surely, strutting in heels couldn't be that hard. White women did it. Why couldn't I?

"Very good, then. Carry on practicing the violin until Flora requests your assistance in setting the table."

"Yes, ma'am." I tried again to stand. I kept myself upright that time, though I tottered back and forth like a tree about to timber. I took a careful step and then another, thinking through my every move. I would need plenty of practice to not walk all stiff like. I could practice at night in the attic.

When Flora came in, she said nothing about setting the table for mealtime. She'd come to fetch me for the missus.

"The missus wants to see you." A sly smile spread on Flora's face. "Something about someone wanting to hire you out."

"Oh!" I attempted to rush to the great room and see if it was true, if Susan had called for me after all. But I could not rush in those golden heels.

Flora laughed as I wobbled. "Those shoes look three sizes too small for your big ole feet, Mercy."

"Oh, shush now. They fit fine." I stood straighter as if to prove I told the truth.

"Uh-huh." Flora chuckled, eyeing me up and down.

I managed to waddle into the great room to greet the missus without tumbling to the floor.

"Mercy." She looked me over much like Flora had done. "I received word that a Susan Renald has requested your assistance. Do you have any objections to working for her for the afternoon?"

I tried to hide my surprise in the missus asking my permission for anything. "No, ma'am."

"Very well. She requested for you to arrive at noon on Monday."

"Monday?"

"Yes. Do you object?"

"No, ma'am. It's just ... I thought I'd be back on the plantation on Monday is all."

"Oh, I see. My husband has some business in town that he will be attending to, likely until the end of next week. We shall return after he's finished."

"Yes, ma'am." I attempted a graceful exit. But I did a wretched job of that, seeing as keeping my balance seemed even harder when my mind swirled like a storm. Another week? Another week without Mama. Another week without Jonah. I could see Susan, but only at the expense of the others I longed to be close to.

* * *

October 2nd, 1842

Flora and I spent all Saturday morning gathering pine and cedar limbs to decorate the house for the party. We put them over the pictures and around the mantle boards until the house looked all fancied up. The smell of roast duck and hen filled the place until my mouth began to water. I was getting more used to walking in them shoes, though I still couldn't rush my steps. The missus told me to change out of the silk frock so it'd stay clean for church, but I kept the shoes on so I could get used to them.

When guests started to arrive, I helped Flora tote water from the kitchen to the dining room and serve mint juleps to all who favored them, while Monday and June helped Bella in the kitchen. Excitement shot around the house like a bolt of lightning, with everyone all dolled-up and bright-eyed.

I kept an eye out for Susan, but she never came. I served at the table with Flora. After we delivered the final course and the guests finished stuffing themselves, I ambled to the great room and snatched the fiddle.

I played as the guests filed in. The men wrote down their names on cards and handed the cards to June. She would go to the gal in question, drop a curtsy, and hand her the name of the man who fancied a dance. If she agreed to dance with him, she would look at him and flick her fan. If not, she ignored him entirely.

Fans flicked all over the room as I played lively reels and women twirled. I didn't have no jar to collect coins in, and I missed hearing that clink. Missus hadn't said a thing about me getting any earnings from my playing, and probably the privilege of fiddling instead of working in the fields was payment enough in her mind.

I didn't have a freedom jar anyway.

My hands were tougher than they had been years ago, calloused and hard from work in the fields. They didn't look as pretty plucking the strings, but they worked just as good. Better, even, since they were used to moving and not allowing tiredness to get the best of them.

I played late into the night, my tunes accompanied by the swirling colors of dresses and the sound of glasses clinking. When the guests began to leave, my heart grew hollow. Fiddle playing wouldn't likely be a regular happening. This night was all I had, and it had faded away too quickly.

When the last guest left, the missus charged us with cleaning up and then headed upstairs. Flora and I collected glasses, and Monday and June swept and mopped the floors. Bella spruced up the kitchen.

Master and Missus didn't believe in any working on the Sabbath, 'cept, of course, what they needed for their comfort. We had to get the house in shape before sunrise, which we managed to do with about an hour to spare. I collapsed on my pallet, sinking quickly into sleep, for the bell would startle me awake before I was ready to give up my dreaming.

Sure enough, the clang of the bell roused us before we even had time to snatch a dream. I stumbled down the steps, groggy and with my head in a fog, and readied the table for breakfast. The missus had some last-minute instructions for church.

"When we arrive, head straight up to the gallery. Remember your manners, to restrain yourself, and be dignified. You are not to make any audible expressions of your feelings. There will be no crying, groaning, or noises of any kind. Your conduct reflects on Mr. Miller and me. Is that understood?"

"Yes, ma'am." What did she think I might do to disgrace them? Hoot and holler? I barely did that at the prayer meetings in the woods and certainly wouldn't do so in a white church.

When we had dressed and gotten ready, we followed the Millers to the Episcopal church on the corner. My breath caught at the sight of the beautiful stained glass depicting the Christ with light shining out from around His head, His arms stretched out all welcoming-like. The church stood tall and proud with a cross erected on top of its bell tower. Yet a graveyard surrounded it.

There was a few minutes before church would start and people congregated outside. White people stood together, fans in hand, standing among the graves of the important white people of the town. Colored people, slave and free, stood together among the graves of their people. Though my heritage was as much white as black, only one part of me determined which group I belonged to. If I died today, I'd be buried in the colored graveyard that lay right next to the white graveyard. Even in death, they'd keep us in our place. Yet even in death, we couldn't truly be free from our masters.

Flora engaged in conversation with a few other women. Instead of joining them, I walked about the graveyard reading the names, dates, and descriptions of the people who lay beneath my feet. The colored headstones were far less elaborate than the ones in the white graveyard, but at least they had headstones. These must have been mighty important colored folk to get their names chiseled in stone for all to see.

Only one of them had the year that they were born on the stone. How did they know when they were born? Was it because they were the master's child? So was I, and I still hadn't a clue when I came into the world.

I found a marker with the name Mary etched into it. I traced it with my fingers, this name I'd stolen for a bit. It was Emma's true name before some little girl, who couldn't even do her own hair, snatched it away from her. Had Emma made it to freedom? Had she found her husband?

I walked the line between the colored graveyard and the white one. That was right where I belonged, on the line between black and white.

A group of men huddled together having a spirited discussion I couldn't help but overhear.

"How could black slaves be in the promised land of America except through the providence of God? Tell me, Richard, don't you agree that this is part of the divine plan for their salvation?"

"Then it's our duty to Christianize them, isn't it? God brought them here for that very purpose. To strip from them their heathen ways and enlighten them to the truth of the gospel."

"Precisely. It is our Christian duty. And the more slaves we own, the more slaves we can Christianize."

"It is the Great Commission, then, isn't it?"

I walked away, back into the colored graveyard, a sick feeling rising in the pit of my stomach. Even now, their words haunt me. It's just men figuring things up in a way that makes them feel better about themselves. But they don't give a care for how that makes the rest of us feel. The ones on the other side of the line.

People began to make their way to the entrance. I found Flora and followed her through the tall wooden doors and straight up the steps to the gallery where we sat peering down at all of the white men and women enclosed inside box pews. Gazing at the blue ceiling, it seemed I sat close enough to heaven to nearly touch it. Below me, the greenery released a fresh scent and contained a subtle beauty.

Before long, the bell tolled, and the organ played. We stood and sang "There is a Fountain Filled with Blood" and "There Is a God Who Reigns Above," our voices matching those of the sea of white parishioners below us.

Then, we recited the Lord's Prayer, the Apostles' Creed, and the Ten Commandments before beginning the catechism, which took me a minute to figure out. I finally found the page so I could rightly follow along.

Q: Is God present in every place?

A: Yes.

Q: What does He see and know?

A: All things.

Q: Who is in duty, bound to have justice done to servants when they are wronged or abused or ill-treated by anyone?

A: The master.

Q: Is it right for the master to punish his servants cruelly?

A: No.

Q: What command has God given to servants concerning obedience to their masters?

A: Servants obey in all things your masters according to the flesh, not in eye-service as men-pleasers, but in singleness of heart, fearing God.

Q: What are servants to count their masters worthy of?

A: All honor.

Q: How are they to do their service of their master?

A: With goodwill, doing service unto the Lord and not unto men.

Q: How are they to try to please their masters?

A: Please them well in all things, not answering again.

Q: Is it right in a servant when commanded to be sullen and slow and answer his master again?

A: No.

I read the words. I mouthed them. But I couldn't make a sound come out of my mouth. I heard the voices rising around me in sullen resignation, but I couldn't join their chorus. They quoted Scripture, and though I'd never "answer again" to the Millers when they done given me a task to do, my voice bucked at this harness of a catechism they were trying to put it in.

There were masters down below who came to church every week spouting this catechism. On Sunday mornings, they admitted they weren't supposed to up and beat their slaves, and then when they got home, they wielded the lash in the most brutal of ways. It seemed bizarre and false to me, and I waited for it to end, for the cadence of voices to fade.

When we finally sat down, they did their Bible readings, and we said, "Thanks be to God" after each of them. After another hymn and reading, the priest finally began to deliver the sermon.

I sat forward, eager to hear of Moses and the Red Sea again, of the Israelite slaves breaking free for the promised land.

"Ephesians 6:5 tells us 'Slaves be obedient to them that are your masters according to the flesh, with fear and trembling, in singleness of your heart, as unto Christ.' Now we turn our attention to Onesimus, the slave of Philemon. Paul calls Philemon 'Dearly beloved' and a fellow laborer, one known for his love and faith.

"Philemon had a slave, Onesimus. And how was Philemon repaid for his great love and charity to mankind?

Was Onesimus grateful for his paternal care? Did Onesimus follow the command of Scripture to be obedient to his master with fear and trembling? No, he did not. Instead, he ran away.

"Yes, he committed a grievous sin in the sight of the Lord Jesus. But Almighty God in His sovereignty had him run straight to the apostle Paul. The apostle Paul, knowing Onesimus was the property of Philemon and that running away was thievery of the most grievous kind, sent him back to his master."

I sat back in the pew, confused and disoriented. While a chorus of "Amen" echoed below the gallery, I opened the Bible provided on the pew. The edges and the spine were frayed, the papers loose and threatening to spill out onto the floor.

I had read Philemon before and remembered it quite differently than what was being preached. I opened to the chapter and read it silently, with no fear of anyone seeing that would give a lick of care since I sat among my own.

I read how Paul called Onesimus his son, asking Philemon to accept him as a brother. *A brother.* Oh, to be brethren in the Lord, white and colored, slave and free. *Brethren.*

The priest in his white robe and highfalutin ways drabbled on about thievery, citing the Ten Commandments and declaring wrath on those slaves who would dare defy their masters in this way. I pressed my lips together, anger rising inside me. What about the thievery of stealing one's freedom? Was that not a grievous sin? What about the verses proving we were all made in the image of God? The priest seemed to be reading out of a different Bible than me. Loathing stirred in my soul. I swallowed past a thick throat. The Bible said that anger in the heart was akin to murder.

"We can look, too, at Eliezer," the preacher continued. "Abraham's servant is the supreme example of a model slave. Look how he took care of his master's property. Did he steal? Certainly not. Eliezer was supremely faithful, a diligent and attentive worker. For this, he had the honor of being chief among Abraham's slaves as well as storing up great reward in heaven.

"In contrast, Elisha's servant Gehazi was unfaithful, a thief, and a liar. His master could not trust him. For these sins, God cursed him with leprosy, and he became an outcast. Let us always remember that our actions—good and bad—have rewards or consequences. May we honor the Lord with our service. Let us pray."

Oh, I could pray right then. Like James and John, I had the hankering to call down fire from heaven and fry up that preacher on the spot. When he said all our actions had consequences, he looked up to the gallery, as if them white folks got a pass for all their bad actions against us.

We were the ones who God would strike with leprosy if we stepped out of line, but they could beat and bully us to no end and be fine 'cause they were doing their Christian duty? While the Millers had been good to me, I couldn't stand for the likes of that white preacher and all he stood for.

All of a sudden, my feet began to ache. If only I could strip off the golden heels and hurl them down into the crowd of pompous people. But then a beating would follow, lynching even, at such a public display of disrespect. I settled back into the pew and prayed to God to cool the heat burning inside me.

We responded to his prayers and sang another hymn as they passed the offering plate. The whites stood and came forward for communion. We watched as they knelt, as the priest placed the bread in their mouths and passed them the cup of wine.

The blood of Jesus covered their sin as much as mine. A sobering reminder. My blood ceased its boil, and I fell into a kind of numbness. I had never gotten the chance to partake in communion, neither as a free woman nor as a slave.

The whites filed back into their pews.

The priest said, "Now, any slave who has been good and obedient is welcome to come down and partake of communion."

We filed down the stairs and to the front, eating the same bread and drinking from the same cup as the white people had moments before. Did they find that odd? Contradictory? But no, they smiled and nodded, the women fanning themselves.

Ignoring their staring eyes, I walked up to the nave and accepted the cup. This was the blood of Christ washing me clean. Making me new, just like Mama said. Was it all official now that his body and blood churned inside me? Was Christ part of me? Was I part of Him?

We climbed back up the stairs to sit for the final prayer and recessional.

How different this was from Isaac's preachin' in the woods? How stiff and odd it seemed, though others around me, black and white, seemed comfortable enough. It didn't make sense, the ease in which the flowed and followed. From my spot, this service was as awkward as walking in them shoes. But when the missus asked me later how I enjoyed the service, I managed a polite "Lovely, ma'am."

18

October 5th, 1842, Georgetown, South Carolina

When Monday came, I took off my fancy shoes and walked the two blocks to the address the missus had printed on my card—Susan's address. The home had a stately appearance. The porch off the upper level turned around the house just like the one below. Three brick steps led up to the wooden porch, its slats nice and neat. Four rocking chairs adorned it and its ceiling was blue like the Millers'. Perhaps they needed the bad spirits away just as much. But there weren't any blue bottles on the bushes, so maybe not.

My hands shook as I knocked at the door. I shouldn't let nerves get the best of me. This was my friend. And yet, how was I to act, how much submission should I put on? Phoebe answered the door, and my breath caught a little. Of course, Susan's faithful slave would be here.

"Why, Miss Mary." Her eyes crinkled.

"The name's Mercy." I curtsied.

"Oh yes. I heard 'bout you. All about you. Word spreads quick 'round here. Come in, Mercy."

What had she heard? Gossip among the quarters often proved more false than true, and she could've heard a whopper. I stood right inside the door, fidgeting.

"I'll fetch the missus." Phoebe disappeared down the hall.

Susan sashayed in but a minute later, her smile setting me at ease some. "Mary!" She done walked up to me and took my hands in hers. I stared at them, our hands together, mine only a shade darker. There was a time when I wouldn't take off my gloves for fear that she would see the black in my blood. And yet, here she was, knowing the truth and grasping onto me anyway.

"My name is—"

"Mercy. Oh my. For years, I've thought of you as Mary. You'll have to excuse my repeated blunders."

I gave a slight nod, still taken aback by her hands in mine.

"Come into the dining room, Mercy. I'll have Phoebe bring us some tea."

I stopped and stared. Phoebe to bring me tea? A slave waiting on me? Another slave? "I thought you were going to give me some tasks to do."

Susan waved her hand in front of her face. "Oh no, I couldn't do that. I only said that to cover up our meeting is all. Now if Sam stops by, I'll have to give you a chore or two for appearances, but he should be at the bank well until evening."

I followed her to the dining room. She signaled to the chair across from hers, but I gawked at it. Would it really be okay for me to sit on the pretty red fabric?

"Mercy, honestly. Have a seat." Susan gestured to the chair, and I obliged. She rang a little bell, and Phoebe appeared, eyeing me all suspicious-like. Sitting in a dining room chair as if I were equal to her missus was surely a way to make enemies.

"Bring us some tea." Susan folded her hands on the table in front of her, and Phoebe disappeared again.

My insides began to puddle with guilt. Guilt that I sat while Phoebe fetched.

"So, I want to hear all about everything, from the beginning. From before we met. How did you get passage on a steamer?" Susan's eyes shone bright as ever. Her intense curiosity eased my fears as I told my story. My shoulders relaxed. When Phoebe came in with the tea, I barely looked up at her.

"Fascinating," Susan exclaimed as I spoke of walking right up to the carriage, pretending I had a right to. I continued recounting my time on the steamer before we came into an acquaintance, and then how, after we parted, I set out directly to Old Master's plantation looking for Mama. When I told her that I spoke with my old missus, Susan picked up her fan and began waving it in front of her. And when I told how I found Mama, I glimpsed a tear in her eye.

"Oh, what a lovely story."

My eyes widened. Her assessment sent a shiver of shock through me. She had said unfavorable things back on the steamer about slaves who ran away. "Really?"

"Oh, yes. You went through all of that to be with your mother. Heartwarming, really. The connection with your kin that compelled you, not a rebellious nature in the least."

"I suppose."

"Suppose? Mercy, you're as loyal as they come. Your loyalty for your mother just outweighed your loyalty for your master."

I had neglected to tell the truth about that master and the puffy marks his lash had left.

"So, the Millers are good to you?" She put her fan down and took a sip of tea.

"Yes, very good." It was the truth. No one had ever whipped me when under their care, and they fed us well and let us tend our own gardens.

"Lovely. What's it like, living as a slave?" She leaned forward as if to receive a secret.

What could I say to that? How could I bottle up slavery to let someone peer at it up close? "I'm tired," I finally said, as if it were enough.

She placed her hand on mine again. "Well, you can rest for now."

She didn't understand that the tired I talked about had weight and length and breadth outside of a sore back and aching feet. It dug down deep into the soul, but I couldn't rightly explain it. "Thank you."

"Do you have a beau?" Her voice tilted up in a tease.

"I have a likin' for a man named Jonah, and it seems he fancies me as well. There's nothing official though." Only a yearning.

"Oh!" She squealed. "Is he terribly romantic?"

I laughed. Only if she considered tossing rice into my hair and calling me Mercy Girl as romantic.

"In his own way." Which included a kiss that had curled my toes. When would I be able to see him again?

"You're blushing."

I pressed my hands to my cheeks. "Tell me about Sam. How did you meet? When did you marry?"

I sat back and listened then, sipping my tea. Susan recounted their meeting, courtship, and wedding. She bounced to life, talking up a storm, her face about to burst with the excitement of it all, just like when we'd met before. She continued prattling on until the door creaked open. I jumped up, heart thumping, and looked at Susan with my mouth agape.

"Here." She slid me her fan. "Fan me."

I ran around to her side of the table and did just that, waving the fan inches from her face, keeping my eyes down to the carpet.

"Sam?"

His footsteps rounded the corner, and my hand trembled.

Susan waved, her voice climbing far too loud for the indoor space. "Oh, hello, darling. I thought you'd be occupied with work until later this evening."

He came over and kissed her on the top of her head. "Finished up early."

"Did you have company?" He eyed the other teacup across from her where I had sat.

"Oh, Mrs. Willis stopped by for a bit." A bead of sweat popped onto her forehead.

I fanned a bit quicker.

"That's nice." He turned to me. "Put these cups away, will you, and grab me a bit of port."

I nodded, snatched the teacups, and turned to leave.

"Oh, Sam." Susan's voice sounded thin. Strained. "It's about time for her to go back to the Millers."

"She can take a few minutes to get me some port, Susan. What are we paying her for? Just to fan you?" His moustache twitched.

I disappeared through the door and nearly ran right into Phoebe. I gasped, but she snickered. "He sure put you in your place right quick, didn't he?"

I didn't smile. "Where is the port?" I asked.

"Never you mind. I'll get it."

I stood there outside the dining room, telling my pulse to slow and my palms to stop sweating. When Phoebe handed me the glass of port, I brought it to Sam in his study where he sat reading the *Georgetown Times*. He didn't thank me. Only said, "Run along now." I left for the Millers without telling Susan goodbye.

* * *

October 6ᵗʰ, 1842

When the wagon rumbled into Hopecrest, sweet relief washed over me—the kind that can only be found when coming home. It seems strange to me now as I write this that a happy breath blew over me at the sight of the oak trees bent over the drive like a canopy. A sight that I should rather associate with hard labor in the fields. With an aching back and tense shoulders. With a longing glance at the North Star. How quickly I had nestled myself at home with bondage. But it wasn't the place that fostered the delight of coming home. It was the people.

I jumped off the wagon and started straight to the cabin to see Mama. So focused on my goal, I overlooked the presence of another until a twig snapped underfoot. I startled, but then Jonah fell into step next to me.

"That took longer than a week."

I grinned up at him. He'd tipped his hat low over his eyes, as if he be hiding a secret. His smile gleamed—white teeth against dark skin—drawing my attention to his mouth.

My cheeks warmed. "Just wanted to give you longer to miss me." I shrugged as if I were above it all.

"I did miss you, Mercy Girl. Very much." His arm swung up, and he caught my hand in his. I slowed my steps. Best to make this moment last.

"You're walking funny." His gaze dipped to my feet.

I'd gotten right used to the slight limp. Them shoes had done a number on my feet.

"You've got fresh blisters."

"Yeah. The missus gave me a pair of her old shoes to wear while I was in town. They didn't rightly fit."

"That's fo' sho. Don't your feet hurt?"

"I'd forgotten about the pain on the drive here. I just couldn't wait to see Mama again." I lowered my eyes, suddenly bashful. "And you."

"We'd best be doctoring them up." His brow scrunched up with concern.

"Aw. They'se just blisters. Ain't like I never had a blister before." My feet were hard and calloused at the heel and toe from years of planting rice. The bottoms of them were hard as rocks.

"These blisters are fresh, though, and not in the usual spots."

I waved my hand in front of me to blow his concern away as no big deal. All the while, it warmed my heart that he noticed. That he cared.

"So, what's happened 'round here while I've been gone?" I tried to steady my steps as we came around a bend, to make him forget 'bout my poor little feet.

"Master wants to clear space for another three or four fields. We's gonna be busy transforming the swamp. Champ says I'll be chopping down trees."

Champ was the driver, second in command to the overseer. His huge muscles made him an intimidating figure, even without the whip he usually carried. He'd seemed to forget he was a slave, same as we was. When he gained favor with the master, he'd changed and started walking 'round like he owned the whole world. As long as you did what you'se supposed to, you didn't have to worry about him. If you crossed him though, oh my! He turned venomous.

"Then I guess that's what you'll be doing." I patted his muscular arm in admiration. His strength didn't intimidate me; it made me feel safe.

"Sho is hard work, clearing them swamps."

I nodded, though I hadn't been there long enough to have done so.

"After we clear the land, we got to build dikes." He squared his shoulders. "Got to bring in the sand from the higher land and the red mud that hardens."

"Then, you make the trunk docks?"

"Yes'm. Then, we put the trunk docks in the dikes to control the water flowin' in and out."

"Sounds like a mighty hard job, but something you can be right proud of when you're all done."

When we rounded the bend, Mama was sitting on the porch of our cabin, peering toward us. She stood and waved. I broke out in a run, rushing toward her. The pain in my feet throbbed then, with the running, but it didn't stop me none. I bounded up the steps and wrapped her in an embrace so tight I might crack her bones.

"Oh, Mama! I missed you."

I hadn't been away from her since I'd found her, and the ache of being apart had burned almost like it did the first time. As I stood there wrapped in her arms, I was like a little girl again.

"Oh, Mercy." She reached up and patted my head like she used to do when I was a child. "You best let me go 'fore you squeeze the life out of me."

I stepped back and looked her over. She looked far stronger than she had on her last day in the fields. The rest had done her good.

"Hello, Jonah." Mama's smile dawned like the sun.

Jonah came up to the base of the steps. "Good afternoon, ma'am." He tipped his hat toward her, all gentleman-like, which made my fondness for him rise a mite taller.

"You got salve and strips of cloth in there?" He nodded toward the front door of the cabin.

"I reckon we do." Mama put a hand on her hip. "Want me to fetch some?"

"That'd be right good of you, ma'am. Mercy done did a number on her feet."

Mama's gaze dropped to my feet, and she winced. "You're bleeding, Mercy."

I looked and saw it was so. "Just a bit."

Mama disappeared inside, and Jonah coaxed me to sit in the chair on the porch. Mama came out with a basin of water, salve, and some bandages. Jonah knelt down and gently took my feet in his hands. His touch sent a spark flying up my spine, and I shuddered.

"You don't have to trouble yourself." Heat spread in my cheeks.

" 'Tis no trouble at all." He washed my feet then. How could a man so strong possess such a soft way of treating a girl? When his fingers brushed my blisters, I winced, and he looked up at me with an apology in his eyes. Such kind eyes. So full of tender care. And something else. Desire?

The air between us tingled with electricity. When he looked up at me, his gaze dropped to my mouth, which then went dry. Oh, if only he would kiss me. Right then and there.

But he took a deep breath and kept washing. Finally, Mama handed him a towel, and he dried my feet so soft and careful. He slowly applied the salve before wrapping the bandages 'round my feet. My eyes took him in as I set to memorize every detail of him. The crinkle around his eyes. The small scar on his left cheek. The way he twisted his mouth when concentrating. I etched every detail of him in my mind.

"There you go." He brought his lips down to tenderly kiss the top of my feet. My toes curled, and my heart thudded in my chest.

"Thank you." The words came out as a whisper. The kiss had stolen my breath.

Mama looked between the both of us, then took the basin and salve inside with a small smile dancing on her face.

When the door closed, Jonah crept closer to me, still on his knees. He took my face in his hands. "I'm mighty fond of you, Mercy Girl."

I tilted forward, my lips reaching to meet his. The kiss was stronger than last time, a statement instead of a question. I drank it in. When he drew back, I wanted to shout, "No! More!" But instead, I leaned into his fingers that were caressing my cheek.

"Does that mean you're fond of me too?"

My mind swirled with so much I longed to say about this man and my affection for him, but I could only muster, "Yes. I reckon so."

"Well,"—his grin stretched wide—"that's mighty good to hear."

I smiled back at him as he stood and grabbed my hand, pulling me up close to him. He wrapped his arms around me. Something like excitement burst through me.

But I had to keep my bearings. "I best be going. I gots to work my garden. The sun is already starting to tip its hat goodbye for the day."

My smile faded. No matter when he left, my heart would leave with him, stretching down the path after him. Whether he hoed in the moonlight, or toiled in the sun, his arms were meant to hold me.

"See you tomorrow?" I asked.

"Tomorrow," he repeated as he stepped back, bringing my hand to his lips without breaking his gaze. His whisper of a kiss left my hand tingling while he backed away, down the steps and toward his cabin, never taking away his gaze until he was nearly out of sight. Then, he turned around, and did a little skip before he faded into the distance.

* * *

October 8, 1842

I didn't see Jonah the next day. I heard that Champ needed all the men in the swamps to log the cypress trees. The overseer would need us to tap pine trees to make turpentine soon and then to prepare the fields before too many days passed by. But for the moment, the missus had given Mama mending to do, and I spent the day helping her. I had trouble being careful with my stitching. My mind wouldn't focus. One minute, I replayed my time with Jonah the day before. The next minute, I developed a plan to see him again. I had to tear the stitches out and redo them several times. If Mama noticed my blunders, she didn't say a thing about them. Just continued humming and stitching.

I told her about going to the church in town. She told me how the Millers had decided to build a chapel on the property and how a white preacher would come 'round once a month to teach us catechisms and deliver a sermon. They'd allow us to use the chapel for our own prayer meetings, provided Isaac met with the white minister's approval. We wouldn't have to hunker in the woods anymore. We'd have our own place for worship.

Would the preacher be the same one I had fumbled with in church? Would he teach us to obey our master? To be good slaves? Probably, but that was the price we'd have to pay for a space of our own.

It's not that I wished the Millers any harm. They were good to us, but the resounding melody of freedom called to me from the Bible I read by candlelight each night. I can hear it's echo even now, and if there was a chance to have both Mama and freedom, I would have taken it, would still take it … as long as that chance included Jonah.

As the time alone with Mama was borrowed, I used it to ask a slew of questions I'd kept bottled inside since I was a little girl. When I first set foot on Hopecrest, Mama told me that Old Master had sold Pa years ago. She hadn't a lick of an idea where. It was punishment for being ornery. She didn't give me more details, and I didn't pry. But now that affection for a man blossomed within me, I needed to know more about the man I called my pa, though everyone knew we didn't share a drop of blood.

"Mama, did you love Pa? Did you …" I lowered my eyes as heat rose in my cheeks. "Desire him? Did you love him like that?"

"Oh, child." Her hands stilled, a frock lying limp on her lap while her eyes caressed my face. "I couldn't afford to love your pa that way. I knew that. We all did. There was too much to lose. So much that had already been lost." Her gaze trailed out the window as if she could see Pa outside, working their small plot. "And yet, without us even meaning to, a hunger for each other entwined itself around us like the vines that try to overtake the garden. It snuck up on us and grasped on tight. Yes. Yes, I loved him. Far more than I intended."

She picked up her needle again but didn't resume her stitching. Instead, she seemed to examine the specks of dust dancing in the shaft of light.

"How did you meet?" My question drew her gaze.

She brightened. "In the fields. Worked Golden Hill together." A smile stretched on her face. "Oh, that boy could sing. Do you remember that? His voice rang out deep and pure in those fields. Seemed to push all my worries away with a melody."

I shook my head. "I don't remember."

"He sang to you. Every night when you was a baby. He loved you like you was his own. You know that, right?"

I closed my eyes, trying to summon an image of Pa. I could only see his face twisting with pain when Old Master came calling for Mama. I couldn't seem to find any space in my memories that included the two of us bonded together. "I only remember you."

"That's a shame."

I didn't feel much of an empty chasm where my father should have been, seeing as Mama's love abounded and overflowed over every crevice of memory.

"Did you despise Old Master?" I cringed at the horror. It was some kind of evil for a man to take what he wanted with no care to the affections of the woman.

Her brow knit, and I braced myself for a torrent of wrath and resentment, but then Mama returned to her stitching. "Despise? Who has time for that?"

Her question threatened to unravel something inside me if I would let it. Instead, I held myself together, avoiding all thoughts of Pa and Old Master, focusing only on my Jonah. When the sun set with no sign of him, I lay down in bed to meet him in my dreams.

* * *

October 9th, 1842

I awoke to a light tapping sound. Darkness still lingered, but out the window, dawn stretched herself, preparing to awake into a new day. I crept over and opened the door, careful not to wake Mama. Jonah stood there. My breath caught at the sight of him, and I slid myself out onto the porch, gently closing the door behind me.

"Good morning." His smile invited one of my own.

"Good morning."

He held something in his hands that I couldn't quite make out in the darkness.

"I brought you something." He handed me a pair of shoes.

"What?" I whispered, turning them around in my hands. They were feather soft, made of leather. I peered through the dimness to make out the delicate stitching. Beautiful.

"Try them on. I want to make sure they fit you good."

I sat down in the chair and slid them on my feet. They enveloped my feet like a gentle hug. I wiggled my toes around inside them, exploring. "They fit like a dream."

"Good." His smile broadened, and his teeth reflected the pale light that was beginning to creep on the horizon. "You won't be able to wear them in the fields, of course, but they'll do you some good walking 'round here."

"Jonah, this is so thoughtful. Thank you." I stroked the sides of the soft shoes.

"Anything for you." His gaze held mine. I dared not blink to keep from missing a moment of time with him.

Champ's horn blew.

"I have to get going." Regret dripped from his voice.

"I know." My disappointment pooled with his.

"Tomorrow is Saturday. I'll have more time after work. I'll come to see you."

"I'll be waiting."

He turned this time and rushed away, only looking back once to put his fingers to his lips and cast a kiss in my direction. I caught it and held it to my heart.

19

———

Natassa peered over at Brandon as he drove their family to St. Anthony's Baptist that Sunday morning. She searched his face for a clue regarding his mood. It was their designated Sunday to attend the city church, and no one had mentioned doing otherwise, but after her appearance on the front page of the local paper, his stiff edges toward her remained. How did he feel driving into the very city he so desperately wanted her to avoid?

He shifted his jaw back and forth, but not in anger. He looked as if he churned something over in his mind, contemplating pros and cons, wrestling with ideals and reality. He caught her staring at him and gave a slight smile, which she returned. Daniel's favorite song came on the radio, and he asked Natassa to turn the volume up. As she did so, the children belted out the lyrics, and her smile broadened at the sound. Brandon still seemed deep in thought, oblivious to the cacophony around him.

At church, they checked the children into their classes, and Bethany took Mercy into her arms. The last church bell rang, and the organ began to play. The choir director told them to turn in their hymnals to page 451. Though Natassa could sing "When Peace, Like a River" by heart, she grabbed the faded green hymnal in front of her and flipped the worn pages. But when she got to the correct hymn, she gasped.

Someone had sketched a picture in the margins of a man with hands outstretched to heaven while a river rushed around him. Her mouth slid open while she stared at the drawing. As rudimentary as it was, she recognized DeAndre's technique. *He grabbed them old hymnals and doodled in the margins. We got dozens of hymnals with his drawings in them.* Bethany's conversation with Janell echoed in Natassa's memory. She snapped the hymnal shut. Brandon raised an eyebrow in her direction.

She shrugged, attempting to look unaffected. "I know this one."

As she sang, "It is well, it is well with my soul," the drawing tugged at her heart. *No. I won't look it.* And yet …

She opened the hymnal to 451 again and traced the picture with her fingers. Ten-year-old DeAndre sat in a pew with a stubby pencil, creating this sketch. *Ugh.* What was she doing? She slammed the book shut again. This was her rapist, not some sweet child with a dream. The man who brutally attacked her. The man who ruined her life.

She stilled for a moment, listening to the voices singing around her. She looked to her right and saw her husband, still by her side after everything. And next to him Bethany, her adopted Mama. And next to her, Mazy held her beautiful daughter Mercy. Ruined her life? That was a lie. Her life was far from ruined. *I have far more power in my story than he does.* And God had—and was still—making beauty from ashes.

She leaned past Brandon and asked Bethany if she could use the church office for a couple of minutes. Bethany tilted her head in a question.

"I need to make a couple of copies."

Wordlessly, Bethany handed Natassa her keys. Natassa slipped out of the pew and past the singing parishioners with the hymnal in hand. Their voices drifted after her. She returned to the sanctuary right before the sermon.

By the time Pastor Jaden stood up to preach, Natassa had nestled into the words of that first hymn. She leaned into the crook of Brandon's arm. His arm around her felt protective in the best way—not controlling but safe. Her husband cared for her, looked after her. She could be thankful for that and relax in that love. She smiled up at him and mouthed, *Thank you.* He questioned her with his eyes, but then the pastor arrested their attention.

"Our city is in crisis. People are angry, and they're hurting." The room filled with soft sounds of agreement. "Some people who don't even live here are coming into our city to cause trouble, and others are causing trouble because they're troubled inside. I want to thank all of you who've been attending our evening prayer meetings." Pastor Jaden rocked on the balls of his feet, hunching forward. "You are the hope for our city. You are the example of unity that our city so desperately needs. You are the light that we need in the darkness.

"While some take matters into their own hands, we are coming before the court of heaven, believing that we have the ear of the only One who can make true and lasting change." He pointed upward; his eyes fixed beyond the ceiling.

Some people clapped, some offered their "Amen" and "That's right."

Natassa nodded her agreement.

"You see, you could burn down a building. You could burn down ten buildings. But that ain't going to satisfy your soul, now is it? Only Jesus can come into that place and make things right inside." His voice grew louder, more passionate. "Only Jesus can change a heart and bring peace and healing. Jesus is the only hope for our city, and that is why we pray." The pastor's forehead glistened with sweat

The assents grew in volume, and Brandon took Natassa's hand and squeezed. He didn't let go of her hand for the remainder of the sermon.

Afterward, a middle-aged woman named Grace stopped them to shake Brandon's hand. "Thank you so much for letting Natassa come to the prayer meetings. We love having her. Her being here is such an example of unity in our city." Brandon smiled at the woman, but maybe only out of politeness.

Two more people came up to them and said similar things. Then as they walked out the door, Pastor Jaden stopped them. "I'll see you tonight, Natassa. You're coming, right?"

"Um, I'm not sure. We'll see." She eyed Brandon, who gave no indication either way.

"Okay. Well, I hope so. We love having you participate." He flashed a grin at Brandon. "And we'd love to have you come as well."

Brandon's tight-lipped smile gave enough of an answer.

They waved good-bye and piled into their van. On the drive home, the pastor's question tumbled around in her mind. Should she ask Brandon if she could go? Surely not. The answer would most definitely be no. No more prayer meetings in the city. Ever. And she could be okay with that. Really. Content with her life.

Only Brandon brought it up before dinner. "Are you going tonight?"

"Going tonight?" She bit her lip. Was this a trap?

"To the prayer meeting. Are you going?"

"I didn't think you'd let me."

He smiled wryly. "I didn't think I could stop you."

"I won't go if you don't want me to." She meant it this time. She could stay at home. Watch Netflix.

"Go." He tilted his head, voice gentle.

"Go?" She did a little clap.

Brandon laughed. "I heard what it means to the community. You are important to them. You need to be there. Plus, Brett will be at the protests tonight. I told him if he sees you down there, he is to handcuff you, throw you in the back of his car, and drag you home." Brandon crossed his arms, attempting to look stern, but the sides of his mouth wobbled and eventually betrayed him, curving upward.

"I will stay at the church. I promise." She crossed her heart for emphasis.

"You'd better. You don't want to mess with Brett."

"I definitely don't want to mess with Brett." She mock shivered, but in reality, after their last interaction, she'd stay as far away from him as possible.

His big convictions had made hers seem small, foolish. Or maybe that wasn't true. They had pulled something pretty big out of her as well. But the friction between them made sparks fly. Yeah. She'd rather avoid the man.

"Stay safe. You're important to me." Brandon drew her close, kissing the top of her head and rubbing the small of her back.

"I know. I love you." She drew back and kissed him full on the mouth, showing him the appreciation that had been simmering inside all day.

* * *

Natassa and a group of twenty-five others from St. Anthony's Baptist gathered on the front steps of the church with candles. They stood in a semicircle and took turns praying for peace and unity in their city, for the healing of the deep wounds of racism, and the safety of all involved.

The streets were quiet, somber even. Though some people stumbled in and out of the liquor store down the road, no one came close enough to the church to bother them. They continued praying, some loud and passionate, some quiet and pensive.

Nearly twenty minutes before their meeting was scheduled to end, a police car cruised down St. Anthony Street and stopped in front of the church. Brett got out, and Natassa walked down to meet him.

"What's going on? Why are you here?" She peered at him.

"A large group of protestors crossed over the highway and are headed in this direction. You need to get out of here. It's time to go home, Natassa." The glare of the streetlamp above them accentuated the deep lines etched on Brett's face and the dark bags under his eyes.

Natassa puffed out her cheeks and glanced back at the group of intercessors on the steps. "The meeting's almost over. How fast is the group moving? Do you think we have another twenty minutes? Or fifteen?"

Brett looked like he wanted to say "You've got to be kidding me." Instead, he ran a hand through his hair. "Let me go check. I'll be right back."

Natassa waited in the parking lot, voices from the prayer meeting wafting to her ears in waves. Brett's police car sped away, headed back down the street, and turned right. Someone came out of the liquor store down the road. A young black man stumbled in the middle of the street … talking to himself?

She strained to hear.

"It's not my fault. It sure ain't my fault. It's this street's fault. That's what it is." He stumbled over to the mural DeAndre had painted on the wall of the abandoned ice cream shop. He pointed his finger at the painting of DeAndre himself. "It's your own stupid fault, D. Your fault. Not mine, bro. Yours."

Her breath caught. Was this? Could this be?

Footsteps. Another figure appeared at the very end of the street.

"Yo, Reg, c'mon man." The figure beckoned Reg to join him. "They're busting into the pawnshop on Eighth. You need a new TV, right?"

Laughter echoed from the distance. Indistinct shouting. A muffle of far-off voices.

"Yeah, man. I'll be right there."

"Hurry up, or all the good stuff will be gone."

"Alright."

The other man left and she stared directly at Reg, the man who was most likely the accomplice in her attack. The man who said, "Have at her, D." She wrapped her arms around herself and shuffled back into the shadows.

Brett's police car appeared in the distance, but it didn't start down St. Anthony Street. It stopped at the corner. He got out and started to walk toward her, oblivious to Reg standing in the shadows near the mural. Brett's radio blared.

"All officers in the area, please report to Eighth and Knight."

Brett held up a finger to her and spun around, jogging in the opposite direction. He pulled out his radio before turning the corner. "This is Officer Bloomington. Roger that." Brett's voice echoed in the nearly empty streets.

"Bloomington?" Reg shouted, beginning to sprint after him. "Bloomington? Like Natassa Bloomington? Bloomington, it's all your fault."

What happened next happened fast. Reg hauled out a gun and disappeared around the corner after Brett. Natassa heard a shot fire, then another. She screamed Brett's name and tried to run after them. Suddenly, Bethany's arms came around her, holding her fast while she waited for Brett to come bounding around the corner, reassuring her that he was okay.

He never came.

Natassa's wails melted into the sound of sirens.

20

November 1, 1842, Georgetown, South Carolina

"**I** love him."

I whispered my confession into the wind as I carried the freshly stitched clothes up to the Big House. Saying them words lifted my feet right off the dirt path. A little leap in my new, soft-as-a-feather shoes. I tried those words on for size and found with a rush that they fit me well. A mockingbird sang out and a giggle escaped my lips.

"I love you, Jonah." My voice rose a little louder, emboldened by the rightness of it all. Yes, it was right. Like it was always meant to be. As if when I was running south to find Mama, my heart was stretching out for Jonah, though I hadn't had a scrap of an idea. Love had found me when I hadn't even been looking. My cheeks warmed at the thought.

I exchanged the stitched clothes for a stack that needed mending and turned right around to bring them to our cabin.

"Mercy?" Missus Miller called out after me, hands clasped at her waist.

I lowered my head. "Yes, ma'am."

"Why don't you come play for us tonight. Only Mr. Miller and me. There will be no guests. I miss hearing you play."

"Yes, ma'am." I bowed.

"Come at sundown."

"Yes, ma'am."

My heart sunk. I had hoped to spend the whole evening with Jonah. Once again, it became clear that my life was not my own. My steps to the cabin were slower, heavier.

Back there, I laid the clothes on the table and then took a pair of trousers to stitch while Mama began working on a blouse.

"So, tell me about your young man." Mama's voice crinkled with exhaustion.

"Jonah? You know Jonah, Mama. He's the one who carried you up from the field."

Warm light filled the cabin, casting a gentle glow on Mama's features.

"I don't know him like you do, Mercy. Tell me."

I beamed. "He's the most tender, thoughtful man I've ever known."

"Mm-hmm," Mama mumbled, her eyes briefly raising to meet mine with a twinkle. The corners of her mouth twitched as if she held back a smile.

"He listens to me, Mama. Really listens. As if I were the most fascinating person in the world. He got me these shoes." I lifted my feet out, rolling my ankles. "Because he cares about me and doesn't want to see me hurtin'. His voice is like honey, thick and sweet."

"And his kiss?" Mama couldn't hold back her smile anymore. It broke out into the open.

I tossed my head back and laughed. "A bit like honey too, I guess." A blush heated my face up real good.

"Well, there you go, Mercy. Sounds like you're in love." Mama chuckled.

I kept smiling as I stitched, my cheeks beginning to ache from it. In love! How did I fall in love?

The day stretched on as I waited for Jonah. The monotony of stitching made my eyes ache. My knee jiggled up and down, messing up my mending. Finally, Mama banished me outside to do some washing. The trip to the creek to fetch water did me some good. Being three-quarters of a mile away, it allowed me to release some of that nervous energy pulsing through me.

I hunched in front of the cabin at the branch that we used for launderin' and rubbed the clothes with lye soap, then beat them with the paddle.

Jonah rounded the corner, and I dropped the clothes and soap in the basin with a plop and ran to meet him, drying my hands on the front of my dress.

He lifted me up and spun me around.

"You free to take a walk?"

I nodded. But no, I had to do the wash. I turned around and spied Mama standing on the porch watching us.

"I got to finish washing the clothes, and then I got to iron them." Resignation dripped from my voice.

"Go on now." She waved us off. "I'll finish up here."

I broke into a grin. "Thanks, Mama."

Jonah held out his hand, and I took it, squeezing tightly. Our arms swung back and forth as we walked, like they was dancing together. My steps were so light, I could have floated up with the clouds.

"Where are we going?" I asked.

"I want to show you the chapel we're building."

"You're building it?"

"Me and a dozen others. The Millers want it ready by the end of next month.

"That soon?"

"That's when the white preacher wants to start coming, so yes."

He led me into a clearing where a dirt rectangle stood amongst the green grass.

"Right here?" I asked.

A dove cooed in the distance.

"Right here." He caressed my hand with his thumb. "I have to come work on this chapel after clearing the swamps each day. They'll be some late nights until we finish it."

"I won't get to see you much, then?"

"Not for a while. But when it's finished …" He looked at that dirt rectangle as if he pictured the chapel all done up and beautiful. Wistful and longing.

"What?" I prodded. A breeze teased my hair.

He took his hat off and turned it in his hands. He suddenly looked unsure, nervous even. I had never seen that side of him, and my head tilted of its own accord, examining him.

"Well, I wondered if I could take you there … for a weddin'."

"A weddin'?"

"I mean to say, Mercy, would you want to get married? Here? In the chapel?"

My hand flew to my mouth, then to his chest, then back to my mouth. "You want to marry me?"

"Very much." His eyes peered deep into mine, and something flopped around in my insides.

"Me?" I asked again.

"Only you." His voice dripped with emotion, and my imagination swirled with possibilities. Walking down the aisle in a beautiful chapel. Jumping the broom with Jonah. Sharing a cabin with him, a bed with him. Waking up next to him each morning.

Children? Would we have children? Children who loved their mama as much as I loved mine? An extended family. Protection. Provision. Comfort. Love.

"Of course, I'll marry you." I jumped into his arms. He held me high off the ground, feet floating like clouds, his strong arms wrapped around me so tight and secure. My head hovered slightly above his, and I bent down for a kiss. He set me down and cupped my face in his hands, kissing me long and slow.

Like honey. I was right, he tasted like honey.

He broke away. "We'll have to get Master's permission."

"That won't be a problem. They adore me." I had no doubt they'd say yes. The missus would probably lend me a dress and make me a veil to boot.

Jonah sat down on the grass by the place where the chapel would stand and patted the ground right next to him. I joined him there, my hand seeking his again, lonely and naked without its company.

"Let's dream." He talked about the cabin he would build for us. There was space next to his mama's cabin, and we could share a garden. He knew how to make furniture too and, in our imaginations, we filled our little cabin with a table and chairs, a bed, and a bench. I could quilt us a nice blanket and fill the mattress with rice husks.

"I've almost got enough money saved up to buy me a horse. Think of it, Mercy. A horse!"

A squeal escaped my mouth. With a horse, Jonah could manage twice as much land of his own, selling his own crop for profit. A horse meant good eatin'. It meant security for the entire family. Medicine when someone got sick, clothing to protect from the cold and rain. A horse would mean we could nestle into a safe place, me and him. Me and him and …

Finally, I gathered up the courage to ask what I'd been thinking. "What about children?" I lowered my eyes, embarrassed by speaking of such things.

His smile faded, and he looked far into the distance. "I don't know about children."

"Why not?" I asked, cringing a bit. Did he not want to have children with a lighter shade of skin than his own? Did he think our children would look too white?

"I don't know how I feel about bringing slaves into this world." His eyes still searched the horizon as the sun began to dip, splashing colors across the sky.

"Oh." I stroked his thumb with my own. If we had children, they'd be slaves. Forced into a hard life of labor with freedom only a dream.

He looked at me then, his eyes searching mine. "Don't get me wrong. There's nothing I'd want more than to have beautiful babies with you … if they were free. If *we* were free."

"I understand." My heart sank. I understood how he felt, but I yearned for children of my own.

"We have a good master," I prodded. Perhaps he would yield.

"Yes, but a master just the same."

A tear slipped out of my right eye. Then another. I couldn't help it, couldn't hold them back. Jonah swiped them away with his thumb.

"Oh, Mercy Girl, don't cry." His voice sounded so soft that I fell into it, laying my head on his shoulder. "Maybe I'm wrong. Maybe we can." He kissed my wet cheek.

"You're right," I managed, voice cracking. "But I's so sad at everything I'll miss, everything slavery has stolen from me."

He wrapped me up tight in his arms and kissed the top of my head. "Let's do it. Let's have lots of babies and raise them the best we can."

"Really?" I pulled back and searched his eyes.

"Really. If that's what you want. I want to see you happy."

We sat there snuggled up together as the colors in the sky danced their way down. We talked about what our children might look like, might be like.

"And when you're pregnant, I'll spoil you."

I stretched. Oh, to do less work and receive more rations as a pregnant woman. Then, after having the baby, I'd get to take a month off from working in the fields. What a luxury.

"I'll fetch you whatever you're hankering to eat. Oysters, crabs, clams, possum. I'll make you Hopping John, Limpin' Lizzie—"

I done bust out laughing at the thought of that.

"What?"

"I ain't got no trouble picturing you picking up some oysters when the tide goes out or catching a possum when the water swells, but I cannot figure you cooking up peas and hominy!" Laughter began rolling again, and Jonah's smile spread wide.

"Don't you underestimate me, Mercy Girl!"

We kept on dreaming. He'd be promoted to head trunk minder, and our son would do the job of tasting the water to see if salt had snuck in. Jonah would train him to be a trunk minder too, and our family would rise to the top of the ranks.

We talked about our wedding, and who would be there to celebrate with us. I cuddled closer into Jonah's warmth, but then straightened with a start.

"Oh no."

"What? What is it?"

"I was supposed to be at the Big House at sundown."

"What? Why?" Jonah sat up, his gaze concerned.

"To play for them. To play the fiddle. Oh, dear. I'll be so late. I hope they don't scold me." Or beat me. But the Millers would never beat me, would they? Not for a simple infraction.

"You best be running." Jonah stood.

He reached his hand out to pull me up and into his embrace. "I love you, Mercy Girl." He bent down and kissed me, stronger and more passionate this time. The earth swirled around me.

"I love you too." My words came out breathless.

"Now run."

I did so, waving back at him as I left.

* * *

November 2nd, 1842

"There you are. I was concerned." Missus Miller sat on the rocking chair on the front porch when the Big House came into view. She stood as I got closer.

"I'm so sorry, ma'am." I bowed my head, out of breath. "I lost track of time."

"Oh?" The missus crossed her arms around herself, and I sunk in humiliation.

"It's just that … Jonah asked me to marry him, ma'am. We were wanting your permission." I didn't mean to say it. Not like that. Not without Jonah at my side. It slipped out in my mix of worry and exhilaration.

"Oh." Her voice dropped in a sad little way. She sat back down in her rocking chair. I walked halfway up the steps and stood, awaiting her answer. Waiting in a long stretch of silence.

"Ma'am?"

She sighed, her gaze not quite resting on me. "I'm afraid that won't be possible."

"What?" My head snapped up in panic. My eyes stretched to meet hers in a way that was far from proper. "Why?"

"Mercy." She stretched my name out long and thin. "We were going to wait until after Christmas to tell you this, but it's a fact we can't avoid. You and your mother are being sold."

21

DeAndre turned the envelope around in his hand several times, testing the weight of it. Thick and heavy. Why did Natassa write to him? What did it say? And with so many words? He hadn't seen her since the food visit. His throat closed at the memory. The softness in her eyes as she watched him eat. Kindness extended. Mercy. It was almost too much.

"You gonna open it already or fondle it all day?" Chris—the leader of the six-cell—scoffed at him from his bunk as DeAndre sat in the corner examining Natassa's envelope. Chris's glassy expression betrayed him as high again. Drugs seemed to be as prevalent inside prison as they were outside, and in many ways, it was like he had landed back in the hood.

"I ain't opening it now." DeAndre tossed the envelope onto his top bunk. There was no way he was going to open its contents in front of Chris. That boy mocked him incessantly. At least that was all he did, but DeAndre didn't want to invite more of the same.

Each cell had a leader, an inmate who assumed control of the cell, demanding and commanding, but sometimes protecting his cellies from jerks pressing them for their food or stamps or money. Chris had a mouth on him, but he wouldn't stand for any bullying besides his own.

It was Rob's turn to peek through the hole, and he sat still as if mesmerized. The others remained glued to the TV, not even giving DeAndre a cursory glance.

Chris continued heckling, and DeAndre attempted to drown him out by retreating into his internal world.

He did this often, using his mind to transport him to the far-off places he'd seen in Mama's old travel magazines. Italy and France, Brazil and Mozambique. He mentally flipped through the thin pages that were bursting with color and culture. Then, he'd paint what he saw on the canvas of his imagination.

The Colosseum and Trevi Fountain. The Eiffel Tower and the Palace of Versailles. *Christ the Redeemer* and Sugarloaf Mountain. Beaches. Wildlife. And in every picture, a beautiful woman off to the side, studying him with pensive eyes. Waiting for him. Still choosing him despite everything.

Janell. She remained in every dream of the day and dream of the night. In every hope of his heart and every fear he held. If he could hold onto her in this place, maybe he could make it out alive without losing himself.

Chris grew quiet beneath him, and as DeAndre rolled over on his bed, he rolled onto something.

Natassa's letter. He'd forgotten about it.

He pried the envelope open and slid out a dozen pieces of paper. He didn't find a letter at all but photocopies of hymns. He scanned through the stack of papers. No note from Natassa. No explanation. Just a stack of hymns sent from her to him.

The first hymn on the stack was "What a Friend We Have in Jesus." In the margin, there was a drawing of Jesus sitting shoulder to shoulder with a boy, both of them smiling. DeAndre gasped. He'd sketched that picture. She must have photocopied the hymn out of the St. Anthony's Baptist hymnal.

He closed his eyes. Memories flooded over him. Sitting in the wooden pew, sketching away with his two-inch pencil, its eraser worn down to the nub. The words from the song washed over him then, and they did so now. The deep tones of the organ and the blend of rich voices urged him to take his burdens to the Lord in prayer.

Encouraged, DeAndre turned to the next page. In the margins of "Be Thou My Vision," he had drawn himself as a boy walking down a dark path while holding a lantern before him. A little lower, he had drawn someone in full armor. Again, the sound of voices singing, asking God to be their armor and sword.

He poured through the pages Natassa sent until lights out. He studied the pictures he drew in the margins of the hymns "Rock of Ages," "How Great Thou Art," "O for a Thousand Tongues," "Take My Life, and Let it Be." When the room darkened, he remained full of light and song. And bittersweet memories.

* * *

Luis caught up with DeAndre on the way to Bible study, smiling. "Dude, I got to talk to you. You want a job?"

"Huh?"

"They transferred Fred. He worked on the cleaning crew with me, so now his spot is open. I put in a good word for you. You haven't caused any trouble and can be a trustee."

Having a job in jail was a privilege afforded to a few with good behavior and great reputations among the staff. Trustees were free to move around the jail without an escort guard and even got paid a few dollars a month.

"Mostly sweeping and mopping." Luis rubbed his chin.

"Yeah, sure." The ability to walk free of his cell sounded like a slice of heaven.

"Cool. I'll tell my boss. Come back to the common room at nine, then. I'll show you the ropes."

"Thanks, man."

They walked side by side to Bible study, a wisp of hope threaded between them.

* * *

That very first morning, his job turned out to be something special. DeAndre swept and mopped the chow hall. Afterward they headed to the day room. It consisted of four tables, a few benches, two phones, and a TV. A toilet and two showers sat off to the side. Luis set to cleaning them.

"You can straighten all of the books and magazines. Put them back on the shelf. Or take any that you want."

DeAndre eyed the reading material strewn across the tables. He'd never spent time in the day room before, never felt safe among the other inmates. Some guys slept in there instead of in their cells, but DeAndre couldn't risk someone assaulting him.

As he grabbed a stack of magazines and arranged them on the shelf, a copy of *Art in America* stuck out from the rest. His mouth fell open as he thumbed through the pages. "I can take this?" He held the magazine up for his friend to see.

"Sure, you can." Luis waved the toilet brush in his hand. "Take anything you want. People donate them."

DeAndre thumbed through the other magazines, excitement building. There were seven editions of *Art in America* and five editions of *Juxtapoz*. He even found a travel magazine just like the kind Mama used to have. He couldn't wait to pour over them when his shift ended.

For the first time since he came to prison, he had a purpose. Hope. A future beyond the bleak walls of the jail. Maybe it was the job. Or the magazines. It could be the friendship with Luis. Or maybe it was the music still pouring over his mind and his soul, beckoning him forward when everything else wanted to leave him behind.

* * *

At two thirty, DeAndre's lawyer came for him. As he led DeAndre to the meeting room, DeAndre's thoughts began to swirl again. They'd set his sentencing for the next week, and Mr. Graz was going to pressure him to talk about his accomplice one final time.

He steeled himself to stand firm against the pressure. Tia and Reg had a baby on the way. He couldn't destroy that. Besides, Pa used to look at Reg with such hope in his eyes as if he could love that boy into goodness. As DeAndre sat down across from Mr. Graz, he gritted his teeth. He wouldn't let the whole truth slip out.

"DeAndre, there's been a development in your case." Mr. Graz's face looked like worn leather, the bags under his eyes evidence of all he carried.

"There has?" DeAndre sat forward. How could there be a development when he hadn't said a word?

"It seems that the accomplice that you didn't want to reveal has confessed to his assault on Natassa Bloomington."

"Reg confessed," DeAndre spoke low, almost to himself.

"Yes. Reginald Maley confessed to third-degree assault charges. He confirmed your story of the incident nearly word for word, only he added one detail that you neglected to tell us. Perhaps because you were unaware."

"What's that?"

"He told us that he injected narcotics into your drink the night of the attack. Therefore, you were under the influence of narcotics when you sexually assaulted Mrs. Bloomington."

That would explain the feeling of flying, of being shot into the air. He'd thought it was the mixture of alcohol, power, and anger. He shook his head, mind reeling.

Mr. Graz shuffled the stack of papers in front of him. "The judge will take this new information into consideration at your sentencing next week."

DeAndre nodded, studying the pattern of the tiles on the floor. A dirty cream speckled with green.

Reg must have turned himself in. Tia would be sitting on that worn couch by herself, waiting for Reg to walk in the door. Only he'd never come back.

"Reg is in jail?" he whispered.

"For a very long time." Mr. Glaz cleared his throat. "DeAndre, Reginald is in prison for murder."

DeAndre's head snapped up. "What?"

"Reginald was arrested for the first-degree murder of a police officer on Sunday evening."

"What are you talking about?" DeAndre catapulted to his feet, shoving his chair back. "Reg killed somebody! Are you crazy? He was cleaning himself up. He was just here!"

"Sit down, DeAndre."

"Sit down? You come here and tell me that my best friend done killed somebody, and I'm supposed to sit down?" But he did, dropping his head in his hands.

"He murdered Officer Bloomington."

DeAndre's head whipped up again. "Bloomington? Natassa's husband?"

"No. Her brother-in-law."

"Oh my God. Oh my God." DeAndre's stomach swirled. He might retch right there in the meeting room. All of a sudden, stifling heat saturated the room. The food visit. Natassa pushing the bag toward him. The hymns she sent. If the murder happened Sunday, she must have sent those beforehand. What was that woman going through right now?

"It's my fault." He let out a train of curses. "It's all my fault."

"Excuse me?" Mr. Graz angled his head in DeAndre's direction.

"If I would have turned him in, he would have been in jail. He couldn't have … He wouldn't have … Oh my God. It's all my fault!"

"As your lawyer, I would advise you to keep those musings to yourself. I'm sorry things happened this way, but we do have his confession now, which will do wonders with your case." Mr. Graz offered a tight nod and let himself out of the meeting room, leaving DeAndre alone with his gnawing guilt.

22

—————

November 6th, 1842, Georgetown, South Carolina

I lay awake well into the night, heart pounding, thoughts swirling. I hadn't told Mama what the missus told me, didn't have the gall to. I didn't tell Jonah, but only because I hadn't seen him yet. I think if I had, the words would have tumbled out of me with the tears I had kept pent up while playing slow and sad on the fiddle.

The missus had given me a minute to ponder what she said.

"Don't worry, Mercy. The trader promised he wouldn't sell you farther south. He promised to find you two a good placement, a kind master. I thought to keep you here as long as possible instead of shut-up in the slave pen until he was ready to move you."

I'd just stared. What could I say to that? Should I be grateful to be here instead of in a slave pen? To have the chance to fall in love, only for the missus to snatch it away? If only I could ask why, but my mouth wouldn't form the words. The missus must have read the question in my eyes.

"Mr. Miller has some bad debts he needs to pay off. Trust me, Mercy, it's nothing personal." She put a hand to her chest. "You know how I don't like to split up families. We need to sell two slaves to make good on my husband's obligations. If we sold anyone else, we'd be breaking up a family. This way, you two can stay together." She spoke in an even voice, as if doling out a perfectly reasonable business transaction. Logical. Calculated.

"You had a good harvest," I finally said, my voice little more than a scratchy whisper.

"Yes, and thankfully, that covered most of it. Otherwise, we'd have to sell more than two."

I shook my head,. No, I couldn't take it in. I wouldn't grasp onto her words and let them make a new reality.

"Now, don't you fret. Come in and play for us. It might be the last chance we have to hear your music." She motioned for me to follow her inside.

How my feet brought me inside was a mystery. Was I disconnected from my body? There I was walking into the Big House. There I was picking up the fiddle. There I was playing a dirge. If the missus and master objected to my song choice, they said not a word. Just sat, sipping their tea, staring at nothing at all, lost in their own worlds.

A stray tear slipped out only once before the missus banished all emotion.

"Mercy, wipe your face, and don't cry again."

I did so, stuffing my sadness down until it churned in my belly. I kept pressing it deeper and deeper as I played. Maybe I was like David playing the harp for Saul. The Bible said when David played, a tormenting spirit would lift from Saul. Could Missus and Master have a demon? Could my playing lift it off them, or would they pin me to the wall with a spear?

When they released me to go home, my steps dragged and my spirit sagged.

Laying in my bed that night, sleep eluded me, running this way and that, hiding behind every bush and tree. If only I could sink into it, forget the harsh truth, and melt into my dreaming from earlier that day. Jonah and a wedding. Building a life together. Why couldn't I go back there in my dreams, to get relief from the weight of reality that pressed on me? Instead, I lay still and silent, thoughts rushing like a flooded river.

Suddenly, I sat straight up. "Susan," I whispered to the night.

If anyone could stop this madness, it would be Susan. She could talk to the missus. Make things right. Turn things around to where they'd make sense again. I had to get word to Susan.

No sense waking Mama, so I took a candle outside along with paper and a pen. There in the enveloping darkness, I penned a letter to Susan, telling her what the missus said, begging her to intervene. First thing in the morning, I'd give the letter to Eli and ask him to deliver it when he went to town for supplies.

I tramped back inside and lay down again, finally succumbing to a fitful sleep. Snatches of dreams flitted around my head. One where I was a child again, white arms wrestling me away from my mother and plunking me on the back of a wagon. One where I clung to Jonah's ankles while hounds tore at me, dragging me from him, biting my flesh. One where I walked down the aisle of a chapel only to have vultures tear away my veil. I woke feeling nary a bit rested and full of trepidation.

At the first sight of dawn, I ran to Eli's cabin, letter in hand. He stood stretching on his porch, looking surprised to spot me coming. Relief splashed over me as he told me he'd be driving into town on Monday. In days, not weeks, Susan would know. Susan would rescue me.

Leaving the letter with Eli, I spun around and headed to Jonah's cabin, but I met him on the way.

"There's my girl." He grinned when he saw me from a distance. "I was just goin' to fetch you, see if you would take a walk with me."

I buckled under his kindness, the lilt in his voice. I stopped walking toward him and crumpled onto the path, bent over, heaving with tears.

His footsteps rushed toward me.

"Mercy Girl, what's the matter, love? What's wrong?"

His strong arms wrapped around me, the heat from his body warmed up the outside of me, thawing the cold and numb parts.

It took me some time of trying to stifle my sobs 'fore I could squeak the words out. "Missus said … Missus said …"

"Shh now, Mercy. It's okay. I'm here." His calloused hands lifted my chin, cupping my wet face. "What did she say?"

Another sob erupted from me, and my tears puddled in his hands. I took a couple of sharp, shaky breaths.

"She said we can't marry. She said …"

"Shh now. What's that?" He pressed his forehead to mine. "She said we can't marry?"

I nodded, fast and forceful.

"Well, I'm sure I can change her mind. I'll talk to her, Mercy. I'll convince her."

I shook my head, squeaking out the word, "No."

His eyes questioned mine.

"She's selling me, Jonah. Me and Mama."

He flinched as if someone had whipped his back.

"Selling you?" His voice wavered.

I nodded.

"No. No, Mercy Girl. She can't sell you. I'll talk with her. Plead with her. They had a good harvest. There's no need to sell anybody." He held me, rocking me in his arms, smoothing my wild hair, kissing my temple. Finally, I calmed down enough to tell him about Susan.

"Yes, that's a good idea. I'll beg the missus, and Susan will talk some sense into them both. It'll be okay. You'll see. We'll marry soon as the men finish the chapel. I'll build us that cabin …" As his voice trailed off, uncertainty crossed his face. The dreams that were so solid the day before seemed like only a mist now. Something we could see but not grasp.

He picked me up from the dusty path and settled me in the crook of a tree, nestling in beside me. 'Twas Sunday, our day off, and we spent most of it sitting cuddled close together, not saying much of anything. Holding hands, our thumbs met and caressed as we looked into the thicket, searching for hope.

"I love you," I whispered. "I'll always love you, even if—"

Jonah cut me off with a kiss, slow and warm. I pressed into it, exploring the spark between us.

We sat together all day and into the night, forgetting to eat, shifting when the ground under us felt uncomfortable. I told him about the time I was nearly free, about how I ran away but headed south instead of north.

"You're a brave one, Mercy. Loyal and brave."

"I certainly didn't feel like I had a lick of courage at all, as frightened as I was."

"And yet you did it. Struck out. Found your mama. I'm so proud of you."

I curled into his praises.

"You could do it again. If they sell you. You could run and find me, and we could head north together."

I shuddered. "It's so dangerous, Jonah. I don't know if I have it in me to do that a second time."

"But maybe you could. Maybe we could both fight to be together."

"We're spinning a web of dreams now, ain't we?" A faint smile tugged at my lips, then fell away.

He sighed into the night. "I supposed we is."

"They're good dreams, though."

We played a game of "what if" then, thinking up different scenarios of what life might be like if we was free in the North. If we dropped the cloak of slavery and danced a dance of freedom. I yawned and stretched against him, burying my head in his chest.

"We best be getting you home." Jonah propped me up. He stood and reached for my hand. I let him pull me to standing, then fell into his arms. He kissed my hair until I tilted my head up, my mouth meeting his. Sweet and slow. Then, he picked me up and carried me.

Before we got to the cabin, he set me down. My mind felt hazy, and it took me a minute to gather my bearings and see where we were, why he had stopped.

We stood on the path next to the slave graveyard. Jonah stared straight ahead. My eyes followed his gaze and settled on the lilies throughout the yard. A few markers stood, announcing the names of more prominent slaves who were laid to rest here, but mostly, the lilies told the story.

The lilies remembered.

When a slave died, we buried him here and planted lilies over the spot. Each year the ground sprouted at the remembrance of that soul. The soft rumble of the river sang its melody. Why were we here? Where did Jonah's thoughts carry him?

How different graveyards could be. At the church, the white graves stood with beautiful etchings, but only one colored gravestone with a date of bith. A luxury. An honor. I tottered the line between those two worlds. How would my life be marked?

Finally, Jonah's voice pierced the silence. "My grandmother is buried right there." He pointed to the far right. "She came straight from Africa. From Gambia. Tricked onto a ship that brought her to Charleston, then to here. She didn't want to learn English, hardly spoke a lick of it. I didn't know her language, but I understood her, you know?" Jonah's eyes met mine and held on for a moment, earnestness in his gaze.

I nodded.

"She loved this graveyard. Said it was the only place our people were truly free in America. She told me to bury her by the river because the river would carry her sould back to Africa.

"She lived with an awareness that this was not home. She was a stranger in a strange land. I never understood that. Never longed for a home country as she did." He dug his big toe into the dirt. "As far as I was concerned, this be my home, and I best be making the most out of it that I can. I've worked hard to make a life here, to abide by their rules, work my way up, gain the favor of the master." He snatched his hat off and slapped it across his knee. "But what does it matter? It all can be snatched away in a minute, can't it?"

What could I say? I remained silent, a melancholy washing over me at the freedom represented by the grave.

He tucked his hat back on his head and cast me a glance. "If you go—and I pray to God that you won't—but if you do, I'm gonna plant a lily right here." He pointed to a place front and center. "So, this land will remember you, now and forever."

"Can you do that?" I couldn't stop the question from leaking out. Would that be disrespectful to the dead to have a lily mark the living?

"Who's gonna stop me?" He squared his shoulders. "Sure, I can do it, and I will. Then I'll come here and look at that lily and remember my Mercy Girl."

"But you won't have to. 'Cause we're gonna fix this. We'll fix it." My voice came out strong and forceful, far more confident than reality. "No need for lilies."

Jonah scooped me up in his arms again and carried me back to my cabin where Mama sat waiting for me.

"Where you been, Mercy?" She rose out of the chair.

"Oh, Mama." Jonah set me down, and I wrapped Mama in my arms. Somehow I hadn't included her in our web of freedom dreams. But Mama couldn't make the trek north, as feeble as she was. How could I ever leave her behind?

"What is it? What is it, Mercy?" Mama patted my head, her voice oozing concern.

Jonah spoke first. "We is wanting to get married, but when Mercy asked the missus about it, she said they'se selling both of you."

Mama gasped, and my chest tightened.

"Don't worry none, Miss. Mercy and me, we gots a plan to change the master's and missus's minds. Don't fret."

But by Mama's shaky breath, frettin' was exactly what she was doing.

* * *

November 9th, 1842

After Eli set off with my letter in his pocket, I prayed the whole day. I pleaded with the Almighty for Susan to respond with sympathy and the boldness to do something about it. The missus had me do their washing, and I worked extra hard on them clothes, in efforts to prove myself to be a slave worth keeping.

When Eli returned that evening, I rushed out to the wagon.

"You got a letter for me?" I pleaded.

"Afraid not." Eli's mouth dipped in a frown.

"She didn't write anything in reply?"

"Nope. Sorry, Mercy."

Tears pooled in my eyes again. What was going on in Susan's pretty little head? Did my plight move her? Perhaps I'd offended her by leaving so abruptly the last time. Maybe I had angered her. Or maybe she felt bad at the thought of the Millers selling me but didn't have the gumption to do anything about it. She had cowed to her husband, telling me to fan her when he walked in. That last scenario made sense. "Sorry, Mercy, but there's nothing I can do," she'd say.

Jonah had to work on the chapel after he finished in the swamps. He wouldn't have time to come see me, so I ambled over to the dirt rectangle to see him myself. Champ stood there watching on, arms crossed, whip in his hand. I couldn't rightly barge in and talk to him, but he did manage to meet my eye, and I shook my head no. His brow furrowed, but he mouthed, *It's okay*, to me. He would keep up hope that things could change until the very end.

I sat down in the grass and watched him work. His muscles bulged and flexed with the lifting. I memorized the sight of him so that if I was sold, I could keep him with me forever.

He heaved beam after beam as if they were but twigs. While others hemmed and hawed, not taking a step without Champ barking a command, Jonah worked without waiting for an order. He spoke gently to the other men, giving friendly slaps on the back and patient instruction. He seemed like the big brother to all of them, even the ones that were older than he. My heart burned at the thought of leaving this man.

Finally, I needed to get back home to Mama, see how she fared. She'd been quiet since Jonah had told her what we knew. I raised myself and tried to meet Jonah's eye. He wasn't looking my way, intent on framing the chapel. I blew a kiss in his direction anyway and walked toward the cabin.

I found her sitting in the wooden chair, darkness wrapping itself around her. Winny and her family were nowhere to be seen.

"Mama? Why you sitting here in the dark?" I lit a candle. She said not a word.

The flicker of the candlelight licked her face, exposing wrinkles deeper than they seemed the day before. As if she'd aged right before my eyes.

"Mama?" I put my hand on her knee. She didn't move.

"Mama, Susan didn't write back yet, but I'm sure she'll get word to me soon. Jonah hasn't had the chance to talk to Master and Missus yet, I'm sure. But he will. They'll listen. They have to."

Mama blinked. Swallowed.

"Everything's going to be okay," I offered, bluffing confidence. "Do you need supper?"

Still no answer.

I set to making ash cakes, pork, and greens. I hummed Mama's favorite hymns as I worked. Maybe they'd breathe life into her, but each time I glanced in her direction, she sat motionless. Perhaps this was her strategy. If she proved herself useless—mad even—the missus wouldn't be able to fetch a good price for her, making selling her next to useless. It might work but could cause the misses to sell her off quick if she gathered she'd have no further use for her.

"I'm sure we'll hear from Susan soon." I set the food on the table and told Mama that dinner was ready. "Come on, Mama. Eat."

"I'm not hungry." Her voice cracked from lack of use.

At least she was speaking. I smiled despite myself. "Try." I stepped over to her and put my arm around her shoulder. "Try to eat a little, for me. Okay?"

Mama sighed and raised herself up, leaning on my shoulder, her steps toward the table stiff. But she sat down and forked a few bites into her mouth before pushing her plate away.

"Okay, Mama. Time for bed." I reached down to help her up and lead her to bed. She lay down, and I tucked the quilt around her nice and tight. As I began to step away, I heard her soft voice speak.

"I've lived a long, hard life. I only wanted better for you, Mercy. I wanted more for you than what the Good Lord handed me."

I knelt beside her bed, putting my palm on her cheek. "I know, Mama. And I love you for it."

"Run away, Mercy. Now. While you can." She propped herself up on her elbow, eyes searching mine.

"I can't leave you. I won't leave you."

"Leave me, Mercy. Leave me be. Let me live and die knowing you found your freedom."

I shook my head, tears trailing down my cheeks. "I can't, Mama. I tried before, and I couldn't do it. I need you. We live and die together."

Mama's face shone wet with tears, and I brushed my thumb across her cheek, smoothing some away only to have them be replaced a moment later by others. I clutched her hand.

"How'd you go and get so stubborn?" Mama let out a humorless chuckle.

"It's in my blood like it's in yours." I offered a small smile as an olive branch.

She squeezed my hand, and I whispered again, "We live and die together."

23

───────

Natassa writhed in her sleep, flinching as he turned toward her, his eyes glowing with rage, his glare slicing through her. "It's your fault. It's your fault, Natassa Bloomington." She stood paralyzed as he reached behind and pulled out a gun, aiming straight for her chest. She screamed as the sound of the bullet shot through the night.

"Babe? You okay? Wake up, honey. It's okay; I'm here." Brandon's arms wrapped around her, stabilizing her. Grounding her.

Her eyes snapped open, and she searched his face in the dimness. She reached out and touched his solid arms. Real. This was real.

"Another nightmare?" He rubbed her arm.

She nodded. The gentleness of his touch counteracted the rapid thumping of her heart. Gradually, her breathing slowed. She pressed her face into his chest, absorbing more of his strength. Needing to find peace there. Somewhere.

She started to sob then, and Brandon's T-shirt dampened with her tears. The nightmares weren't real, but one thing stood true.

It was her fault.

Brandon kissed the top of her head. His warm kindness soothed her, and yet it stung.

Because she didn't deserve it.

"I'm sorry. I'm so sorry!" Her shoulders shook.

"Sweetheart, we've been over this. It wasn't your fault. None of this is your fault."

If only his words would wash away the guilt, clear her conscience. But the truth stood blatantly in front of her. Piercing. If she would have left when Brett told her to, he would still be alive.

She grabbed onto his shirt, grasping for emotional footing as her body racked with sobs. What had she stolen from the man next to her? His only surviving kin. His brother. His best friend. How could he stand to be close to her?

"I don't blame you," he whispered against her hair.

He said that now, but what about after he had time to process? After the grief lifted enough to see the facts in front of him. What then?

* * *

Natassa sat numbly on the couch, staring into space. Her hands fiddled with the crocheted blanket draped over her, finding the holes, twisting the threads around them. The sound of her ringing phone came from somewhere in the house. She didn't move. It was probably her mother.

Though her mother had brought several casseroles by the house, they came with a price. A subtle shake of the head and a tsking sound. Or a question that dripped with accusation. *Why did you insist on going down to the city and praying with those people?*

Brandon entered the living room, her phone in his hand. "It's Bethany."

She waved him away. She didn't want to talk to anybody.

"Honey, talk to her. You've got to talk to her. Please?" He looked as if he had aged ten years in the past two weeks. The stubble on his chin seemed more gray than brown. The lines around his eyes spoke of sleepless nights, and his own struggle that he kept locked away.

He handed her the phone, and she took it, staring at it for a minute before bringing it to her ear.

"Hi, Bethany." Her voice cracked.

"Sugar, how you doing, baby? We all been worrying about you." Bethany's voice was a soft cushion to her soul, and she leaned into it.

"I'm okay," she lied, wiping away a stray tear.

"Natassa, we's so sorry you're hurting so bad."

Natassa nodded as tears began streaming down her face.

"But baby girl, in times like these, you've got to press into your people, not run away from them. We all need community in times of tragedy. Please don't push us away."

She didn't mean to. "It's not so much you. It's more the location." She sniffed. "I can't go down there anymore. Not right now. That street … It hurts too much." She put her fist to her mouth, trying to keep the pain in. Once she let it out, it would run rampant. Trample her. Hijack everything.

"Then let us come to you."

And they did. That night, members of St. Anthony's Baptist Church flooded into their home, laden with casseroles and condolences. Bethany brought Old Ezra. Mazy came with Grace. Nearly every member of the prayer group perched in Natassa's living room. Their presence warmed her, drawing out words. Memories of Brett. Admiration of the type of man he was, the life he'd lived.

Only she didn't speak of her guilt, of her part in the snuffing out of his flame.

She let them hug her, hold her hand, push close. She glanced at Brandon, the line of his mouth stiff. He stood on the outskirts of the throng, nodding politely, shaking a hand when offered.

He kept so much locked inside, hidden right below the boundaries of propriety. She'd walked by their bedroom to hear him weeping once. She had put her hand on the door, yearning for her grief to melt into his. In the end, she continued down the hallway. He needed his space, and he kept his tears aloof from hers. To her, he stood as her rock. She loved him for it, but fear crept around the outer edges. How long before he crumbled?

* * *

Natassa sat on Brett and Laura's bed. Only it wasn't Brett's bed anymore. She looked at the end tables on both sides of the bed. Tissues were strewn all over one. The other had a stack of books with reading glasses on top. She squinted to see the titles on the spines. She could only make out *How to Win Friends and Influence People*. She closed her eyes and breathed deeply. She had to be strong for Laura.

Laura stood in front of the closet with her face buried in one of Brett's dress shirts. She inhaled the scent of her husband and rubbed its softness across her cheek.

"He loved this shirt. I bought it for him last Christmas." She clutched the bright blue shirt to her chest as if grasping for the man that was no longer inside of it. "It brought out the color of his eyes." Laura's voice broke, and she crumpled onto the floor. In a flash, Natassa kneeled next to her, wrapping her arms around her sister-in-law and rocking her softly.

"If it's too much, we can do this later." Natassa smoothed Laura's hair from her face.

"No. No. I need this, to walk through the valley of the shadow of death." Laura leaned into her, and Natassa sat up straight and strong, steeling herself to be a wall of stability.

"It's just … I don't want to be here. I don't want to walk around alone in this house that we shared. Is that bad? Is that like abandoning him?"

"No."

"It's like he's everywhere, but nowhere. Sometimes, I think I hear the creak of his footsteps as he creeps in after a late shift, not wanting to wake me. I made him coffee this morning." Her gaze flitted to the ceiling. "Out of habit. Then, I stared at the mug as if it had fangs. I want to get away, start someplace new. I think I should sell the house."

Warning bells blared in Natassa's brain as she remembered her counselor admonishing her not to make any rash or permanent decisions while she waded through grief.

"Don't sell it. Not yet. Take some time to make sure that's really what you want. The thing that haunts you now might comfort you later."

"I don't want to be alone." Laura's body shook as another wave of tears sprung forth.

Natassa bit her lip as an idea hit. If she moved Hope into Faith's room, it might work. "Stay with us."

Laura sat up, searching her face. "What?"

"Stay with us. I mean, I have to run it by Brandon, but I'm sure he'll agree."

Laura shook her head. "You don't have the room."

"Are you kidding me? We have tons of room. I'll move the girls in together. They'll be thrilled. It'll be like a perpetual slumber party." *Hopefully.*

"But I'm going to have a baby." Laura's hand cradled her stomach.

"It's only temporary. Until you figure out what to do with the house."

Laura nodded. "Okay."

"Okay," Natassa echoed. Could it be true? Would everything be okay now?

* * *

When Brandon finally broke at the funeral, a wave of relief washed over Natassa. Then, guilt followed. But wondering when it would hit, when he would crumble, was like watching heavy storm clouds overhead and hearing the thunder but not the release of rain. He couldn't carry the weight of grief inside forever without a torrent drenching the parched ground around him. It just so happened that the downpour came publicly.

Several newspapers covered the story and reporters stood outside the church. Cameras rolled as mourners filed out of the service, then piled into their cars, steeling themselves to see Brett's coffin lowered into the ground.

Brandon emerged into the piercing sunlight with red-rimmed eyes, his suit crumpled from doubling over in gut-wrenching sobs during the service. The pastor had to speak over his wailing, his fist pressed up against his mouth doing little to conceal his grief.

Natassa had rubbed his back, ignoring the looks of pity tossed their way. Ignoring her mother's glare at the lack of decorum. She fixed her gaze on the pastor and silently prayed as her husband unleashed what he'd bottled up inside since the moment he heard of his brother's death. She barely noticed the tears streaming down her own face.

This time, Brandon made the front page of the local paper.

24

November 13th, 1842, Georgetown, South Carolina

Four days passed, and I didn't hear nary a word from Susan. My palms began to sweat all regular. I teetered in this state of in-between. Not yet sold. Not yet safe. My body didn't fight sleeping no more. It welcomed it, just to ease the tension. Dreamless, I floated between two worlds, here and there.

Mama sat lifeless most of the time, save when I persuaded her to take a few bites of supper. She should keep working, proving herself useful to the master and missus. But hope had flitted away from her, and she didn't see the point. How could I blame her?

On the fifth day, Winny came barging into the cabin as I made candles for the Big House.

"Mercy, the missus wants you." She put her hand on her chest, catching her breath.

My mouth went dry. Was this it? Was I being sold today? Not yet, right? They said they weren't going to sell me until after Christmas.

"Just me?" I asked. "What about Mama?"

Winny's forehead puckered. "She didn't say a word about your mama. Just you."

I dropped the candle mold with a clank and rushed out the door. It had to be word from Susan. Had to be. Missus wouldn't sell me without Mama. She said so herself.

I ran all the way to the Big House, heart pounding, my soft-as-a-feather shoes pummeling up dust with each step. I came up upon the Big House and bounded up the steps, knocking on the door. Flora answered.

"Mercy, come in. The missus is expecting you in the parlor."

I followed Flora to where the missus reclined on the settee. I forced my breathing to slow. I bowed my head and curtsied.

"You wanted to see me, ma'am?"

"Oh yes." She reached to the table next to her and picked up a letter. "It seems that Mr. and Mrs. Renald from town were quite taken with you. She said you mentioned you play the violin, and they would like you to play for a party they are hosting tomorrow evening."

"Yes, ma'am." My accompanying nods were far too eager. A smile leaked onto my face. I reigned my excitement in and gave another curtsy.

"Very well. Be ready to depart with Eli after breakfast. She wants you to have time to settle in and help prepare for the party as well." The missus laid the letter back down and picked up her tea, a signal that our conversation was through.

I bowed, and turned to leave, forcing my feet to walk instead of race as they desired to. Once I closed the front door behind me, though, I bolted toward home.

"Mama! Mama!" I burst through the door to the cabin. "It's Susan! She must have a solution. She must. She's requested me to play for a party tomorrow." Mama sat in her chair by the window, and I knelt before her and took her hands in mine. "She wants to talk to me. I know she does. She has something to say, something so important that she couldn't write it in a letter. She's gonna help us, Mama."

Mama's eyes lit up. A small spark but something of hope, nonetheless.

"We're gonna be okay." I looked deep into her eyes.

"We're gonna be okay," Mama echoed.

"Yes." I twirled around the room, then turned to see Mama rising out of her chair.

"What are you doing?"

"We're gonna be okay." The spark brighter now, color returned to her cheeks. "I best get to stitchin'." She walked over to the basket of clothes in need of mending and picked up a dress. "Now where did I put my thread?"

I grabbed the spool from the table. "It's right here, Mama."

My smile spread so wide my cheeks began to ache. I pressed the palms of my hands on them. My whole body was filled with life. "I have to tell Jonah!"

I bounded to the cabin door and threw it open.

Mama called out. "Child, Jonah's in the swamps now. Just you wait."

"I can't wait." I hollered back, banging the door closed behind me. When I reached the bottom of the steps, I stared down at my shoes. I couldn't wear them down there. The mud would ruin them. I slipped them off and dashed back up the stairs, tossing them in the cabin. "Bye."

I took off then, jogging at first, then running full out, then slowing to catch my breath after I passed the second field. I put my hand on my side, pressing against the stitch of pain from the exertion.

I passed Big Bear Field, then Great Hawk Field. The bottoms of my feet that had scratched against the parched dirt at the first field now sank in the softness of the ground, and a squelch of mud rose each time I heaved my foot away. I heard the men before I caught a good sight of them. Heard their voices singing, low and rich:

> I know moon-rise, I know star-rise,
>> Lay dis body down.
> I walk in de moonlight, I walk in de starlight,
>> To lay dis body down.
> I'll walk in de graveyard, I'll walk through de
>> graveyard,
>> To lay dis body down.
>> I'll lie in de grave and stretch out my arms;
>> Lay dis body down.
> I'll go to de judgment in de evenin' of de day,
>> When I lay dis body down;
> And my soul and your soul will meet in de day
>> When I lay dis body down.

Finally, I came to the border of the farthest field and approached a line of downed trees ready for chopping. Cypress still stood proud and tall at the farthest edges, but men worked in twos with saws pulling and pushing, working to bring them low. I spotted Jonah to my far right and trudged toward him, my feet sinking deeper into the mud and murk with each step. It reached halfway to my knees before I reached him.

"Jonah!" I shouted above the grind of saws and songs.

His head snapped in my direction. "Mercy, what are you doing here?" His face transitioned from shock to sheer pleasure, then to concern. "What's wrong?" He turned from his work and faced me, though his eyes roamed all around me before they settled on my face.

"Nothing." A giggle escaped me, and his eyes flickered in confusion.

"Then why you here? Champ is gonna run you right out as soon as he spots you."

"I had to tell you. Just had to. Susan called for me. I go to her tomorrow. She wrote the missus a letter asking me to play the fiddle for her party, but it's an excuse to speak with me. I know it. I'm gonna be safe, Jonah."

His smile dawned. "Well, I'll be. I told you, didn't I? I told you everything would be alright."

"Yes, you did."

"You better run now 'fore you get a lash. I'll try and come by and see you tonight."

"I'll be waiting." I blew a kiss in his direction and then turned and squelched my way back to firmer ground.

When I got back to the cabin, Mama sat humming to herself, stitching up a storm as if she'd been doing so all week. I finished making the candles, then sat down to help her mend. After supper, I sauntered out to the porch and sat in Mama's chair, waiting for Jonah.

Night sounds surrounded me as darkness fell. Crickets and screech owls. Laughter in the distance. The crackle of a fire in the hearth. A deep sigh escaped me as I released the tension that I'd been holding onto the past four days. Mama was back to normal. Susan would help us. We'd be fine. I'd marry Jonah as soon as they finished the chapel.

I must have nodded off because I awoke with a start to Jonah kissing my forehead.

"Hi, Mercy Girl."

I smiled, rousing. Shifting my weight in the chair, I rolled my stiff neck back and forth.

"It's late. Just wanted to say hi and goodbye as I won't be seeing you tomorrow, I reckon."

"Hello," I whispered. "Goodbye." My eyelids refused to open fully.

"Here. I'll put you to bed." He reached down and lifted me, cradling me like a child. He creaked open the door and padded over to me and Mama's bed, laying me down next to Mama as soft as a whisper. He tucked the quilt around me, then bent to kiss my forehead again. "Sweet dreams, sweet Mercy."

"Goodnight." I yawned and listened for the soft click of the door before succumbing to deep sleep.

* * *

November 18th, 1842

When Eli drove the carriage up to Susan's house, she stood on her porch, hands clasped together in front of her.

"Mercy, how nice to see you again." Politeness wrapped around her voice. "Thank you, Eli, for bringing her to us. You can pick her up tomorrow morning."

"Yes'm." Eli nodded and left.

"Do come inside." Susan gestured toward her front door and then stepped into the foyer. I followed. As soon as she shut the door behind us, she turned and grasped my hands, squeezing tight. "Oh, Mercy, I couldn't believe it when I got your letter. Sold? How could they sell you? It's too awful."

"I know." I spoke all slow and cautious-like. "I hoped you could help us. Persuade Master and Missus not to do it."

"Oh, I've done better than that. But let's slow down. Come here and sit." She lowered herself onto the settee and patted the spot next to her.

Better than that? What could she mean? I sat down, awkward and stiff, yet hopeful.

"Sam works until shortly before the party begins, so we have some time to talk together. You wouldn't believe the lengths I went to in order to get you here. I had to fabricate a reason that would avoid Sam's suspicions. He adores parties but hadn't hosted one yet. Oh, the work that goes into these things, and at such short notice."

"Thank you." I nodded for her to go on.

"At any rate, when he comes … well, you know what you must do. Fall into the role of a slave. Assist with setting up and serving the guests until it's time to play."

"Yes …" Did I need to add a *ma'am*? Surely not. Not until Sam arrived at least.

"So, I asked around and found out more about the slave trader that's been in town. You told me he promised not to sell you farther south, but that's not what I heard, Mercy." She brought her hand to her mouth. "He's headed to New Orleans with a whole lot of slaves. I'm sure he intends to sell you there too, to toil in a sugar plantation."

"New Orleans?" My voice sounded small, choked. Why was she telling me this?

"I couldn't bear the thought of you down there, Mercy. Couldn't stand it. So, I started pressing Sam about how we need another slave. It took a lot of convincing, but he came around. I'm with child you see. Isn't that wonderful?"

I forced a nod, my mind swirling and trying to make sense of her words.

"I'll need someone to help care for the baby. At least that's what I convinced Sam that I need. He said we should wait until the baby comes, but I told him that I was quite taken with you and how you served us when you were here last. I told him that you're about to be sold and asked if we could purchase you instead."

"Me?" My mind felt fuzzy.

"Yes, you. Sam agreed, Mercy. He agreed that we can purchase you."

"Purchase me?" I mumbled, reeling at the possibility.

"Think of it! You could work for us here, only it wouldn't be much work unless Sam is home. He has different views of slavery, you know, and he'll expect you to be dutiful and productive. But when it's just you and me, Oh, Mercy, it'll be delightful!" She clasped her hands together, her eyes dancing.

"Purchase me?" I repeated.

"I'll be good to you. We'll be good to you, I promise. You won't have to labor in the fields anymore. You'll get good food, be taken care of. I remember you telling me of baby Elizabeth and how fond you were of her. You'll get to help care for a baby again."

Susan beamed, and I stared. Blinked. Live here? Leave the fields? Care for a baby?

"And Jonah. Think of your beau, Jonah. You two can marry, and he can visit you on weekends, or you can visit him. I think your love story with him is as precious as can be. You can keep penning that story."

"Jonah," I whispered, filled with longing for the man. It wasn't the life we had pictured, but it was a life together. I smiled at Susan, and a laugh escaped her lips.

"It will be splendid." She grasped my hand in hers again, and I stared at our hands together. The subtle difference in our skin allowed her to purchase me, to direct my fate.

"It sounds splendid …" But then, my smile faded, and I bit my lip. "But what about Mama?"

Susan frowned, and a sick feeling crept up in my stomach.

"Surely you understand. There's no way I could convince Sam to purchase two slaves, even if your mother is significantly less costly than you." Her forehead puckered. "We simply haven't the need, or the extra funds right now, to justify purchasing two slaves. It took much persuasion to convince him to purchase one. Surely you understand."

"You want me to stay here while Mama is dragged to New Orleans?" My voice shook, and I removed my hands from hers, readying them to swipe at the tears that were already pooling in my eyes.

"I'm sorry, Mercy. Truly, I am. But think of it this way, your mother will be taken to New Orleans no matter what. You can't change that. Missus Miller is set in her decision to sell you both. There's no convincing her otherwise. You can't save your mother, but you can save yourself."

We live and die together.

My own words echoed in my mind.

Mama, despondent at the thought of being sold. Mama, back to humming and stitching at the prospect of remaining with the Millers. What would she do if she was taken away? She would die, of course. Her broken heart would break her body. She would fade away into nothing. I couldn't let her do that while I lived easy and comfortable with Susan.

We live and die together.

"Please," I whispered, tears freely flowing. "Buy Mama."

Susan's frown dipped low, and her eyes welled with regret. "I told you, I can't. Sam won't hear of it. We cannot justify purchasing two slaves. I'm sorry. I'm so sorry."

I shook my head. "No, buy Mama instead of me."

Susan sat back with a tiny gasp. "Instead of you? And allow you to get sold to New Orleans?"

I nodded. "Please." It came out a desperate whisper. I reached out and grasped her hand, meeting my eyes with hers, pleading with my gaze.

"Mercy, I couldn't. Oh no. I couldn't watch you get shipped off …"

"Take care of Mama. Take good care of her and treat her well, and she'll be good to you too. She'll be strong here. Let me do this for her, please." I squeezed Susan's hand, applying gentle pressure. I needed her to agree. I couldn't conceive of any other option.

We live and die together.

But if we were together, Mama would die. And I couldn't live with that.

"Okay," Susan eked out, breaking my hold to wipe her eyes with a handkerchief. "I'll talk to Sam about it. If he agrees …" She took a shuddering breath.

"Thank you. I won't forget this. Not ever."

"But what will you do?"

"I'll survive." I gulped in a breath. "And I'll write. I'll find a way to get word to you."

We heard a commotion outside, and Susan rose and glanced out the window.

"It's Sam. He's home. Just speaking with a neighbor, and then he'll come in. Oh my." She waved her hands in front of her face. "We both look a fright. I need to freshen up. Go back to the kitchen, will you? Help Phoebe with whatever she needs?"

I nodded, taking note of the question in her voice. She didn't feel comfortable commanding my service. Hopefully, she would be the same with Mama. Kind requests. Gentle inflections.

"Thank you." I rushed off to the kitchen.

That night, I lost myself in the playing of the fiddle. Simply leaned into it and disappeared. As couples danced around me, I closed my eyes and faded into memories and dreams, forgetting where I was and what was on the horizon. It was the best I'd ever played.

I slept on a pallet in Susan's attic that night with a warm quilt over me. I was full of good food—all the leftovers from the feast Phoebe had prepared. I was warm and safe. I grasped the comfort and held on since it wouldn't be mine for long. But Mama would have it, and that settled a dose of peace deep inside me.

I was doing the right thing, the only thing I could live with. That didn't dispel the fear.

* * *

When Eli jostled back onto Hopecrest the next morning, Jonah stood right there, waiting. His eyes flittered from eager expectation, to worry, to trepidation. I tossed him a sad smile. Eli slowed, and Jonah hopped on board, settling himself close to me. Our legs touched, sending a warmth rushing over me that brought tears to the back of my eyes.

"What happened? Did Susan talk to the Millers? Did she change their mind?"

I looked up at the tall oaks lining both sides of the path. "See the resurrection fern, Jonah?" The fern covering the branches of the oaks looked brittle and lifeless. "It looks like it's dead, like there's no hope for it. But all it takes is a good rain, and that fern will come roaring back to life, full and beautiful as ever."

"Mercy, what are you saying? You ain't making sense." He put his hands on my shoulders, giving me a gentle shake.

"Susan couldn't convince the Millers to keep me, Jonah." I peered into his eyes, seeing them fill with tears before I could even finish. "But she did agree to buy Mama."

"Buy your mama?" His voice cracked, and he shook his head.

"I'm being sold down in New Orleans. I don't know what will become of me. The fern looks to be dead, as near as me. Plumb dead and shriveled up like there's not a hope in the world. But somehow, some way, the rain will come, and it'll spring to life again."

Jonah wrapped his arms around me then, clinging to me. "No, Mercy Girl. I can't let you go."

His enclosing arms filled up the parts in me that were empty. I stood safe. Loved. Wanted. Everything I wrote about when I was still a girl.

Being wanted is a powerful thing. It's all I wanted alls my life.

How fortunate I was to have a man loving me, wanting to keep me near. How it broke my heart to tell him the whole story, that I had a chance to be his but turned it down. His body shook with sobs as I relayed my conversation with Susan.

"I'm sorry, Jonah. I love you. I do. But I can't let Mama be sent off to New Orleans when I have the power to stop it. I can't."

"I know." He swiped his fists over his eyes. "If you could, you wouldn't be the Mercy I've come to know and love."

Eli stopped the wagon, and Jonah jumped off, offering his hand to help me down. We meandered hand in hand to the cabin, not saying much of anything for a while.

Finally, I broke the silence. "Don't be afraid to marry, Jonah. You got your whole life ahead of you, and you best not stop living it on my account."

"I couldn't—"

I put my hand to his mouth to stop his nonsense words. "You must."

"But I love you."

"I know. And I love you. Go ahead and plant that lily, but then take a wife. I won't be responsible for you being all pathetic and miserable your whole life." I managed a smile.

He returned it, snatching my hand and bringing it to his lips for a feather-light kiss.

When we neared the cabin, I gripped his hand hard. Mama sat on the porch, stitching. What if I broke Mama's spirit while trying to save her? The creek of a twig told on us. Her head snapped up, and she stood.

"Mercy? Come here, child. Tell me what's going on."

I bounded up the steps and wrapped her in a hug, tight and long. If I pulled away, I might lose her forever. "Oh, Mama."

She stilled, her fear so real and solid I could almost taste it.

"You're safe, Mama. Susan is going to purchase you. She'll treat you well, and you can take care of her baby. You'll have plenty to eat, and your eyes won't ache from stitching all day. You'll be warm and safe."

"Susan's buying us?" She tilted her head, and I read her confusion.

"You, Mama. She's buying you. I'm being sold … elsewhere." I couldn't bear to tell her where.

"Oh no! Mercy. No!" Mama shook her head, plopping down so hard in her chair it screeched underneath her.

"Yes, Mama. It's okay." I patted her hand. "I'm going to be okay. I'll be okay knowing you are taken care of."

"You should have run north when you had the chance." Her voice came out as a harsh whisper, stinging like an accusation.

"Mama." I bent in front of her, my eyes searching for hers until they met. "I wouldn't have traded these past few years with you for a lifetime of freedom without you."

She huffed, and I took her hands in my own.

"I chose you then, and I'm choosing you now."

Her eyes fell from defiance into a pool of sorrow. She understood what I meant, what I had done, and why I did it.

"What'd I ever do to deserve you?" She reached out and patted my damp cheek.

"Everybody needs a little bit of Mercy." The whisper of a smile graced my face.

* * *

January 1st, 1843

Before I left, I had one last Christmas with Mama and Jonah. Missus Miller hadn't even planned on telling me they were selling me until Christmas had passed. Perhaps it would have been better that way. How could I rightly enjoy the festivities around me, knowing it would all be ripped away?

Each Christmas, we got three days off. Master and Missus butchered a cow so we could feast on beef. Our rations were special at Christmas too. We got a half bushel of rice, ten pounds of beef, and a pint of molasses. The men got tobacco.

The missus gave Mama and me the holiday rations the same as anyone else like they was pretending nothing was unusual at all. Like we was supposed to go along and act like it was just another Christmas and not our last one together.

For our present, Missus gave each of us four or five yards of homespun cloth to make our own clothes with. It had been a year since I'd sown the light blue dress I wore when I first kissed Jonah. Now, I had beautiful white and red checkered fabric to make a new dress out of. A new dress for a new life? A life I did not ask for. I dropped my fabric into Mama's hands.

"You can make yourself an extra. I don't want it."

"Don't you start that, Mercy. You don't know what they'll be giving you down there and what you'll be needing."

"This last year was perfect in my perfect blue dress. I'll be keeping this one."

Mama chuckled low. "Perfect?" Her eyebrow lifted toward the sky.

I dipped my head. She'd collapsed in the heat, and I'd spent most of the year complaining about fieldwork.

I picked up a pine cone and started fiddling with it, snapping off pieces until it looked less than perfect. Until I could see holes.

I sighed. "I guess love covers up a lot of imperfections."

Mama patted my cheek, and I tilted my head into her palm. "Make yourself a new dress and wear it with your head held high. Remember who you are, Mercy."

Jonah didn't drink a lick of whiskey those whole three days. While the other men stumbled around, singing and laughing, he stayed by my side. Said he didn't want liquor to make him forget a moment with me.

We didn't talk much, didn't spin webs of dreams. What use were they to us now? We clung to each other. His hand stroked my arm, keeping me warm as the sun set and the coolness nipped at us all. I laid my head on his shoulder. The whole world seemed less weight to bear when I had someone to share it with. My last Christmas was one for sitting and then listening as Jonah began to sing:

> Dark was the night, and cool the ground
> On which the Lord was laid;
> His sweat, like drops of blood ran down;
> In agony he prayed.

Jonah called on the Millers and begged them not to send me away. When that didn't work, he begged them to sell him right along with me, to sell us together. The Millers were appalled at that suggestion. His position as a trunk minder made him far too valuable to them to up and sell. He pleaded with tears for any possible way to keep us together, but the more he cried, the more resolute they became.

His tears ripped at my insides. I shall always love him.

When I pulled away from Hopecrest for good, I sat huddled in the back of the wagon. Jonah followed on foot with big fat tears sloshing in the dirt. He followed until he couldn't keep up anymore. I could still hear him wailing even after we turned the corner, and I couldn't see him any longer.

We're in town now at the Millers' house, and sometimes the echo of his wailing is still with me. My mind keeps playing those tricks on me. I have one more night here. In the morning, I will be sold to the trader and taken off toward New Orleans in a big boat stuffed full of other slaves.

I can't take this journal with me. It's too risky. I would be caught before reaching the shore. What would they do to me if they discover I can not only read but also write? I shudder to think of it. So, in the morning, I will hand this journal off to Susan for safekeeping. She promised to see me before I go. And once again, I will say goodbye to all I love and head off to the unknown.

Whether or not Mama and Jonah agree with my choice, they respect it. And this is the source of my strength, at least now: it's my choice.

25

"Why are you doing this?" The concern in Breanna's voice bled through the phone. And was that warning in her tone?

Natassa pushed past it.

"I don't know. Curiosity, I guess." Natassa merged onto the highway, holding the phone to her ear with her shoulder.

"I don't think it's a good idea."

"Probably not," Natassa admitted. "But if I don't go, I'll always wonder what he wanted to say, why he asked me to come."

"Look, I get last time. You needed answers. But now you have them. All the answers, all the puzzle pieces. If I were you, I would stay away." Breanna was likely folding her arms, confident in her verdict.

"Well, you're not me."

Breanna sighed, loud and dramatic. "Point taken. Call me when you're done. Please?"

"Will do."

When Janell called her to say DeAndre requested to see her, Natassa's initial reaction mirrored Breanna's. But soon, curiosity gnawed at her.

What could he possibly want? Another burger? She scoffed to herself. His buddy—the one he had tried to convince her was a good man just trying to make his life right—killed her brother-in-law. And planned her assault. He should stay locked up for life.

A half hour later, Natassa sat across from DeAndre, arms folded tightly around herself. She hardened her resolve. She wouldn't soften at the weariness in his eyes.

"Thank you for coming." His shoulders sagged.

She said nothing, merely stared straight at him.

"I heard about your brother-in-law, and I wanted to say that I am so sorry." His voice wavered, and he coughed to cover it up.

She shifted in her seat. "Is that all?"

DeAndre sat back, looking as if he'd been slapped. But then, he leaned forward again, hands out as if pleading. "If I had it all to do over again, I would have turned Reg in. Right away. Then this wouldn't have happened."

She flinched. He was right. In his desire to protect his friend, he had created another victim. He'd traded one life for another, a decent man full of integrity for a hardened criminal. A wave of nausea rose as did the desire to bolt.

She scooted her chair back. "Is that it, then?" Her voice sounded hard in her ears. Bitter.

"No. Don't go, please." He inched forward more. If only she could push him back. Away. "Reg is an idiot. He always has been. Loyal, yeah, but a fool. He deserves whatever he's got coming. But Tia—"

"Tia?"

"Tia's his girl. She's not like that. She was a good kid. Just got mixed up with the wrong crowd is all."

"What's your point?"

"Tia's pregnant, and now she's alone. Her baby's daddy is behind bars. She's probably sitting in that house, wondering what to do."

Natassa crossed her legs and held herself tighter. "And?"

"And I wondered if you'd check in on her. The address is 118 Wingrave Place. Just make sure she's okay, that she's got a plan and has what she needs."

Natassa sat up straight, enraged. "You want me to do you a favor? Are you kidding me? You. A criminal. Asking for a favor on behalf of my brother-in-law's murderer? What's wrong with you?"

DeAndre rocked back in his seat as if her words punched him in the gut. "But you brought me food. You sent me those hymns. You're a Christian, right? I thought you would be forgiving. Show mercy."

She gritted her teeth, speaking slow and deliberate. "You thought wrong."

Her chair tipped over onto the floor as she stood, the clattering an exclamation point in the silence. She spun around and nearly sprinted out the room and down the corridor. *The nerve of that man.*

She seethed and shook when she got out to her car. She picked up her phone to call Breanna, then stopped herself. She wasn't ready to talk. She needed to drive, to clear her head. But first, she texted Janell: *Tell your boyfriend to leave me alone.*

26

———

"Y"ou gonna wash up today, or are you gonna lay there and mope all day again?" Chris sneered.

DeAndre rolled toward the wall in response.

"You're pathetic. You know that?" Chris lumbered out of their cell for the showers.

"Yeah. Add that to the list," DeAndre mumbled. "Pathetic. Criminal."

Natassa's words haunted him. *What's wrong with you?* The way her entire face twisted in disgust. Her eyes flaming and fierce, full of the hate he turned on himself.

His breakfast sat untouched. Steel-cut oatmeal didn't appeal to him at that moment. He'd been feeding on self-loathing for days.

What *was* wrong with him? What kind of idiot would ask the woman he victimized for a favor? Why did he do it? Why did he ask *her*? What kind of sentimental naive cloud had he been riding on? Those stupid hymns. That stupid hope. He should have asked Janell.

He tossed onto his back again, uneasy. Why didn't he ask Janell?

The answer came to him as easy as the image of Tia's face, soft in the glow of the streetlight as she waited for Reg to get home that night many years ago. Her smile never stretched wide, her mouth always cautious, looking for who to trust.

But that night DeAndre drew her out, if only a little, as he invited her inside to wait for Reg. She came to make things right, to reconcile a relationship that was probably doomed from the start. How many times could one couple break up and get back together? How many times would she take him back?

Yet Tia was Reg's girl, and they both knew it. Even if they were, at that moment, broken up. Her lip had trembled as she confessed how she feared she would never amount to much. They connected that night, heart to heart, fear to fear.

Reg finally showed up at one in the morning, tipsy but not full-out drunk and somehow still able to lay on the charm. He snagged Tia into his embrace. The backward glance she cast DeAndre still haunted him.

Tia was never his, never meant to be his. After he met Janell, he understood why. There was no comparison. And yet, how could he not care? After he had seen Tia's heart, he couldn't bear to think of it being trampled. Not like this.

But how could he ask the woman he loved now to be the one to reach out to the woman he loved then?

So, he had asked Natassa.

And Natassa had breathed fire.

What about *I forgive you. God will forgive you too?* What about that?

Some things were beyond forgiveness. Some people were too much. Some people went too far.

He wasn't only a rapist. He was an accomplice to a murder.

What's wrong with you? Criminal. Criminal. Criminal.

DeAndre reached under his pillow and yanked out the stack of hymns Natassa had sent. "Amazing Grace." He scoffed at the picture he had drawn of himself as a boy smiling under the kiss of the sun, the favor of the Son. He clenched his fist, crumpling the paper in his hand, then threw it against the wall.

"DeAndre, where you been?" Luis's voice startled DeAndre, causing him to jump.

He sat up in bed and peered down. Luis was standing in the entryway. "Hey."

"Dude, you been sick?"

"Something like that."

Luis squinted up at him, tilting his head to the side. "You have a job now. You can't skip out on work. They'll give someone else the position."

He had forgotten about his job. "Sorry."

"Is it your sentencing that's got you all gloomy?"

Rather than explain that his sentencing didn't matter now, he grunted and sat up.

"Well, come on." Luis knocked on the bars of the cell. "Get ready. Let's go."

He opened his mouth to give an excuse but stopped himself. He didn't have a single good one. Luis had already reached the end of the hall before he made it out of his cell.

The monotony of mopping the floors came as a welcome distraction. He soaked up the grime by moving back and forth with the mop, only to expunged the dirt in the bucket. *Though your sins are like scarlet, they shall be as white as snow.*

The phrasing of that verse served as further evidence to the world that white was good and black was bad. It was insulting, but oh, to have the cleansing that it spoke of. He reached for it, but it seemed just out of his grasp.

If only his wrongs could be eradicated like the grime on the floor. They were, of course. Jesus took them all away—technically. But then, why did everything he touch seem to get filthy? How come he could still feel the grit on his soul?

* * *

When DeAndre had shuffled into the courtroom, he'd expected to see Natassa sitting out there, eyes ablaze with hostility. Poised with a letter in hand to read to the judge, to him, enumerating the heinousness of his crime and what it had cost her, cost her family. But she wasn't there. Janell sat perched on the edge of the back pew, arms wrapped around her middle, eyes cloudy.

Where was Natassa? This was her chance to speak, to spew out allegations against him. To make a statement that would make the judge's stomach churn, make the gavel pound clear and loud.

He attempted to make eye contact with Janell, but her gaze was fixed on the judge. His pulse kicked up a notch as he sat down next to his lawyer. This was it. It was really happening. Could he fast forward to the verdict and get this over with? Or better yet, could he rewind years of his life to remove himself from this courtroom?

The judge sat high above the courtroom, ensuring she could see everything. Even the stains on his conscience. She had her hair pulled back in a bun so tight it seemed to stretch the skin around her eyes taut.

Of course, he'd get a female judge. She'd undoubtedly sympathize with Natassa, putting herself in the victim's place with ease. Her voice came out hard. No-nonsense. It didn't bode well for him. Then again, what did it matter? The length of his sentence wouldn't change the weight of his guilt.

He only half-listened as the prosecuting attorney spouted the technicalities of his case. It seemed as if they were talking about a different person, even though he could recall every detail vividly. Like he had dreamt it or drew it. But not lived it. His attorney stood and approached the bench, railing about Reg and his part in the crime. The mastermind, his lawyer called Reg, and DeAndre assented with a small nod. It was true, only not the whole truth. Who could fit Reg and DeAndre's history into mere words? It lived and breathed and moved until it didn't anymore.

The judge called DeAndre to the bench, and he came. Hopefully, this would be over soon.

"Mr. Scott, do you agree that Reginald Maley exerted a negative influence on you?"

DeAndre dropped his head. The truth. He needed to tell the truth.

"Yes, Your Honor." His shoulders drooped. "Reginald and I grew up together, as close as could be. We were like brothers. He looked out for me, and I looked out for him. My pa— my father—always believed that Reg could break free from his lousy upbringing and redeem himself, so I did too. While I am responsible for my own actions, Reg came up with the plan against Mrs. Bloomington. I went along with it. Afterward, I realized what a negative pull he had on me, and I moved out, cut off our friendship. I wanted to be a better man. I believe I was on my way to becoming one."

"Were you aware of the narcotics Mr. Maley put in your drink that night?" The judge looked over her glasses.

"No, Your Honor. I remember feeling strange, but I wasn't sure why. I drank in excess, which is not something I usually do, so I thought it was only the alcohol."

"Why did you turn yourself in, Mr. Scott?" The judge's glasses slipped a half an inch down her nose as she peered down at him.

"Because it was the right thing to do."

"I see." She peered at him, eyes piercing. What did she see? His guilt, plain as day? Or his desire for something better? "That will be all."

DeAndre returned to his seat while the lawyers and the judge whispered amongst themselves. He turned to steal a glance at Janell. She bit her lip, leaning forward as if she could possibly hear the conversation at the bench. She didn't meet his eye.

The lawyers returned and sat down. The judge perused the paperwork before her.

"Mr. Scott, I am willing to extend a shorter sentence for a felony charge on the grounds that Mr. Maley is held responsible for his crimes. You have no prior criminal history and turned yourself in of your own volition. I hereby sentence you to four years at a medium-security prison."

His jaw dropped, and Janell gasped behind him. Four years? He was only getting four years? He thanked the judge as he stood to be led out of the courtroom.

His lawyer angled toward DeAndre and whispered, "As long as you behave yourself, you can most likely get out in two."

"Thank you, sir." DeAndre smiled and shook his hand. "Thank you."

"Behave yourself." He turned to walk away.

As the guard led DeAndre out, he locked eyes with Janell, and she gave a soft smile.

Four years, she mouthed.

His heart flipped at the way the side of her mouth turned up in pleasure.

He didn't deserve this sentence, and he thanked God with every step he took.

27

DeAndre's shackles clanked and rubbed at his ankles, but he ignored the irritation. He gave the lady at the front desk a little wave with his shackled hands as the guard led him out the front door. Sunshine beat down, spreading warmth on his face and causing him to squint against the glare. He took a deep breath of the fresh air.

They were transferring him to prison, and he had a sixty-five-mile trip to the diagnostic center. He ducked into the van and sat next to the only other inmate there. The man didn't introduce himself. It was just as well. If the man found out DeAndre had a sex case, there could be trouble on the drive. The less they interacted, the better.

Big windows stretched across the back of the small van, and DeAndre stared out of them, transfixed. He could see so much more blue and green than he could squinting out the peephole of his old cell.

The other inmate fell asleep within minutes of the drive, his head jarring from side to side with every bump. But DeAndre didn't want to miss a minute of the view. Then suddenly, they passed El Mexicana, and he slammed his eyes shut, pressing back the memories from his first date with Janell. Her cheeks bulging with chips and salsa. *The king is held captive by your tresses.* He was drowning in nostalgia. He both welcomed and resisted it. Could his heart burst with longing?

He opened his eyes. Whew. They'd passed the restaurant, but where might they drive next? *Please don't make a left at the light. Please don't make a left at the light.* And yet, they would since that was the way to the highway.

He sucked in his breath as they neared Java Joe's, pressing his hand against the glass. Was Janell there right now? He didn't see her car. What about Rob? James? He glimpsed the bell above the door as a customer walked out onto the sidewalk. His mural screamed at him, echoes of another life. One he probably couldn't ever return to. He held onto the sight until it faded completely in the distance.

They turned onto the highway. Each day, he'd commuted from the city until he finally moved in with Rob. He'd been nervous about driving into the county. James had taken him to the police station to calm his nerves. The cops hadn't pulled him over after that, but the guilt of what no one knew weighed on him every day. Would it always? Or would paying for his crime absolve his conscience?

DeAndre continued to gaze out the window at the life contained in the world out there. A world he would rejoin in two to four years.

Years.

Though the judge had significantly shortened his sentence, years of his life would still waste away on the inside. He sighed and refocused his mind on the fragments of beauty that met his eye.

When they slowed and pulled onto a long drive leading to the Department of Corrections, he shuddered. The barbed wire and fences surrounding the place intimidated him. Empty. Void of color. They turned into a big parking garage with a large door. He looked out the back window as the garage door closed behind them with finality, leaving the outside world behind.

Guards led him and the other inmate into a room with twenty or so other men and relieved them of their shackles. DeAndre rolled his ankles. They were almost rubbed raw.

The guards told the men to strip down to nothing. One of them came up to DeAndre and commanded him to open his mouth so he could peer into it. Then, he told him to show his hands and open his fingers. They sprayed the men with a cold, smelly liquid to kill body lice. DeAndre followed the directions without a word while shame swelled up and bubbled over. How had he come to this?

He stood in line to get his clothing, and a man gave him a pair of hand-me-down underwear and a T-shirt. He tried to ignore the stains on both. The T-shirt was far too large. It made him appear even smaller than he already did. They herded him to a hallway to sit alongside a dozen other men awaiting their orange pants. When someone finally handed him his pants, he commented that they weren't the right size either.

"That's all we have. Move on."

He waddled down the hall, holding onto his paperwork and pants at the same time. After a nurse weighed him and checked his temperature, he sat down to watch a video that explained what to do if someone placed a candy bar on your pillow. Don't eat it, or you'll owe someone for it.

The man in the video stated that they should not tell anyone about their legal case, owe anything to anyone, gamble, or socialize with people who were up to no good. DeAndre's head spun from the abundance of stimulation compared to life confined to a cell.

A guard led him off to his wing, and he followed, eyes roaming over every space.

"The common area." The guard nodded to his left where a large area had been crammed with a big television, a couple of phones, and showers. A few men jogged laps. The showers stood mostly open to the room, the push button ones, the kind that gave you twenty seconds before they shut off. He glanced over to the control room next door where the correctional officers could see the men showering.

He entered the B wing, dozens of eyes staring him down as he walked. The guard led him to a two-person cell. His new cellie jumped up when he entered. He stood slightly shorter than DeAndre. Skinnier too. DeAndre could probably take him if it came down to that.

"Hey, I'm Kurt." The man stuck out his hand.

DeAndre shook it cautiously.

"Don't worry, man. This wing is like 95 percent sex offenders. You don't bother us. We won't bother you."

How could Kurt tell he was one of the 95 percent?

"DeAndre."

"Cool."

DeAndre took in the cell. It was bigger than his last two-person cell by at least six feet.

"Hey, a window." DeAndre's voice buzzed with excitement.

"Yeah, man. You can see thunderstorms. Snow. People coming and going."

DeAndre strolled up to it and stared out. Two oak trees stood in front. What an interesting painting that would make: luscious green trees with barbed wire in the background.

"You got the bottom bunk." Kurt slouched against the wall.

"Cool." At least no one would wrench him to the floor and bust his head.

* * *

The first thing DeAndre did was figure out when they held a Bible study. He missed Luis. Could he find another friend like him here? He'd find out Monday night from seven till nine in the chapel.

Until then, he kept busy with mandatory kitchen duty, playing basketball with some of the guys from his pod, and avoiding Mitch, one of the prison gang leaders. So far, his secret hadn't come out, and he intended to keep it that way. No one needed to know he had a sex case.

When Monday rolled around, DeAndre counted down the hours until Bible study while drawing in the margins of his Bible. His stubby pencil brought scenes to life. He would read, then draw, then read some more. Birds. More and more, he drew birds in flight. If only he could soar like them, gliding free and unhindered. The good thing about prison was that he could walk outside, see the sky. But the birds flew over the yard without a care to the bondage beneath. The barbed wire didn't faze them; they soared above it all.

When DeAndre rolled into the chapel, about a dozen others were already there, holding worn Bibles. Sitting down next to one of them, he introduced himself. The man to his right stuck out his hand, and DeAndre shook it.

"The name's Griffin, but they call me Preach."

"Nice to meet you, Preach."

"Over there," Preach nodded to his right toward an older man, "is Schmitty. And there's Mark, James, Johnny, Gabe …" He continued naming the other men in attendance. When they heard their names, they turned and nodded toward him. DeAndre smiled. Maybe these were his people.

The teacher came up front and sat down, opening her Bible. "Let's get started."

Her gaze landed on DeAndre, and she asked his name. He stood up and introduced himself. He would be safe here. He could let his guard down around these people. The teacher opened in prayer and told everyone to turn to Galatians. He did so, sitting forward and absorbing every word. This was good.

* * *

DeAndre wrote Janell every week, sometimes twice a week. He prayed she'd visit, but he couldn't ask her to. She'd have to drive over an hour to see him now. Still, he asked God to bring her to him.

He lived for Monday nights and ate with Preach in the chow hall. They lifted weights together, too, sometimes. DeAndre didn't ask about Preach's case and didn't offer any info on his own. Freedom from his mistakes was priceless, but he was on borrowed time. When the truth of his case came out, he wouldn't be able to walk the yard freely, at least not without paying Mitch off.

And then it happened.

Mitch and his gang approached Preach and pushed into his space as he rounded the corner to meet DeAndre in the yard.

"Well, if it isn't the Preacher man." Mitch's eyes gleamed. "You've been hanging out with a pervert, Preacher man. Did you know that?"

Preach tried to sidestep them, but Mitch blocked his path. "Your new friend DeAndre is a sex offender. You know how I feel about sex offenders, don't ya? Before I deal with him, I'm going to need you to pay up too. Call it a socialization fee."

"I don't get paid until Friday." Preach caught DeAndre's eye and signaled with his gaze that DeAndre should beat it.

"I guess you didn't hear me. I said I'm gonna need it right now."

"I don't have it, Mitch. I'll give it to you Friday."

Mitch looked at the other guys. "You see how he talks to me? Is anyone allowed to talk to me like that around here?" He crossed his arms.

DeAndre froze. This wouldn't be good. But he couldn't do anything to stop it.

Four guys at once began to pummel Preach. He ducked down and put his arms over his face. Protecting himself. Punches and kicks flew.

Rage fired through DeAndre. He lost all sense of reason and raced toward them. His face burned with heat as he body-slammed Mitch at full speed. He punched one of Mitch's cronies in the left eye. The man stumbled backward. DeAndre kneed another guy in the gut, eliciting a curse as the man doubled over.

"DeAndre, what are you doing? Stop! They'll send you to the hole. Stop it!" Preach cried out from behind his arms.

A fist came flying toward DeAndre's face. He ducked. Swung again. Hit the guy in the jaw.

Mitch kicked DeAndre in the stomach hard, sending him sprawling. Pain sliced through him. He gasped for breath but couldn't get any air. The other three took turns kicking him while he was down. A crowd gathered, jeering until guards broke them up and took DeAndre to the hole.

* * *

DeAndre sat shackled and cuffed on a hard steel bench, waiting for a cell. His hand throbbed, and his chest burned. Maybe from a cracked rib or two. At least an hour had crept by. The correctional officer sat at a desk a few feet away from him, reading a magazine.

"What's the deal with the newbie," someone asked from a cell down the row.

"I heard he raped a lady."

Men from all over the pod mocked.

"Rapist scumbag," they spat, among other things.

DeAndre steeled himself against the verbal onslaught when something hard hit his shoulder from behind. A bar of soap attached to a string. The man reeled the soap back and then flung it again. Others followed suit. The soap smacked into him from all sides. DeAndre looked toward the CO, but the officer barely glanced up from his magazine. Until a bar of soap nearly hit his foot.

"That's enough," he yelled.

The roar died down, with only a few men throwing wads of toilet paper at him. Finally, the CO took him to his cell. DeAndre stood awkwardly by the door. His cellie stared at him from his cot but didn't speak.

Another small cot sat in the corner. A sink. A cold steel toilet bolted to the floor. The mesh bag the officer had given him contained a toothbrush, toothpaste, a bar of soap, and a comb—the only items allowed in the hole.

He stepped inside, and the steel door slammed behind him with finality. Two days for a first offense. He collapsed on his cot, then grunted. He should have landed more gently to cushion his aching ribs and back. The florescent lights glared down at him, and he covered his eyes with his arm to block out the light.

Outside of his cell, a television blared. Guards shouted at some inmates. The words were muffled but the tension in the voices mirrored the stiffness in his shoulders.

He rolled over and faced the wall. Tiny scratches lined the wall. *So, this is how prisoners spend their time in here.* He ran his fingers over the markings, though his swollen, bruised hand still throbbed. They made notches in the wall, then counted them? And this kept them from going insane? Maybe he could sleep most of his sentence away. Make it go by faster. But it didn't take long for him to figure out the impossibility of that plan. The noise never stopped. No silence to take refuge in.

He tried to do push-ups but couldn't manage it with the pain splicing through his hand. He tried sit-ups and stretches instead. He tried to retreat into his mind and paint scenes from the beautiful places he had read about. Even places from the book he'd only started reading. If only he could get his hands on a brush again, try out the techniques. But the inmate in the next cell howled like a wild animal, day and night, and he couldn't seem to get there, couldn't seem to find the beauty.

And then it hit him: *Stay out of trouble.* The words his lawyer spoke to him reverberated in his mind. He'd done the opposite of staying out of trouble. Would this ruin his chances of an early release?

He had just tasted something life-giving, and now it disintegrated almost as soon as it came. A waft in a breeze.

Morning eventually came, and with it, toast and oatmeal through the chuckhole. He brushed his teeth, combed his hair, and did sit-ups again. When he couldn't do anymore, he recounted the notches on the wall.

At some point, the guards alerted him that it was time to shuffle outside and enjoy his hour of fresh air. He paced back and forth with four other guys inside the small concrete slab surrounded by high chain-link fences. Dog kennels, they called them. Appropriate since he was like a caged bear, lumbering back and forth on the concrete between steel bars, pining for its natural habitat. A prison within a prison.

He breathed deeply as if trying to soak up enough oxygen to last him for the day. He couldn't breathe deep enough to still the panic that assaulted him when the time came to go back in and face the hole.

Back in his cell, Janell's face danced through his mind. All the simple, poignant moments with her played on an endless loop behind his closed eyelids. Then, he dared to dream of future moments as well. Foolish. But a way to pass the time. Even if it made him hurt inside for what he could never have.

Lunch hadn't even arrived yet. How was he was going to make it another day and a half? People put themselves here? On purpose? Yeah, many did. To avoid persecution. Tears stung his eyes, and he faced the wall and let them come. His cellie had fallen asleep. There was no one to see. No one but God.

God. Did He see? Did He really still see? Because it didn't seem like it. And yet … there wasn't anything else to do but pray.

He tried. But somehow, he couldn't force the words out past the lump in his throat. Past the pain that he had caused others, that he had brought upon himself. He'd tripped himself up and couldn't find his footing again.

What a friend we have in Jesus, all our sins and griefs to bear …

The words to the hymn came flooding into his mind, washing over him, loosening his tongue. Before he could censor himself, he began to sing. He sang through that hymn and then "Come Thou Fount," "Abide with Me," and "In Christ Alone."

He hadn't sung those since he was a boy, but the words were fresh in his mind since Natassa sent him the pages from the hymnal. As he sang, timidly at first and then with increasing confidence, peace began to envelop him. His cellie shifted in his cot. But he didn't yell at him to keep it down. In fact, he didn't move again and said nothing.

"Hey, over there. Don't stop singing," A voice called from a neighboring cell. The whole place had gone quiet. No howling or shouting. The sharp tongues of the guards fell silent. Maybe everyone else needed those hymns as much as he did. So, he sang "How Great Thou Art" and kept singing until lunch arrived.

And then he prayed. He prayed that God would right the wrongs he had inflicted on others, that God would make up for his many, many mistakes. He prayed for Tia and Janell and Natassa. Luis and Preach. And he prayed he would make it out of prison without losing himself.

28

Natassa sat across from Bethany in The Corner Coffee, a quaint little shop about halfway between where they each lived. The decor reminded her of a cheap hotel. The artwork on the walls was drab, and exactly what she needed. Entirely different from the engaging paintings hanging at Java Joe's. The Corner Coffee was mediocre in every way—and safe. Like their conversation had been.

Bethany updated her on people from St. Anthony's Baptist. She noted that the protests had died down and their prayer meetings moved to only once a week.

"How's Brandon? How are those sweet children?"

Natassa stared over Bethany's shoulder to where the waitress wiped down the table behind them. "The grief comes like waves, you know. Washing over different ones at different times. But then retreating long enough to make space for laughter and lighter moments." She flicked her gaze back to Bethany. Took a sip of her coffee.

"You mentioned you met with DeAndre. You didn't tell me what he said." Bethany's eyes bored into her, gentle yet insistent.

She wiggled under the intensity of her mama's stare. So much for sticking to safe subjects. "He wanted a favor if you can believe it." Her jaw firmed at the memory of the interaction.

"A favor? Well, that's humbling now, isn't it?" Bethany didn't avert her gaze.

"Humbling? More like infuriating."

Bethany shrugged. "Depends. What did he ask of you?"

"He wanted me to check in on Tia, Reg's girlfriend. She lives on Wingrove Place." Natassa rolled her eyes. "Apparently, she's pregnant, and now that Reg is in jail, DeAndre's worried about her." She rubbed her thumb across the embossed lettering on the mug.

"Hmm."

"Can you believe his nerve? Why in God's name would he ask *me*? Reg killed my brother-in-law, and now I'm supposed to waltz over to that murderer's house, knock on the door, and become BFFs with his girlfriend? That guy is insane." Her face heated, and her body tensed. If DeAndre were here, she'd take her coffee and fling it in his face.

"That's interesting." Bethany sat back and took a sip of her coffee, looking as relaxed as could be.

"Interesting?"

"Why *do* you think he asked you?"

Natassa shook her head. "He said something about the hymns I sent him. The ones I photocopied from the hymnal that Sunday morning when I asked to borrow your key for the office. I mailed him a stack of hymns that he had drawn on as a child." Natassa fidgeted with her shirtsleeve. "I'm not sure why. I felt like I should, like God wanted me to, I guess. I didn't know he'd use that and shove it in my face."

"Hmm." Bethany picked a piece of lint from her sweater.

"Is that all you have to say?"

"Are you about done, sugar?" Bethany set her mug down. "I hoped you'd come to the store with me. There are some things I've got to get."

Natassa glanced at her lukewarm coffee. It wasn't worth finishing. "Sure."

Moments later, they were in Bethany's car on the way to the grocery store.

"I finished Mercy's journal." Natassa switched the subject and attempted to change her mood into a more pleasant one. "But I know it's not finished, so if you could *please* not wait three years to give me the next part, I'd appreciate it."

Bethany glanced at her from the driver's seat. "Oh no, baby girl. That's the end of the journal. It's all we have."

Natassa sat forward, eyes widening. "What? You're kidding me. There's got to be more. It can't end like that."

"Once they sold Old Mercy, there were no more journals. There wasn't no way she could keep a book full of her writings down there without someone finding her out and punishing her."

Natassa sat back, stunned. It was like something had been stolen from her. She had so many questions. Would she never have answers? The weight of loss began to settle over her until Bethany spoke.

"We do have some letters from her, though, if you be wanting those." Bethany grinned.

Natassa playfully swatted her arm. "Bethany, don't you ever do that to me again!"

Bethany laughed. "I'll get those letters to you. There's not too many of them, but enough."

"Is it bad?" She cringed. Old Mercy deserved health and happiness. But had things gotten worse for her?

"Yes, child. It's bad. For a long time, it's bad. It's slavery in New Orleans."

Natassa blew out a breath. "I can't imagine. I guess I'll never really know what it was like. I can read the stories, but I can't completely step into them. No one's ever looked down on me because of the color of my skin."

Natassa looked at the woman next to her. The lines on her face told of years on earth that was less than kind to people who looked like her. What had she seen? What had she been through?

"But you have." Natassa angled toward her. "You don't talk about it, at least not to me. But I remember my mother saying right in front of you that she was glad Mercy didn't look too black, as if looking black was a bad thing. You shrugged it off, as if it were nothing at all."

"That's because it wasn't nothing. Not unless I let it be something." Bethany gave a nod.

"How can you do that? Let cruel words roll off of you like that?" Natassa's face warmed again. "I mean, my mother."

"Oh, sugar, words can slice deep, for sure." Bethany shook her head. "But offense is more like a cloak or a coat than a cut or a bruise. It's something that's handed to you, and you gots the choice whether you'se gonna pick up that cloak and wear it or not.

"My people, we done been handed so many cloaks of offense since our ancestors were ripped from their homes in Africa, shoved on ships teeming with disease and haunted with despair, and sold to the highest bidder as human cargo. Over two hundred and forty years of chattel slavery—think of how long that is, sugar—then when we finally think we're free, we find out we in bondage again to sharecropping, lynchings, Jim Crow laws, housing discrimination, the Klan, injustice in the legal system and with the police." She tapped the steering wheel with each infraction.

She cast a glance at Natassa. "Baby girl, that's a lot of cloaks been handed to us, over and over and over again. And they might look like they'd be mighty fine to wear, but let me tell you, they's heavy. Offense weighs you down fast. Then, parents pass their cloaks down to their children, and you got some generational weight going on.

"It's hard to hold your head high and be proud of who God made you to be when you're walkin' under all that weight." Bethany slumped her shoulders. "But the thing is, you can choose not to pick up that cloak. You can choose to drop it in the dust. Sometimes, I don't even realize I've put it on until I start to feel my shoulders droop. Then I take that ugly thing to the cross and leave it there. I don't want it on me. I want to run my race free." She straightened, jutting out her chin.

"And you know the color of my skin don't have nothing to do with what I'm trying to say to you, right, sugar? Your black brothers and sisters, we've just had plenty of practice at this, but people of all colors are weighed down and weary. And angry. Hurt people hurt people. But healed people heal people."

Natassa sat quietly. *Hurt people hurt people.* She'd told Laura as much. *But healed people heal people.* She didn't own that one, not deep inside. Could she grasp onto it? She rolled her shoulders, conscious of the heavy feeling there.

Had she put on a few cloaks of offense lately?

Yes. She had.

Was she ready to take them off?

She didn't know.

They arrived at the grocery store and made small talk about the soup kitchen and church as Bethany picked out an array of vegetables, fruits, and staples. Spaghetti, marinara sauce, French bread …

"Looks like you're planning quite a meal."

Bethany smiled and nodded at her, then instructed her to grab a few boxes of cereal, granola bars, fruit juice, and some mixed nuts. When Natassa finished grabbing those items, Bethany was already halfway through checking out, the cart half-full of bags.

Natassa put the rest of the items on the belt.

"Thanks, sugar."

Natassa pushed the cart out to the car.

Bethany plucked out a cigarette. "Do you mind loading the trunk while I grab a quick smoke?" She fished the keys out of her purse and held them out to Natassa.

"No problem." She snatched the keys, opened the trunk, and nestled the bags inside.

"Do you ever think of quitting?"

Bethany blew out a puff of smoke. "All the time. Now, my turn for a question. When are you coming back to St. Anthony's Baptist?"

She thudded the trunk closed. "I don't know. Maybe never."

"I'll take that as a 'Not yet.'" Bethany flung her cigarette down, grinding it with the toe of her shoe.

Back in the car and several miles later, Natassa stared out the window. Nothing looked familiar. In fact, the buildings around them looked pretty run down. She wrapped her arms around herself. Hopefully, they'd arrive back at her car at The Corner Coffee soon.

Someone had spray-painted Black Lives Matter and BLM on the sides of buildings and sidewalks.

"Can I ask you something?" Natassa ventured.

"Sure."

"Why do people get so upset if you say all lives matter? It's true, isn't it? Every life is precious and important."

Bethany cast a glance in her direction that she couldn't decipher. "Of course, it's true, sugar. Your life is just as important in the eyes of God. All people have value. But just because someone says "Black lives matter," doesn't mean your life doesn't.

"Look at it this way. The Good Shepherd left all those ninety-nine other sheep to go after the one, didn't He? Did those ninety-nine sheep not matter to Him? Of course, they did. But He pursued that one lost sheep because that sheep needed His attention at that moment. The other sheep don't need to be holding a rally shouting, 'All sheep matter,' now, do they? The house that's on fire is the one that needs the firehose, baby girl."

"I guess that makes sense."

A moment later, they pulled up in front of a dilapidated house with a hole in the porch and a couple of boarded-up windows.

"Bethany—"

"Do you remember the number of that address on Wingrove Place?"

Natassa spoke the words with resignation. "I think it was 118."

"Perfect. Now, sugar, I understand completely why you didn't want to check up on Tia. And I respect that. But thinking about that girl, pregnant and alone … about how scared she must be, and how she probably ain't got any money for food or for her bills. Like I said, I understand why you don't want to help her, but that doesn't mean I can't help her now, does it? So, if you don't want to come in, that's perfectly fine. You can wait here. I won't be long. I'm only gonna bring these groceries in and see how she's doing. I'll come back some other time."

"Bethany." Natassa flung her hands in the air. "I can't believe you did this to me. You kidnapped me!"

"I wouldn't exactly say kidnapped, sugar."

"I don't know what else to call it."

"Don't you worry none. You sit tight here. I'll be back in a few minutes." Bethany got out, popped the trunk, and took out two paper bags. She struggled to carry them up the rickety steps. *I should help her* collided with *how dare she*. Natassa's indignation won, and she sat, arms crossed, watching from the passenger's seat.

Bethany put a bag down and knocked. Waited. Knocked again. The door cracked open, and an ebony face with full tight curls appeared. Tia's eyes scanned her surroundings nervously, her mouth in a straight line. Her overalls clearly displayed her baby bump. The women exchanged a few unintelligible words before Tia let Bethany inside.

Natassa senses tingled on hyperalert in her surroundings. She locked the doors and watched for activity on the street.

This was a bad neighborhood, and she was sitting alone in a car. Granted, it was only three in the afternoon, broad daylight. And of course, this was Bethany's neighborhood. Her friend felt comfortable here, and it made sense that she wouldn't consider the fact that Natassa didn't.

But she didn't.

She weighed her options: stay in the car or go in. The trunk remained slightly ajar. Several more bags needed to be taken in. Could she do it? Could she take off that cloak for a moment and carry in a couple of bags? But this was Brett's murderer's house. She sank firmly in her seat. No. She couldn't do it. It was too much. Too much to ask.

As the minutes passed, she kept replaying what Bethany had said. *People of all colors are weighed down and weary. And angry. Hurt people hurt people. Healed people heal people.*

Only months ago, she was cruising along the path to bringing healing to others. If only life hadn't thrown her a curveball. And then another.

Could she get back onto that path again?

Heaviness pressed on her shoulders again. Why would she choose to live weighed down and weary?

With a heavy sigh, she unlocked the car, got out, and grabbed a couple of bags, then carried them to the door. She knocked and waited as she heard Bethany call out, "One minute."

"Oh, sugar, glad to see you." Bethany beamed and opened the door wide. "You can put those over there in the kitchen." She pointed to her right, and Natassa followed her direction.

"Tia, sweetie, this is Natassa. Natassa, this is Tia." The two women looked at each other over the kitchen counter. Tia nodded at her, eyes pensive. Natassa offered a small smile.

"It turns out we done bought Tia all this stuff to make a meal, and she doesn't cook. Do you think we have time to help her fix dinner, or should I come back tomorrow?" Bethany prodded Natassa with her eyes, asking the questions left unsaid. *Is it too much? Can you do it?*

Could she?

Natassa pressed her lips together. Took a deep breath. *Who do I want to be?* "I'll chop."

"Wonderful." Bethany gave a little clap. She beamed, and Natassa soaked up her mama's praise.

She started to unload the bags on the kitchen counter. Diapers. Wipes. When had Bethany gotten those? *That must be why she had me grab those other items, all from different places in the store.* Sneaky.

"Where do you want me to put these?" Natassa asked.

"Oh, I guess in here." Tia led Natassa into a bedroom. "This is the extra room. We was going to turn this into a nursery. I don't know what I'm gonna do now."

Natassa sucked in a breath at the paintings on the wall. The extra room. DeAndre's old room. A wave of nausea rushed to the surface, but she took a deep breath and pushed it down.

"What do you mean, Tia?" Bethany came up behind them. "What's going on?"

"There ain't no way I can pay the rent on this place. I already got a letter that they gonna turn the lights off on the fifteenth if I don't pay them a hundred and fifteen dollars. Where am I gonna get that?"

"Do you work?" Natassa asked.

Tia's eyes narrowed. "I did. I got fired when they found out I was pregnant. I applied down at the diner, but I didn't get the job."

Tia turned away from Natassa and toward Bethany. "I don't want to end up on the streets again. Not with a baby. I want better than that for my baby, and I don't want 'em to end up in foster care like I did. I don't know what I'm gonna do."

Bethany embraced her, smoothed her hair, spoke tenderly. "It's okay, child. We're here for you. We're here for your baby. God will make a way."

"You really think so?" Tia sniffed.

"I know so." Bethany spoke with far more confidence than Natassa could have.

"So," Natassa scooted past the two women, "I'll start on dinner."

She finished unloading the bags and washed the vegetables. She scoured through the kitchen but couldn't find a full-sized cutting board. She did end up finding a miniature one. She put some water to boil and added vegetables to the sauce.

"Wow." Tia came up beside her. "This is so fancy. I'm used to eating TV dinners."

"Well, this will be far more filling. And better for the baby."

Tia laughed.

"What?" Natassa's mouth twitched.

"That's funny. Like the baby cares what I eat."

"Actually, eating well during pregnancy is very important. Your baby needs the right vitamins and nutrients to grow strong and healthy. Are you taking prenatal vitamins?"

Tia shook her head.

"We need to get you some, then. Didn't your doctor tell you to take them? Sometimes they'll give you free samples at your doctor's office."

"I ain't been to the doctor." She looked at the floor.

Natassa stopped stirring. "You haven't been to the doctor? Tia, how far along are you?"

Tia shrugged. "Not sure. Four or five months?"

"And you haven't been to the doctor?"

"I don't have insurance."

Natassa's mind swirled with all of the worst-case scenarios. What if Tia was anemic? Or had gestational diabetes? Preeclampsia? Placenta previa? What if the baby wasn't growing correctly? So many complications were treatable, but not if the expectant mother didn't get medical care.

"Okay, I am taking you to the doctor. Next week."

"I ain't got no money for that."

"Don't worry about that. This is important."

Tia's eyes narrowed, "Why you doing this? Why you being nice to me?"

Natassa raised an eyebrow. "Us moms have to stick together, right?"

Tia shook her head. "Girl, you don't make sense."

"Mmm, something smells good in here." Bethany emerged from the other room. "How can I help?"

Natassa put Bethany on salad duty and then showed Tia how to mince garlic.

And by the time the three women sat down and ate dinner together, they had formed a tenuous bond. Hard to believe that just an hour ago, Natassa had refused to even enter the house.

29

June 12th, 1843

Dearest Susan,

I hope this letter finds you well. How is Mama faring? Is she in good health? I trust she is enjoying your baby. I am thankful she is well-fed and safe. That is my one consolation.

I'm sorry I took so long to write to you. I'm in a different world down here, and it's taken me a bit to get my bearings and figure out how to send word to you. I'll be honest with you, Susan, but please don't share these details with Mama. Her heart would break to know how I've suffered.

We came here on a schooner named *Free Bird*—my insides twisted with the irony. We were all stuck so tight together I couldn't stretch out my legs or my arms without pushing into another. The swaying back and forth caused some to vomit and others to moan. I squeezed my eyes shut, and the movement transported me back to dining on the steamer with you, tasting our fancy meals while listening to your lively chatter. I tried to climb high above the stench and groaning in that way, lifting myself up in my memories. Imagining the girl that I was then, white and free.

The women there bantered back and forth about me. "What are you doing here?" one asked. "You're too light-skinned for New Orleans."

They argued about whether the trader would be able to find a buyer for me down there or whether I'd have to be taken up farther north. "No one will want you in Louisiana," one woman said. "They only want dark-skinned slaves. You look too much like a Creole."

But another woman claimed that she heard of them selling a mulatto at an auction in New Orleans straight away.

"Probably as a mistress," another woman said.

I didn't say nary a thing. Pretended not to hear their speculations. All the while, their words roared like waves inside me. Was I once again too white? Back when I was a girl, that seemed like such a wretched thing. But I'm grown now and have some sense. There'd be nothing better than for no one to want me in New Orleans. I couldn't be so naive as to think they'd bring me right back to you, but I'd be a mite closer at any rate.

The ship docked. As they prodded us to stand and exit the ship, I stumbled into a woman holding her infant. Pins and needles sliced up and down my legs from being stuck in the same position all that time, and I couldn't feel my feet. I offered an apology, and my gaze found hers. They were the softest eyes I'd seen since leaving Georgetown, the kind of eyes a mother has when looking at her sweet baby. They didn't hold a touch of cynicism or begrudging in them, even though shackles encircled her ankles same as mine.

"I'm Mercy." I could be friends with this woman. Good friends.

"I'm Octavia. This is Manda." She rubbed her lips on the baby's curls. "And this here is Daffney." She wrapped her arm around a young girl, five or six years of age. Daffney snuggled closer to her mother, burying her face in Octavia's blue skirt.

"It's nice to meet you." I angled my eyes at both mother and daughter.

"I'm sure thankful to be in Louisiana." Octavia's eyes darted to and fro.

"Why is that?" We ambled toward the dock, my ears tingling from all the hustle and bustle in front of me.

"They don't sell your children away from you here. It's against the law, don't you know it? They won't rip my babies from me here."

I didn't know that about Louisiana. Seems like everything I heard contradicted each other. Some said it was the worst place to be sold; some said it wasn't so bad. And if they had laws saying they had to sell families together, how bad could it be? It gave me a sprout of hope, though I might not end up in New Orleans at all.

After being paraded through the docks and streets, they shoved us in slave pens right there in the middle of everything. Men and women both came 'round gawking, sizing us up, and talking 'bout us as if we couldn't hear a thing. Pointing to some of us and saying words like "sturdy" and "solid." One man whistled and asked why this lot of slaves wasn't bare-chested like the last.

A man in a suit and tie answered him. "These slaves come from up north, not from Africa."

"I thought they weren't allowed to bring in slaves from Africa anymore," I whispered to Octavia.

Octavia shrugged, but the woman behind us spoke up. "Oh, honey. They ain't so big on following the rules here, is they?"

Octavia stiffened. She had to be thinking about the rule keeping her and her girls together. For her sake, hopefully, that was one law they'd follow.

Dozens of people had walked by whose skin looked much like mine. They walked free on one side of the bars. I stood on the other.

"Creoles." Octavia caught my gaze, confirming my suspicions. "If you could break free, you could melt into the sea of them."

"If only." I slid my hand through the bars. The free air fluttered over my fingertips. It stood only a breath away and yet utterly out of my grasp.

It rained that night, and we slept huddled together in the pen. The iron bars surrounding us did little to keep us dry. We didn't suffer much from cold, for even though it was February, the air only held a slight nip. Nothing like them frosty winter evenings in Kentucky, remember? But the dampness made for a miserable night, nonetheless.

In the morning, they opened the gate and took us women behind this building, where they had us strip off our clothes and stand for a washing. When we were all cleaned up, they handed us these fancy gowns and painted rouge on our cheeks. They had me dress in this dark green frock with a big ole hoop. We looked like we was getting ready for a ball, 'cept there wasn't a smile to be seen in the place. We waited for the auction with nervous energy. What would be our fate?

Finally, they paraded us under the rotunda of this ornate hotel that was already filling with gentlemen and ladies. The people were all dressed up, and eagerness and excitement shone on their faces. Servers walked around offering plates of food and glasses filled to the brim with alcohol, like at a big party. Their laughter and gaiety grated on my nerves.

We sat in back, waiting for our turn to go up on the auction block. The young boys went first, those without a ma or pa with them. Then, the men. The day wore on, and we sat listening to the bidding. Some took their hand at guessing what each one would go for. I didn't play along. I nestled next to Octavia and her girls. What would my life have been like if Mama and I had been sold together back when I was a little girl? Maybe then we could have run together and crossed the Ohio River to freedom.

Finally, it was Octavia's turn to stand up there with her girls. I watched rich ladies start a bidding war over the trio, but in the end, a serious-looking gentleman won the bidding at $600 for the lot of them.

When I stepped up on the block, the auctioneer announced another "negresse americane" for sale and cautioned everyone that no bids under $100 would be accepted. The silence rang loud in my ears, and my pulse quickened as I looked out to all the faces of those who were too nervous to purchase me. Just when it seemed I wouldn't have a buyer, the same gentleman who bought Octavia signaled that he would have me for $100. No one challenged his bid. The man ended up buying ten of us.

I sold for the lowest bid of them all.

Here, my light skin made me worthless. With the ever-changing rules, how was I to navigate the white and black within me, around me?

They loaded us on the back of a wagon that drove away from the city. It took all that evening and into the next evening before we arrived at the sugar plantation. We didn't even stop for the night. Two drivers took shifts. The man who bought us followed in his carriage.

When the day dawned, I awoke from a restless slumber to find Daffney's head resting on my shoulder. She stretched and rubbed her eyes, reaching out to make sure her mama was beside her. Octavia kissed her on the top of the head.

"Mama." Daffney sat up and looked around her. "Why are the trees cryin'?"

"They look like they cryin' to you, child? Oh, hush now." Octavia smoothed Daffney's hair.

I studied the trees. I agreed with the girl's assessment. In Carolina, the oaks looked as if they were lifting their hands in worship, only they got a bit twisted along the way. Here, the trees looked as if they were weeping, sad and slow. A foreboding pounced upon me then, and though I tried to shake it off, it followed, leaping from weeping tree to weeping tree.

Once we unloaded at the plantation, I never saw the man who bought us again. An overseer met us near the Big House and led us six miles away to our cabin. Cabin S.

We work in field S. There be no cute names for the fields here. Everything is cut and dried. There are no gardens to tend, no chapel to build, no fiddles, or drums. We work "can see to can't see," at least twelve hours a day, sometimes up to seventeen. The bells call us to work in the morning and let us know when we can go back to our cabins. At least Octavia and her girls and I share a cabin, along with an older woman named Henrietta, and Rebecca and Cecil, who are married.

The overseer doesn't care a lick about my name. He calls me "You There," and it's caught on to where some of the other slaves think it's my name. I've been Mercy and Annabelle and Mary and now You There. It doesn't bother me much anymore, but maybe it should. Am I losing pieces of myself along the way?

Working cane isn't a thing like working rice, and it's taken me some time to learn how to hustle fast enough to meet my quota. I got whippings every day my first week here for failing to meet the quota in time. Then, I did okay the next week, only to slice my finger on the sharp blade of the sickle, which caused me to work slower for nearly a month. It don't matter if you're injured here. You still got to make your quota, long as you're breathing. They would have whipped me for sure, 'cept Octavia worked extra hard to help me cut enough cane. I owe her a debt of gratitude.

Each night, I listen to her sing to Manda while she nurses her. Her voice, her song, is the purest thing I've heard in a long while. I drink it in, taste its sweetness.

I used to sing to baby Elizabeth. How is she doing now? Has she learned how to hate those with different skin than her own? Or is a thread of innocence still woven within her? Does she remember me? Probably not possible for her to, but it's a nice idea.

Jonah is on my mind always, along with the dreams we wove together. My heart may be growing dry and cracked, but tears still spring from my eyes at the memory of him. We were going to have children, me and him. I could have been with child by now, on the verge of welcoming a sweet baby. I would have sung to our baby as I did to baby Elizabeth. Whether her face came out dark like her daddy or light like me, she would have been beautiful. I would have found love in a way that's new and fresh and vibrant. Now I can only watch it as a spectator, the love that dances between Octavia and Manda and Daffney.

Octavia married a free man, but her children are slaves, nonetheless, and she'll never see her free husband again. At least she has a piece of him in her girls.

I have nothing.

I must go now. It's very dangerous to be writing. I made friends with Robert, who takes the pirogue boat into the city for supplies and to take produce to market. He doesn't go unsupervised very often as we have most everything we need on-site, but when he does, he comes back with a copy of the *New Orleans Bee* and tales of his time dancing in Congo Square. While listening with fascination to him recounting the sights, sounds, and tastes of the square, I devour what bits and pieces of the newspaper I can read before he takes it to the Big House.

The advertisements for runaway slaves interest me, as does the way he describes the beat of the drums and movement of the dancers. If only I could sneak off with him and melt into the crowd of both free and enslaved negros, dancing and singing, remembering who I am and forgetting who I ain't. But I'm stuck here, so I hang on his stories and take them for my own.

They meet at Congo Square every Sunday, but he rarely gets to go. Come harvest time, going into the city is quite an ordeal, so my letters may be few and far between. He promised to mail them whenever he can, and I pray to God he's trustworthy and won't tell on me. You probably won't be able to write me back, but I trust that you and Mama are well.

With all my
love,
Mercy

30

J anell breezed in, the red in her hair accentuated by the florescent lighting, her floral cardigan billowing slightly behind her with the movement. And DeAndre could breathe deeply for the first time in weeks. Fresh air seemed to emanate from her. As if he could inhale hope itself. Beautiful. So beautiful it pained him.

"Hey." She tossed him a small smile.

"Hi."

They sat across from each other, the glass barrier between them, silent for a moment, drinking each other in. She looked like every painting in his mind, except had he forgotten that freckle to the right of her nose? Had he remembered her dimple was so pronounced? Her eyes held specks of emerald. Had he never noticed, or simply forgotten?

He picked up his phone.

She picked up hers. "It's been a while." Her mouth twitched.

"Sorry about that." He winced. At the county jail, he had put her on the back burner, choosing Reg, choosing to advocate for Tia. And yet, all the while, this woman held what he needed.

"How have you been?" Her face scrunched up, clearly fearful of the answer.

He could lie to her, but she was too intelligent for games. "I spent some time in the hole. So, let's just say I've been better."

She sat forward. "What? Why?"

"I got in a fight."

"Another accident?" There she went again, scrunching up her nose.

"Not this time. A bunch of jerks were beating on my friend. Not cool."

She sat back and nodded, lips pursed. "Did you win?"

DeAndre chuckled. "Yeah, maybe. For a while, at least."

Her smile spread and snagged one out of him. Oh, if he could kiss that mouth. Stupid glass.

"The hole wasn't all bad." DeAndre shifted the phone to his other ear. "I got to deliver the food trays, and they gave me an extra one."

"Well, isn't that special?" Her smile faded. "DeAndre," she leaned forward again, "I don't know if you've heard about anything that's gone on in Crawford County. Do you get the newspaper? Watch the local news?"

He shook his head. He could, of course, but chose not to. Seeing the world outside spinning on without him stung. Life continued on, passing him by.

"They did a story on you. On your art at Java Joe's. I didn't know if that was a good thing or a bad thing, but a couple more of your paintings sold, and I've been keeping the money in an account for you. For when you get out."

He angled his head, disoriented. His paintings still hung in Java Joe's? They were still selling?

Janell's brow scrunched. "About a week after the story ran, some people broke into Java Joe's and destroyed the rest of your artwork." She got choked up and put her hand to her mouth. "They slashed some paintings, broke others in two, and spray-painted over others."

He slammed his eyes shut, a deep sense of loss plummeting inside of him. In Rob's garage, he'd spent hour after hour on painting after painting, making sure he perfected each brushstroke, made every color and nuance exactly perfect. *Gone.* All of his work was gone. He groaned.

"I'm so sorry."

He opened his eyes. Tears were streaking down her cheeks. "It's okay," he conceded. "I deserve it."

"What?" She shook her head. "No. No, DeAndre, you don't, and I don't know what happened to you that makes you think you do."

"News flash, Janell. I raped a woman."

She didn't flinch. Why didn't she flinch? "Old news."

He stared at her, confused.

"Old news. New you. You're a new creation. The old is gone. The new has come. You used to know that, Dre. You believed it. What happened to you?"

It sounded true, but it sure didn't ring true in his heart. He shook his head, staring at his hand in his lap. "I don't know."

"DeAndre, I need you to paint something for me."

He looked at her and laughed. Then he saw the sincerity in her eyes. She was serious? "This isn't exactly Picasso's studio."

"They destroyed the picture you painted for me. The bridge. I never took it home. I hung it in Java Joe's so I could look at it every day. It kept me going, Dre. And now it's gone."

"What'd they do to it?"

She shook her head, wide-eyed.

"Janell."

"They painted horrible words on it."

"Tell me." He kept his voice gentle, yet insistent.

"I-It said, 'Nigger burn in hell.'" She barely choked the words out before dissolving in a mess of tears.

"Well, then." DeAndre's shoulders sagged. If only he could wrap his arms around the woman in front of him, but he could not. If only he could make things right, yet he was over here. She was over there. And the world was far less forgiving than Janell.

"Paint another bridge for me, DeAndre. Please. Paint a bridge for me."

He gazed at the woman in front of him. Why was she even here? Why was she bothering with him? She had every reason to give up on him, and yet she begged him not to give up on her?

"I don't have any paint. I don't have a canvas." Tears pricked the back of his eyelids, but he took a deep breath and steeled himself.

She straightened, a spark of light filling her eyes. "Don't worry. I talked to the lady up front. They have painting classes every Monday, Wednesday, and Friday at six. I'm sure the classes wouldn't teach you much, if anything, but you'd get to use the materials."

"I'd get to paint?" A spark of hope ignited within him.

"Yes. Didn't you know about the classes?"

He shook his head. "I knew they had some beading and leathercraft class because the guys make fun of it, but not painting."

"She said inmates teach most of the classes. You could teach art someday."

He cocked his head. "Who are you, woman?"

She chuckled. "What?"

"You're here. I can't believe you're here. Why?"

She leaned forward, looking deep into his eyes. "I'm here because I believe in you, DeAndre. I see who you are. Not who you were. Not the mistakes you made. I see you. I believe in you. I love you."

"I don't deserve you."

"Of course not." She quirked an eyebrow. "But you're stuck with me."

DeAndre shifted in his seat. "I want to believe as you do. I just …"

"Stop. Just stop." Janell's voice startled him, sounding sharp in his ears.

"Stop what?"

"You keep doing this. This penance thing. Stop trying to earn forgiveness that you already have. It's done. It's over. Jesus paid for your sin. Start living like it."

"Then why did God want me to do this? Go to prison? Why did He send me here if not for penance?"

"I don't know, Dre. You might be making things right with others and with the law, but He erased your sin. Now can you go and be the light in the darkness?" She waved her hand around her. "Because this place sure seems like it needs some light. Bad."

He steeled his jaw. "I can try."

"Good." Janell's eyes shone. "Four years is so much better than ten or fifteen. So much better."

"My lawyer said as long as I stay out of trouble, he can almost guarantee I'll get out in two." His gaze dropped to his lap. "I'm not sure what will happen now that they sent me to the hole."

"Two? Only two years?"

"That's what he said, but—" He glanced up.

"I can wait for two years." Her eyes sparkled with life.

"It might be longer now."

"Well, then, I can wait for four."

"So can I." He could wait forever for her if he had to.

"See you next week?"

"See you next week." DeAndre hung up the phone and put his hand to the glass.

Her hand met his there, dark and light, hope sparking hope.

31

"**O**h, you're leaving?" Disappointment dripped from Laura's voice as she peered over the banister to where Natassa knelt strapping on Mercy's shoes.

Natassa squinted up at Laura, sunlight from the upper windows gleaming in her eyes. "Yeah, sorry. We'll be gone for a few hours. There's leftover ravioli in the fridge for lunch if you'd like. Or I bought you that nitrate-free turkey if you want to make yourself a sandwich."

"Okay." Laura tightened her robe around herself. She wore the same pajama pants she'd sported for the past two days, and it didn't look like her hair had seen a brush in at least that long either. Natassa should have offered for Laura to come with her, but where she was going was *not* the place for the lady inhabiting Hope's bedroom.

Which reminded her … "Laura, when is your next OB appointment?"

"Tuesday, actually." Laura stared off into space.

"Want me to take you?"

Laura shrugged. "Sure. Okay."

Natassa nodded up at her. "It's a date, then." Probably Laura would shower and dress by Tuesday.

Natassa turned to Mercy. "Ready, Freddy?"

Mercy dashed out the door to the van.

Natassa's mind hummed with activity as Mercy chattered for the entire ride to Breanna's house. She answered with "Really?" and "Is that right?" but didn't truly hear her daughter. Bigger issues took over her focus. Like how Laura's entrance into their home had altered their lives.

Natassa had shifted from grief mode herself to comforting the grieving, a frustratingly futile endeavor. Laura spent massive amounts of time in her room and responded with one- and two-word answers to many of Natassa's questions and attempts at conversation. She seemed in some other place entirely, and when Natassa did manage to summon her back to reality, Laura only seemed to want to drift away again.

Laura's sullenness had begun to affect the children as if a rain cloud moved inside and hid the sun. Before she moved in, the grief hit in waves with reprieves of laughter and playfulness, but now the dreariness was constant. Natassa needed to shake it. She needed a break in the clouds.

"You are my sunshine," Mercy sang from the back seat. Natassa joined her in the song she had sung to all of her children since they were babies.

She glanced in the rearview mirror. Mercy beamed at her. Those dimples. Those wide, expressive eyes. Her heart could explode with love for her daughter. Laura would soon experience that feeling as well. And then? Natassa prayed that joy would overtake the mourning. The grief would never go away, but they could all find new mercies

She cruised into Breanna's driveway to find her friend already waiting on the porch. Breanna came around to the driver's side window, which Natassa rolled down.

"You're sure about this? Me going with you? You don't want to revert to plan A?"

The original plan had been for Breanna to watch Mercy while Natassa went by herself, but ten minutes before she headed out the door, she called Breanna and asked to switch to plan B. She needed a supportive presence. Again.

"Yeah. I'm sure. Get in."

Breanna walked around and strapped herself into the passenger's seat. "Alright then. You know me. Always up for an adventure." She winked at Natassa.

Natassa smiled.

"Where we going?" Mercy asked.

"We are going to see Mommy's new friend." Breanna turned and tickled Mercy's tummy.

Mercy giggled.

Natassa coughed.

"What?" Breanna raised her eyebrows. "What would you call her?"

"I don't know." Natassa adjusted her seat belt, suddenly feeling confined.

Breanna chuckled. "This is going to be fun."

After stopping at the grocery store to get fresh fruit and vegetables, whole-grain bread and cereal, organic milk and eggs, and prenatal vitamins, they merged onto the highway and headed toward the city.

"So, is this place in a bad neighborhood?" Breanna peered out the window.

"Yes. But Bethany didn't seem bothered."

"Well, she's used to it." Breanna hit the automatic lock on the doors even though they were already locked. They pulled up to Tia's house. "Wow."

"I know." Natassa popped the trunk. "Watch out for the hole in the porch."

She carried the groceries, and Breanna carried Mercy. Tia let them in right away, and Natassa plopped the bags on the kitchen counter.

"Tia, this is Mercy and my friend Breanna." Natassa began to unload.

Breanna, normally extroverted to the max, stood quietly near the front door, still holding a tentative Mercy.

"I wasn't sure what kind of cereal you like, so I got Honey Nut Cheerios and Chex."

Tia nodded, her smile barely discernable.

"I got all the trappings to make a great big salad. You should still have some dressing from last time, yeah?" She checked the fridge. "Yes, you have plenty."

Tia stared at her.

"And some strawberries, blueberries, bananas, carrots. Oh, and I got you some prenatal vitamins." She checked the bottle. "These are the one-a-day kind, so you're supposed to take one every morning with food."

"Where's Bethany?" Tia's gaze darted to the front door. "Hmm?"

"Bethany. The black lady. Where is she?"

"Oh, she didn't come with me this time."

Tia tilted her head, and Natassa couldn't discern her expression. Was she confused? Or did she think Natassa was crazy?

"Why you here?" Tia crossed her arms around her chest.

"Wh-What do you mean? I'm here to help." Natassa shifted a pint of blueberries from her right hand to her left.

"Am I your charity case or something?"

"What? No. I … It's just …"

Breanna put Mercy down and stepped into Tia's line of sight. "Look, DeAndre asked Natassa to look in on you, and she's doing so. She noticed that you needed a few things. That's all."

"DeAndre?" Tia's mouth spread into a smile. "He asked you to check up on me?"

"Yes." Natassa tried not to cringe.

"Aw, that boy." Tia shook her head, affection dawning on her face.

Mercy ran up to Natassa and hugged her leg. "Mommy, can we go now?"

"Wait, you're her mama?" Tia studied Mercy's face.

Natassa nodded.

Tia stared at Mercy, taking her in.

She set down the blueberries and put a protective arm around her daughter.

"Oh." Tia folded her arms. "I get it now. That's DeAndre's kid. She's got his nose, his cheekbones—"

The room begin to tilt, and Natassa put her hands on the kitchen counter to steady herself.

"Why don't we go wait in the car, huh, Mercy?" Breanna swooped in and took Mercy by the hand. "Let's go, baby girl. Mommy will be right behind us."

"She looks so much like him," Tia continued.

"Stop," Natassa choked out. "Just stop," she said again with more power.

Tia shut her mouth. Blinked. The door closed behind Breanna and Mercy.

"DeAndre raped me. Raped me." Natassa squared her shoulders. "He might be your friend or whatever, but to me, he's my rapist. I came here to help you because I care about babies and their mothers. But I swear to God if you say another word about DeAndre or Mercy, I will leave and never come back."

Tia stared back at her, feet apart as if measuring her up.

"Have you ever been raped?" Natassa asked in a challenge after a minute of silence.

"Yes."

Natassa took a step back.

"I been raped by my daddy and then by my daddy's friends. Then later, I been raped by a foster brother."

Natassa closed her eyes for a minute. So many violations, it was unthinkable. She took a deep breath and then opened her eyes. "Then you can understand not wanting anyone to call the person who raped you a nice guy."

Natassa held her gaze until she nodded.

"Not one word about DeAndre or Mercy. Not one word. Do we have a deal?"

Tia gave a solid nod.

"Good. I made you a doctor's appointment on Thursday at 2:00 p.m with the information you gave me. I'll come to pick you up at 1:15, okay?"

"A doctor's appointment? Where? With who?"

"With my OB. She delivered Mercy. She's excellent."

Tia shook her head and laughed. "You want to take me to some white doctor in your white county, right?"

Natassa's mouth tightened into a straight line. "She's a good doctor."

Tia scoffed. "I'm sure she is. I ain't going."

"Tia, please." Irritation crawled up Natassa's spine.

"Find a different doctor. One around here."

"I don't know of any around here." Natassa rubbed her temples.

"Ask Bethany. She'll know where black folk can get good care in our own neighborhood."

Natassa sighed. "Okay. I'll cancel Thursday's appointment and try and find a different OB. I'll text you and let you know."

"Alright." Tia nodded again, a signature move it seemed.

"Do you need anything before I leave?" she asked.

"Money for cigs?"

"What? No. You can't be smoking while pregnant. It's not good for the baby."

Tia smirked. "I'm messing with you. You shoulda seen your face."

Natassa gave her a smile with both eyebrows raised. This woman could be a challenge.

Back in the car, Breanna made her opinion known as they drove home.

"I'm just saying, this shouldn't be your responsibility. There's got to be some kind of program out there for single pregnant women. Help her get in somewhere and then sayonara, sister." Breanna punctuated her statement by slapping the car's dashboard.

"I looked. The only two programs that came up on an internet search said they were full and not taking any new applicants."

"Perhaps you didn't look hard enough. I'll do some research tonight. Or what about Bethany? Can't Bethany take her on?"

"Take her on?" Natassa cast Breanna a sideways glance.

"You know what I mean."

"I don't know if she *can't* or *won't* because she wants me to."

"That woman expects too much from you."

"Yeah, maybe."

"Maybe?" Breanna blew a raspberry which made Mercy laugh.

Natassa chuckled. "I think you're more upset than I am."

"I'm only trying to look out for you."

"I know." Natassa struggled to find the words. "It's just that if I look at her as Reg's girlfriend or DeAndre's friend, I want nothing to do with her. And when she reminds me that's who she is, I want to bolt. But then, there are these times when I look at her and I see … a person. A woman. A woman who is more like me than different. A woman who has been hurt like I've been hurt. And who has been afraid like I've been afraid. At those times, I think Bethany knew what she was doing when she brought me to Tia's house."

"I just don't want to see you get hurt." Breanna spoke so softly that Natassa barely heard her.

"I know. But think of all the things we do—or don't do—in the name of not getting hurt. How many of those things could actually be agents in our healing?"

Breanna arched her eyebrows. "This is far too deep for my liking, sage one. Let's go get some ice cream."

Natassa conceded, but when they were nearly at the ice cream parlor, she turned the car around.

"Where are you going? The rocky road is calling me!" Breanna reached toward her window.

"I want to go get Laura. We'll drag her in a straitjacket if we have to. She needs to get out."

"Aha! Mission kidnapping for ice cream." Breanna slid on her sunglasses and began to hum the *Mission Impossible* theme song. An hour later, the three women and Mercy sat at the ice cream parlor, eating ice cream and playing a ridiculously lame game of twenty-questions. Breanna made Natassa laugh so hard she nearly spit out her ice cream. Laura cracked a smile. And Mercy sang.

32

November 1, 1843

Dearest Susan,

I am writing tonight with a shattered heart.

I've come to love Octavia as if she were my sister, and I've been an auntie to Daffney and Manda. Daffney often sleeps in bed with me, burying her head in my chest, entangling our fingers together. I watch her sleep, smooth her hair, kiss her on the tip-top of her head. And Manda.

Sweet Manda. She was starting to take her first tentative steps, exploring the world around her with wonder and delight.

Then, she got sick.

It started with a cough. The spunk drained out of her so that her arms hung limp at her sides. Her forehead burned with fever. Octavia and I took her to the sick house. We have a hospital here on the plantation. Vieux Cecilia is in charge of it

(*Vieux* means "old" in French). The elderly granny is half-blind but has a good sense about herbs.

She took one look at Manda and put a hand to her chest. "Sweet Jesus." She set to making holly brush tea. Holly brush tea! Forgive me, but I didn't have much faith in that tea reviving our sweet baby girl when the life was draining out of her so fast.

So, I sent for the overseer.

I'm the one who did it, Lord forgive me. I was ignorant of their ways here. If only he would have sent for the doctor. The doctor could have given her medicine to mend her; I'm sure of it. I should have waited, trusted Vieux Cecilia. But I put my trust in the compassion of the overseer. Lord, can you ever forgive me?

He murmured complaint the entire walk to the cabin. His driver Mark followed behind him, eyes low to the ground. He stomped all annoyed as if I had taken him away from his work of barking orders and slashing the whip. I saw the hard look in his eyes but figured it would soften when he saw the baby.

I figured wrong.

He took one look at Manda and uttered a curse. Stomping over, he put his hand on her forehead. Then, he stepped outside. I followed to hear how he was going to help her. But he leaned over to Mark and said, "Drown her." Then, he started to walk away.

"What?" I trailed behind him. "You don't mean that. Please, you don't mean that."

"It'll cost more in medicine than she's worth." He spit out his words. He might as well have knocked the breath right out of me. I tried to breathe in but couldn't. Tried and couldn't.

Finally, I gasped, sucking in all the humid air around me, then releasing it in a wail. I flung my head back, blurry eyes searching the star-filled sky for intervention as tears cascaded down my face. The sting of a slap on my cheek forced me to the ground.

"Shut up, you stupid nigger."

Then, a surreal, feral sound came from behind. A groan. A growl. I whipped around. Octavia grasped on to Mark's ankles as he kicked her off. Manda lay limp in his arms, whimpering quietly. Her eyes looked glassy, but even then, they were searching for her mama.

Octavia stumbled to her feet, scratching and clawing at Mark, vainly attempting to rescue Manda from his clutches. He kicked her in the gut, and she doubled over. Three women from Cabin T came over and restrained Octavia, whispering futile comfort, telling her to be strong. Vieux Cecilia looked on, face solemn but devoid of tears. She turned, and her eyes met mine in the moonlight. The slice of my betrayal was evident in them, the cut of accusation, the weight of my guilt.

I followed Mark, pleading with him to reconsider. His skin shone as dark as the night—a shade darker than the baby he carried. He couldn't be that callous, could he? He ignored me, answering not a word. I stayed back a good enough distance to avoid physical retaliation, hurling my pleas in his direction.

When he got to the swamp, he thrust Manda in, holding her down. I screamed. Oh, how I screamed. I tried to wade into the waters to snatch her from death, but Mark grabbed my dress and held me back, all the while holding Manda under. I watched bubbles float to the surface, and then all fell still. He picked up Manda's lifeless body and tossed it farther out before turning to leave.

I jumped into the swamp straightaway, searching in the murky waters for the body. No worries about alligators or snakes at that moment. Only Manda. My hands brushed her, and I reached forward, finally grasping onto her. Her body lay wet and cold in my arms as I waded back to shore. Then, I collapsed in the grass, clutching her to my chest, pleading with God to breathe life into her again.

I've read all the stories of Jesus raising the dead, and I rocked back and forth in the night, crying out for Him to do it again. Yet, she remained still and cold. Eventually, I stood and carried her to her mother.

Octavia sat on the ground in the same spot I had left her, wailing and weeping. Women stood together in groups nearby, whispering among themselves, leaving her alone in her grief. I placed Manda in her arms, and her mourning washed over her baby girl.

"I'm so sorry." My throat felt swollen. "I tried to save her. I tried …"

Daffney ran up to me from her place on the steps of the cabin, clinging to my legs, tears plunking on the ground like rain. I lifted her into my arms, and we clung together, our grief melting into each other.

I write this letter now in the quiet of the night. No one stirs. No baby cries. We are numb with grief.

It's roulaison, grinding season. Everyone uses French words here. In a few hours, the bells will toll, and they'll expect me to work. They'll expect Octavia to feed the hand-cut cane through rollers to squeeze out the juice. There will be no time to reflect, no time to wade through the sadness and memories and dreams.

This place has hardened me. The Mercy you knew was soft and light, hopes for her future floating like wispy clouds. Now I've turned brittle; I can't feel anything anymore. I would burn with anger at the injustice of it all, but I'm tired. So very tired. The tears I shed hours ago have disappeared leaving a vast emptiness in their wake. Hollow. I am hollow.

I know now why the trees weep.

Love,
Mercy

November 30th, 1843

Dearest Susan,

In South Carolina, each winter, after the first hard frost, about the same time the Millers would come back from their summer house in Charleston, we would burn the rice fields to prepare them for the next spring. If I were back home, the fields would be burning. I would smell smoke, and the radiance of heat would press in around me. The old burning away made room for a new life, new birth. New harvest. Life there held a rhythm that we aren't graced with here, and I long for the purging.

Octavia has run away to the swamp, leaving Daffney with me. She feared it would be too dangerous to take her. At first, she begged me to go with her, but I couldn't bring myself to risk it. When it was clear I'd not be going with her, she asked me instead to take care of her daughter. Daffney and I are kindred spirits, a part of each other almost. The sweet girl has lost so much. Her father, her baby sister, and now her mother.

Sometimes we'll go down to the edge of the swamp and sing:

> Roll, Jordan roll,
> Wish I had been there to hear sweet
> Jordan roll.
> Look over yonder, see what I see,
> A band of angels comin' after me.

Then, we'll hear Octavia singing back to us:

> Roll, Jordan roll, you oughter been there
> To see sweet Jordan roll.
> Roll, Jordan roll, you oughter been sittin'
> in the kingdom
> To hear sweet Jordan roll.

It helps Daffney to know her mother is alive and well. Helps me too.

I pray for Octavia to stay away and clear of the overseer's searching. She's been gone three weeks now. If she's gone for a month, and they catch her, they'll cut her ear off and brand her. If a slave runs a second time, they cut their hamstring and brand them again. The third time warrants execution according to the law. I shudder to think of someone catching her and dragging her back here.

I'm working the Jamaican Train each day. We pour the sugarcane juice into a large kettle and leave it there until the water evaporates. I help pour the thick liquid into smaller and smaller pots as it thickens. We best not be burning the sugar, but it's hard to keep it at the right temperature. Three burn marks grace my arms and hand, mixing with the scar from the sickle blade. I'm a sight to see. If only I had Octavia to talk to as I work.

I finally saw the master again. He strode around, surveying the property. He stopped and eyed me up and down, then asked if I was married.

I replied, "No, Master."

He asked, "Why not?"

I didn't have an answer. None that he'd want to hear, anyway.

He came around again an hour or so later hollerin', "You There," with a negro man following in his wake.

I turned to face them. "This is Odel. Do you object to marrying him?"

I stood, shocked and silent, my eyes open wide, taking in the man before me.

Odel stood with his hat in his hands, eyes low to the ground. Muscular and not unhandsome, but quiet and reserved. So unlike Jonah.

By Le Code Noir—the Black Codes that form the laws concerning slavery here—he couldn't force me to marry against my wishes But what would he do if I refused? There were multitudes of ways to make me miserable.

And, God help me, I would do anything for a child of my own.

I answered, "No, sir."

He asked Odel if he objected, and Odel answered the same.

"Then it's done. You There, move into Cabin D."

He moved on, leaving Odel and me to stare at each other, strangers who'd been yoked together.

So, I am married. There was no ceremony, no jumping the broom, no veil or dress. No great love story. I am ashamed that I accepted and almost didn't tell you because of it. I moved into Cabin D this morning, bringing Daffney with me. What do I do? How do I entwine my life with that of a man I do not know?

Jonah's face comes to me often, the way his smile stretched wide, the lilt of his voice. His every word sounded like a song. I am betraying him, and yet, how could I not? I told him to find someone else, though I'd rather not hear when he's done so.

He'd not expect me to forego marriage, to never mother. His love for me proved true enough to grant me wings.

But I do not love Odel.

I don't even know him.

Perhaps, in time, love will blossom and bloom between us. Will my heart ever thaw enough to let that happen? It's as cold and limp as Manda's body on that day.

Mama always held tightly to her faith in the Almighty. Her words and her ways testified of Him, even throughout great heartache. I always admired that and tried to imitate it. But God is far away from here, completely absent from this land. How can I grab hold of Him? If only Isaac were here, preaching in these woods. Maybe his words would bolster me.

But there is no preaching or praying here. Even saying His name will give them reason to whip you. They've run God off and hope right along with Him. I am left directionless, wading through a muddy swamp of hopelessness, no solid ground in sight. Perhaps that resurrection fern will never raise back to life.

Don't tell Mama I said this. It would break her heart.

Love,

Mercy

33

"Why are you doing this now?" Natassa threw her head back, attempting a deep breath, but she was a minute away from losing it.

"I need purple socks! I don't want the white ones!" Mercy threw her shoe across the room and crossed her arms, staring her mother down.

Natassa looked at her watch again. She would most certainly be late if she didn't leave about five minutes ago.

"Out to the car. Now." She spoke through clenched teeth while picking up both shoes and pointing toward the door.

Mercy glared. "I don't want to go to Aunt Breanna's. Why can't I stay here with Aunt Laura?"

"Because Aunt Breanna is babysitting you."

"I can watch her." Laura plodded in from the kitchen, coffee in hand, looking back and forth between Natassa and Mercy. Though still in her pajamas, she looked clean and kempt. And present. But …

"That's not necessary. Breanna agreed to watch her."

"But I'm here. All day. Why would you take her somewhere else when I can do it? Especially if she doesn't want to go?"

Natassa's arms collapsed at her sides. "She loves Breanna's. She just woke up in a mood."

Laura stared.

"I would hate to inconvenience you." Her words sounded lame and fake in her ears.

Laura locked eyes with Natassa. "I can do it."

She looked at Mercy, still scowling in the corner.

"You won't be late if you shave off the twenty-five minutes it would take for you to go out of your way to drop her off." Laura sipped her coffee.

Natassa hated to concede a power struggle, but Laura did have a point. "Okay."

Laura's slight smile assured Natassa that she was doing the right thing.

She squatted in front of Mercy. "All right, Mercy Girl. We've had a rough start this morning, haven't we? When Mommy gets back, we need to talk about obeying with a happy heart, but right now, I'm sorry for losing my temper. Please forgive me."

Mercy wrapped her arms around Natassa's neck. "Sorry, Mommy."

She hugged her daughter tight, then pulled back to look Mercy in the eyes. "I forgive you. Now, Aunt Laura is going to babysit you, and I need you to be super-duper wonderful for her and listen to everything she says."

"Okay."

Natassa turned to Laura. "If you need anything, anything at all—"

"I know your number." Laura waved her off. "We'll be fine."

"Okay." She nodded, let out a breath she'd been holding, gave Mercy a final goodbye hug, and left.

She called Breanna on the way.

"You're sure Laura can handle it? I mean, she's stable enough and everything?"

"Yeah."

"You think the counseling is helping?"

"Yeah. Maybe." Laura had said little about her sessions but seemed eager to go.

Breanna scoffed. "Listen to us. We're acting like Laura's some twelve-year-old who has never babysat before. Of course, she'll be fine. This is silly. Does she know where you're going?"

"No." Then it hit her. "Wait, she did say that not dropping Mercy off would mean that I wouldn't have to go twenty-five minutes out of my way. I'm not sure how she would know I would be going out of my way unless …"

"You've never talked about Tia to her?"

"No, Of course not."

"But you talk about it with Brandon?"

"Yes." She talked. He listened. He rarely said more than *If you feel like that's what you're supposed to do*. What he really thought of her reaching out to Tia remained a closely guarded secret. He'd turned inward since Brett's death.

"She might have overheard."

"Ugh." Natassa hadn't considered that possibility. "Ugh."

"Or it could have been a random comment. Any word on how long Laura's going to be staying with you?"

"No. She hasn't made any decisions yet and doesn't seem any closer to making any. But it takes time. No rush."

"Oh, you want that baby, don't you? You want her to stay with you while she has a newborn so that you can be some kind of surrogate mother." Breanna sounded proud of her discovery.

"She might need a lot of help," Natassa defended.

"You're not the mother." Breanna's singsong tone mocked her, and though she only jested, it jabbed at Natassa's heart.

"I know that. But I can help."

"This baby might be what Laura needs to rise out of the pit of depression she's been in. You better not try to take that away from her."

Natassa huffed. "It's not like I'm going to kidnap the kid and run off to Canada. Look, I've got to go. I'm almost there."

"K. Have fun. Bye." Breanna sounded completely unaffected by their conversation.

Natassa was shaken to her core. Was she dreaming of taking over Laura's mothering role?

Brandon had wanted to try for another baby but finding out about DeAndre followed by Brett's death halted those plans. No baby for her, at least right now. But that didn't mean she was trying to live vicariously through Laura, did it? Wasn't she, at her core, simply a mother? Doing what came naturally to her. Taking others under her wing. Perhaps she could be … too much at times. Learning to let go was a process, but not one she should feel guilty for, right?

She arrived at Tia's house five minutes ahead of schedule. As she walked up the front porch steps, her gaze landed on something hanging from the door. Her stomach sank as she read the eviction notice. It said Tia had ten days to pay the full amount due or evacuate the premises, but it was dated four days prior. *Six days.* She had six days.

Natassa knocked tentatively at first. Would she be the first tell Tia of the notice? But when Tia didn't immediately answer, she began to knock louder and louder, picturing the woman crumpled up in pain on the bathroom floor.

"Hold up," Tia called from inside. "Geez. What's your problem?"

Tia opened the door wearing faded blue pajama pants and a spaghetti strap top that showed half of her pregnant belly. Tia rubbed her eyes, then adjusted her headscarf.

"Tia." Natassa stepped through the doorway. "You have a doctor's appointment this morning. Did you forget?"

Tia rolled her eyes. "No. I didn't forget. I knew you were coming."

"But we're supposed to be leaving in," Natassa checked her watch, "three minutes."

Tia chuckled. "Man, you white people are so uptight. We'll get there."

Natassa pressed her lips together and took a deep breath before speaking. "Doctor's offices tend to work on schedules."

"They're always late anyway." Tia walked toward her bedroom.

She couldn't argue, so she stood looking around nervously for a few minutes. She looked past the burn marks on the carpet to where the couch was missing a leg on one side, making it lopsided. DeAndre sat on that couch, watching … What would DeAndre watch on TV? She shook her head. She couldn't do this to herself. She needed something to occupy her mind.

She walked over to the kitchen, grabbed a handful of paper towels and a squirt bottle of cleaner she found under the sink and began wiping down the counters. Vigorously. As if she could wipe away every trace of DeAndre, every trace of

Reg, from that dilapidated house. A stray tear slipped out, and she wiped it on her sleeve and scrubbed harder.

"Girl, it don't matter how clean you make the place. I'll be out on the streets next week anyway."

Natassa's head snapped up in surprise. She hadn't even heard Tia come into the kitchen, but there she was, dressed in jeans and a red T-shirt that covered her belly bump slightly better than the previous shirt. She stared at the woman in front of her, belly bulging with life but eyes devoid of any such thing. It was so fundamentally wrong that something began to bubble up within Natassa. As if she just couldn't stand one more wrong thing in the world.

"No." Natassa's jaw tensed, resolve steeling her spine. "You will not be on the streets. I'm going to make sure of it. I'm going to do whatever I can to make sure you and your baby are safe." She punctuated her statement by dunking the paper towels in the trashcan. The lid swayed back and forth, reverberating with her sentiment. She grabbed her purse and strode out the door.

Tia followed. "I told you, I ain't your charity case."

"You're right. You aren't."

The women got in the car.

"You don't have to do nothing for me."

"You're right. I don't."

They sat in silence for most of the short drive to the OB's office. How should Natassa begin a conversation. *She's lived on the streets before.* Like what? In a cardboard box under a bridge? Tia merely stared out the window.

"That's where—" Tia pointed at a building on the corner. "Never mind."

Natassa glanced in the direction she had pointed and surmised what she had been about to say.

She'd recognize DeAndre's artwork anywhere, and the auto body shop had his signature touch all over the exterior— a black man driving a green Cadillac with musical notes drifting out the window. She gritted her teeth and kept driving. At least Tia had remembered to keep her mouth shut.

"So, you knew about the eviction notice." Natassa glanced at Tia as they parked.

"Yeah. They been sending me stuff for a while now."

"Why is it still on the door?"

Tia shrugged.

"We'll figure out something." On impulse, Natassa awkwardly reached over the boundary of the gearshift and grabbed Tia's hand, giving it a slight squeeze, then withdrew hastily when Tia's eyes opened wide.

She snatched her keys and opened the door. What was she doing? Tia had been nothing other than standoffish from the moment they met. *Where do I get off trying to be buddy-buddy with her? She's made it clear that she barely tolerates me.*

Natassa checked the paper in her hand to confirm the building and suite number and forged ahead.

Tia waddled behind.

"Looks like we need to take the elevator to the second floor."

"Whatever you say," Tia mumbled, rubbing her back.

Natassa stopped and waited for her to catch up. "Are you having back pain?"

"Yeah."

"I know of a great chiropractor …" Natassa trailed off when it appeared that Tia's eyes would roll into the back of her head. *Shut up. Just shut up.*

They rode in silence up the elevator and strode down the hallway to suite 214. Natassa marched up to the window, told the receptionist that they were there for Tia Raymond's appointment, and grabbed a clipboard and a pen.

"I'm perfectly capable of answering for myself. I ain't no child you need to talk for," Tia said as they sat side by side in the waiting room.

Natassa handed the clipboard to her. "I'm sorry. I thought I was helping."

"You white people always do," Tia mumbled under her breath.

Natassa attempted to ignore the comment by picking up the nearest magazine and sifting through it. Only she wasn't paying one bit of attention. She put it back down.

"What? You don't like *Ebony*?" Tia's right eyebrow lifted.

"Huh?"

"The magazine. You were reading *Ebony* magazine. Is it not your style?" The side of her mouth tipped in a knowing smile that irked Natassa.

"I wasn't paying attention."

"Uh-huh." Tia continued to fill out the paperwork in front of her.

She angled herself to face Tia. Riding a sudden wave of boldness, she asked, "Can you explain something to me? You keep saying 'you white people' like everyone with white skin is the same. Do you really believe that?"

Tia put her pen down and stared at Natassa. "You don't even see it. You want to swoop in and rescue the poor black woman, like all of the other 'white saviors.' You do your thing, and you feel better about yourself for a while—did you ever stop to see me as a person? Did you ever stop to think that something about me could save you? White woman raising a black daughter—you think I *might* have some insights for *you*?"

Natassa sagged in her chair, mulling over Tia's words. Pained by them. Here she was, giving her time and energy to help Brett's murderer's girlfriend, and it wasn't enough? She was doing it all wrong? A tear slipped down her cheek, and she wiped it with her sleeve.

"Just," Tia snapped the pen under the clipboard, "stop trying so hard."

The waiting room door opened, and a nurse called Tia's name.

Natassa looked at Tia. "Do you want me to come back with you? I mean, I can stay here. You can go by yourself, and I can wait here until you're done … or I could come. Whatever you want."

Tia studied Natassa's face. "You can come back."

"You sure?"

"Girl, I said you can come back. Why would I say that if I wasn't sure?"

Natassa found a small smile spreading and stood to follow Tia to the exam room. Since she had no prenatal care thus far in the pregnancy, there were a lot of questions for Tia to answer. Natassa sat as a quiet observer. Tia had an easy repertoire with the nursing staff and the doctor—all African Americans. They slid naturally into conversation with none of the initial distrust Natassa experienced from her.

Tia's voice seemed louder, her facial expressions more pronounced, and her laugh glided into the air with no filter. It was as if Natassa faded into the background, observing Tia in her natural environment, as her best self. Tia was beautiful. Her unguarded personality transformed her into a radiant, lovely woman.

Blood work was in order, but first, the doctor wanted to do an ultrasound to see how far along Tia was. She sent Tia and Natassa to the room three doors down where the ultrasound technician would be able to fit her in.

"Are you excited?" Natassa spoke for the first time since the waiting room.

Tia's eyes flashed surprise at the sound of her voice. "I don't know. I guess so. Nervous."

"Nervous? Why?" Natassa almost poured forth all of the wonders of ultrasounds and how amazing it would be to see her baby, but she held back. This was Tia's story. And Natassa needed to listen.

"I had one before, but they didn't let me see it. When I had an abortion, I mean."

She put her hand on Tia's arm, heart welling with compassion. "Tia? You had an abortion? You didn't say anything to the doctor when they asked if you had any previous pregnancies."

Tia shook her head. "They don't need to know all my business."

"They might."

Tia shook her head more vehemently.

Natassa scooted her chair closer to Tia and grabbed her hand, confident this time. "It's going to be okay. This time will be different. So, so different. They're going to show you that screen, and you're going to see that baby. You are going to fall in love."

Tia yanked her hand away. For a second offense crept up inside Natassa. Until the tears streamed down Tia's face. "But then, I'm gonna know what I missed."

"I'm sorry. I'm so sorry." What else could she say? How could she make this better? How could she "sweep down and save" this poor black woman now?

Tia reached over and grabbed Natassa's hand. "Thank you for being here."

"My pleasure."

* * *

At every stoplight on her drive home, Natassa glanced at the ultrasound picture lying on the passenger's seat of her car. *A boy.* Tia was twenty-three weeks along with a baby boy. Despite going through over half her pregnancy with no prenatal care, both baby and mom were healthy and well. And as predicted, Tia fell in love.

Love looked good on her.

After taking Tia to get blood work, Natassa dropped her off at the house she would inhabit for less than a week. Tia gave Natassa one of her ultrasound pictures to keep. That simple gesture brought Natassa to tears, which made Tia roll her eyes. Which made Natassa laugh. When Bethany drove up to Tia's home that first day, even a tenuous friendship with this woman had seemed unlikely. And now Natassa had a picture of her baby.

When she got home, she slipped the ultrasound picture into her purse. She couldn't exactly hang it on the fridge. Not with Laura living there.

Natassa rushed inside. The appointment had taken longer than anticipated.

Peals of laughter erupted as Natassa opened the front door. She followed the sound to the playroom where Laura and

Mercy sat engaged in a round of charades. Tears streamed down Laura's face as Mercy flopped around on the floor.

Natassa grinned. "Is she doing her seal impression?"

"Oh my gosh, she's hilarious." Laura wiped tears from her cheeks.

Mercy grinned and continued her goofy antics. Natassa laughed. "She loves to make people laugh."

"I can't even tell you how much I needed this." Laura hugged Natassa. "Thank you. I … I just needed some Mercy."

34

———————

eAndre stepped into the room and surveyed the easels lining the perimeter. About half stood with blank paper. The other half were in various stages of progression. One boasted a rudimentary green apple on half of a wooden table. Another appeared to be a woman's face, whether in abstract or from lack of talent, who could tell? A few pieces held nothing but angry lines and splotches.

"Hello. Welcome to Beginning Acrylic Painting." A Hispanic man standing at least six feet five strode over to him and shook his hand.

"DeAndre." He nodded to the man.

"Paul."

"You an inmate here?" DeAndre asked.

"Yeah. Been here for five years. Been teaching this class for three."

"Woah. Cool." DeAndre scanned the canvases up front. They were considerably more advanced than the ones on the easels around the room. One of a skyscraper reminded DeAndre of a piece he did during his first year of art school.

Could he ask about Paul's qualifications without appearing rude?

"So, have you painted before?" Paul cocked an arrogant smile.

"Yeah." DeAndre nodded, his own smile stifled. "Yeah, a bit."

"Oh, good. With acrylics?"

DeAndre deepened his nod. No need to leak info or brag.

"Sweet. I won't have to go over the basics again. Every time someone new comes in, I have to spend twenty minutes telling them about the different brushes, how to wash the brush, and how the paint sets. Today I'm planning on going over the stippling technique. You familiar?"

"Yep."

"Great. You can help me with Stramby. Some dude knocked that kid against a wall a couple of months ago, and he ain't been right in the head since. Needs things explained to him nice and slow."

People started to file in, and soon there were twelve men in the room standing in front of easels. A couple of them had already started painting, tuning out Paul's tutorial on how to add a mass of tiny dots to create texture to the painting and how to apply it to add subtle variations of color. Paul demonstrated the stippling technique and then encouraged everyone to try it at their easels.

DeAndre caught Paul's eye and mouthed, *Where's Stramby?*

Paul pointed to a young, scrawny kid, three people to his left.

DeAndre sauntered over to him.

The kid stood with a paintbrush in hand, staring into space.

"Hey, Stramby. I'm DeAndre. How you doing?"

Stramby startled. "Fine."

"Good." DeAndre smiled to put him at ease. "Did you understand the stippling technique?"

His eyes glazed over. "Huh?"

"The thing Paul just showed us?"

Stramby stared.

"Here, let me show you." DeAndre took the brush from his hand and dipped it in the blue paint in front of him. Stramby watched as DeAndre used short, sharp brushstrokes to make dots on the top of the easel paper, varying the shades of blue as he angled down toward what became the horizon line. He, then, mixed white into the palette, and after that, purple, pink, orange, and yellow, transforming Stramby's paper into a brilliant summer sunset.

He added grass and wildflowers, losing track of time, losing all sense of where he was and what he was supposed to be doing. The brush took him on a journey, and he went with it, not conscious of anything until he put it down.

He sheepishly turned to Stramby. "See. That's how you use stippling."

The kid's eyes widened. He stuck out his hand. "My name's Luke."

DeAndre wiped his hand on the cloth hanging from the easel and shook Luke Stramby's hand. "Nice to meet you, Luke. Sorry for taking your paper."

As he turned to go back to his easel, Paul came around and looked at what he had painted.

"Wait a minute. You're DeAndre Scott?" Paul narrowed his eyes. "Hold up. You are, aren't you?"

DeAndre turned and nodded. Why did it matter?

"I saw you on the news. You're a famous artist, and you done waltzed in here like you're going to take my class." Paul puffed out his chest. "'Yeah, I painted a bit.' What was that?"

DeAndre put his hands up, uncomfortable with everyone's eyes zeroed in on him. "Famous is quite a stretch."

"Uh-huh. Bobby—the guy that used to teach the class—he had real training. He was a great artist. When he got out, he chose me to take over the teaching because he said I was the best." Paul widened his stance. "That I got promise. I've been teaching for three years, and no one has had a problem."

DeAndre popped his knuckles. "I'm only here because I want to paint again."

Paul tilted his chin. "Well, then. As long as that's all you're here for, we won't have any problem with each other, will we?"

"No, man. No problem at all."

* * *

"What's with you lately, man?" Preach sat forward in the blue plastic chair, draping his elbows on his knees.

DeAndre tossed his head to the side. "I don't know. Depressed, I guess."

"Depressed? Why?"

DeAndre laughed without humor. What a ridiculous question to ask while locked away in prison. He eyed his friend, who folded his hands between his knees. Preach cared. Preach was safe.

DeAndre leaned in. "It's just, Janell says I need to stop doing penance. I'm a new creation and all of that. My sins are gone." He closed his eyes. "I know. I know. And yet, here I am in this place that reminds me every single minute of every single day what a sinner I am. Of how I screwed up my life. And every time I break free of that, I feel guilty, like who do I think I am?

"I painted today, Preach. For the first time since I came behind these walls, I picked up a paintbrush, and it's like my soul could breathe again. A weight lifted, and I wasn't here anymore. I was there, in the sunset with my feet in the grass." He wiggled his toes at the memory. "But then, I put down the brush, and I saw my prison clothes, and I felt … condemned. I don't deserve that sunset or the grass or the air. Any of it. I deserve bars. I can't seem to get past it."

Preach opened his mouth as if about to say something, then closed it again. He bowed his head for a minute. When he raised it, he looked straight into DeAndre's eyes with the weight of sincerity. "DeAndre, how many times did Jesus have to die?"

DeAndre shifted in his chair. "Once."

"Are you more powerful than God?"

"No."

"Then what makes you think your sin is stronger than the cross?"

DeAndre winced. He didn't think that, did he?

"Man, get over yourself." Preach reached into his back pocket and pulled out a Sharpie. "Here, give me your hands."

"What?"

"Just do it."

DeAndre put his hands out in front of him. Preach turned DeAndre's palms up and wrote *Forgiven* on the left palm and *Redeemed* on the right.

"And when that washes off, I'll do it again."

DeAndre raised his eyebrow.

"Hey, sometimes we have to be reminded. I walked around with those words on my hands for almost a year. I don't need them anymore because they're written on here." He tapped his chest.

"If you say so."

"I do."

Bible study began, and DeAndre directed his attention to the front, but he kept stealing glances at his palms. *Forgiven. Redeemed.* This was the truth whether it felt like truth or not. The Bible confirmed it. So, all the other voices telling him he was still a rapist and a screwup … they must not be from God. And every thought that was not from God, he was commanded to resist.

Stop trying to earn forgiveness that you already have.

Since he had come to prison, he had misidentified the enemy as his past. But he had a true enemy, the same liar that came after Adam and Eve in the garden. The same deceiver that shackled the human race with sin and shame. He had allowed that adversary to whisper lies and gain ground. But no more. It was time to fight.

35

January 5th, 1845
Dearest Susan,

So much has happened this last year. Where to begin? I'm sorry for not writing sooner. At first, I had nothing to say. Nothing at all. And then, after a while, so much to say that I became overwhelmed by the words flowing through my mind. However would I pin them down? But now, I will try to do so and trust the Good Lord to fill in the rest.

Octavia remained a "maroon" for months, living in the swamps with a band of disgruntled slaves. Each would take turns returning to their plantations for food, though they cultivated corn, squash, and rice out there and had plenty of wild fruits for the picking. Octavia said she'd gotten quite good at trapping birds, though she never mastered fishing.

The first time Octavia returned to the plantation to retrieve food, I 'bout lost my breath with worry. She went to Cabin S, not knowing 'bout the change in circumstance. Henrietta and Rebecca gave her a little something and then told her where to find me.

No one noticed the tapping on the door at first, but then it grew a smidgen louder, and I investigated. When I saw Octavia, I gasped and flung my arms around her. I asked if she'd come home for good, but she shushed me by putting her hand on my mouth and slipped inside, bringing a stench with her.

Her eyes roamed 'round the cabin until they spotted Daffney, sound asleep on the straw tick. Her breath caught. "Oh, my baby!" She clasped her hand over her own mouth, seeming all surprised 'bout how loud her voice had come out of her. She glided over to her daughter, bending down and brushing the hair out of her face, as gentle as a whisper. She stood and wiped her face with the back of her hands. It was too dark to see her tears, but the weight of them pressed on me.

"Give me whatever you've got to spare," she whispered.

"You're going back?" I stared at her. My heart flopped around in my chest. Why would she want to go back?

She came up to me and hooked her arm around my shoulder. She said that she was doing quite well in the swamps and would stay there forever if she could. Many of the men were armed with stolen rifles, and they could defend themselves if caught. They pillaged the meat houses from neighboring plantations and shared whatever food they could gather from their families.

"But what if you get caught here?" My nerves stood on edge, fear for her threatening to swallow me whole.

"Don't you worry none." She put a hand on my arm. "I put bay leaves on the bottom of my feet and walked in some fresh manure. No dog will be able to track me."

Manure indeed caked her feet, which explained the poignant aroma emanating from her.

"And we're praying to Juan St. Malo to help us." I eyed her and spotted her sincerity.

I'd heard about Juan St. Malo, the patron saint of runaway slaves. He led a large band of maroons for quite some time but ended up getting caught. Why would anyone would put their faith in someone that the white men hung in the public square? But I didn't tell Octavia that she be putting her prayers in the wrong place. Instead, I nodded, my belly still turning in fright, and began gathering what I could.

Our meals consisted mostly of some assortment of rice and beans, and that was the majority of what I piled into the sack that she brought. Black-eyed peas, rice, marsh beans, some couscous made from rice, a little bit of what Odel called lax sow, which is the Wolof name for grits with sweetened sour milk. We were fresh out of okra and gumbo.

Then as quick as she came, she left. When I awoke in the morning, it seemed like a dream, but for the dingy footprints and spattering of rice and beans on the floor—what I had spilled in my haste.

She came three more times after that, always without warning and always when her baby girl slept soundly, unaware of her mother's presence in the cabin.

And then it happened. The local militia organized an expedition to gather up maroons from the swamp. They captured thirty-nine of them, four from our plantation, Octavia among them. They branded her with the fleur-de-lis on her right shoulder and cut her ears plum off.

She never fully returned to us. Not really.

The Octavia who came back to live in Cabin S wasn't the same woman who had stayed there before. She paced 'round like a caged animal, seething wrath in her eyes. Octavia scared Daffney stiff, and the sweet girl ended up staying with Odel and me rather than going back with the woman who looked like her mother but acted nothing like her. Everyone whispered about her when she was out of earshot, saying she had them fits of madness and wasn't right in the head. I didn't add fuel to the fire of gossip, but I had to agree with them.

Octavia mumbled constantly, jabbering on in half sentences and spewing nonsense none of us could piece together. She couldn't hold a normal conversation like before, and most of her talking was with herself. What was I to make of her? I would draw close, wanting to love her back to normal only to back away when her strange ways frightened me.

And then one day, she up and disappeared again. We all assumed she ran back to the swamp, but we haven't seen her since. She's been gone three months now without coming back for food or a glimpse of Daffney. Did she escape this cruel place by taking her life?

I dare not express my worry over this. I wouldn't want word of such to get to Daffney. It's much better for her to think her mother is safe and well in the swamp than at the bottom of it, drowned like her sister.

Odel is good to me, tender and soft like a quilt. His voice hangs deep and low and has come to soothe me. He doesn't speak when words aren't necessary, but he harbors great wisdom inside.

He asked me if I knew why Master had wanted me married off, and I told him I did not. He said that it's because those with family are less likely to run off and more likely to be content with their lot of slavery. My light skin, coupled with the fact that my best friend had run off, qualified me as a flight risk. If Master could tie me down to a husband and settle me with children, he would have greater assurance that I would stay and work diligently. That makes a great lot of sense, in a terrible kind of way.

I am with child again, for the second time. I lost the first baby nearly as soon as I learned of her existence. Odel says it's the hard work in the fields that makes miscarriage so common here. The strain on our bodies isn't any good for nurturing a child in the womb. My heart ached and bled over the loss of this child I imagine was a girl, but then at least she is with Jesus now, perfectly at peace, never to be forced into bondage. She was born free.

Some man named Rillieux invented a machine to process the sugar and do away with the Jamaica Train. Many planters weren't willing to take the risk on something so new and daring, but ours was. No longer do I have to suffer burns from striving to keep the temperature just right as to not burn or spill the sugar. And better still, before his invention, we could make 190 hogsheads of sugar a season. Now we can make 250 or more.

Hopefully, there are no more floods like the one that swept through in August. Breaches—they call them crevasses here—broke through the levees, and we had to work day and night to repair them and dig deep canals to drain off the floodwaters into the swamps. Rice might be mighty happy in flooded fields, but sugar needs well-drained soil. A bad flood can ruin a whole crop.

Right now, it's planting time, which is less strenuous than cutting cane. Perhaps the baby tumbling 'round inside me will live to see the light of day and his mama's face. I think it's a boy, though I can't know for sure. Odel does, too, and has taken to telling him stories, bending low over my belly and relaying the tales he heard as a child.

Odel's mama came to the plantation straight from Senegal, of the Wolof tribe. She died a few years ago. From what Odel has told me, she was quite a feisty one. Now she lives on in the stories she passed down, which her ancestors passed down to her in Senegal.

Our child has already heard much of Bouki, the stupid and greedy hyena, and Lek, the weak but cunning hare, who is forever tricking and swindling his companion.

Before Odel starts the story, there is a ritual. He says," Bonne foi! Bonne foi!" and I reply "Lek! Lek!" though others around here call him Lapin. At the end of the tale, Odel always says, "Fa la lèèb jogee tabbi gèèj" which means "from there the story ended its journey in the ocean."

He will never tell a story before dark, as tradition states that to do so means risking the life of your mother. His mother is already gone, and he doesn't truly give heed to such superstitions, but he hangs his hat on these traditions. They make him feel knitted together with his people.

Odel's birth name was actually Lindor, but it got mixed up on the overseer's tongue. First, he called him Ordel, then eventually Odel. Seems a mighty big stretch to me, but then again, he calls me You There, so he doesn't pay much attention to names anyhow.

Odel thinks the man purposefully twisted up his name out of spite, not wanting to speak a Wolof name, though who's to say for sure. He's been Odel for so many years he doesn't miss his Wolof name, but he wants to give our child one to honor his heritage. I think that's mighty sweet and don't mind a bit. His African heritage fascinates me.

Odel worships the Good Lord, unlike his mother and those before her. He is as quiet about his faith as he is regarding most things, but we are steady together, praying to the same God. Sophie and Philipe live in Cabin D with us and also worship the Good Lord.

They sneak out late at night to go and pray in the fields. They've asked me to go with them, but I declined. If we were caught, the consequences could be severe. Odel stays behind, not wanting to leave Daffney and me by ourselves, but he would probably go otherwise. I am holding him back, yet I am not sorry. His protectiveness is a gift. He watches over me and Daffney, nurturing our hurting places with his quiet attentiveness.

If what is blossoming between us is not love, it is akin to care. A kindness and gentleness dances between us, and the timidity that I came into the marriage with is slowly taking flight as I find a safety here with him. Slowly and carefully, I am peeling off layers of defensiveness and allowing him to see the tender places where my soul resides. If I am not happy, I am settling into a contentment with my lot with him.

This was the master's aim. I could resist it on principle, yet I've lost the will to defy such things. Perhaps God was behind the master's plans. Perhaps when it seemed He was the furthest away, He stretched out His arms to me in the form of Odel. Maybe His mercy is following me still, even in the darkest of places.

I hope you and Mama are faring well. If only you could write me back here, but it is still not safe. Please take care and send my love to Mama.

Yours truly,
Mercy

May 15, 1845

Dearest Susan,

Something has shifted deep within me, and I am no longer consumed with my preservation. I used to spend time working situations to my favor. Making it through each day unscathed. Unbeaten. Keeping peace. Not making a fuss. If I could just do everything I was supposed to do, then I could keep my back from bleeding and keep my heart in one piece.

But the cost I paid to do so was too high, Susan. The Bible says, "For what shall it profit a man, if he shall gain the whole world, and lose his own soul?" I've been endeavoring to do just that—gain the biggest parcel of peace that I could muster in exchange for the very soul inside me.

Now the overseer doesn't abide any praying to the Almighty. Not any gospel singing either. We can hum, but if he can tell we're humming a church song, he'll put an end to it right quick. He's of the mind that religion makes us hunger for freedom and gets us to think we're good enough to have it too. There ain't no way they can keep us down if we're thinking the Almighty is lifting us up.

But one day in the field, my back ached something fierce, and I stopped in my tracks and cried out to the Lord for mercy. My voice carried itself to the overseer's ears. In a flash, he jumped down off his horse and dug a hole right in front of me. Trembling, I begged him to reconsider. I told him I'd been doing my job fine and that I'd keep working hard without a lick of complaining, but he gave me no heed.

With the hole dug, he barked at me to lay down. My swollen belly protruded into the hole, sheltered from the cruel world above. I sucked in my breath as the hot lash licked my back again and again. I scrunched my eyes shut, but tears leaked through nonetheless, watering the ground.

I begged God to protect the baby inside my womb. We'd come so far, the baby and me. We'd made it through months of bone-breaking work and utter exhaustion. My belly continued to grow despite not having the best food to nourish the life within me. I could not lose this child now.

I might never see freedom, but perhaps this child in me has a chance to. To stand on free soil. To breathe free air.

I didn't even have the words to pray all that I held inside for this child. My prayers came out as groans and cries. The overseer must have thought I moaned from the pain of the lash, but as he sought to extinguish prayer from my lips, he only succeeded in drawing it out of the depths of my soul. When he finished the beating, he poured brine over my back and ordered me to return to work.

Most of my praying up to that point had been for myself. Shallow prayers. Prayers for safety. Prayers for comfort. Prayers to make it through another day. But when I turned my prayers toward another generation, something got unlocked inside me. I have no words to explain it, Susan, except to say that I came alive.

And suddenly, fear fled from me.

Suddenly, nothing could stop me from praying.

I told Odel as much when we got back to the cabin that night, and he laughed all hearty and full. "Well, look at you! You done grew wings."

Then he told me he wanted us to go pray that night, with Sophie and Phillipe. He said we'd wait until Daffney fell fast asleep, and I agreed, nerves and exhilaration tumbling around in my belly right along with the baby.

I sang to Daffney like I do every night, the same song I sang to baby Elizabeth:

Mercy. Sweet mercy.

Good Lord, we need Your mercy.

Every morning. Every morning.

Your mercies are new.

I will sing this song to our baby in another month or so and to any other children the Good Lord gives us.

When the night melted deep and silent and Daffney lay heavy in sleep, the four of us crept out of our cabin and down to the cane fields. We didn't take a candle or a torch, and it took a few moments for my eyes to adjust to the inky darkness. The moonlight alone guided us. Owls hooted from far off. In the distance, the shadows of others crossed the fields, and they were carrying something, though I couldn't make out what.

We ducked and dodged through the cane until we came to a place in the middle where a dozen or so were gathered. A kettle sat upside down on the ground, and we all lay down on our bellies—I on my side—around it. One by one, we began to whisper our prayers into the kettle, and they reverberated loud enough for each other to hear, yet they remained safe from anyone else's ears. The kettle caught and contained each hope-filled prayer like that bowl from the book of Revelation.

I listened at first, being the newcomer to the group. As I lay there, face in the dirt, voices rising up all around me, He appeared. It was probably all in my head, but it was as clear as if I saw it straight in front of me.

Jesus hung on the cross, bloody and beaten even worse than a slave. Only, unlike the whipping I had earlier that day, He chose to be mistreated. He chose it on purpose for me, because of His love for me. On that cross, He smiled at me.

Smiled!

It unwound something in me that was wound up all tight. And I began to pray. I poured out my soul with the rest of them, crying out for freedom for the next generation, crying out for justice and liberty, for God to set all the wrong things in this world right.

We prayed even for the master, the overseer too. We prayed for God to break into them and save their souls. Then, another face came to mind. The driver who held Manda's body under the swamp water until all the life drained out of her. With a lump in my throat, I prayed for God's mercy to overshadow him, to yank him out of the swamp of darkness that he's drowning in.

Everybody needs mercy, and if I've received it, I can extend it in prayer.

Oh, Susan, to pray this way was so good, so right and holy. To join with others who believe in the same God I do and who have the same passion for Him that is bubbling up inside of me makes all the difference. I've been holding the Lord at arm's length all my life. Mama's told me about Him from the time I was big enough to listen, and I heard what she said without truly hearing.

I read the Bible she gave me, but not until that moment did I meet the man who loved me enough to give His life for my freedom. If only I'd been baptized like Mama there in the Pee Dee River in South Carolina when I'd had the chance because here it won't be an option. But at least now, I don't have to be afraid of dying or of whippings because there's nothing they can do to me that can take me out of God's hand.

I've been going to the fields and praying every night. Sleep is no longer a coveted thing. and I am more energized than ever before. There is a grand purpose to my life. In truth, history will have a different narrative because of my prayers.

Give Mama my love. Read her this letter. It will warm her heart.

Love forever,
Mercy

36

───────

Natassa tucked Mercy's journal back under her bed with trembling hands, tears tracking down her face. Old Mercy's letters undid her. Only three more remained, unless Bethany kept more from her, and then … this journey was over? It couldn't be. She wasn't ready to let go. Old Mercy had become as much of a friend and mentor as Bethany herself. And the tenacity—the bravery—inside that woman… She longed for it. Did one inherit it through blood? Or could she obtain a piece of it simply through yearning?

She wiped her face with the sleeve of her pajama shirt and looked around at the comfort surrounding her. A massive king-sized bed with a plush down comforter. A closet full of designer clothes. She lived in the "Big House." And yet, she wrestled with the same issues as Mercy. Mercy found her way to freedom. Could she?

"Oh God." Natassa closed her eyes. "Can You remind me again how much You love me? Messed up as I am with all my faults and mistakes? Let me feel Your pleasure over me. Because I love you, Lord. My love is weak, but it's real." She released the tension in her shoulders and allowed God's love to wash over her, splashing the corners of her heart that had caked dry. Saturating. Renewing. A smile edged its way up her lips.

God loved her! Just like this. Beautifully broken. She exhaled the stress she'd been holding onto.

She'd been praying for Tia daily, petitioning heaven for provision for this woman and her unborn baby. A home. A place to stay. But even more than that, Tia needed what she had never truly had before: a family. The more Natassa prayed, the more burdened she became.

She scoured the internet again and again. Made calls. Went to the local pregnancy resource centers. Encountered dead end after dead end. Frustrated and heartbroken, she came back to God in prayer, full of questions. *Where are You, God? What are You doing?* The only answer she could seem to find could not possibly be from Him because it wasn't logical. It was cruel. And she could not give it voice.

As ardently as she'd interceded for Tia, she had yet to utter DeAndre's or Reg's name before the Lord. But now, as peace filled her, she slid her Bible from her nightstand and flipped to Matthew 5:44. *But I say to you, love your enemies, bless those who curse you, do good to those who hate you, and pray for those who spitefully use you and persecute you.*

It stood out, highlighted in yellow, the word *pray* underlined. It sounded great, in theory, but she had yet to pray for her enemies. She hadn't spoken one word of blessing over DeAndre or Reg.

Lord, forgive me.

I choose to forgive.

Lord, bless those two men. Show them Your great love. Reveal Yourself to them and show them Your saving grace. Show them the power of the cross. Transform their hearts and lives and set them free of all their bondage. Let them walk in the freedom and peace and joy that comes only from You. Use them to impact others for Your kingdom.

Natassa took a slow, deep breath. The weight on her shoulders … lifted. Something had shifted inside her.

Brandon walked in the room, straightening his tie. He smiled. "Good morning, babe."

"Good morning." Her smile back was more genuine. Lighter. Issues remained, and yet she'd begun a journey with the Lord. A destination of healing was on the horizon. She leaned toward it.

In a rush of boldness, she spoke up. "Hey, honey, could we talk tonight? I have something that's been bothering me that I'd like to process with you." She bit her lip. Hopefully, he wouldn't press for details right then. She needed time to prepare what she would say and how.

"Yeah. Sure." He shrugged on his sports coat. "My last meeting should end around four thirty today. I'll be home after that." He kissed her forehead and left for the day. His kiss and the earthy smell of his aftershave lingered long after she heard the front door close.

She'd chosen to do life with a good man. She had spent so much time judging him wrongly, complaining of everything he was not, everything he was not doing. It was time to be thankful for who he was. She chuckled to herself. That day at the soup kitchen Bethany had tried to tell her as much.

A cacophony invaded her bedroom as her children ran in and climbed—or jumped—into bed with her. Hope asked about breakfast. Faith chattered about a dream she had. Mercy sang about monkeys jumping on the bed. David reminded her that he needed poster board for his science fair project, and Daniel lamented about not being able to find his favorite black button-down shirt. As the voices reached a crescendo, Laura peeked her head in the doorway and smiled.

"What are you smiling at?" Natassa laughed.

"It's the most beautiful sound. A house full of children."

She smirked. "I enjoy it better after I've had my coffee."

She got out of bed, and Laura helped to get the children breakfast. It was good to see her up and out of her room so early. When she first moved in, she wouldn't emerge until afternoon. Progress. Healing. They each had their paths to walk. It was time to trust the process and the One guiding them along the way.

* * *

"So, what did you want to talk about?" Brandon slumped on the couch, arms stretched over the back of the sofa, feet propped on the coffee table with a bowl of popcorn in his lap.

Natassa angled herself across from him on the chair, sitting forward, hands between her knees. She took a deep breath and prayed for strength. And for the right words. All she had to do was to share her heart and trust God with the rest.

"It's about Tia."

"Tia? Reg's girlfriend?" Brandon removed his feet from the table and sat forward.

"Okay, so, I don't see her like that anymore."

"But that's who she is, right?"

Natassa shook her head. "No. Not anymore. Tia grew up as a foster kid. Her mom was a meth addict. Her dad raped her and then pimped her out to other men. The system took her away from her parents when she was ten. Ten, Brandon." She held up both hands. "So, she bounced around from foster home to foster home, some in the city where she grew up and some in the county where she didn't know anyone.

"Some were nice families. Some were only in it for the money. Others were horrible. A foster brother raped her multiple times, and she ended up pregnant at fourteen. Her foster dad paid for her abortion and made her go to school the next day." Natassa grimaced. "DFS finally yanked her out of that home and put into another home where they kept their emotional distance, but at least she was safe."

Natassa waved a hand in front of her. "Throughout all of this hell, there was one guy in the neighborhood where she grew up that was nice to her and treated her well. Reg was her on and off boyfriend through high school. On and off because she kept having to move away whenever she got a foster placement in the county. When she aged out of the system, where was she supposed to go? She had no family. She had no one. She reverted back to him."

Brandon shifted on the couch but didn't break eye contact.

"He made promises. She believed them. Once, she ran away from an abusive foster home and lived on the street for a few months. She was so hungry she decided that a little abuse was worth the price of food." Natassa tented her hands together. "Brandon, Tia is a person. She's pregnant. She's scared. And she's about to get kicked out of her house. She has nowhere to go. Nowhere.

"I've called every housing opportunity listed for pregnant mothers, and they all have long waiting lists. She is now on them, but she'll have the baby by then. She has two days. Bethany said she can stay with her, but when Tia visited, she could barely make it up the stairs. She had an asthma attack. There is no way she could do that daily, plus Bethany's apartment smells like smoke, and it's only a one-bedroom. There's not enough room."

Brandon nodded slowly. "So, what do you want to do?"

Tears welled up in Natassa's eyes. "I don't know what to do, Brandon. I keep thinking that we have room here. The boys could share a room. I mean, if the girls can do it, the boys can too. But I couldn't ask you to do that, and I couldn't ask Laura to do that. It would be cruel of me to ask such a thing from the two of you. But my heart is breaking for Tia, and I can't stand for her to be on the street."

Brandon's jaw firmed. "I could do it."

She caught her breath.

"But you're right. It would be unfair to ask Laura."

"You could?" She shook her head in disbelief. "You lost your brother. You lost your best friend."

"Tia didn't pull the trigger. She had nothing to do with it."

"But she would remind you—"

"Natassa, I live with what happened every day." He leaned close, his gaze plunging into hers. "Every day I wake up and remember again that Brett's not here. That I can't call him and ask what he thought about the game last night or what he's doing this weekend. And what's the alternative anyway? Forgetting?" He raked a hand down his face. "I'm just going to have to walk through this, and sometimes the best way out of pain is to reach out and help someone else who is in pain."

She sat back. "Wow."

"But Laura …"

"Can I say something?" Natassa and Brandon whipped around to see Laura standing at the bottom of the staircase, arms wrapped tight around herself.

Natassa winced. "We didn't hear you come down."

"Obviously." Laura smirked.

"Did you hear everything?" Natassa asked.

"I think so."

"Sorry."

Laura sat down on the coffee table, looking between the two of them. "Listen, I appreciate what you guys have done for me. I do. I felt paralyzed for a while there and I just couldn't find a path forward." She rubbed her bulging stomach. "But being around your family, the whole, noisy, chaotic family, it resuscitated a part of me. I needed this. Family. Life swirling around me. I think that probably soon I'll be able to go back home and try living there and see if I can do it or if I need to find a new place. I just need a little longer here."

"Take as long as you need." Brandon's lips formed a steady line.

"One thing that's bothered me a bit while I've been here." Laura looked up toward the ceiling. "I'm not your sixth child, Natassa. I'm an adult, and I can make my own decisions."

"I know that." Natassa's hand flew over her heart.

"Do you? Because ever since I've gotten here, I feel like you've babied me." Now Laura's expression turned parental. "And maybe I did need to be babied at first. But not now. I'm used to making the decisions in my home. I don't need you to make lunch for me or decide my agenda for the day or make decisions about what I can or cannot handle."

"Okay."

"So, when you guys have this meeting about Tia—who, by the way, you've tried to keep a secret from me this entire time—and you sit here and make a decision together about what I cannot handle, I feel like you are treating me like a child. Holding me powerless."

Natassa shook her head. "That's not what we're trying to do. I was only saying it would be unfair to expect—"

"Perhaps, but you could include me in the discussion."

Natassa closed her mouth.

Brandon broke the silence. "Well, what are your thoughts on this? Maybe … we could pay for her to get a small apartment?"

"Does Tia have any job skills?" Laura asked.

"No." Natassa's mouth twisted. "I don't think she's ever held down a job. She doesn't even really know how to cook besides microwaving meals. I need to teach her. She never had a mom who taught her those things. She dropped out of high school and has never had any other training. I think basic people skills would be helpful."

"So, she needs to learn how to support herself?"

"Yes. And she's going to need to learn how to care for a baby because I'm sure no one's ever taught her that either."

"Then I'm willing to try. And if it gets to be too much and I can't take it, then like I said, I am about ready to move back home anyway. It sounds like Tia needs to be in a functioning family and learn how to do life here."

"Are you sure?" Natassa asked.

Laura nodded. "As Brandon said, Tia didn't pull the trigger. She had nothing to do with it."

"There's another thing." Natassa looked between them. "Tia doesn't like being anyone's charity case. She can't stand the white savior mentality. So, she can't be like this project to us."

"Then how do we help her?" The lines around Brandon's eyes crinkled.

She shrugged. "I don't know. Just … see her as a whole person. Someone who has something to give us too, not just someone who needs something from us."

That night, Natassa fell asleep with Brandon's strong arms wrapped around her. Her protector. And the one who stood by her side as she followed the path of healing spread out before her. He was right. Tia didn't pull the trigger, so they could all extend mercy and blessing to her.

But what about the one who did pull the trigger? She had prayed for DeAndre. She had prayed for Reg. But could she extend forgiveness and blessing to them and finally let them go into the Father's hand?

37

"**Y**ou kidding me? This is like Beverly Hills." Tia gaped through the car window as they entered Natassa's subdivision.

"Except in the Midwest." Natassa kept her tone light. Cheerful. Trying to counteract the palpable anxiety rising from the woman next to her.

"How could you expect me to feel comfortable in a place like this?" Tia crossed her arms and slouched like a sullen teenager.

"I think you're gonna like it here," Natassa belted out awkwardly.

Tia looked at her as if she had lost her mind, head down, eyes up. Apparently, the reference was lost on her.

"It's from *Annie*. The musical?"

"You saying I'm an orphan?"

"No." Natassa waved her hand in front of her. "I was just—"

"Whatever." Tia shifted in her seat. "You think you're my Daddy Warbucks. It's a hard knock life for me. Come rescue me, powerful white daddy."

"They actually made a new version with a little black Annie and a black Daddy Warbucks," Natassa offered.

Tia merely rolled her eyes.

"Which is good, I think." Natassa glanced in Tia's direction. "I mean, I think it's good for Mercy to see. People that look more like her, I mean."

"You can stop talking now." Tia angled herself away and stared out the window.

Natassa sighed. This had to be a culture shock for Tia. The world had shifted under the feet of the woman sitting next to her. Everything was changing, and Tia had little choice in the matter.

How did she react when her own world spun out of control? Her natural inclination was to get a bit catty herself. Could she blame Tia if she wasn't displaying her best self right now?

You saying I'm an orphan?

Actually, yes. Tia had grown up as an orphan and operated as if she still was one. She had no understanding of being adopted into the family of God. Natassa prayed right then that while under the Bloomington roof, Tia would be overtaken by the love of the Father and know what it was like to be a child of God.

Moments later, they cruised into Natassa's driveway. "Here we are."

"This is your house?" Tia asked.

Natassa nodded.

Tia shrugged. "I've seen nicer." The corner of her lip tilted up in the slightest of smiles.

"I've had snarkier houseguests," Natassa countered.

That brought Tia's smile to full circle.

"That's all I am." Tia lifted her suitcase from Natassa's trunk. "A temporary houseguest. I'm going to get on my feet and get my own place."

"That's exactly what we want for you."

The two women stood staring at each other. Natassa stuck out her hand and Tia shook it. "Deal."

"Let me carry your bag." Natassa reached for the handle.

Tia started to shake her head.

Natassa added, "Not because you can't carry it yourself but because you're pregnant. Pregnant women are supposed to take it easy, Tia."

"Yeah, okay."

Natassa hefted Tia's bag onto her shoulder and led the way into the house. Five excited children greeted the two women, eager to meet the new addition to the household.

The girls shoved pictures they had drawn in Tia's direction. The boys asked if Tia needed anything. Brandon stood behind them, and far in the background, Laura stood near the staircase tentatively watching. Tia seemed to be shrinking within herself. She took a few steps backward and bumped into the door.

"Guys, guys, give Tia some space."

The boys got the message and retreated to the kitchen. The girls merely took half a step back and continued to wave their papers in the air.

"Those are beautiful pictures, girls." Natassa crouched down and admired the drawings. "Why don't you go put them on Tia's bed so she can look at them later?"

They ran off like a flash.

"It's nice to meet you, Tia." Brandon nodded toward her. "I'm Brandon, Natassa's husband. If there's anything you need, please feel free to let me know." He followed the boys' lead and left for the kitchen. Out of the corner of her eye, Natassa saw Laura slink off toward her bedroom.

"Who was that?" Tia whispered.

"That's Laura. Brandon's sister-in-law."

"Sister-in-law?"

"Yes."

"His brother that … died?"

Natassa swallowed. "Yes."

"The one—"

"Yes."

"She visiting?" Tia's voice held caution.

"She lives here."

"Oh no. No, you can't do that." Tia shook her head frantically. "She's gotta hate me, Natassa. She's gonna kill me in my sleep."

Natassa put her hands on Tia's shoulders. "She doesn't hate you."

"She has to. Reg—"

"Exactly. Reg. Not you."

"You didn't tell me this."

"Because it doesn't matter."

"I'm gonna sleep with one eye open."

"Tia, relax. We believe in forgiveness here. And love that overcomes fear. We're not perfect at it, but we're growing."

"I don't know what you're talking about." Tia bit her fingernail.

"Oh, but you will." Natassa rubbed Tia's back. "Come on. Let me show you your room."

After a brief tour of the house and a short nap, Tia reappeared just in time for dinner. She didn't eat much and was fairly quiet.

What could Natassa do to put her more at ease? Perhaps a family movie night was in order to keep the chaos to a minimum. Everyone discussed movie possibilities.

Tia chipped in with, "I heard there's a new *Annie* out." She cast a sly glance to Natassa, who couldn't help but laugh.

Tia's idea caught on, and soon everyone settled on sofas and chairs with bowls of popcorn, watching *Annie*. Laura crept downstairs and silently found a spot on the couch next to Daniel. Her sister-in-law smiled and nodded at Tia, who returned the gesture. Mercy snuggled up right next to Tia and ended up falling asleep with her head on Tia's lap. This was family. Hopefully, Tia felt it too. Enough to sleep with both eyes closed.

* * *

Natassa's heart pounded as she thrust her car into park. She needed to do this. For her. For him. She thought back to the day she had left the bottle with the note. The absence of the clinking in the car had felt like freedom then. She needed that freedom now. Full and total freedom. And it was only found in complete forgiveness.

When she had called Janell last week to ask her to tell DeAndre she wanted another visit with him, Janell had resisted. "Why, Natassa? So that you can crush him again?"

"What? No."

"Last time you visited, you completely obliterated him. You tore his heart out. "

"I want to forgive him," Natassa blurted out, defensive. Exasperated.

"Forgive him? Maybe you should ask him to forgive you."

"Okay. That too?" Natassa had said, though it was an offensive suggestion. Had Janell forgotten that *she* was the one who had been *raped*?

"Alright. I'll tell him. But you'd better be nice."

"I will."

The conversation had gotten Natassa's blood pumping and defenses rising, but the long drive gave her time to appreciate Janell's fierce tenacity. She loved him with the kind of love that transformed a person into who they were created to be. She would settle for nothing less. And she would not tolerate anything getting in the way. *Janell's actions mirrored those of Jesus.*

So, yeah, Natassa's actions last time had not been … like Jesus. And she could own that. And she could forgive. *Oh God, guide my words and don't let myself get in the way.*

She walked into the prison with her stomach flip-flopping, and she pressed her hands on it to steady it. As they led her back, she prayed. As she saw his face, she prayed. As she sat down, she prayed. His somber eyes searched hers. What were they looking for? Judgment? Mercy?

"Hey, Natassa." DeAndre nodded toward her. "Nice to see you."

"Thank you. You too."

He sat straighter. His countenance looked clearer. He seemed wrapped up in well-being as if he had smuggled in peace and kept cocooned in it. "To what do I owe the pleasure?"

She took a deep breath and went for it. "DeAndre, I have done you a great wrong."

He flinched.

"I've proclaimed to forgive you, and then I took it back and stockpiled bitterness and resentment. I've been so angry.

Hurt and angry, and it's like I had to direct it at someone, and you were the logical target, so," she dipped her head, "there you go. But the truth is, you've asked me for forgiveness, and everything you have done since then has shown that you are a man of integrity. Whatever you were before, I don't know. But now, that's who you are. I should and would forgive you if you were still a jerk. But it's ridiculous for me to hold this bitterness toward you when you're not. And for me to keep seeing you as someone you are not."

DeAndre's lip trembled, and his misty eyes looked up to the ceiling.

"DeAndre, I'm so sorry for how I have dishonored you. And how I've misrepresented Christ. Please forgive me."

DeAndre shook his head. "Natassa, I … Oh God … I'm so sorry. If only I could take it back."

"I know." Natassa leaned forward. "And I forgive you. DeAndre look at me. Look me in the eye."

Slowly, his eyes met hers. In them, she saw not a criminal but a brother. A brother in Christ.

"I forgive you. I release you from any debt you think you owe to me. You are free. When you get out of here, you're free to go. Go and marry your girl. Go and find a place where you can have a fresh start. Go buy your studio and sell your art. Go have a family. Go live a big, beautiful life. Enjoy this life God gave you. You are free."

Tears coursed down DeAndre's cheeks, and he didn't even attempt to wipe them away.

"I was going to ask you … I'm making some money selling these paintings and if you wanted some money for Mercy?"

She shook her head. "No. You don't owe me anything, DeAndre. Thank you for the offer, but no." She tapped her chin. "If you're really looking for a place to put your money, you could create an account for Tia. We're working to get her on her feet, but she's going to need a little help for a while since she'll have a baby soon. You don't have to—no obligation—but it could help her out."

DeAndre nodded. "Yeah. I'll do that."

"She's living with us."

"Tia?"

"Yes." Natassa smirked. "Just until she can get on her feet. But we love having her."

New tears began to flow. "Thank you. I've been worried about her." Now DeAndre swiped his cheeks with the back of his hands. "Man, the guys would give me a hard time if they saw this."

"It's good for the soul."

"Yeah. Until you get decked."

She winced.

"Don't worry. Most of the guys leave me alone now that they know I'm famous."

"Ah." She nodded.

DeAndre smiled, and she returned the gesture. But her smile faded when she turned her mind to what she had to do.

"Now, I need to extend the same forgiveness to Reg. Only I'm not able to visit, so it has to be through a letter."

DeAndre's smile waned. "Reg is a hard one. I can never tell if he is sorry for what he did, or if he's only sorry he got caught."

She pursed her lips. "Yeah. It's harder to forgive someone who's not sorry, right? And yet, in the end, it's not about whether they are sorry or not. It's about whether you want freedom or whether you want bondage."

DeAndre stared straight ahead as if contemplating her words.

She swallowed hard and pushed the words out. "I'm tired of feeling this way inside. I can't wait for an apology. I want to be free."

DeAndre seemed to shake himself out of a trance. "For sure. Yeah."

"Well, goodbye. I bless you. I bless your life. I bless your art. And I will continue to pray for you."

"Thank you." DeAndre looked surprised but waved.

Natassa turned to leave with a lightness in her step. Why had she been so nervous?

Back in her car, she opened the glove box and fingered the envelope that contained the letter she had written last week. Every time she went to mail it, she stopped herself. I'm not ready. And she held on a little longer. But why? Wasn't she ready for freedom?

Pressing her lips together, she drove up to the mailbox on the corner and dropped the letter to Reg in. With the descent of the letter, pounds were released from her grasp. She left the window down, took a deep breath and, let the fresh air fill her lungs.

* * *

DeAndre lost himself, tangled in each strand of her hair, in the layers of depth in her eyes. He forgot to breathe, or he could have inhaled too much of the dream of her because for a moment, he lost balance. He nearly fell into his canvas, tumbling off the bridge and into the turbulent water below.

"Dude, you using? Is that your secret?" Paul shouted from the front of the room.

DeAndre gave a quick shake of the head as if shooing off a fly. He had to find his way back to the heartbeat of his brush. He needed to add color to her cheeks, volume to her lips, life to her countenance. He had to bring her back to him. Make her as real as she had been when he'd first painted this. Then he'd been able to hold her in his arms, her breath mingling with his own. Distance. There was too much distance. He had to close the gap.

He lengthened her fingers minutely so that they stretched out for him ever so slightly. He caused her dress to ripple toward him farther, reaching, grappling for him. There. That nearly captured the desperation he felt for the woman he loved. Almost. He added a single teardrop in her eye and in his and stepped back.

Perfection.

This was worthy of his signature, so he signed *DAS* in the bottom right corner.

Paul whistled from right behind him.

"Is that your girl?" He smacked DeAndre on the back.

"Yep." DeAndre wilted, every ounce of energy having been utterly spent on the masterpiece in front of them.

"That's going in a museum somewhere." Paul crossed his arms, his gaze roaming the painting.

"No. This one's for her."

Paul flattered him. Always for a price, but DeAndre didn't mind paying. He wasn't yet museum-worthy, but his paintings sold. Perhaps it had to do with pure talent. More than likely, it was due to the scandal of a prison artist. Having his art on the wall could be a great conversation piece.

At least he'd been able to set up a fund for Tia and save for a future with Janell—the woman who helped him believe there was still a future to save for.

"Okay, Michelangelo. Time for my lesson." Paul rubbed his hands together and ambled to the front of the classroom.

DeAndre drew his eyes away from the new bridge he had painted and walked to where Paul's blank paper stood, awaiting eager strokes. He'd struck this deal with Paul in order to get his hands on the canvases his art teacher hogged. While all the students painted on paper, canvases lined the front of the room, all graced with Paul's work. DeAndre had already gotten on Paul's bad side, so he treaded carefully in asking Paul about where the canvases came from.

"They're donated by the same group that donates all the art supplies. A charity arm from the art museum." Paul huffed. "There's not enough for everybody."

"Of course not." DeAndre rubbed his chin. "But maybe you'd be willing to offer me some for the right price?"

The right price turned out to be 10 percent of any profits he made as well as private art lessons three times a week. For that, DeAndre could have half of the canvases donated. Paul helped arrange for the same group who dropped off the art supplies to pick up DeAndre's finished canvases and take them to the art museum where Janell would pick them up.

Things finally seemed to be falling into place. Only two more years to go.

But he would keep his focus on the mercies that God had provided. On her last visit, Janell had referred to him as an artist, and it hit him anew. He *was* an artist again. His creative side had come alive in here. Whether doodling in the edge of his Bible or designing tattoos for the guys, he was bursting with ideas. Mercy. This was pure mercy. And he would embrace every minute that God so freely granted him.

38

———

October 1, 1846
Dearest Susan,

I regret that nearly a year and a half has gone by since I wrote you last. The last time I put pen to paper was but days before Mingo was born. My awakening came, and then his birth swiftly followed. Our little chief entered the world.

Mingo means "chief" in the Wolof language. This boy will be one of great importance among his people, breaking forth from my womb when he did, nearly in the middle of a passionate time of prayer in the inky blackness of the cane fields.

The pains came upon me so sudden-like, no one knew what was happening. Everyone thought I was gripped with emotion, crying out to the Lord. I rolled and writhed this way and that, groaning and moaning, unable to form any string of words to let my fellow intercessors know that our meetin' was about to get a tad more interesting.

Finally, I managed to get on my hands and knees and rock back and forth, which took my voice out from under the kettle and got their attention. Odel put his hand on my back and asked me if I be alright. I hissed at him then, and you should have seen his face. It looked like his eyes were going to pop right out of his head.

"Mercy?" he asked, all afraid-like.

All I could say was "baby" in between gasping breaths.

Realization dawned on his face like a trunk dock lifting. "Baby?" he spit out in a whisper.

I managed to nod.

He jumped up and spun around as if he was looking for someone somewhere to tell him what to do.

The others sat up then in stunned silence as if afraid to make a commotion.

"Nancy," I groaned. "Get me to Nancy."

In one giant step, he hitched his arm under mine to support me and help me walk. We stumbled forward, stopping each time a birth pain hit me hard. I squeezed his hand until it turned white in order to keep from making a sound, but he didn't complain a bit. We were but a stone's throw from Nancy's cabin when I couldn't go a step farther. The baby was coming and wasn't about to wait another minute.

I crouched down and put my hands out to catch him, and Odel's hands came right beside mine. We caught our boy together. Nancy heard Mingo's newborn cries and rushed out to see that we'd done most of her work for her. She led me inside the cabin and shooed Odel away, but I'll never forget how his hands met mine when we brought our boy into the world.

They gave me two days to rest then expected me back in the fields. I left my precious Mingo in Nancy's arms in the morning until the noon break and then again until evening. Nancy cares for all the children as if they were her own. Mingo is in good hands, but it rips at my heart to leave him. It did then when he was so fresh and new, and it still does now. Nancy saw him take his first steps while I worked in the cane.

My memories from childhood seem all twisted now that I'm a mother. It seemed like Mama and me had all kinds of time together, but she worked in the fields too. So, it must have been less than she wanted as well.

Mama made brooms from broom sage cooked on the fireplace. Isn't that an odd thing to remember? So simple, but the scent of it wafts through my memories. If I gather my own broom sage to cook, will Mingo smell it and remember me forever?

Odel is always spouting off this African proverb: "When memory goes a-gathering firewood, she brings back the sticks that strike her fancy." Something deep in me testifies to the truth in that.

Mingo is turning out to be dark like his father. Dark like Mama. It makes me proud to see his coffee skin. It's the color of people I love, people I take great pride in. Good people. And yet, there is no chance for him to flee north, passing as white. That was a luxury afforded to me alone. If only I could give him that chance.

When Mingo was born, I had to stop going to the prayer meetings in the cane. We couldn't risk a newborn's cry giving us away, and he was far too little to leave with Daffney. Odel offered to stay back with me, but I told him to go.

I began holding my own little prayer meetings in the cabin by myself. I'd rock and pray as I nursed. Pace and pray as I soothed Mingo back to sleep. I kept my voice to a hushed whisper, not even loud enough to bother Daffney if she were to stir awake.

I left my old Bible with Mama, too afraid to risk taking it with me to New Orleans, but Odel got me another one. He didn't tell me how. But he showed me how to hide it under the floorboard. Every night I'd dig it out and read and pray, pray and read. This has been a special time for me to grow roots deep and thick.

Last week I started going back to the kettle meetings. Mingo sleeps soundly through the night now, and he's fine with Daffney beside him. The flame inside me licks the night air, hotter and brighter than ever before. I am a mother now, and my heart has grown in capacity. My larger heart contains larger hopes, larger dreams, and larger prayers. I am hungry for the more that only God can supply.

I am with child again. Can my heart hold any more love?

I hope all is well with you. Give my love to Mama.

Yours Truly,
Mercy

November 12, 1847

Dearest Susan,

Another year has passed, and so much has happened. Our sweet Faja has come and gone. She stayed with us for two months only, gracing us with her sweet coos and eager, exploring eyes. Her name means "dawn," for a new day dawned upon us here with her arrival. But she was taken from us too soon.

She came down ill, and I couldn't look to the overseer for help, for fear he'd order her to be drowned in the swamp. I didn't even to take her to the sick house, but Vieux Cecilia came to our cabin and made poultice for her. It did little good. She wasted away in my arms and took her last shuddering breath as my tears cascaded over her. Some men cut timber from the woods and made a little box to bury her in.

Gatherings to mourn the dead are outlawed here, so I stood alone by the gaping hole in the earth and whispered a hymn I dared not sing aloud, lest the funeral be broken up by the lash.

> Hark! From the tombs a doleful sound,
> My ears, attend the cry;
> Ye living men, come view the ground where you
> Must shortly lie.
> Princes, this clay must be your bed,
> In spite of all your towers;
> The tall, the wise, the reverend head, must be as
> Low as ours.
> Great God! Is this our certain doom?
> And are we still secure?
> Still walking down to the tomb, and yet prepared
> No more?
> Grant us the power of quickening grace,
> To fit our souls to fly;
> Then when we drop this dying flesh,
> We'll rise above the sky.

Mingo doesn't understand what happened to his baby sister. I told him she is free.

So many here have lost children. I would be hard-pressed to find a woman who hasn't. Mama used to talk about joy and pain being all mingled up together. Faja brings that truth home to me. The joy of her birth. The pain of her death. All mashed and mingled up together so tight I could never untangle the mess of it if I tried. I just got to let myself wade through it all. Eventually, I'll come out the other side a truer version of myself.

I'd be amiss to tell you that the devil doesn't come sneaking around my mind trying to bargain off his fear to me. He tells me that Mingo is next to die and that I'll never have a child live to be more than a child. I have to keep shooing him away like them pesky mosquitos causing so much bother around here.

I tie a bit of asafetida in a rag and put it around Mingo's neck to ward off colds and help him when his teeth start thinking of poking through. I try and catch belly aches right from the start and then pour cold water over hot ashes, having him drink it all up when it cools. I do what I know how to do, putting soot or cobwebs on every cut to stop the bleeding right quick.

But in the end, I can't keep my boy from dying. He's in the Good Lord's hands, and all I can do is pray for his safety, pray that he makes it to see the end of slavery.

It's the hardest thing I've ever had to do, trusting God with this piece of my heart.

Now that Mingo is older, he isn't fed at Nancy's breast. For the noonday meal, the children all eat from a trough in the yard. Like animals.

When Faja was alive, and I'd come to nurse her, I had to turn my head. It broke my heart. My little chief plopped down in front of that trough and scrounged around like a pig for his food. I'd press my eyes tight and tug on that place in my memory where I sat with my shoulders square and ate roasted duck off fine china while on that steamer right next to you,

Susan. For that thin slice of my life, people looked me straight in the eye, and I looked right back like I had the right to. When people called me miss instead of You There. I pull on that image so hard sometimes, like I could grab it from the air and hand it to my children.

At supper time, we give Mingo a plate and spoon and teach him to hold his head high like he's an important man. Because one day his outsides are going to match what is inside of him, and people are going to know he's a man to be listened to. Not an animal eating out of no trough.

We lie in bed at night and count the stars through the cracks in the roof. Mingo's gotten right good at counting. I taught him a rhyme to chant while parceling out kernels of corn one by one, and he caught on straight away. Counting the stars together, though … that's something special. We count until he and Daffney fall asleep, and Odel and I sneak away to pray.

We got a new overseer. The rumor is going around that he came from the North. But Northerners are supposed to be sympathetic to the plight of slavery and all. This one here is as mean as hades. Riley don't like praying or singing any more than the last overseer did, and it seems that he's spent all his time inventing ways to make us miserable and get us to keep from seeking the Good Lord. There ain't no way he's gonna stop me from praying, but he sure seems bent on trying.

The first time he caught us praying in the cane, only Phillipe and I were caught. The others ran and managed to get away. Instead of just whipping us like normal, he stripped us naked, put weights on our ankles and wrists, and put us in big ant piles.

The ants crawled all over our bodies, biting, while we were powerless to swipe them away. My whole body was on fire with scorching and itching. He left us out there from before sunrise until after the sunset that day.

The sun beat down on me, and my mouth was so parched. Was this what Jesus felt like when He said He was thirsty? Jesus went through such torture, just to bring me closer to God. I would go through a million ants a million times over if it meant being closer to the One who loves me that much.

We moved our meetings to the woods after that, and I began to lead them. Crazy how the girl who was too scared to even go to the meetings became the woman who led them. But time and fire seem to do some marvelous refining.

We still find our way to the meeting with only the moonlight as our guide, and we pray in the dark, but when it's time for me to read Scripture, I have a can of grease that I burn. I sit over the can and read and as soon as I'm done, I snuff it out. When Riley caught us the next time in the woods, he saw that I was clearly the leader of the meeting. Everyone got a whipping. I got a whipping, and then I also got the cat claw.

Riley stripped me and tied me up to the post, lying down with my face in the dirt. Then, he got the master's cats all riled up and had them scratch at my back until my back was all clawed up and bleeding.

The lash hurts fiercely, but it's predictable. One blow at a time. Bear down during the pain, breathe in between. Them cat scratches slice you at random. It messed with my mind and left me with nightmares for weeks afterward.

And then there was the time he put me in the stocks because he caught me reading my Bible during the noon break. It was risky to bring it out in the fields. But I hungered for something more than rice and beans, something more than this life.

I tucked my Bible into my dress so as to carry it with me in secret, and during the break, I snuck off to the far corner of the field, found a high patch of cane, and nestled in the middle of it where no one could see me. But Riley caught me, and oh my, was he riled up. He grabbed my wrist and dragged me to the stocks where he ripped my Bible from my hand.

The stocks here is this big piece of wood on a stand with holes in it. He put my neck in one bigger hole and my wrists in other smaller holes. There I stood, hunched over. While I was locked into place, Riley took my Bible and ripped it up in front of me, scattering it to the wind. Then, he spit in my face and walked away, leaving me there for the rest of the day and half of the next.

As I stood there, back aching, the heat of the sun glaring at me, the suffering of Jesus resurfaced in my mind. The Scriptures say that Jesus "who for the joy that was set before him endured the cross, despising the shame." Scoffers spit upon Him, but His disciples considered it a joy to be counted worthy to suffer for His name. Why shouldn't I?

When darkness fell, Odel gathered all of the stray Bible pages he could find blowing around and stashed them safely under the floorboard. When Riley came to loosen me from the stocks, I thanked him. Think of that! I didn't tell him what I thanked him for, and he didn't ask, but unknowingly he had handed me a jewel on my heavenly crown.

The next night, I got baptized in the pond where we draw water for the sugar house. We couldn't have any kind of formal ceremony or carrying on. Odel baptized me in the stillness of night with Sophie and Phillipe watching. When I came up out of that water, peace settled over me. Nothing's gonna hold me back anymore, Susan. Not a thing.

I send you and Mama all my love.

Yours truly,
Mercy

May 2, 1861

Dearest Susan,

So much time has passed. This letter may not even reach you. Are you still in Georgetown? It seems the whole world is shifting and changing. How long has it been? Ten years, at least.

I used to give my letters for you to Robert, but he was sold. Afterward, I couldn't get word to you. So many here seemed like they would betray anyone for a chance of favor with Riley.

But now Riley's gone. Master's gone too, off to fight the war. There's a new overseer here, Simon. He's not so bad. He doesn't seem so concerned with what we do as long as we keep the plantation running as it should. Master took Odel with him to the war front, and if worry did a lick of good, I'd be sick with it. He is so close to danger. What is he doing? He thought he might dig trenches or the like, but he didn't rightly know what he'd be doing or when he'd be back.

Why did Master choose him out of everyone? Why does God allow Odel to aid a cause we are praying vehemently against? But there are no accidents with the Almighty, so there must be a purpose in all of this. Just because we can't see the purpose doesn't mean it's not there. So, I will trust Him and rest in His goodness.

Ten years. My, what these eyes have seen in these last ten years. We've been hit by catastrophes and disease. Yellow jack and cholera swept through like a cruel storm, stealing many among us. An odd frost fell upon us as the cane was springing up in '58. Then another flood burst through the breaches in the levees in '59. The two together devastated that year's crop. We still haven't recovered really.

And some years ago, one of our boys was playing with a white boy, and they got into a tussle over something silly. The white boy got rustled up and shot the colored boy in the head. Killed him right there for no good reason. Of course, that white boy didn't get in any trouble, and we weren't even allowed a funeral for our boy.

Hurts like that twist deep into people and change the way the eyes see and the ears hear. Jesus is the only one who can heal wounds this deep, and we pour out our souls to Him like water.

Mingo is a strong young man now and can hold his own in the field and under the kettle. Mama would be so proud of him and of the fine young woman he's sweet on. Mayme will make a delightful daughter-in-law when Mingo works up the gumption to ask her. Odel and I also have Omey, Mirsa, Liberty, Kolle, and Ayda. Our precious Pape was taken from us when he was four years old, and I lost two others before they had a chance to be with us on earth. Six children living. Five children waiting for us in heaven.

I am known as a mother to not only my own children. I am called the Mother of Israel around here and looked to by the younger slaves to help guide them in their walk with the Lord. I still lead the prayer meetings, and I preach in the woods, more so now that Riley and Master are gone. Last month I baptized fourteen others in the pond by the sugar house.

And I am teaching children to read! I don't have any McGuffy readers, but I do have Bibles. I got a handful from

Mindy at the neighboring plantation. She got them from the colporteurs who peddle devotional literature and Bibles around these parts. I'm using them to teach the children in the woods on Saturdays, using pine torches to see by when the night descends. We cut out blocks from pine bark and smooth them out for tablets. For pens, we cut sticks from white oak, and for ink, we soak knots from oak trees overnight.

The freedom we've been praying for is coming, and they must understand how to navigate it.

Of course, some of the children's mamas don't want nothing to do with their babies learning to read and write. One mother caught her son reading a Bible and burned it up. Lord have mercy on her soul. She's just afraid.

Patrollers are liable to invade plantations around here, searching for books and papers in our cabins and whipping anyone they find thirsting after learning. If you persist at it, you may get your finger cut off. That's the way it is, but I can't let fear stop me from doing what's right. I put my trust in the Good Lord.

However this world may look when this war ends, I believe the North will win. I believe the Lord has heard our prayers and is moving on our behalf. My children and grandchildren will breathe free air. They will walk on free soil. Every tear I've cried, every drop of blood that's been ripped from my back, has not been in vain. My prayers for my children will be answered.

When I left Georgetown, I tried to grasp onto the hope that the resurrection fern that looked dead and brittle would spring to life again with one heavy rain. For so long, I was like Elijah's servant, looking in the sky for a cloud to show me there was rain coming, only to be crushed by the weight of disappointment.

No cloud. No rain.

But now I look and see it: the cloud that holds promise.

The true transformation has happened not in my outward circumstances but in my heart. I am freer now than I have ever been. Free of fear. Free to love.

I hope to come to you when the war is won.

Yours Truly,
Mercy

39

———

The timer beeped. What am I supposed to do now?" Tia waved the wooden spoon in the air.

Natassa paused slicing apples. "Take the rice off the burner and stir it, then put the lid back on and let it sit for a few minutes."

Tia did so. "I never knew you could put apples in a salad."

"Oh, sure. You can put all kinds of fruit in salads, or even nuts. We can play around with it. See what you like."

Tia wrinkled her nose and sat down on the barstool across from where Natassa worked.

"Look at all you've learned already? You know how to bake chicken and potatoes, how to cook pasta. Now you can make rice."

Tia grunted. "All you've been teaching me how to make is healthy food. What I really want is a piece of cake."

"Tell me about it." Laura stepped into the kitchen. "What's for dinner tonight? Kale?" She stuck out her tongue at Natassa.

"Oh please, no. Not that again. That tastes like wiper fluid or something."

Natassa and Laura both laughed.

"No, not kale." Natassa made a face back at Laura. "You two are worse than the kids. I know better than to try to sneak that in again. This is a plain iceberg salad. At least I won't have to listen to the grown women complaining."

"So, what else? Besides salad?" Laura slid onto the barstool next to Tia.

"Chicken tacos and rice."

"Tell me it's not that plain brown rice again. What about Spanish rice? Tia, have you ever tried it?" She leaned over to Tia and mock whispered, "If you want, I can teach you how to make Spanish rice some time. It actually has flavor."

"Naw, but anything is better than that plain brown rice. Y'all's food is bland as heck."

Natassa silently marched to the refrigerator and retrieved a bottle of hot sauce. She walked up to the counter and set it in front of Tia without saying a word, then continued tossing the salad.

"Hallelujah!" Tia lifted up her hands.

"That's it." Natassa burst into laughter. "Laura, you and Tia are on dinner duty tomorrow night. Cook whatever you want."

Laura high-fived Tia. As Natassa watched the two women conspire together, she sent up a prayer of thanksgiving. They were both coming into their own, blossoming before her eyes. Healing. Finding freedom. Together.

Later that night, after Natassa finished singing to Mercy, she meandered downstairs. Tia sat on the sofa staring into space. The television was off, and the space around her swirled in contemplative silence.

"What's on your mind?" Natassa settled down next to her.

"That's pretty. The song you was singing. What is it?"

"Oh, that's Mercy's song. It's from a journal Bethany gave me. One of her relatives—a slave named Mercy—used to sing it. Now I sing it to my Mercy."

Tia hummed the tune. Her voice was deep and rich. There were many things about Tia Natassa could never possibly have known without drawing closer.

"Do you like it here?" Hope and trepidation vied for first place in Natassa's gut.

"I do." Tia spoke slowly enough that something else was trailing on the end of her statement. "It's just that I miss my community. Everything here is so … white. I've been in this place before, where I was yanked out of my home and put in a neighborhood where I looked different from everyone else. Never this nice of one, but still. I said to myself, 'You've done it before, Tia. You can do it again.' But just 'cause I'm used to it doesn't mean I like it." Tia rubbed her swollen belly.

"Your family is great. You've done all this stuff to make me feel welcome, make me feel at home. But I'm not at home here. This ain't my people. I want to be around my people."

Natassa mouth twisted. The tenderness of Tia's response revealed what her friend needed. A wave of nausea rose in the pit of her stomach, but she pushed it down and said, "How do you feel about going to church?"

"Aw, no." Tia shook her head. "I just told you I don't feel comfortable around all these white people. You gonna drag me to some uppity white church? I don't think so."

Natassa smiled. "No, not that. I know just the place."

* * *

None of them had been there since the day Reg murdered Brett. Brandon drove around the back route, avoiding driving his car's tires on the street where his brother's blood had been spilt. No one spoke. It seemed like no one even breathed.

Breanna had taken their children for the morning, though Mercy begged to go with them. Their emotions rode too high at the moment. They would bring the children back to this place to find their own closure, and soon. But for now, Brandon, Natassa, Laura, and Tia rode together.

Laura and Tia are here together? Is this nuts? Natassa gripped her seat belt and craned her neck to look toward the back seat. Both women stared out their opposite windows. This may have been the stupidest idea she had ever come up with, or it could be from the Lord. At that moment, it could go either way.

Brandon pulled into the back parking lot of St. Anthony's Baptist and parked the car angled away from St. Anthony Street. Natassa looked over at him. He shifted his jaw back and forth, but when he noticed her gaze, he returned it. He reached for her hand and ran his thumb along hers before getting out of the car.

Walking around to the front of the church, the four of them stared down the street to the scene of the crime.

"Let's let Laura have a moment first." Brandon pressed his lips together.

"I don't want to walk down there alone." Laura inched closer to them, her high heels making scratchy sounds on the worn concrete.

"I'll walk with you." Brandon squared his shoulders.

Natassa watched the two of them walk side by side down St. Anthony Street. Laura gripped a bouquet of assorted flowers in her hands. The blue, yellow, and red blooms contrasted with the dullness of the gray street and plain brick buildings until they reached DeAndre's mural, where the colors seemed to greet each other and dance together.

The last time she had stood in that spot, she'd been watching, waiting for Brett. It had all happened so fast. Realizing the drunken man in the street was likely the same man who had conspired to rape her. The race of her pulse rising. Hearing her last name shouted in the street. The blast of the gun.

She shuddered.

"You okay, sugar?"

She gasped. She hadn't heard Bethany come up beside her.

"Yes. I think so. I'm going to be."

"Ain't that the truth." Bethany gave her a warm side hug, then joined her in staring down the street.

"I introduced Tia to Mazy. They're in there chatting up a storm."

"Oh." She had completely forgotten about Tia. Also, Mazy was early for church? Strange.

"It was good for you to bring her here."

Natassa nodded absentmindedly.

Bethany touched her shoulder. "I mean it, baby girl. This is what she needs. A family. And a Father. It's what we all need, ain't it?"

Laura knelt on the pavement and lay her flowers on the street. Natassa couldn't hear anything, but Laura's shoulders shook. Brandon's too. Weeping for the one they lost.

She looked Bethany in the eye. "Yes, it is."

Bethany wrapped her in a bear hug, and her defenses melted at the gesture. Tears began to leak into sobs that racked her body.

"It's okay. Let it out, sugar."

And she did.

When the wave of grief lifted, she drew back and wiped her eyes. "I'm sorry I soaked your dress."

"Oh, don't you worry 'bout that." Bethany waved her off.

Brandon and Laura were walking back. Natassa turned to Bethany. She had meant to tell Bethany something a week before. "Oh, I finished the rest of Mercy's journal. The letters, I mean. Is that it, really? You're not holding out on me?"

"That's all we have from Old Mercy. It's a shame, ain't it?"

"I feel like I'm saying goodbye to a good friend."

"I know." Bethany patted Natassa's back.

The first bell rang as Brandon and Laura reached them.

"I'm gonna go inside and see how Tia's doing," Bethany said.

"You ready?" Brandon held out his arm.

Natassa sobered and threaded her arm through his.

She walked arm in arm with Brandon down St. Anthony Street. So many times she had walked down this street that was shrouded in significance. Waves of emotion rolled over her, and she rode them, up and down, forward and back. Her eyes misted, and she grasped tighter to Brandon's arm, but she held her head high.

This street was where she lost herself and was found again. And again. And if she were ever to get lost once more, she would be found yet another time. She had a God who wouldn't leave her lost and broken.

When they reached DeAndre's mural, she let go of Brandon's arm and drifted toward it. A smile tugged at the edges of her lips as she once again saw herself on the wall, in the story. It was as if her feet yearned to dance. They started a miniature shuffle right there in front of the mural before her brain shut them down. She wasn't a dancer. She was in the middle of the street. Her husband was staring at her. People were watching. There was no music. She came here to grieve. To find closure. This wasn't the time or the place to dance.

She stepped back. Rejoined Brandon. Came to the place where flowers lay strewn in the street. She knelt beside them. Why hadn't brought some of her own? She picked up a flower in her hand, rubbed the softness of the petal.

"Goodbye, Brett. Thank you for your sacrifice."

When they got back to the church, Tia and Laura were standing next to each other staring out at the street toward them.

"Did you want to walk down there?" Brandon asked Tia.

"No, no." Tia shook her head, looking down at her shoes.

"Okay. I'm going to head inside." Brandon bent to peck Natassa on the cheek.

"It's not because I don't care," Tia said in barely more than a whisper. "It's just that I'm so sorry 'bout all of this, Laura. I feel so … covered in shame 'bout it all. You done lost your husband, your best friend. I feel so bad …" Tia covered her face, her body trembling.

Laura turned to her. "Tia, look at me."

But Tia didn't. She wouldn't lift her head.

"Tia, it's not your fault." Laura wrapped her arms around Tia and stroked her back. "It's not your fault. And even if it were, I'd forgive you. I'd forgive you a hundred times over. You're forgiven, honey. You're okay. It's okay."

The church bell rang again, and Natassa turned around and headed up the steps. She would save the two women a seat next to her.

* * *

Two weeks had passed since the four of them ventured to St. Anthony's Baptist. Time enough for the stirring of emotions to settle, lying peacefully surrendered. Time enough for the yearning to build to be back in those stiff wooden pews.

"Can we go to black church?" Faith asked.

Natassa smiled. She wasn't the first one to ask if or when they could go back to St. Anthony's, but it meant something different—something more—coming from her.

Natassa's gaze met Brandon's, asking the question. Could they? Was it time?

He took a deep breath and exhaled slowly. "Yes, Faithcakes. We'll go today."

Faith squealed at Brandon's proclamation while Hope beamed. Daniel and David nodded at each other with a mature knowing. Mercy was in the other room, but when she found out, she jumped up and down in excitement.

The girls chattered among themselves on the ride there, but the rest of them were quiet. Tia came with them, but Laura opted to go to her regular church. When they got there, Tia stood talking with Mazy and Bethany on the steps while Brandon and Natassa took the children down the street to see where their uncle died.

Mercy ambled slower than the rest so Natassa hung back with her while Brandon walked on with the others. When they neared the mural, Mercy stopped. Stared.

"Why is that wall so pretty?" she asked.

A lump grew in Natassa's throat, but she pushed words past it. "Because someone painted it."

She walked closer, stood toward the middle, her head moving from one side to the other as she took it in. Then an intake of breath. "Mommy! Mommy! That looks like you." She pointed to the picture of Natassa.

She cleared her throat, pushing her hand against the lump. "It does, doesn't it?"

"The wall is so beautiful."

"Yes." *Beauty from ashes.*

"It makes me want to dance."

Mercy began swaying side to side and then twirling and jumping in her little three-year-old style. Stumbling here and there, tongue out in concentration, but a smile on her face. Natassa's eyes filled with tears. Before, she had stopped herself from dancing for so many reasons. No music? Mercy didn't care. People watching? Mercy was oblivious.

"Mommy? Dance with me." Mercy stretched out her arm.

Natassa took a step toward her, holding her hand and twirling her, swaying side to side, allowing her feet to move.

You turned my mourning into dancing.

On the very street that could have destroyed her, she found redemption. She found joy. She found mercy.

Epilogue

When Tia's baby boy Zion greeted the world with his first newborn cry, Natassa's eyes puddled over. She couldn't stop crying, even when Tia lovingly chided her.

"Stop blubbering, will you? I'm the one who had a baby."

Natassa laughed then, but the tears didn't stop flowing. The sound of newborn whimpering and suckling, the smell of baby lotion, the soft feel of Zion's skin, the general anticipation of newness—new life—in the air. It stirred the pot of Natassa's emotions until they spilled over the sides in the way of tears and bubbles of laughter. And inner sighs of gratitude that Tia had wanted her there in the delivery room with her. Natassa had gotten to walk through the journey of eighteen hours of labor with her new friend, providing comfort and encouragement.

Tia kept checking her phone when the nurse came and gave instructions on how to change the baby's diaper and care for the cord. Natassa made a note to go over it all at home when Tia was less distracted. She could help out until then.

When they got home, Natassa put Tia's and Zion's things away in their room and came down to find Tia changing Zion's diaper as if it were the most natural thing in the world. She stood and watched the ease in which Tia handled her newborn, not a trace of first-time mom jitters.

"I didn't know you knew how to do that." Natassa gaped at the scene in front of her.

"You never did give me a chance." Tia buckled Zion in the swing, went to wash her hands, and returned.

"I figured you'd need help. Never having had a baby before, I mean."

"I've taken care of a lot of babies before, though. As a foster sister. All them foster families want babies, and I learned how to change them and feed them bottles and keep them from crying when they wasn't supposed to." She scooped Zion up and settled on the couch with him, beginning to nurse him.

"Wow." Her mind stretched to think of Tia as a little girl faced with such a grown-up job. So much more than a big sister, Tia had been training to be a mother. All that training had brought her to this.

"See, you assume a lot of things, Natassa. But I'm gonna be a great mama. You'll see." Tia gazed at Zion, her eyes full of love.

"I know you will, Tia."

* * *

One Year Later

"Turn here." Natassa pointed right. Something had come over her. This feeling, this knowing, flooded her out of nowhere. They were on their way home from visiting Tia and Laura when she saw the sign. *Open House 1-3 p.m.* They had to go.

They weren't looking for a new home.

But maybe …

Tia and Laura moved out of their home six months earlier, Tia with six-month-old Zion and Laura with four-month-old Bella. Once Laura saw how amazing Tia was with babies, they developed a plan. Laura returned to work, and Tia watched Bella during the day. Laura sold her house, and she and Tia rented a decent house in a nicer part of the city, on the "good" side of Park Avenue.

The neighborhood was safe and yet far more diverse than Crawford County. Tia felt comfortable, more in her element, and Laura felt stretched but not overwhelmingly so. They were much closer to St. Anthony's Baptist, where Tia attended. Laura attended a different church ten minutes farther north. Both women were satisfied with the compromise.

"Why am I turning?" Brandon narrowed his eyes.

"I don't know," Natassa mumbled, almost to herself. But when she saw the house, it made sense. The towering turret, the expansive patio, the stained glass windows. She let out a soft gasp. "Pull over. Please, pull over."

As soon as Brandon put the car into park, she stumbled out of the van and up to the front porch.

The second story window snatched her breath. Stained glass cut in diamond shapes in the same colors of yellow and blue as the windows at St. Anthony's Baptist.

She had to see more.

Brandon questioned, "Honey?" in the background, but she waved him off. She was in another world.

She strolled from room to room, gaping. All of those times that she searched Zillow for farmhouses, and *this* was where she was meant to be. In the city.

All of a sudden, Brandon and the children were beside her. He didn't say anything. He looked at her with question marks in his eyes.

"Ours." She gestured around her. Eleven-foot beamed ceilings. Venetian plaster walls. An eat-in kitchen with marble countertops. And the window—a reminder of what led her to St. Anthony's Church in the first place. To Bethany. To hope. "This is ours. It's where we are meant to be."

"Are you serious, Mom?" David raised his eyebrows.

"Babe? We weren't planning on moving." Brandon spoke slowly.

"I know. But this is right. I know it in my gut. Can you see it, Brandon?" She closed her eyes and prayed for Brandon to see what she saw. When she opened them a moment later, he was smiling.

"You're crazy, you know that?"

"Yeah." She nodded.

"Do you remember how much work moving is?"

"Yep."

"Let me go talk to the agent."

"Whoa, Mom. Really?" Daniel pumped his fist in the air. "Which room is mine?"

"I get dibs on the one on the left." David headed up the stairs.

"Will I have to switch schools?" Faith asked.

"I'm not sure, baby." Natassa tousled her hair. "I know if this is God, which I think it is, then it's good."

* * *

Another year later

DeAndre squinted against the sunlight as he stepped out into the faint breeze, the fresh air of freedom. And there she stood, twenty feet in front of him, shimmering like a mirage. Only real. She was real.

He ran. Embraced her. Twirled her around until she squealed. Then, he set her down and planted a firm kiss on her mouth, tasting the salt of her happy tears.

She drew back, ran, and grabbed something from the car. When she returned, she shoved a ring box into his hands.

"Here. Now." Her voice sounded commanding and desperate.

"Not here. Let's go out to dinner. Somewhere nice. I can—"

"No, I've waited two years for this, and I can't wait another minute. Here. Now."

"In the prison parking lot?" He looked around. This was how she wanted to remember her proposal? Gravel and dust?

"Yes."

She was right. There was no reason to wait. DeAndre got down on one knee and, with his finger, drew in the dust a rudimentary outline of her and him holding hands in the sunset.

Janell squinted. "Is that us?"

"Yes."

"And a … deflated basketball?"

He chuckled. "It's a sunset. Give me a break. This isn't exactly the easiest medium to work with."

Her mouth tipped. "It's beautiful."

He wrote the words *Will you Marry Me?* and wiped his hand on his pants. He pulled out the ring and held it up to her.

"Janell, your love has spoken hope to my dry, dying heart and made it come to life again. You are beautiful in every way, and I want to spend the rest of my life calling forth the beauty inside of you. Marry me?"

"Yes."

He slid the ring on and stood, and she wrapped her arms around him again, their lives intertwining without bars between them.

"Now, let's go." Janell tugged his hand.

DeAndre slipped into the passenger's seat. "Where are we going?"

"Where do you want to go? The world is ours." Her smile illuminated the car, the adventure in her eyes calling to him. They could go anywhere, make a fresh start in any place. But the only place that came to mind was a place he'd already been.

"Chicago?"

"Sure." She beamed. "I would love to meet your mom."

He settled back against the seat, staring at her profile as she pulled into traffic. The ring glinted on the steering wheel while she turned the vehicle. A beautiful ring for his beautiful fiancé. How had God in His great mercy continued to grant him so much? The trunk and back seat were stuffed to the brim with their worldly possessions of utmost importance. But they only really needed each other.

MERCY WILL FOLLOW ME

Book One of *The Mercy Series*

Natassa seems to have it all – a devoted husband with a good income, beautiful children, a faithful best friend- but it only takes one night for her world to crumble, catapulting her into a journey of trauma and healing, old pressures and new friendships. Will she learn to stand her ground or will she always live in someone else's shadow?

DeAndre longs to break free from the neighborhood that keeps dragging him down, but the streets are made of quicksand. Dreams can hardly take flight there, even if he paints them wings. And when he does the unthinkable, could mercy ever be a possibility?

In the 1800s, a mulatto enslaved girl is torn from her mother and left to figure out who she is on her own. Through her time as a house slave in Tennessee and Kentucky, Mercy grapples with her deep ache for her Mama and her understanding of black and white. Which is more important to her? Freedom or loyalty?

Join these three characters, see how their stories intertwine, and dare to believe that mercy will follow you.

Available in Paperback, Kindle, and Audiobook.

MERCY'S LEGACY

Book Three of *The Mercy Series*

Four stories merge in this compelling conclusion to the split-time Mercy series.

After being released from prison, DeAndre struggles to make a new life for himself and his family. But when his past shows up in the doorway of his art studio, begging for a place in his heart and life, he is forced to make decisions that will alter his life forever.

Nine-year-old Mercy has questions no one will answer. That is, until her brother reveals that he knows the whereabouts of her birthfather. Is the man whose blood runs in her veins a bad man like her parents told her? Or a good one? Could he fulfill the longing in her heart to truly belong?

Natassa's been hit with one heartache after another, and she's finding it difficult to bounce back. She longs to keep her loved ones safe and secure, but her arms don't seem big enough to shelter everyone. Not when COVID hits, and certainly not when her daughter takes off to meet her birth father. Will Natassa find the strength she needs to pull everyone through?

In 1868, Liberty's safety is threatened by a band of night riders and she must flee for her life. Her mother—Mercy—pleads with her to find refuge with an old family friend and Liberty's grandmother in Georgetown. What will Liberty find when she gets there? And will she find herself along the way?

Available in Paperback, Kindle, and Audiobook.

ABOUT THE AUTHOR

Sarah Hanks is an award-winning author of Christian fiction in both the contemporary and historical genres. After spending over a decade mostly writing and teaching Sunday school curricula for churches in her community, she finally jumped into writing fiction full time.

She and her husband have nine children of their own, a couple of whom seem to have inherited their mother's love for playing with words and crafting stories. Though Sarah dreams of a cabin by the beach, the family lives jammed together in beautiful chaos near St. Louis, Missouri. She buys ear plugs in bulk.

You can find Sarah Hanks on Facebook and Instagram as @authorsarahhanks, or connect with her on sarah-hanks.com. You can sign up for her newsletter list on her website.